THE CHECKERED BUTTERFLY

GEORGE OX

First Printing, 2020

The White Rose Society

United States of America

ISBN 978-1-7347887-0-9

For Mom & Dad

Just like the butterfly, I too will awaken in my own time."

- DEBORAH CHASKIN

Human affairs are always checkered. No one knows this better than Tala Stone, whose mother climbed thirty-three flights of stairs in red stiletto heels. When she made it to the top of the historic Miami Beach's Hotel Statler, she accessed the rooftop, stood on the ledge, and looked down at the masquerade party she had fled, as her thoughts drowned in the dark ocean afore.

She took the revolver from her purse, put the barrel to her head with such force her fingertips turned white. The moon's glow reflected off the silver nomenclature. The wind billowed her raven black hair. One drop of sweat ran down her forehead underneath her domino mask.

She pulled the trigger.

Her lifeless body fell forward like a doll tossed out a window. Her gown billowed up as she raced down to meet the earth. She smashed against the pool deck, sending the masked revelers into hysteria. Eight-year-old Tala ambled over amidst the chaos and screams and realized it was her mom who had fallen out of the sky like a ghost, her body askew, her polka dot dress caked with blood, her unmasked face, still beautiful.

Why Yona Stone killed herself remained unknown.

That unanswered question was the catalyst for Tala's depression, anxiety and nightmares.

Her childhood memories were fogged, but she remembered running to Pleasant Valley, an office festooned with butterflies, and her mother's smile. She wished she could remember more of mom and less of the masquerade party, but the tragedy replayed in her mind endlessly.

Mom splayed and broken.

She remembered her mom reading her scary Stephen King stories which she oddly loved. When Yona tucked her into bed, she'd smell her neck and give her the usual goodnight kiss on the forehead, whispering, "Goodnight, Little Red Riding Hood," into her ear.

Every

single

night.

Besides those fragments, nothing else remained. Even her mother's smile had dissipated with time. She wondered if her mother's smile was real. Now that she knew the truth.

Happy people don't kill themselves.

David Stone couldn't understand why his wife would do such a thing. People brought food, told him it was God's plan, and said they understood his pain. He opened one of his books and picked a random town on the outskirts of New York. He took Tala to Urbana and left everything behind. Shortly after settling in, David shared his pain, and everyone learned their secret.

He hoped that one day he could make sense of the whole thing and explain why Yona had ended her life to leave them alone forever.

It wasn't his fault. It wasn't hers.

At least, that's what he told himself.

He suspected the gossip in Urbana must have hit a fever pitch. Nothing interesting had happened in Urbana in thirteen years—since Richard Bachman, drunk off his ass turned off a cliff and went nose first into a fifty-foot ditch that killed him instantly.

Small towns have long memories, and Tala soon became "The girl whose mother killed herself." Others nicknamed her, "The suicide girl." David knew in a small town like Urbana, these names would follow her like a dark shadow.

Tala tried to ignore the people who snickered behind her back, but there's only so much weight a kid could carry. She was growing into an antisocial teenager, her grades were dropping, and Charles O'Conner, the undertaker at Pleasant Valley complained he would often see Tala spread the flowers left at tombstones to other ones that had no flowers. It was considerate in a flower stealing kind of way. But David became concerned with Tala's off manner.

The memory of the office festooned with butterflies came when she met Dr. Richard Moss, a psychiatrist who had been practicing for many years before he started treating Tala. He had a reputation for using unorthodox methods. It was said he got *favorable outcomes*.

David ran into a childhood friend at LaGuardia, and that friend handed him the doctors business card and sung his praises. He told David he had quit smoking, lost weight, gotten a promotion, and re-married, all because of him.

Nothing was helping Tala.

David felt he was due for a favorable outcome.

People told David he should have her talk to *someone*. Maybe they were right. Maybe Tala needed a professional. Therapists came and went until he found Dr. Moss's business card in his jacket. Tala met Dr. Moss about a year after Yona's suicide.

Dr. Moss was a peculiar man who wore ostentatious bowties. He was soft spoken, affable. He looked like a science guy. David guessed he was, to a degree. David liked him from the start.

WHEN NINE-YEAR-OLD TALA walked into Dr. Moss's office for the first time she was taken aback by his butterfly collection. She had never seen so many butterflies up close before. They were frozen in time, framed on his walls. She could get close. She could almost touch them. Tala ran her fingers on the glass as if bewitched by their beauty. These were *real* butterflies. Once alive and free. A kaleidoscope of colors. His collection had hundreds, and he had decoratively hung them to form a large butterfly shape.

Tala had never seen something so peculiar and beautiful.

His wooden desk was spartan save for two butterflies. The first one had beautiful orange and black wings that looked like stained-glass windows, with the scientific name *Danaus Plexippus* underneath in beautiful cursive letters. Next to it, a white butterfly with black checkered wings, the scientific name *Pontia Protodice* underneath in the same cursive letters.

She didn't know why, but she wanted to touch them.

She wanted to go beyond the glass.

"They're my favorite," he said, sitting on his desk, looking down at the frames, pensive. "That's why I keep them close." He picked up the orange and black Monarch butterfly.

"Tala, would you like to know something interesting about this butterfly?"

Tala nodded. Wanting to be agreeable. Wondering who this strange man was. He seemed familiar. He had friendly brown eyes, a clear calm voice, and a polka dotted bow tie. Her dad told her he was a doctor, but this wasn't a hospital.

Dr. Moss put the frame down the same way it had been positioned, turning it so Tala could see it again.

"Did you know the Monarch butterflies go south during the winter? Their lifespans are so short they die during the voyage. But their offspring grow and continue the voyage south. Did you know that, Tala?"

She shook her head no.

Dr. Moss appeared to be in a trance.

"It's amazing," he said. Looking into the distance. A horizon with a settling sun that was only an office lamp.

"It's like they're programmed since birth. They know where to go, even though no one is there to give them directions. It's in them. It's extraordinary."

"Can I leave?" Tala said, parting her dry lips.

"Ah, there's no place like home," he said. Suddenly cheery. "You just got here! I guess I can't make you stay. But before you go, would you like to know one more thing about this butterfly? A secret?"

Tala nodded again. Wanting to be agreeable but wanting to leave more so.

He leaned in closer over the desk.

"My wife Lola loved butterflies."

He pointed at the wall. "Most of these were hers. I just continued collecting them to... remember her. She got sick. I couldn't help her. And I'm a doctor. So, I know what it's like to lose someone you love. To feel bad sometimes. I know it's hard Tala. So, I want us to be friends. And I want to help you. And if you let me, I will. But you have to trust me."

He pushed off his desk and pointed at the wall.

"Come take a closer look," he said.

There were hundreds of butterflies, in different colors, sizes, variations. The frames themselves, arranged like a large butterfly. Tala ambled to the massive wall, examining the butterflies the best she could. She looked up, narrowing her eyes at the butterflies higher on the wall.

She felt two hands come up behind her. Dr. Moss hefted her high into the air. She was startled and yelled, "LET ME GO! LET ME GOOOOOO!"

"Take a look, Tala!" he said. "I can't hold you forever. You're thin, but I'm getting old." Tala jerked and swayed from side to side, trying to break free.

"Let me go!"

Dr. Moss put her down. She ran to the door, turned, and looked at him with disdain. How dare he *touch* her. David, who waited in the small lobby, went to the door without opening it.

"Everything okay in there?"

"Everything's fine, Dave. Give us some time."

David lightly tapped the door. "Red, you okay?"

Dr. Moss nodded as if giving her the answer.

"Yes," she said.

She had never been more frightened.

"You can trust me," he said. Then revealed a warm smile. "You're safe here."

Tala turned her head but eyed him from the corner of her eye.

"Did you see one you like?"

She looked at him suspiciously.

After a short while, she nodded.

"Which one would that be?"

She pointed at the checkered butterfly.

"A fine choice." He took the frame from his desk and slowly walked to her. She looked like a scared animal. He hoped she wouldn't run outside when he got too close.

"Here," he said. "I want you to have it."

Tala hadn't made direct eye contact and was upset he had carried her. She almost took a step toward him. Instead, she bolted out the door.

The open door got David's attention. He put his coffee and magazine down and stood up.

"Red, what's the matter—"

"Why did you bring me here? I want to leave," she said, crying. She was holding on to his leg like a child in a toy store.

David looked at Dr. Moss, who now stood in the doorway of his office. Dr. Moss nodded at him.

"Okay, go wait in the car," David said. "It's okay. Go wait in the car, baby."

She shook her head violently and cried.

After Tala finished her shower that night and went into her bedroom, she saw the mysterious Checkered White butterfly frame propped up on her pillow, inside, inscribed in red cursive letters.

> You made a fine choice.
> I hope to see you again,
> Your friend,
> Dr. Moss

Tala ran her fingers over the glass, studying the intricacies of the butterflies' veined wings. She put the frame next to her nightstand, smiled, and went to sleep.

[2]

WHEN TALA HEARD the showerhead come on, she crept downstairs with her Mickey Mouse backpack strapped across one shoulder. She saw David drinking from a bottle of whiskey, but she closed the old wooden door quietly, anyway. She took off to Pleasant Valley Cemetery as it began to snow again. After all, David had told her Pleasant Valley was a place where people went when they died, so it made all the sense in the world for Tala to go there.

To be closer to mom.

There was nothing pleasant about a cemetery at night.

Tala strolled now through the graveyard that had tombs, crypts and mausoleums of men and women buried from the Civil War. The cemetery's land was hemmed in trees, hills and frozen flowers. She passed angel statues three times her size and crosses that looked beautiful yet menacing. She kicked at the snow on the ground to uncover ancient name plaques. She read the names aloud as if she had company, but she had none except for the ravens, who watched her from the Oakwood trees above.

She moved snow off the tombstones that looked like

grey thumbs. Her freezing hands revealed names that had been forgotten, and when she spoke these names, some louder than others, the heat her mouth released made her feel like an ice dragon. The more names she read off the tombs, the more she cried, her tears like ice.

Just weeks before she had left her life behind and arrived in Urbana. Her father had knelt in tears and frightened her more than any monster ever could. He gave a loud animalistic wail, hugging her at the waist, she knew then that what she saw was real.

Momma was gone.

Dead.

She was never coming back.

Tala didn't want to run away; she just wanted things to be as they were but staying in the house made her feel like the walls would suffocate her.

***

THE COLD SHOWER helped David sober up. He came out of the bathroom calling for Tala. When he saw she was gone, he jumped into his car and drove west on Main Street. His gut told him he'd find her at Pleasant Valley. To his relief, he was right. As he exited the car, he could see her at a distance, kneeling before a peculiar rock that shone with the moonlight and looked like a medieval stone from another time.

It was a ferociously cold night, and snow fell from the heavens. Tala held her palms together, reciting words he couldn't understand. He stood too far. David took a step closer, careful not to disturb her.

He wanted to hear what she was saying. Her incomprehensible words sounded like a gothic lullaby. Just as he began to make out her words, the ravens squawked from the tall oaks, as they set off flying through the inky sky.

David looked up, startled.

"Why did she die?" Tala said, still on her knees, the wind billowed her red hair. She didn't turn her head to acknowledge him. She kept her eyes on a large jagged tombstone.

David trudged through the snow and knelt next to her. She turned her head.

David saw she was crying.

"Who will read to me?" she said.

Her father bit down hard on the side of his lip. "I will, kiddo."

"Why did she die?" she said, her voice high and haunting, snow on her brow.

"I don't know, baby," he said. "I don't know why."

3

TALA YAWNED.

Tired from running track, she sunk into Dr. Moss's leather sofa. She stared at the butterfly frames on the wall and recalled the first time she'd seen them when she was a little girl. She couldn't believe she had just turned sixteen.

Dr. Moss's secretary, Frances Gumm, popped her head in.

"Hello, Beautiful. Didn't see you come in. Cookies?"

Tala smiled. "Homemade?"

"Oh please!" she quipped. "That's insulting."

Frances came bobbing her shoulders, dancing to music on her earphones while holding a plate of cookies as gracefully as an experienced waitress. Showing she was in a good mood. She was *always* in a good mood. Tala didn't know how that was possible. She took a cookie and bit into the warm familiar taste of fresh dough and chocolate. It melted in her mouth. Tala met Ms. Gumm shortly after Dr. Moss and felt like she was practically her aunt. Frances had been sneaking her sweets, chocolates, and homemade cookies behind his back ever since.

"You're going to give this child diabetes!" he'd say in good humor. Frances called her every birthday and mailed her handwritten postcards in purple ink from around the country when she traveled. Always ending with a valediction:

> I love it here! But there's no place like
>   home!
> Love Frances!

The phone rang.

"See you soon, Honey." Frances went back to her desk to answer the phone with the same enthusiasm she did coming in.

Tala loved it here. This was her safe place. It was as if the world stopped when she walked in and closed the door. She was someone else.

Someone *strong*.

"Can you hear me?"

"Yeah, sorry. I was kind of spaced out." She sat up.

Dr. Moss had his peppered hair slicked back, his skin shined like he had moisturized, and he wore a black and white polka dotted bow tie.

"It's okay. Lay down. Lay down." Dr. Moss smiled. "Long practice?"

She nodded.

When something was troubling Tala, she reverted to nodding and shaking her head. As opposed to saying "yes" or "no". Reminding him of when he first met her as a little girl. She had gotten much better at talking but the process had taken a long, long time.

"I spoke to your dad. He's ambivalent about the job offer in Miami. He said you don't want to go."

She shook her head.

Dr. Moss sat next to her and leaned in. "Go, Tala. Live your life. This is the new chapter you and your dad need. I'll miss you. But I need you to go. Remember, to learn who you are, sometimes you have to go to the beginning."

"What about you and Ms. Gumm? What about my meds?"

"We'll be fine. You haven't taken your meds in some time. You've been taking placebos, Tala. I've been weaning you off the medication. It's time."

"You have?"

Dr. Moss nodded.

"I'm scared. This town's all I know," Tala said.

"Trust me, Tala, everything you want is on the other side of fear. David told me something your mother once said. It always stuck with me. Your mother told him life's an adventure or it's nothing. Maybe you'll even find those wolves," he said. "Have they visited you again? In your dreams?"

"You mean nightmares," she said.

"Yes, if you see them that way."

"The same one."

He said, "The wolves."

She nodded.

"Have you seen the white sand beach with lions? You're happy dream."

She shook her head.

Not in the least happy she was still having the nightmare.

"Did it wake you?"

She nodded.

"Well, let's get to it, Tala."

She started the same routine of deep breathing exercises. She closed her eyes and listened to his deep voice. She had been doing this since she was nine years old, and she was now sixteen. With that much practice, it became easy to enter a suggestive state of mind. He asked her to count to thirty-three and then back to one. Tala did that a few times. He didn't swing a pocket watch from side to side like the movies. That would be silly.

"Take me back into your dream," he said. Dr. Moss dimmed the lights. Tala didn't notice. Her eyes were closed, and she was already in a faraway place. Inside her nightmare.

Her body became cold.

I don't like it here, she thought.

"I'm with you, Tala," he said. As if looking inside her head with a microscope.

"This place scares me," she said. Her voice cracking from fear.

She had been plagued with dreams of wolves since the masquerade party. Lately, the dreams had become surreal. Nightmares returning with a vengeance. Tala often woke up crying at night, panting for air.

"I'm there," she said. She tried to force the dream out of her mind. To materialize the white sand beach with lions but it was no use. The nightmare always won.

She was standing somewhere high, between the clouds. On some sort of balcony. Over a dark rainbow. The haze from the clouds looked like smoke or fog or maybe death.

It was raining.

"What do you see?" Dr. Moss pressed. "Tell me everything you sense..."

"I feel cold. I'm wearing a white blouse. I can smell sulfur or burned wood. The air is smoky."

"How do you feel?"

"I'm afraid."

"I know, Tala. But where are you?"

"I don't know. I'm in a forest. There's trees everywhere."

"Are you alone?"

Her eyes blinked rapidly underneath the curtain of her eyelids. She could see someone.

"There's someone here."

"No. Tala. It's just you. There's no one here..."

She shifted in her chair. Her eyes remained closed.

Something was coming toward her. It looked like dogs. When they got closer, she could see they were wolves. They ran past her.

"The wolves are back."

"How many?"

Dr. Moss began jotting notes.

"I don't know. A pack... They're so big. There's a girl too."

"What girl?"

Tala had never mentioned a girl.

Dr. Moss continued to write notes inside his notebook.

"Oh my God. She's so little. She's running around, playing. She's biting her hand. Where are her parents?" The wolves saw her.

Tala began to pant. She took deep breaths. Her eyes remained closed.

"Who is this girl, Tala?"

"I don't know. She's small," she raised her voice, panting. "She doesn't see them. Where are her parents? My God. They have yellow eyes, sharp fangs. They're running toward her. The wolves cut through the fog.

Tala yelled *STOP* at the top of her lungs.

"Are you there? Tala listen to me. Are you there?" Dr. Moss said.

"NO!" she cried. "I don't know. I'm too far. I'm there, but I'm too far."

She hyperventilated. Struggling for air.

"Do something," Dr. Moss said.

"I'm running to her."

"Can you save the girl?"

"They're so big. I don't have a weapon. I don't have a stick. There's nothing. They're gonna kill her. I don't have a weapon."

The wolves gained ground. She ran as fast as she could, but she couldn't save the girl. The wolves were on her. She was a rag doll. They tore her to pieces. There was blood everywhere. She could see it even in the darkness. Tala knew when she woke up that there was something inherently wrong with her.

4

DAVID STONE TRIED hard to cope despite his wife's suicide. He found himself drinking, smoking, and taking long walks in reverie. He talked to Tala less and less. Looking at her brought him pain because she had her mother's blue eyes. David became a wanderer who contemplated the point of life.

He didn't think he could go on. The only light remaining in his miserable life was his love for Tala and the sky. He had to be strong for her. He tried his best. Before he took notice of his deteriorating health and depression, other people did. Primarily at work, and before long, people began to gossip.

David found himself drinking at the airport bars after his flights. But that drinking sometimes carried on for hours and on some occasions even until the airport closed. It looked bad. He didn't notice. He didn't seem to care. Would-be flyers didn't feel comfortable seeing a pilot in uniform drinking at a bar. Word spread like wildfire. The FAA opened an investigation into David's drinking habits.

They followed and observed him for two weeks. Different day. Same routine.

David had found solace in drinking. If he was flying or not was irrelevant. He'd have a cup of whiskey with a shot of sprite. Once he started it was hard to stop. David had found alcohol to be the only barrier that could help him cope with the fact that his wife killed herself and his daughter was estranged. He felt lost, and only alcohol brought him to the dream state where his wife and daughter would co-exist.

John Palmer, the FAA's lead investigator on the case, reviewed several complaints of David Stone drinking before his flights. Palmer was a tall black man who dressed impeccably. His clothes were always pressed, and his shoes were always shining.

He took great pride in everything he did, especially his work. It was his job to ensure pilots maintained integrity and responsibility when flying. So many lives could be jeopardized because of David's alcoholism. Palmer's plan was simple. He'd make an example out of David. Palmer knew about Yona's death. He had read the police report.

Cause of death: Suicide.

Palmer reasoned her suicide was the primary reason why David, a reputable pilot for years, had become an irresponsible drunk. Palmer empathized with him more than the average Joe would. His son Toby killed himself at nineteen. Toby was tall, dark, and handsome with a bright future. But he was gay.

When someone hacked his phone and posted explicit photos of him on the web, he became a constant target and fell into a downward spiral of depression and drug use. He ate a gun shortly after at a nearby park. Palmer understood the detrimental effects of suicide on a family. His own son had died damnit. But he had a job to do.

He'd allow David his drinking routine, so when they detained him on board, he'd be forced to blow into a breathalyzer and the evidence would be irrefutable.

His team had begun to compile surveillance video and sworn testimony from bartenders. Palmer liked his investigations to be tight. With Palmer in charge, Urbana Airlines could fire David without him having a chance of getting his job back through arbitration.

David walked across the terminal. Agents watched his every move. Several agents manned the surveillance cameras from the security portal of the airport waiting for him to sit at one of the airport bars. A different one every time, drinking until he felt numb. David winked and told the bartenders he was "off the clock." No one questioned him. Maybe because they felt it was his responsibility not to drink and fly or maybe because he always left a generous tip. Either way, it's easy to look the other way when you profit.

As David walked past the terminals, he saw people from all nationalities. Young, old. Happy, sad. Married couples laughing together, going on honeymoons. Some traveling for work or visiting relatives. That sense of family made him long for Yona. Two FAA agents conducting floor surveillance followed him in civilian clothing. They kept their distance from him, but they knew he suspected nothing.

TODAY IS THE TAKEDOWN.

David comes to work and never comes back.

His face plastered on the news, his career over.

. . .

DAVID MADE it to a small sports bar where Anderson Cooper was on the flat screen TV with a CNN Breaking News Alert. David didn't watch much television, but he was a sucker for Breaking News Alerts. Cooper's face looked grave as he reported of an active shooter at Caulfield Academy in Seneca, Kansas.

The screen split and showed a helicopter angle of students running out of the school being escorted by police officers and SWAT team members. Four confirmed dead.

Jesus. It never stops.

The shooting had gone viral as patrons started checking their mobile devices and tweeting on the crisis.

He leaned across the bar, trying to grab the bartender's attention, who was doing some leaning of his own, face first into a de-Christianized Southern girl's cleavage. The seats next to David were vacant but across from him sat several nervous fliers who wouldn't think to get on a plane if not for the companionship of Jack and Johnny. Their eyes glued to CNN.

The bartender made eye contact with David.

David held up his hand. "Give me a second."

His cell phone was going off. It must've been important. Tala was at school, and no one called him much these days. He didn't recognize the number. He stood up, told the bartender to hold again and answered.

"David speaking."

"Listen closely, Mr. Stone. Sit down for as long as you usually do. Order a tonic and lime. And when you're done with that one. Have another. Don't change anything in your routine today."

"Who is this? What are you talking about?"

"This phone call never happened."

"Excuse me? Who is this?"

"Who I am is not important. There are two FAA agents on the floor watching your every move. Not to mention a dozen surveillance cameras. I hope you get your second chance. Good luck."

"Who is this? Why are you doing this?"

The caller hung up.

David swallowed what felt like a cotton ball in his mouth.

Nothing about the voice sounded familiar. David didn't dare look back. He sat down. The bartender came over smiling, telling the girl to wait. He looked at David with a look that said:

Hurry up. I'm trying to get laid over here.

"Tonic and lime," David said. "Keep 'em coming."

David drank about seven tonic and limes. Paid the bill. Got up and scanned around, looking for two potential agents as discreetly as he could. It could've been a prank call, he reasoned. He saw the regular function of the airport.

His gut told him something was in motion. He went to his terminal, scanned his I.D., and boarded Urbana Airlines 711. His first flight of the day was scheduled from New York to Jacksonville, and he wondered if he'd make it down there today. As soon as he stepped on the plane, Stacy, a flight attendant he knew well, gave him an uneasy look. Two agents who had been sitting in first class stood up.

"What's going on?" David said, looking at Stacey.

"Mr. Stone. I'm Agent Johnson." He flipped open his FAA ID like on one of those cop shows.

"You need to come with us."

"What's the matter?" he said. Stacy and another flight

attendant were eyeing him, and the early boarders in first class were staring.

"We need you to come with us," the other agent said.

"I'm scheduled to Jacksonville."

"Mr. Stone, we're not asking you again. We need you to blow into a breathalyzer."

"Excuse me?" he said. "What for?"

He knew there would be no alcohol in his system.

"You're under arrest. Turn around."

"Are handcuffs really necessary? I'm a pilot, not a murderer."

"No," Agent Johnson said. "They're not really necessary, but I want to make sure everyone gets a good look at you."

"So, you get off on this?" David said.

"I'm not in the business of underestimating people."

"I don't deserve this. This is a mistake."

Agent Johnson cuffed him with his hands behind his back. "You're a drunk."

They walked him off the plane.

"My wife died," David said.

Agent Johnson, who walked a little ahead, stopped. "Hold it, guys."

He pressed his index finger into David's chest. "I'm aware about your wife, Mr. Stone. I know she killed herself too. I'm sorry she did, but if you don't get yourself under control, someone else's wife, brother, sister, mother, daughter, son, uncle is going to die. Because you can't get it together." The agent raised his voice. People stopped to watch.

"You don't know what I've been through. Screw you," David said.

Agent Johnson pulled him by the elbow through the terminal and out to the lobby of the airport where thousands of people could see him. Johnson took him to the security office at a leisurely pace. David saw some old friends, people who once came to his house to barbecue and have beers. He tried to stop and look away. Pretend he wasn't in cuffs. Pretend this wasn't happening.

"You brought this on yourself," Agent Johnson said.

Two NYPD officers were waiting in the security office with several agents.

John Palmer entered the room and introduced himself to everyone, then sat down and faced David. He requested the officers change David's handcuffs to the front so he'd be more comfortable. The officers obliged.

"David, I'm sorry. You need help. You won't be flying anymore. These officers will be transporting you to NYPD headquarters for DUI processing."

The problem, of course, was that there wasn't a drop of alcohol in David's system. Today, he was free and clear, and that mysterious phone call saved his job and had put him in a legal position of advantage where he could now sue for defamation of character.

"I'm not drunk," David said.

Palmer leaned forward, "Do I look like a fool to you? You've been drinking for hours. We've been watching you for weeks. You're drunk, and your flying days are over. You can take it up with the arbitrator but believe me. What we have is solid. You're finished, David." Agent Palmer leaned back in his chair, taking a deep breath. "I'm sorry, Mr. Stone. It's my job. Nothing personal."

"I've been through hell—" David started saying.

"I understand about your wife."

David yelled at Palmer, "Don't you ever mention her, you coon!"

Agent Palmer said, "I didn't peg you for a racist."

David's screams had turned into a long hideous cry.

Looking up at Palmer, he said, "I'm not a racist. I'm nothing."

Palmer asked the NYPD officers to step out for a moment. Agent Johnson stayed behind but Palmer signaled him to escort them. When everyone stepped out of the office, Palmer came closer to David and whispered, "You're lucky I owed someone a favor. I hope you enjoyed your tonic and lime. When you leave this place, remember I'm the coon that saved your career. I'm the coon that called you to give you a second chance. I hope you fix your life David; you won't get a second bite of the cherry."

Agent Palmer walked out of the room.

David covered his face with his hands.

He wanted to apologize.

He wanted to say sorry.

But he said nothing.

[5]

WHEN TALA SAW the 757 Boeing that would soar her through the skies, she felt her stomach hollow as she looked outside the large panel windows of the airport and out at the planes rolling in line for their next chance at the sky. Tala closed her eyes and took deep breaths, trying to calm her rising anxiety.

David came back from the kiosk with a *New Yorker* magazine and sat next to her, keeping his eyes on the pages. Tala wanted to say something but decided not to; her dad had a look about him, a certain intensity, when he focused, and she knew he wouldn't pay attention now. She studied his narrow eyes and thin silver spectacles. His customary neat-trimmed beard was rough and unkempt, unlike him.

David said something as they walked through the terminal and boarded the plane, but his voice sounded hazy, like a broken television. Tala's fear spread down her legs and up her arms as she walked down the aisle looking for her seat. She opted for the window seat despite her fear of heights, hoping to face them head on. She wanted to be brave, but the sound from the engine wrapped its arms around her neck, choking her. She gasped for air and found less and less. Her ears got hot, and her palms started to perspire.

The chirpy flight attendant commented on the temperature over the loudspeaker. Tala sat up in her chair and took a deep breath, then another, reverting to Dr. Moss's breathing exercises, trying to find the rhythm.

The airline played a safety video featuring a robotic American Airlines stewardess who gave safety instructions to bring people a false sense of security. To make passengers believe if the steel bird decided to nosedive like a roller coaster, there was something you could do; use your seat as a floating device.

Fat chance.

What about the height?

David stowed his carryon into the overhead bin.

"Ready for the Sunshine State," he said, sounding more cheery than usual. Tala ignored him and unlocked her iPad. Her attention fixed on the glass screen. She played a movie she found in her library. She didn't remember downloading it, but she had bootlegged so many movies it was hard to keep up.

Return to Oz.

"Did you download this movie?" Tala turned the iPad screen to her dad.

David shook his head. "I've yet to figure that out. But you should try watching movies on TV or better yet, in theaters, you know, with other people..."

"I'll try that sometime." She wanted to get her mind off the thought that she was going to be lifted thousands of miles in the air.

She put on her earbuds and hit play.

Urbana's a small country town where everyone knew

each other's business. Tala had a hard time making *real* friends there. She knew people on the track team, but those friendships never solidified. She never trusted them after she heard Carrie, one of her teammates, call her 'the suicide girl' in the locker room.

High school girls could be the cruelest beasts on earth. Part of her wanted to leave. Part of her didn't. She looked forward to a new life without everyone knowing her past. Urbana was all she knew; how could she leave Dr. Moss and Ms. Gumm behind? They were like family. The non-judgmental ones, who listened (albeit they were paid).

When her dad broke the news about his new job in Miami, she tried to convince him to drive down, but David saw it as an opportunity for Tala to face her fears.

Tala paused the movie, resting the iPad on her lap. "Dad, is this the right thing for us?"

"What do you mean?" he said, cleaning his silver eyeglasses with a fiber cloth.

"Leaving."

"It's time to move on, Red," he said.

Tala couldn't focus on the movie, so she stowed her iPad in her carryon bag and stared out the oval window at the concrete runway now covered with snow. She looked at the men in their reflective vests hauling luggage into the aircraft.

David put a hand on her knee. "You okay?"

"You know I hate planes."

"You used to play with my collection of toy models when you were a kid."

"Your toy planes didn't lift me 10,000 feet into the air."

David smiled.

"Don't laugh. You know I hate heights," she said.

"You've flown more than anyone your age. You used to ride these things like nothing. You used to love it."

"Things change," she said stubbornly.

"That they do. But it's going to be fine. Switch with me." Tala was lost for a second, but she realized he meant to switch seats. She decided it wouldn't make a difference. Wasn't her seat a floating device? She looked away. David went back to the *New Yorker* cartoons.

The flight attendant, who sounded like she had one too many espressos came over the loudspeaker. "Ladies and gentlemen, Captain Carroll has turned on the Fasten Seat Belt sign. If you haven't already done so, please stow your carry-on luggage underneath the seat in front—"

It was really going to happen. This pressurized metal tube created by God knows who was going to fly her thirty thousand feet, God knows how, to a place she'd left as a kid, God knows why. Her anxiety drowned out the rest of the announcements until she heard a somewhat fragile voice on the loudspeaker.

"This is your Captain speaking. This will be my first flight..." he said timidly. Tala looked at her father. His face was calm. She looked around anxiously at other passengers and felt a layer of unease. "Of the day..." the pilot said in good humor. The passengers laughed.

"That's one of the oldest pilot jokes," David said.

"Not funny," she said.

The pilot said a few other announcements that brought mild laughter, but Tala had drowned him out again with her earbuds.

She braced herself as the plane started rolling on its wheels like a ride at the fair. It completed a 360-degree turn. Tala's heart barked like a ravenous dog inside a cage; she braced herself for takeoff. She put her hand on her chest and felt her heart beating posthaste. She was sweating profusely and felt a wash come over her, depleting her of energy. She was having a heart attack.

David leaned in. "You okay? You're pale."

Beads of sweat formed over her lips.

She didn't respond. Her skin damp, her left side went numb and her hands shook uncontrollably. She felt a tingle on the left side of her face.

"I think I'm having a heart attack," she managed.

Tears built up in her eyes and ran down her face when she blinked. Her nose started bleeding.

David stood and waved the flight attendant over. "Something's wrong. Hurry!"

Tala's vision dimmed to black.

A PARAMEDIC STOOD OVER TALA, reading her vital signs. He examined her pupils with a tiny flashlight. When he was satisfied, he pulled the cuff off her arm, then removed a small plastic clip from her index finger.

"You okay, kiddo?" he said.

Tala nodded. She fought through grogginess, which made her feel like she'd taken an excess of her prescription medication.

He told David, "Her numbers are stable."

He asked Tala, "How are you feeling? Know what day it is?"

"What happened?" Tala started to get her bearings and realized she had fainted again.

"What day is it, hun?" the medic asked her.

"Friday."

The medic smiled at David. "Best day of the week."

"Her vitals are good. But we can take her to the hospital and have a doctor look." Something in his voice suggested this was nothing. Medics at airports had frequent calls of nervous flyers whose nerves got the best of them. The medic handed David a form.

"What's this?"

"Waiver. Your autograph says we provided care and don't want her transported to the hospital." Tala hated hospitals.

"I'm fine," she said. It had been *weeks* since her last panic attack. This was a bad omen.

David glanced at the form and signed.

"Are you doing this on purpose?" he blurted.

"Really David, you know I hate flying."

David handed the waiver back to the paramedic.

"She has a condition. Her doctor, I guess her old doc, said they're panic attacks induced by anxiety."

"Can't say I'm surprised. It's common here. No foaming to indicate a seizure or something more serious. But it's up to you, we can take her." The medic took a deep breath, like he'd given this spiel many times. "Flying is a scary business. For most folks, anyway."

David would never understand that. He loved the sky since he was a boy. Flying put food on the table.

Tala put her hand on her chest as if to check if her heart was still there. "Why did it feel like a heart attack this time?"

"Sweetie, you're a little young for a heart attack," The paramedic chuckled. "But mind the French fries just in case." He winked at her.

David uncrossed his arms. He shook the medic's hand.

"Thank you."

The medic gave Tala a pat on the back. "You'll be okay, sweetie. Remember Kennedy; nothing to fear but fear itself."

That was a great quote. One she really liked. But she

didn't remember things turning out great for Kennedy. She wasn't even sure he had said that.

Anxiety made Tala feel out of control, like a car hydroplaning on ice. After her mother died, she got the big three, random anxiety attacks, depression, suicidal thoughts. The doctors called it the dark triad. The trio made her feel sick to her stomach, like she had swallowed a helium balloon and she was floating up, staring down at a person she didn't remember.

Tala sat up off the gurney, feeling nauseous, her blood rushing to her head, making her feel lightheaded.

David picked up his cell phone. He chirped away with *her*. Tala knew it was *her*, his new girlfriend, because he changed his voice when she called. When she got her bearings, she left the hospital ward of the airport and sauntered back to her gate to look outside the large panel windows again and out at the runway, knowing the plane she had boarded was now in the sky.

David walked up behind her and softly tugged her red hair.

"Can you do me a favor and not walk off when I'm on the phone? You're going to give *me* a heart attack." He looked at her blue eyes. She was a reflection of her mother. At least she had his freckles. He attributed their recent fights to teenage rebellion. He loved her so much. He rustled his fingers through her hair.

"C'mon, sport, we're due for a road trip anyway," he said.

Tala felt guilty for making this harder than it had to be.

He leaned down and kissed her on the cheek.

"Yeah, I know how much you love traffic," she said.

"I'll be okay." David smiled.

David wasn't looking forward to thousands of miles of concrete foliage on the road. But he had no choice. It was

time to move on and leave Urbana for good. He sued
Urbana Airlines and the N.Y.P.D for false arrest, libel, and
defamation of character, and as Donald Trump would say,
the settlement was HUGE! He got a less than glamorous
job flying cargo for Dotted Blue. Because what else was he
going to do? He was only in his mid-forties. He remembered
leaving Miami all those years ago when the officers came
knocking on his door.

Sir, I regret to inform you...but your wife...

Yes, he had decided to leave Miami for good. He
couldn't stay in their same house, in their same bed. There
were too many things that reminded him of Yona and the
pain was too much to bare. It was all so sudden. Now he
was done with Urbana, it has served its purpose.

Sir, I regret to inform you...but your wife...

After his arrest, he knew it was time. The lawsuit was
the icing on the cake.

Tala needed a fresh start.

This was their chance.

David had lived in Hialeah as a kid and took a liking to
airplanes as a young boy when his father took him to Opa-
Locka Airport to watch the planes take off and land. David
would never forget the roar of those engines and how the
ground seemed to move. That place filled him with hope.
Maybe he'd take Tala there sometime.

David purchased a chic two story house in an affluent
South Florida neighborhood called Miami Springs. He
didn't show Tala pictures of the house because he wanted
to surprise her. On the road, Tala told him she watched
Return to Oz, which she thought was too dark for kids.
She also read half of *The Catcher in the Rye*, but mainly
slept.

Sir, I regret to inform you...but your wife...

David followed the I-95 signs south, hoping this was the right move for them.

The drive was long and uneventful. They stopped every few hours or so to use the bathroom, stretch, eat. Nothing but concrete and foliage. David glanced at her in the passenger seat of the rental. Tala had propped a pillow against the window, her seatbelt fastened. This was their second day on the road, and they had just crossed the Georgia-Florida line. Eight hours later, they were in the heart of David's hometown; Hialeah, or as David called it, the prairie.

Tala stretched out and yawned. "Where are we?"

"This is Hialeah."

"Hia-what?"

"*Hia-leah*, where I grew up. Remember? it means High Prairie," he said, never taking his eyes off the road. "We lived here for a bit."

"How come I don't remember?"

"It was a long time ago." David said.

"Are we close?"

"We're very close," he said. "You know, if you ever want to go to Angels of Mercy, to see your mom. I can—"

"No. I'm not ready to go there," Tala said curtly.

David's eyes went back to the road. "My God," he said. "So much traffic now." He wasn't in bumper to bumper traffic—yet—but he didn't want to imagine rush hour.

"Why are there so many street vendors?" Tala asked.

———

Tala saw Hispanic vendors selling roses and sunflowers out of the trunks of their cars at the corners of intersections. They adorned paint buckets with yellow sunflowers, or red roses. Some vendors sold lemons or bottled water and walked up and down the street during red lights.

"It's a little different here. But hey! No more shoveling snow."

Tala sensed false excitement in his voice. She adjusted her seat to an upright position. Hoping to relieve some of the soreness from her lower back. She took in this new world.

David drove south on East 4 Avenue at what felt like a snail's pace. Urbana's nearest car sometimes wouldn't be seen for miles. He had adjusted to that life and had forgotten the fast city life. Although in traffic, it never felt very fast. Occasional honks made him irritable. He felt nostalgic as he drove adjacent to the Hialeah Racetrack. Its pink deteriorating cursive sign hadn't been replaced.

"Maybe this is a bad idea," Tala said, knowing her father was annoyed. David put on an AM radio station as revenge.

He drove south, exiting the Hialeah city limits, and felt the sense of nostalgia brew as he got to Okeechobee Road. He crossed the Curtiss Parkway Bridge, over the alligator-infested canal that divided Miami Springs and Hialeah.

He yielded right at the roundabout that was called Circle Drive. The roundabout had the local Starbucks, gym, hair salons, barbershops, mom and pop restaurants, a diner called The Cozy Corner, and even a small independent bookstore called Happenstance. This town was nothing like Hialeah.

Clean. Rich. Picturesque.

It looked like a toy town.

Tala loved the green running path on Curtiss Parkway. Rowed with tall shade trees, benches, and a place to park your car, not that she had one yet. She saw ubiquitous red and blue political banners depicting a foxy woman with a crew cut sporting an ultra-white politician's smile.

VOTE
EMMA SOSA!
FOR MAYOR
IF IT AIN'T BROKE DON'T FIX IT!

"I GUESS IT'S AN ELECTION HERE," she said.

"Guess so."

David made a left on Deer Run, and she saw it for the first time, a large acreage of high unkempt grass, some patches green, some brown, burned from the sun. As if God had taken a magnifying glass to examine the land and forgotten the sun was behind Him.

She saw tall oak trees, old and strong, with ravenous roots and vines in a heavily dense area. And beyond that, in the distance, she saw the facade of the Curtiss Mansion. An enormous three-story Spanish villa house made of red clay. Half standing, half destroyed. Like a wrecking ball had smashed into its side and given up. The mansion sat at the center of the acreage, apart from all civilization. There must have been a football field in each direction that eventually kissed a tall black iron fence. Making this a sequestered place.

"What's that?" Tala said, pointing at the Curtiss Mansion.

"That would be a house," her father replied.

"I know it's a house, Dad."

David eased on the brakes to take a better look. The

trees seemed to have quadrupled in size since he last saw them.

David lowered the radio station and pulled over, parking before the mansion. The nose of his rental car only feet away from the black wrought iron gate. The house stood there. Staring back at them.

"The Curtiss Mansion," he said. "My God, it's still here. I used to sneak in here when I was a kid. No one talked about it much, except for us. It's like the black sheep of this pasture."

"Why? Who lived there?"

"A great man who went crazy," he said, then stepped out of the car and lit a cigarette.

"Since when do you smoke?"

David realized his folly. He didn't want Tala to know he was smoking again.

"Just the last couple of months. Here and there. You know, with work, the arrangements to come over here, leaving Urbana. It's helped with stress," he said.

"Smoking causes cancer. Remember?"

David said, "You're one to talk."

"What's that supposed to mean?" she said. "I don't smoke."

"Spare me. I know things have been rough between us, and I haven't been dad of the year by any means. I was your age once. I'm trying here. I want to fix things. You're my daughter and I love you. Can we just not lie to each other?" He sounded exhausted when he said it. Like he was tired of the old. Like something had to give.

He took a deep drag. The cigarette paper burned orange and red, becoming shorter. Ashes stacked up; her father's lungs turned black with every puff. That unkempt beard. He looked like a different man.

Tala rubbed the side of her neck. Realizing the car ride had given her a cramp.

"This is a new start for us. Deal?" he said.

"Whatever."

Her father gave her a stern look.

"Yeah, I guess."

Her dad exhaled. He passed her the cigarette.

"What are you—" she said.

"No more lies."

Tala hesitated, but then took the cigarette from him. She held it like someone who had smoked all her life. Graceful. She took a puff, "You happy?"

"No," he said, "but it's a start. I'm not an idiot. I know you've smoked. I rather you don't."

David looked at the mansion again. "It's kind of surreal being here. This place scared the crap out of me when I was a kid." He leaned on the hood. Tala sat next to him. She too kept her gaze on the abandoned mansion built of adobe rock.

The mansion listened intently to their conversation. The wind came fast and swift. Trees in the distance whispered secrets no human being should hear. The sun hid behind a cloud, darkness fell on the mansion's bed of grass like it had two faces.

"When I was a kid, everyone said that this place was haunted. You see that dense area over there? We used to call it The Sea of Trees. That was no man's land." He took another drag from the cigarette, tossed it to the ground, and stomped it.

He pointed at her. "You're done smoking, by the way."

Tala rolled her eyes.

"Please tell me you don't believe in haunted houses," she said.

David said, "I did when I was a kid, but I also believed in Santa and the Tooth Fairy." He came off the hood and grabbed the gate—

"Ouch." He pulled his hand away. "Static," he said.

Tala chuckled.

He held the gate again, pensive.

"Bad things happened here. The man who lived here is a legend. Can't take that away. He was a genius aviator who dropped out of school. He founded this town and Hialeah when it was nothing but a backward swamp. He's one of the reasons I became a pilot. But he committed a horrible crime. The only reason it hasn't met the wrecking ball is because the city voted and turned it into a historic site.

"What did he do?"

A gust of wind ran a cold chill through Tala's body, giving her goosebumps.

David turned on his heels and opened the car door.

"How about we see our new house?"

"What was the crime? What did he do?" Her eyes on the mansion. In awe of the sheer size of it. David saw she made no attempt to get into the car. He knew his daughter enough to know she wouldn't leave until he said it.

"He killed his wife and children."

"How?"

"Burned them alive."

The sun lingered behind thick clouds, allowing the darkness to seep to the other part of the mansion's bed of grass, now one large black mask.

"Get in the car. This place gives me the creeps."

7

BECOMING mayor of Miami Springs wasn't Emma Sosa's priority, at least not at first. That came later, when harnessing local power became necessary for her to continue her work. She graduated with honors from Harvard Medical School and excelled in her profession, but she had other ambitions.

She entered the world of law enforcement, quickly rising through the Miami Beach Police Department's ranks from officer, detective, then commander.

She was also an education activist and community organizer before ever considering running for office. Fate brought her to small-time politics with big time control. And Emma liked control. Everything in Miami Springs fell under her thumb. Under her sway. She became obsessed with control right around the time she felt she lost it, when she was young.

A man lured her into his car offering to show her a puppy. Emma loved puppies; she always wanted a dog. But when she walked up to the rear passenger door of an old Buick, she quickly realized there was no dog.

Only pain.

The man didn't kill her. But he tore Emma from the inside out, taking any chance of a normal life. The assault messed up her life, relationships, and led her to substance abuse, where she battled her demons for years.

Emma's family was wealthy, so even though she was a misfit teenager, she never got arrested. All it took was a phone call from the Sosa's.

Emma saw therapists who tried to help her with the trauma. In college, she became fascinated with psychology, persuasion, the mind, and control.

She developed a theory that human beings were 'moist robots' who responded to emotions instead of reason and logic. Emotions made humans tick. Emma was only seven years old when that bastard took her innocence. When she told her parents, they refused to believe her.

She knew not to talk to strangers. Not to trust anyone. How could she be so dumb? She had overheard her parents say while bickering in the kitchen. Miami Springs Elementary had the best surveillance video on the market in the eighties, but it had failed to capture the assault.

The police caught the pedophile, anyway. He was hard to miss, standing at 6'9, lanky frame, African American male. His name was Rodnam Jackson, an upcoming basketball star that had gone all conference since his freshman year.

The police arrested him, but the charges were dropped when The Sosa's signed a non-prosecution form in fear the publicity of a sexual abuse case would more deeply scar their daughter or their perfect family image. The bastard walked. At the time of the assault, Rodnam Jackson had several scholarship offers from Division I universities.

The system failed Emma Sosa, which led her to study

psychology ferociously and go down the rabbit hole of the human mind.

Emma retired early and launched a quick and swift campaign for mayor in her hometown of Miami Springs against a local business mogul who owned a chain of pawn shops and gas stations in Hialeah. Emma Sosa won the election with the town's largest voter turnout ever.

People love authority. People love their hometown heroes. Emma had the resume.

Just days after moving into the Mayor's Office in city hall, Rodnam Jackson made his way back to Florida from Jersey. Emma Sosa found him. She didn't kill him.

But let's just say Rodnam Jackson disappeared.

8

BEFORE TALA GOT comfortable in her car seat, David pulled into a pebbled driveway leading to a white Victorian two story house with a red door that could have been cut out of a magazine.

"No way, Dad."

Tala opened her door before her dad parked.

"You have got to be kidding," she said.

David finished parking and came up behind her.

He rubbed her shoulders. "This is it."

She turned back to him, astonished.

"How the hell could you afford this—"

"Language!" he said.

David, put his life savings, and a good chunk of his airline settlement for the down payment. Springs was for rich people. Plain and simple. The house sat on Fairway Avenue. Spanish Moss trees performed curtseys over the road and provided blissful shade.

The house felt strangely old and modern, and had beautiful white, purple and yellow May Bells on the lawn. David unlocked the red door. Tala walk into a furnished home.

She ran upstairs to check out the rooms. The rooms were bigger than her old house, and she felt a tinge of sadness when she saw the large master where her father would sleep alone. She walked back out to the hall, overlooking the living room.

"Why did you get such a big house?"

"Why not?"

"Don't get me wrong. I love it," she said. "It's just so big."

"I couldn't help myself, I suppose. Did you see the pool? Look out your window."

Her bedroom had some of her old furniture. There was an angel nightlight next to her bed that she had for as long as she could remember. The checkered butterfly was in its frame on her dresser drawer. Positioned the same as it had been in Urbana. She looked out the window and saw a large swimming pool. The water looked rich blue, like an ocean she imagined from *The Old Man & The Sea*. Everything looked so new.

So fresh.

So modern.

So Un-Urbana.

David leaned against her door.

"Like it?"

She thought about the empty rooms. She thought about being home alone. She thought about her heart beating, about her breathing. She felt a little off and had a slight headache. Maybe she was hungry.

"Geez, why did you get such a big house?"

"It's for us. I thought you'd be happy."

Tala sat on the corner of her bed, looking at her shoes.

"You okay, Red?"

The empty rooms made her feel empty.

She looked up. "I'm okay." She forced a smile. "The house is great. I'm happy."

Her dad smiled. "Great. There's something I have to tell you..." He looked around. "About the house, it's kind of important. But it can wait."

"Please don't tell me someone was murdered here."

Her dad chuckled. "No. No. Nothing like that." He seemed like he wanted to tell her something but changed his mind.

"Get settled in first. I'll tell you later."

[9]

DAVID HAD PLANNED BEFOREHAND from Urbana. He enrolled Tala at Miami Springs Senior High School. Got a job with Dotted Blue. Junked his black 1999 BMW, a car he had out of habit more than necessity. Purchased a white Porsche from an exotic car dealership, to be delivered via carrier service.

His reasoning was simple: One, he could die tomorrow. Two, he couldn't park the ninety-nine Beemer in a driveway in Springs. It wouldn't look right. Three, he could afford it now. He changed his bills and correspondence to his new home. He had found the Victorian house while surfing the internet and remembered Miami Springs.

The house was the first Google result. He fell in love with it. The Springs filled him with nostalgia. He remembered how, as a kid, he dreamed of living on the other side of the canal.

Later that night, Tala walked downstairs and saw David laid back on his lazy blue chair, doing a word puzzle with CNN on TV solely for background noise. Her father never watched TV but always kept it on for some reason.

David sat up.

"You'll have to walk to school tomorrow. I have to be at work early."

"You're going to make me walk on my first day?" Tala said.

"It's a ten-minute walk. Closer than your old school. Besides, work, you know, pays for all this." He waved his hands around.

"What about the rental?" she said.

"I turned it in. Ben drove me back."

"Who's Ben?"

"Our neighbor."

"You make friends fast."

"I didn't tell you. We went to school together. I saw him when I came down here to see the house. He did good for himself. Not many people get out of Hialeah."

Tala said, "Awesome. Guess I'm walking."

David put the pen to his mouth, pensive. "Maybe you could walk with Mark."

"With who?"

"Mark." Her dad stared at her as if she should know. "He's Benny's boy. You two go to the same school." David went back to his word puzzle.

Tala rolled her eyes. "I'm not walking with some *stranger,* David, I'll be fine."

"Okay, suit yourself."

Tala leaned over his shoulder and saw a word instantly.

"I got one." Her dad handed her the pen. It was skewed diagonally.

She circled the word.

Metamorphosis.

TALA SNOOZED HER IPHONE ONCE, maybe twice. When she got up, she didn't have much time. She washed her face, put on jeans, and a gas station t-shirt that read: BEN OMAHA. She downed some Lucky Charms, hurried out, worried she'd be late. She'd hate being late on her first day of school and having people stare. Most people stick to the same seats the entire year, so she didn't want to get stuck next to some loser.

What if she tripped on her way to her seat? She'd always be *that* girl. Her rules for day one: *Be early. Don't Trip. Smile.* The first rule already in jeopardy.

Tala slung her backpack over her shoulder and opened the front door. There was a boy there, about to knock. He was tall, thin, with a handsome face, short black hair and a sly smile. He had a uniform on. Navy blue blazer, white Oxford shirt, khaki pants, and a necktie.

"Hi...I'm Mark. I live next door. I guess your dad wanted me to walk you—wait." He seemed surprised. "Where's your uniform?"

Tala looked into his brown eyes, then saw the two dimples come alive when he smiled.

Cute.

Wait.

Did he say UNIFORM?

"You been to Omaha," he said, trying to break the awkward silence.

Tala just stood there. Angry at her dad. How could he not mention a uniform? What was she, in elementary? She closed the door in Mark's face and called him.

He picked up on the first ring.

"Red," he said. "Everything okay?"

Tala thought, FANTASTA-FUCKULOUS.

"Did you know this school requires uniforms?"

"I put it on your bed. I told you. I even put a Post It on it."

Tala fought the urge to roll her eyes. She had gotten up in such a rush, she missed what was right in front of her.

"You couldn't tell me yesterday? I'm gonna be so late."

Tala stomped her way upstairs to change.

"Sorry, Red. I thought I told you." He looked at his watch. "Hey, you got time, send me a picture. Hello?"

She had hung up.

She rubbed her temples. "I'm gonna be so late."

She changed into a red-black flannel skirt just above the knees with a necktie. *He wants a picture. Of course, he does.* She thought of the movie *Cruel Intentions* and hoped she wouldn't see girls snorting coke out of their jewelry in the bathroom.

She went downstairs, texting her father,

This isn't over. I told you I would walk alone.

What had gotten into him? The beard. The Porsche.

The forgetfulness. Send me a picture? This wasn't like him. He was definitely having a midlife crisis. Tala hurried out again and found dimple boy on the sidewalk about to take off.

"Atta girl," he said. "I thought you weren't coming."

He might as well have been talking to the birds.

Tala passed him, having Googled her path to school the night before.

"Wait. I'm supposed to escort you," Mark said.

She looked back, still walking fast. "Listen, Matt, I'll be fine."

"It's Mark. Mark Bradshaw."

"Right, whatever," she said.

Tala kept looking at the time on her iPhone as if she could rewind it with her mind. 7:15 A.M.

"Hey, hold on." He jogged up and stood in front of her, blocking her. "Aren't you going to tell me your name at least?"

"My name is shut up."

The dimples returned.

"Listen, we're going to see a lotttt of each other," he said. "I live right there." He pointed to the house next door, which they were now standing in front of. Equally beautiful and picturesque.

"Your dad told my dad I should walk you to school since you're new here."

"Did he?"

The obvious answer was yes. He did. She realized how stupid and rhetorical the question was, but she had to say something. She hadn't stopped looking at his dimples.

"So, is that okay?" he said.

Tala said, "I'm gonna be so late."

THEY WALKED ON FAIRWAY AVENUE. Backpacks over one shoulder, eyes narrowed at the sun. They made small talk. The awkward feeling of two people meeting for the first time evaporated higher and higher into the clouds.

"So, is this school any good?"

"Nothing you haven't seen before. High school is high school, you know, you got the jocks, the nerds, the sluts, the band-geeks, and the downright weird."

"Which one are you?" she asked.

"Jock by day. Nerd by night."

"How does that work?" Tala said, amused.

"I've played soccer since I was a kid. But I love to read books. None of my friends know, so keep it on the low."

"What's wrong with books? I love reading."

He elbowed her softly. "I rest my case. Just kidding. It's just that most of my friends aren't readers. Actually, I don't think any of them are."

"I see."

"How about you? Which one are you?" he said.

"Well, I ran track. I read books. So, we might be on the same team. Although I think I'd fit in better with the down-right weird."

They laughed. Tala liked him. She couldn't stop looking at his dimples. She let him into her space, which she rarely did, and she felt okay. She didn't remember the last time she met someone whom she knew for so little time and had felt so comfortable with. This was that chemistry she had read about in books and seen in movies.

When they walked into Miami Springs High, they were shoved by crowds of students looking for their classes. She thought of bees squirming in a beehive, the buzzing sound growing louder and louder. She envisioned the walls closing, students jumping onto her, smothering her until she could no longer breathe. She felt tightness in her chest.

"What's the matter?" Mark raised his voice to speak over kids who just about yelled at each other in a fusion of English and Spanish, excited to see each other again since last year.

Tala shoved her way out of the hall into the courtyard. She sat down at a bench.

Breathe.

Just breathe.

Relax.

You're fine.

Mark followed. "What's wrong?"

"Nothing. What's with all the Spanish? I don't know what they're saying." She tried to downplay how she felt, putting her anxiety at bay.

"You don't know Spanish?" he said.

She shook her head. "You wanna laugh? I was born in Mexico. I mean, I can say *Hola* and *gato flaco*."

"A Mexican who doesn't speak Spanish, the world must be coming to an end. Can you say anything besides 'Hi' and 'Skinny Cat?'" Mark laughed.

Tala shook her head.

"Tu vas hacer mi novia," he said. *You're going to be my girlfriend.*

She appeared lost. "What'd you say?"

The halls had cleared.

Mark said, "It means, don't worry, I'll teach you Spanish." He looked at his watch. "You better get going. Late bell should be going off."

As if summoned, Tala heard the late bell go off.

Be early. Don't trip. Smile.

She ran through the hall and found her class after asking several people for directions. A couple of girls told her it was by the pool on the third floor. It took her some time to realize there was no pool. Or third floor. She eventually found her class. She peered in through the door window. The teacher stood front and center talking to his students.

Damn it.

She held the cold doorknob in her hand and peered in at an angle so no one could see her. She thought about walking in but knew everyone would stare. How could she be so stupid? This was the very thing she feared. Maybe the teacher would make her introduce herself right there on the spot. You never know what to expect when you walk in late on your first day. On top of that, she was the new girl. She hadn't seen another redhead, so she would stand out like a bear in a kitchen. The horror.

"Are you lost?"

Tala turned around, startled. "Geez, you scared me."

She saw an Asian boy with jet black spiked up hair with no folder or book bag. He had faded lines through the side of his head. He was smiling. Tala had her hand on her chest. He copied her.

"I pledge allegiance to the flag of the United States of America..." he said.

Tala realized he was teasing her and put her hand down.

"Sorry," he said. "I didn't mean to sneak up on you but I'm a ninja."

"A ninja?" she said, cracking a smile.

He stood in a karate stance. "Isn't it obvious? I'm just messing. What are you doing here?"

"Who me?"

"Yes. You. Couldn't be—then Who!" he said. "Yeah, I mean you're here holding the knob. There's no one else. This is 7204, American Government," he said. "Mr. Wilson's class."

Tala looked at her schedule. "Right. Yeah, this is my class."

"I'm Yin Vo." He put out his fist to her. She reluctantly fist bumped him. She had never saluted someone like this before.

"I'm Tala Stone."

"Cool." He put his hand out like a claw and started turning it.

Tala looked around. "What are you doing?"

"This is how you turn the knob." Yin laughed. "Come on, you're late."

Tala blocked him from opening the door. "You mean *we're* late."

Yin shrugged. "So?"

"When we open that door, everyone's going to look at us," she said.

"That's the best part," he said. "I'm late on purpose."

"What if I fall?" She bore a worried face.

"What?" Yin looked confused.

"You know," she said. "You walk in. Everyone goes silent, looks at you, then you fall and you'll always be the loser who tripped in class. Forever."

Yin shook his head and laughed. "You've really given this a lot of thought."

"Nobody cares," he went on. "Besides, you're not going to fall, and nobody is going to see you. You can trust me."

He reached around her and opened the door. She had no choice now. She felt the air conditioner from the class-room. The heavy silence from inside spread as the teacher, who was now leaning against his desk, paused to wait for them to enter.

Tala walked in and quickly scanned the room looking for chairs. All the chairs were taken except for three at the back of the room. She didn't have many options, which was good. She took a couple of steps forward and heard people call Yin's name who trailed her. There was no doubt he was popular.

"Excuse me." Yin said, walking theatrically in front of Tala. He took an exaggerated step forward and fell on the floor, face-first in front of Mr. Wilson. The class erupted in laughter. Yin got up slowly with a fake look of surprise. Holding his lower back like he injured himself. All part of the show.

Tala felt tremendous relief that the attention was off her. She scurried past him, sitting at an empty chair.

"Settle down. Settle down," Mr. Wilson said. In good nature.

The class settled down. Yin sat right in front of her.

"Mr. Vo," Mr. Wilson said. "I thought you'd wait a few days until you started with the theatrics."

"Sorry, Sir, I slipped." He fist-bumped a kid next to him.

Mr. Wilson taught American Government, but he was also the wrestling coach, which gave jocks the wrong idea. He was one of the cooler teachers, but when you were in his class, he liked to run the show. "Of course, you did." He made a note and went back to explaining the syllabus.

Yin looked back. "Wasn't so bad, huh?"

Tala said, "Looks like *you* fell."

Yin winked at her. "I told you, you could trust me. No one even saw you."

BUT THAT WASN'T TRUE. There was a dirty blond boy with a sleeve tattoo who saw her. In fact, he hadn't stopped looking at her.

11

SHERIFF JAMES HOGG stopped on the steps of city hall and watched a couple of deputies raise the American flag. The sheriff was a monumental man. He was the type of man who walked into a room and owned it. He was tall, black like coffee, and his arms looked like tree logs protruding from his uniform.

His size intimidated most men. Citizens told him they felt safe when they saw him in police uniform. Kids took pictures with him every chance they got and asked him if he could bend his gun in half. There was even a town legend about Sheriff Hogg arriving at the scene of a car crash and saving a man who was pinned underneath by lifting the vehicle with his bare hands.

Hogg watched the flag billow in the wind. He thought of this great country and its freedoms. He thought of his daughter Alice who had died years ago. Because of him. He had left his gun within reach. He had fallen asleep and woke to the sound of a gunshot in his living room. He tried to forget what he saw. There was blood everywhere. In a moment, he lost his daughter, his marriage, his future.

There wasn't a day that passed he didn't think of his baby girl.

Emma Sosa's friendship helped give him purpose. To look to the future. But the heartache was always there, lingering. He took the elevator to the third floor and walked into the mayor's office. He was in uniform, stars on his collar. Mayor Sosa held a finger up to him and continued talking on the phone. She had her legs up on the desk.

"Yes, sir. I know. Thank you."

She hung up.

"Well," Sosa said.

"The pilot is here." Hogg said, taking off his Stetson hat.

"And the girl?"

"Of course. She's here too."

Mayor Sosa stood from her desk. Paced slowly across the room and grabbed Hogg by the shoulders.

"We can't fuck this up."

Mayor Sosa's hands went back down to her side. She smiled like an excited little girl who was somewhat scared.

Sheriff Hogg stared down at her like a proud father.

"I know, Em, this is what we dreamed about in college," he said. "We're going to change *everything*. This is what it's all about."

"Is there any way she can know?" Sosa said.

"No. She can't know."

Sheriff Hogg looked deep into the mayor's eyes.

"She looks just like her mother."

Mayor Sosa nodded.

"Well, don't worry. That bitch is dead."

12

THE VICTORIAN HOUSE made Urbana's seem like an old painting at a garage sale. A house she and her dad had never quite lived in. She scrutinized the small cracks on her pebbled driveway and thought of how those cracks resembled her, resembled everyone, really. She wondered what cracks Mark had and if he was home yet. She was glad her dad arranged for them to meet, although she would never admit it.

Tala plucked a white May Bell from her garden and went inside the house. Her nose was overtaken with the smell of food she couldn't make out. Probably microwavable. She had skipped lunch to check out the library. She hadn't been hungry, taking everything in at school. She started having hunger pains.

Her dad stood in the kitchen with a serious face.

"Smells good," she said.

He stirred the canned refried beans. "Tell me I did good."

Tala sighed, tossed her backpack onto the couch. "You

never listen. I don't need some guy I don't know walking me to school. How weird is that? You didn't even mention the uniform."

Her dad gave her a melodramatic look.

"I'm serious. That was so awkward."

"Tell me I did good," he said.

"David, please, You're so embarrassing." A smirk crept onto her face, because her dad's ridiculous look hadn't changed. She wasn't good at hiding her emotions.

David said, "Handsome neighbor, beautiful town, huge house with an awesome pool."

"I could use my own car."

"Don't push it."

"Since when are you so excited about me hanging out with boys? When did that happen?"

"I'm not excited. Believe me, but I happen to like Benny. He's a nice guy. We went to school together, you know, back in the dinosaur era. I know Mark comes from good family. I'd rather you make friends with the right people."

"Who are the wrong people?"

Her dad pressed down on the Foreman grill. Smoke came up to his face. He waved it away.

"Prairie boys are the wrong people."

"You mean like you?" Tala had been at Springs High for one day and had already heard about the Hialeah boys, commonly referred to as Prairie Boys.

"From what Benny tells me, there are good people in Hialeah but few and far in between. Lots of troublemakers across the canal, I don't want you over there. Things have changed since I was a kid. It's different times. Are we clear?"

"I'm glad we're not stereotyping people." Tala said.

"Don't patronize me. I trust Ben. This isn't Urbana, and

this is not a debate. I don't want you hanging with the wrong people. Hialeah kids are off limits. *Capisce?*"

"Yes, your highness." Tala rolled her eyes when her father turned around.

13

AFTER HER MICROWAVE DINNER, Tala remembered she needed school supplies and wanted to get her hands on the new Stephen King novel. She refused to order online because bookstores *mattered* to her. She went downstairs looking for David and found him in his office, clicking and clacking on a keyboard. She pushed open his office door slightly, peering in.

"Dave—"

He gave a slight jump, pulled down his laptop screen a few inches. "You scared me," he said. He was Skyping with Olivia, whom Tala referred to as *her*. He pulled out his earbuds.

"I need stuff for school. Is there a Walmart by here?"

"Hang on." He paused the video call, opened a new tab in Firefox as he noticed the time at the corner of his screen. "Wait. Don't you have to go?"

"Go where?"

David analyzed the room. "I should really put a clock in here," he said.

Tala waited. "Go where?"

"Mark asked if he could show you around Springs with some friends. I said yes."

"YOU SAID YES? That's great, David. Thanks for sharing. When?"

"Now."

"NOW? I'm not ready."

Tala and David covered their ears at the loud shriek that came from outside.

"What in the blue hell was that?" David said, standing. It sounded like a train had parked against his window and blown its horn.

"There are no trains—"

David pinched the window blinds and saw a gang of teenagers inside a black Jeep Wrangler Gladiator. The Jeep had a lift kit, shocking blue headlights, lightbar, and exaggerated mud tires. The teens were laughing, listening to music that always made him want to put on talk radio. David let go of the blinds and followed Tala to the living room, contemplating his decision. Tala looked out the window. She turned to David with a mischievous smile.

"This looks like trouble, David." The obvious fail made her want to burst out laughing, but she was angry too.

"Why do you keep making plans for me? When the hell were you planning to tell me about it?"

"Watch-your-mouth." David stressed every syllable, making the appropriate pauses between the words.

David peered out the window again.

"Looks like Mark brought some friends, alright."

A moment later they heard the doorbell.

David said, "Listen, Red, I should have told you. I understand if you don't want to go."

Tala didn't know if she wanted to go. This had backfired

too perfectly for her to say no. He didn't expect a crazy group of teenagers.

"Oh, no. I'm going." She darted to the door.

David raced her there and opened it. Mark stood bashfully on the doorstep. "Hi. I'm sorry about the train horn, Mr. Stone. My friend is an idiot."

"Is he?" David said.

"Yeah. I've known him for years."

David looked past Mark. "That's his car?"

"Yes, sir, it is."

"Why are his tires so big?" David knew people customized their Jeeps with big tires for show, to make the cars look cool. But he pointed it out as a subliminal insult. No doubt an expensive waste of money.

"He's into cars," Mark said.

"How interesting," David said. "They look very useful." But of course, Tala knew her father, so she just rolled her eyes.

"Tala's not feeling well," David said. His phone went off. He took it out of his pocket and answered.

"Sorry I cut you off on the webcam," he said, his voice changing. It was *her*. Olivia's name always made Tala cringe. Even though she had never met her, she had concocted a million reasons why she hated her.

"It's too bad you're not up for it," Mark said. Looking concerned. David chirped on the phone, laughing like a schoolboy.

"David, I'm feeling better," she said.

Mark's dimples returned. She started walking out with him.

"How come you call him David?"

"It annoys him."

David reluctantly said, "Have her back by eleven."

"Are you and my dad ever going to include me in your plans?" Tala sulked.

David had gone back inside and closed the red door.

"I thought he told you," Mark said.

"He's distracted lately," Tala said, more to herself than to Mark. "It's not like him."

"Let's go. I want you to meet The Hawks."

Tala hesitantly followed him. "Oh God. You guys have a name?"

"Yeah, it's cool, right?"

"Super."

Mark opened the rear passenger door for her. Tala analyzed the three girls in the back seat. She didn't remember them from school, and she didn't know the driver either. She would be sitting next to strangers, close together.

She felt uncomfortable like she always had in tight spaces, but the Jeep's top was off so there was plenty of air. That made it bearable. Besides, she wanted to make friends here. She wanted to be social for a change, and what could be more social than running your thigh against some girl you just met.

"Earth to redhead." Tala realized she had dazed out.

Be early. Don't trip. Smile.

She gave her best smile. There was no real happiness behind it.

The brunette in the middle seemed concerned. "Are you okay? Why are you smiling like that?"

"She's fine," Mark said. He introduced everyone to Tala. "This is Valerie Hale, Makayla Stevens, and Jaen Justice." The girls waved. Analyzing her. Our idiot behind-the-wheel with the train horn would be Lance Vega, but you could just call him idiot."

"Very funny," Lance said. "Dickwad."

"Sorry about the horn," Lance said. "I can't help myself. It's too much fun. Just had it installed. We're probably on your dad's shit-list now, huh?"

"He'll live," Tala said. Taking it all in.

"Nice to meet you all," she said.

The girls continued dissecting her white t-shirt, blue ripped jeans, red curly hair, blue eyes, freckles, not a drop of makeup. There was an awkward silent moment that Jaen broke up when she asked, "Are you really a redhead?"

"Apparently," Tala said.

"Oh." Jaen seemed confused.

"We can't do sarcasm," Valerie said. "Jaen never gets it. Just get in."

There are moments when you meet someone for the first time that are weird. This was one of those moments, but there was a good flow of energy inside the Jeep, and everyone picked up on it. It was an energy of excitement and novelty. Of adventure. The Hawks bantered and laughed at a word Valerie pronounced wrong. They told Tala she did that often and she would adamantly defend her incorrect pronunciations.

"What's your name again?" Valerie said.

Lance raised the volume on the radio which seemed to annoy Valerie, a task he said, he undertook with great pride.

"What?" Tala said.

"Lower the music, numb-nuts." Valerie looked at Lance through the rearview mirror. He and Mark laughed. Mark lowered it to a reasonable level.

"I said, what's your name?" Valerie repeated.

"Tala."

Valerie whispered. "Tala. Tala. Tala. Tala. Tala." Tala gave her a strange look. Valerie smiled. "I'm horrible with names. I hate forgetting people's names. It helps."

Lance upped the volume on the radio again as he cruised on Circle Drive. There were people in the center terrace who apparently knew him. A couple of girls yelled, "Lannnnce!" as he drove by.

He yelled back, "What up, what up! Call me!" and kept driving slowly through the circle with the music blasting and set off the train horn a couple of times just to let everyone know who's boss.

Mark looked across his shoulder. "Who was that?"

"I have no clue," Lance said.

Everyone in the Jeep laughed.

They headed over the canal into Hialeah.

Tala saw where they were heading and started feeling hot and sticky. Knowing David didn't want her in The Prairie. Tala brought her attention back to the girls. She thought it was strange how they were all different but beautiful. Makayla was the only black girl. She had light black skin, curly hair, with green eyes. She figured the girls were analyzing her just the same.

"Where we going?" Tala asked Makayla.

"I'm not driving but looks like Hialeah," Makayla said.

"What's the plan?" Valerie bumped to the music. She took a silver flask out of her purse and took a sip. Tala had never had a drink of alcohol and was amazed at how nonchalant everyone seemed about it. The smell was strong, like the scotch her father used to drink.

Valerie held the flask to Tala. "How rude of me. Want some?"

"No. thanks."

"Jesus, Val, it's a school night," Jaen said in a mocking tone. She asked Lance, "What's our destination please?"

"Don't know our destination. But your destiny is with me."

Jaen gagged. "BARF!" she said.

Everyone laughed.

They were within the city limits of Hialeah. "We can show her the Beach, The Grove, Wynwood, Leah Arts—"

"It's a Wednesday night, man," Mark reminded him. "It's her first time out. We gotta break her in slow, we don't *really* want to get on her dad's shit-list. What are you up for, Tala?"

She almost said she needed school supplies but decided against it. Telling them she'd never been to the beach would make her seem queer. She'd been there of course, but she was in no way ready to go back.

"There's a new King book that came out."

Makayla gave an involuntary snort-laugh. Then really started laughing when she realized Tala was serious.

"O.M.G., you like books," Makayla actually said. O.M.G.

"I like stories. Not textbooks."

"Well, in that case, how about the track? We can tell ghost stories," Jaen chimed in. "It's a shame Yin couldn't come, he loves the track."

"That's right, I almost forgot the track." Lance smiled roguishly, making eye contact with Tala via the rearview. Tala could only see his eyes. Of course, he hadn't forgotten. No one forgot the track.

"What track?" she asked.

Lance said, "The Hialeah Racetrack. Great spot to chill, drink, hangout, hookup—"

"Or murder someone," Makayla said under her breath.

"That too." Mark said, then laughed.

"The only bad part is that it's haunted," Lance said.

As Lance drove deeper into Hialeah, Tala saw the change in neighborhoods and roads. Everything seemed older and dirtier, like the buildings were held together with glue.

"Welcome to the High Prairie," Valerie said.

Mark looked through the rearview. "You up for it? The Track?"

"I'm up for anything, but I don't believe in ghosts," Tala said.

"You will," Lance said. "It's a scary effin' place."

Lance started heading toward the track, and after some small talk with the girls, Tala noticed the car slowed down as Lance turned in. The Hialeah Racetrack was surrounded by high vined walls and tall pines. It looked different than when Tala drove by during the day. She remembered the pink cursive sign.

Hialeah Racetrack.

Lance drove on a dark road into a dark place surrounded by nothing but darkness. The streets of Hialeah had begun to die down. There was no light save for the moon and stars and the Jeep's headlights and HID light-bar, which revealed a dirt road and nothing more.

Lance went off the road. He followed a worn path, made some scary noises which Tala found amusing. He turned over fallen logs and put the Jeep into four-wheel drive. Tala bounced up and down and felt like she'd been in the Jeep for hours.

Lance killed the engine.

Tala saw a blood red moon sitting behind the tall pines.

"Are you sure you wanna come here?" Lance said. His voice deeper now and the look on his face grave.

"Don't listen to him," Valerie said. "He's just trying to rile you up. C'mon turn on the car."

"I'll manage."

"This is your last chance." Lance cracked his voice in a

girlish mocking tone. "It's like a scary effin' place." The Hawks laughed.

"It's your funeral, Tala," Lance said sternly.

He started the engine again.

He drove into another high walled area that Tala saw was covered with vines, foliage, and graffiti. Tala focused on the thick vines, thinking how much they resembled human veins. The farther they drove into the track, the more the city lights faded. The headlights provided the only light they had; that, and the moon overhead and its scattered stars. Tala saw tall trees on both sides of the unkempt road and nothing but a few feet of deteriorated pavement before them.

"Scared yet?" Lance asked. Driving slower than necessary, he made a spooky howling noise.

"So, what about that story?" Tala said. "I love scary novels."

No one said anything for a moment, then Mark said, "Novels are fiction." The car sank into a pothole and bounced back out. "This is real."

Lance drove farther down the desolate road and veered off into a smaller trail that led into more darkness. It was evident that Lance had taken this route many times. He knew the way but branches hit the windshield and side of the Jeep, touching Tala like fingers.

"We have to get off the car." Valerie smiled at Tala. "That's the fun part. Unless you're scared."

"Lead the way." Tala's boldness started to dissipate the farther into the track they went. She could see nothing but pitch darkness out the window now. The thought of a hand reaching into the truck and grabbing her became more plausible with every minute. Tala put her window up.

"You're not scared, are you?" Valerie asked.

"No, branches keep hitting me."

Her face betrayed her.

Tala said, "Ghost stories are fun but fiction. And no matter how scary they are, we know that at night when we turn off the lights in our bedrooms, no one will reach from under our beds and pull our legs."

"That may be true. But this is no bedroom, Tala." Mark adjusted the rearview and winked at her.

Lance parked, turned off the Jeep. "We're here. Let's go."

Tala didn't know where *here* was. She could barely see.

Everyone got off the Jeep. The interior dome light seemed like the only light left in the world, and when they shut the doors, it was gone like a burned-out sun.

Lance led through the tall pines using a flashlight he had stashed underneath his seat. This light brought some relief but also made the woods seem three-dimensional, and the noises made it seem like someone was dodging to hide behind a tree when the flashlight was pointed in their direction. They walked through the woods until they met an enclave in the ground. The rest of them used their cell phone flashlights to guide them.

It was dark, but the blood red moon and stars provided enough light to make out the track. Tala thought of the dead men and horses who had found glory on this very field. She thought of the thousands of people from all over the world who had united here to wager and celebrate great victories and suffer unbearable losses. All those people dead now, she thought. That place of great history now a barren desolate hole in the Earth.

Tala followed Mark through the underbrush with Jaen, Valerie, and Makayla by her side. She thought how, minutes before, she had been in her house wanting to go to Walmart for school supplies and how now she was watching her step out here, in the darkness, with these strangers.

Tala and Mark broke off from the pack. Lance, Jaen, Valerie, and Makayla trailed them, lost in their own conversations. Due to her insecurities, Tala imagined they were talking about her when they laughed. She stayed by Mark's side as they made it around the track. Somewhat uncomfortable she was unable to make out his face. When they walked to the center of it, the track reminded her of a cemetery. Of Pleasant Valley. Of Angels of Mercy. She pushed the thought away.

"How long has this place been closed?" she said. Breaking the heavy silence.

"Many and many a year ago," Mark said.

"Poe," Tala replied.

"Edgar Allen is one of my favorite poets. You're not the only reader here," he said with glee.

"Why'd you stay quiet back there when I said I liked books?"

"Wanted to see if you'd drown. I won't always be there to rescue you, you know." He smiled.

Tala could make out his white teeth now. She couldn't distinguish the other features of his face. It was too dark.

"I see that. Nerd by night."

"Touché."

"This place has been closed for hundreds of years," Mark said. Even though Lance, Valerie, Jaen, and Makayla were a considerable distance, their voices bounced off the trees.

"It's haunted," Lance said. "It's haunted, I tell you!" he screamed and waved his flashlight around like a maniac as he ran around in a circle.

"Is he always this animated?" Tala said.

"Unfortunately."

"What about Yin?"

Mark said, "You know him?"

"We have a class together."

"Him too. Very animated. They're best of friends, raised together."

"How come he didn't come?"

"His parents threw a fit because he tripped in class or something. His parents are strict like the military. They're done with him being a class clown. He said he tripped to get some laughs. Break the ice for the new year. Mr. Wilson didn't think it was funny. He called his parents."

Tala felt guilty.

"You would think his folks would cut him some slack. He's a straight A student, freakin brainiac."

The rest of The Hawks made a Beeline toward them. "Story time. New girl has a curfew," Valerie said.

"Hurry. This place gives me the creeps," Jaen added.

They all gathered in a circle.

"You tell it," Lance said to Mark.

"You go. You're a better storyteller," he replied.

Lance thought it over. "You've got a point there."

Lance pointed the flashlight up from his chin, illuminating his face, giving him a malevolent appearance. His eyes looked distant, like he was in a trance. He turned his head deliberately to Tala.

"There's no fiction in this story," he said, making his voice deep and eerie.

The girls giggled nervously.

His expression didn't change. His eyes looked piercing and evil.

"Let's hear it," Tala said. She felt more comfortable enclosed in a circle. The wind began to pick up and when she looked at the sky, she could see the canopy of pines dancing with stars behind them. It was like dark magic. They stood on lower ground inside the enclave on the track, surrounded by pitch black darkness and nosy pine trees.

"You ever heard of the Curtiss Mansion?" Lance said.

"No," She lied. "Never have." She had a smirk on her face, her natural response to Lance's stern face, but when she looked at Mark and the girls, she saw no one laughing. She felt like a stranger again.

"Glenn Curtiss built this very track, Tala. He founded the neighboring cities here. Most things that bear his name have been considered *haunted*. Strange things. Odd things have happened here and about these towns. Unsolved murders. Disappearances. An unexplainable obsession with the Curtiss Mansion has led many to insanity."

"You mean the house on Deer Run?" she offered.

"So you have heard of it," he said.

She nodded so slightly, it could have been a nervous twitch. She panned her eyes, but she couldn't see anyone's face apart from Lance's since he was holding the flashlight to it. The rest of The Hawks looked like faceless humans.

"The house is evil. Haunted. People have died. Suffered. Burned. Cried. Disappeared. Lost their minds, and some say even their souls."

Tala had heard scarier stories in *Goosebumps* books. She panned her eyes again but still couldn't make out anyone's face, and this began to make her feel more uncomfortable. She wasn't scared of the story. Stories were stories. But being out in the dark was different.

She could only see the shadows on Lance's brow and lips from the upward illumination of the flashlight. Giving him a hideous appearance. She was a little scared but not much. For some reason being near Mark made her feel safe.

If she were alone here, she knew she would run toward the city lights.

Lance continued, "Stories of the Curtiss Mansion go back a hundred years. Everyone knows he locked his family inside the house. He burned them alive. The horses too. Many fucked up things happened, but for the sake of brevity and staying off your dad's shit-list, I'll tell you a recent story."

"Let's hear it," Tala said.

"Years ago, a kid from The Prairie disappeared. His name was Charlie Owens, a senior at Hialeah High School. Kid was a mess, always in and out of trouble, a rap sheet longer than my," He looked down at his pants. "And that's pretty big."

"Oh please. You want us to believe you or not?" Valerie laughed.

"Okay, okay, I'm kidding. But seriously. It's huge. I have a problem."

Everyone laughed.

"Okay, for real," he continued. "Charlie became obsessed with the mansion. He would research it, sketch it, paint it, draw it. Like from one day to the next, he's talking about it all the time. He's obsessed with the God forsaken place, right? And everyone in town knows the legends, some true, some inflated. Charlie can't stop thinking about them. Back then, there was no perimeter fence, so it was a haven for winos and hobos looking for a place to sleep. The city started building the fence and cracking down on trespassers. The cops nail Charlie for trespassing a few times. And the Sonofabitch would come back as soon as he was released. It was like he was in a trance. Hypnotized and shit—"

"And?" Tala said. Not very impressed.

"Let me finish. He's obsessed, right? Kept talking gibberish—not making sense. Talking about rainbows and butterflies, out of his mind crazy. He told people the mansion had ears. It was listening to his conversations. Reading his thoughts. There was other stuff—I can't remember everything, but I remember him saying Glenn Curtiss might've been a good man. Charlie Owens got inside the house, no one knows how. He skipped school, bummed a ride with some friends got off the car, walked towards the door on a dare and disappeared right in front of them."

Lance lowered the flashlight giving him a surreal look with heavy shadows on his face.

"It was broad daylight. His friends told police they waited for him for four hours. Walked around the mansion. And that he had just disappeared. When it got dark, they left. They figured their eyes played tricks on them and that he had gone home. The cops thought his friends were lying. They thought the story was suspicious and brought them in for questioning. I heard they almost charged them with murder.

"Needless to say, Charlie didn't come home. His friends told police maybe he had been playing a joke on them or something, you know, hiding out trying to scare them. The Curtiss Mansion is huge. And the land is massive. He could have been hiding anywhere."

"What happened?" Tala said.

"Police searched the entire property. Not to mention volunteers. K9's sniffed his clothes to try and track him down. The county helicopter canvassed the dense wooded area called The Sea of Trees. No dice. He was gone like a fart in the wind. Detectives checked all the schools, talked to his teachers, friends, Amber alerts on radio, his school picture on the news. You name it."

"What happened to him?" They heard a wrestle behind the trees. Lance quickly pulled the flashlight to the area, but they saw nothing but moving branches."

"What the hell was that?" Tala said.

"I think it's time to leave," Makayla said.

"I'm outta here." Jaen began walking away.

"Relax, ladies. It's just a fox or something," Mark said.

"Do they attack humans?" Jaen said.

"You're safe with me, baby." Lance blew her a kiss.

"Remind me to puke when I get in your Jeep," Jaen said.

"I love it when you play hard to get," he countered.

"Anyways," Lance went on. "A deputy found him six months later."

"Six months?" Tala said. "Where was he?"

"No one knows. But I know where they found him." Tala knew the answer before he said it. *She could feel it.* His eyes focused intently on Tala. "Here. On this very race-track." Tala felt a chill run down her back.

"A cop found him walking this very track, lethargic, speaking another language. The cop who found him told the paper Charlie Owens seemed to be in a trance and was a very disturbed young man."

Lance gave a slight smirk. A nervous smirk. Tala interpreted it as dishonesty.

"Liar," she said. "You had me going for a minute."

"It's true," he replied defensively.

"Bullshit," she said.

Lance kissed his thumb and index finger simultaneously like an Italian. "Swear to God," he said.

"Everyone knows this story," Makayla said. "It's true."

Everyone but Mark concurred. The story had made the

news several years past, and everyone in the Springs agreed it was sensationalized.

"C'mon, maybe something happened but you spiced it up. You know stories change from ear to ear," Tala said. "It's like playing telephone."

Lance said again, "My brother went to school with Charlie and his friends. He told me the story."

"Your brother could have pulled that story out of his ass," Mark said. "C'mon, Owens disappeared in front of them? That's Urban Legend crap."

Lance said, "It's true."

"So where is Mr. Owens now?" Tala said.

Lance said, "I remember my brother telling me Charlie's parents didn't believe it was their son. Like he had been changed into a zombie. He ended up in a mental hospital."

"Which one?" Tala questioned, hoping to trip him up on his words, make him stumble on a lie, but she was unsuccessful. He simply replied, "I don't remember."

"Well, that's pretty convenient," Mark said.

"You don't remember because it's not true," Tala added.

Lance pointed the flashlight at her face, forcing her to bring her hands up.

Valerie said, "Can we get the fuck out of here? I think I hear something. This place gives me the creeps." Everyone hushed, but they only heard crickets chirping and branches wrestling with the wind.

"There's no one here," Lance said.

Tala knew he said it, but she heard Dr. Moss's voice in therapy. *There's no one here. There's no one here. There's no one here.* She was back in the woods. She heard the wolves howling. She was running.

Tala thought, *someone's here.*

"I'm serious, let's go," Valerie said.

"I'm with her. Let's go," Jaen said. "It's getting cold. I think it's gonna rain."

Tala crossed her arms. "Yeah, we better go."

"Who's scared now?" Lance said to Valerie. "We're supposed to be scaring the *new* girl. Why are you tripping? You know this place is overrun with stray cats and foxes."

"I swear he went to a hospital by here; I can't recall the name," Lance said to Tala.

They all looked doubtful at him. There was a rumble of thunder, and out of nowhere a heavy rain started to fall.

"Holy shit balls," Lance said. "My Jeep!"

They climbed out of the enclave of the track, feeling heavier and slower due to drenched clothes. They sprinted back to the Jeep. Lance led the way with the flashlight. Lance turned off his flashlight making it impossible for his friends to see.

"Don't get lost, guys!" he listened as the girls panicked and ran around like chickens with no heads. He laughed. Tala felt the grass tickle her ankles as she ran over bushes and overgrown shrubs. They ran quicker with more precise steps, careful not to fall into the muck.

They wanted to be out of the dark and back on the street where the lights brought comfort. As Lance took off the alarm of the Jeep, the lights beeped. Its short burst of noise ricocheted off the trees. He opened his door quickly, ready to jump in when a bunch of oranges fell off the driver seat.

"What the...?" he said, stepping back, holding the door with one hand. The heavy rain subsided.

"What is it?" Mark opened the passenger door.

Oranges fell off his seat as well. Tala looked behind her and saw nothing but darkness and silhouettes of trees. She peered in and saw no one. Could someone be waiting in the backseat with a machete?

Lance smiled on the outside, but he looked scared. Tala opened her door, and countless oranges fell off the seat. The Jeep had been loaded with them, rotten to the core. Lance reached in and turned on the car. The radio came on and echoed off the trees. Playing nothing but static. The track was a dead zone for radio and cell phones. No one knew why. It added to the legends.

"Okay, what the *fuck* is going on?" Valerie said, drenched from the rain. She had finally caught up to them.

Tala looked around and felt her heart pulsing in her hands, a ball of cotton lodged in her throat.

Lance picked up an orange and looked at it. "The mental hospital..."

"What?" Mark said.

They all looked perplexed. Lance looked possessed.

"I remember the name of the mental hospital," he said in a low voice.

They all waited for an answer.

He inspected the rotten orange in his hand like it was an alien life form.

"He's at Citrus Mental Hospital."

THE HAWKS CLEARED oranges off the leather seats and headed back toward the city lights. They smiled at each other, concealing the fear inside that expanded like a balloon.

On the way back, Lance slowed down on Circle Drive, which was now empty. Most people felt enamored when they saw the circle, and Tala was no different. The historic roundabout permeated with mom and pop businesses and shops.

The Happenstance bookstore made Tala wonder how much of her life had been coincidence. In the center of the roundabout stood a beautiful white rustic terrace with neatly trimmed grass and stone monuments of the town's forefathers.

"This circle is so beautiful," Tala said.

"The old timers say it's the heart of the town," Mark said.

"Want to get off?" Lance said to Tala, slowing down.

"She can see it some other time. I'm soaked," Jaen said.

"Don't be a party pooper. Let her see it. You never want to go home," Valerie said.

Jaen said, "If I get sick, it's on you,"

Valerie said, "You'll live."

Lance pulled over right on the road since traffic had died down.

"This place is lame," Jaen said.

"It's not," Makayla said. "Go with her, Mark."

"Who's getting off?" Lance said.

"I'll take Tala," Mark said. "C'mon."

Mark got off and opened her door.

"What a gentleman," Lance teased.

They walked to the rustic white terrace. Tala shivered when the cold air hit her wet clothes. The silent night at circle drive belonged to Tala and her friends.

"This is neat," she said, running her fingers on the wooden rail.

"Yeah, it's been here a hundred years," Mark said. "It's kind of nice. We take it for granted most days."

Mark came close to her and looked into her blue eyes.

"If these benches could talk." Tala sat down, absorbing

every detail, hardwood floors, rustic benches, a circle at the center of the town. The historical monuments paid tribute to founders like Glenn Curtiss, James Bright and men of the past.

Mark said, "I wonder if I'll ever be worthy of a monument."

"Maybe you will," Tala said.

Mark said, "You know, you look different from any girl I'd ever seen."

"Is that bad?"

"No."

When Tala looked up, she saw several black bubbles on the ceiling of the terrace.

"Are those cameras?" she said.

"Yeah. The town installed them a while back. Prairie scum was coming here to tag and vandalize the circle. Mayor Sosa had them installed. Talk about big brother, huh?"

"So is someone looking at us right now?" she said, putting her hand up and slowly waving it.

"I don't know. I doubt it. I guess it just records. Or maybe it's just there to scare people off."

"I don't think so," she said. "I think it works. I think someone is looking at us right now."

14

SOMETHING ABOUT BOOKSTORES made Tala feel comfortable. During class, Tala googled the Happenstance bookstore. She loved reading novels but lately had taken a liking to autobiographies and memoirs. Her curiosity took charge, and she started thinking about the racetrack and Lance's story about Charlie Owens. What was his autobiography? Or was the tale fiction? She thought of Glenn Curtiss, the genius madman and the horrible murders he committed.

What was his story?

What was her own?

After school, she went to Happenstance and asked a tall girl behind the counter with short hair and thick bottled eyeglasses if she had any books about Glenn Curtiss. The girl barely registered Tala, she kept her eyes down on her iPhone as she texted, Tala knew by the green and blue bubbles on her screen. Tala wondered how some people even got jobs. The employee finally acknowledged her.

"Why do you want books about that *monster?*" She chewed gum like a cow.

Tala wanted to shove a book into her mouth.

The girl fiddled with her computer and said she had one book by Glenn Curtiss, but it sold. The fact Glenn Curtiss wrote a book *himself* made Tala curious. She expected to find books written about him, but like most historical figures, the killer had put ink to paper. *The Aviation Handbook*.

The salesclerk went back to her phone, and Tala finally snapped, "I'm standing right here!" She raised her voice; people browsing nearby aisles looked over. She hated rude people. Her mom always said manners were free.

The salesclerk held on to her Coca-Cola bottled glasses and apologized. She put her phone away. She said if she really needed it, she could probably find an old copy on the internet. So much for bookstores, she thought.

She wanted the book now. Her curiosity grew. She had never read anything penned by a real killer before. She wanted to read his words to see if there was a clue as to why he had committed the horrible crime and tarnished his legacy.

Tala left Happenstance. She saw Mark across the street, talking on his cellphone. He had seen her, and something about the way he looked at her made her think he was talking about her. She smiled and gave him a little wave. She hoped he would come over and offer her a ride home, but he didn't.

When Tala made it home, she found a note on the refrigerator door next to the picture of Tala and her mom at Disney World when she was four.

> DINNER IN THE FRIDGE.
> HAD TO RUN.
> —DAD

David often left home without much foresight. As the sun and moon were trading places, she felt a transformation in her when she saw the full moon shining. It was Friday night, and her first week of school was officially over. Tala checked her phone and saw thirteen missed calls. She had left her phone downstairs and taken a shower. The calls were all from Mark.

She called him back. To find out what was going on. Thirteen calls seemed abnormal. Had something happened?

He picked up on the first ring. "Hello?"

She held her breath, anticipating bad news.

"Hey, you."

"Did you call me?" She felt stupid after she asked. Of course, he called her thirteen times.

"Yeah, about a hundred times," he said. "Come over. The Hawks are here."

"The Hawks?"

"Yeah, the crew. That's what we call ourselves. Remember?"

"Oh. You were serious about that?" Tala teased.

"Very funny," Mark said. "Come over."

"Over where?"

"Look out your window."

Tala looked out her side window.

Tala saw Mark, Valerie, Lance, Yin, Jaen, Makayla, and other kids from school. Right next door. Some she recognized. Some she didn't.

Mark said, "Pop's in Orlando for the weekend on business. Come over. We're having a few beers." David was working too. He wouldn't be back until tomorrow.

Tala heard Lance in the distance laughing and talking loudly, being a clown. He sounded far, but she heard him say, "Tala, where you at, girl? It's Friday. You ain't living on a farm no more."

She sure wasn't.

She heard more laughing in the background and saw others dancing now that the music had been raised to an unnecessarily high level. She felt the tension in her neck evaporate. She hated how she always thought the worst. *You're being invited to a party. Nothing to freak out about.*

"You're coming, right?" Mark said.

"I don't know. I have this book—"

"Oh, please, it's Friday. Come or I'll put you in the downright weird crew forever."

"I won't drink," she said.

Tala almost drank from her father's stash once but decided against it when she saw what it did to him.

"You don't have to do anything you don't want to."

"We're playing beer pong," he went on. "But there's also music."

"I know. I can hear it." She wanted to come over. She wanted to see him. She wouldn't drink. She wouldn't do that.

Tala stayed silent for a moment.

"We're not going to peer pressure you or anything. We're over that. That was *so* last year, so?"

Valerie took the phone from him. "Look out the window, whore!" She was laughing hysterically. Tala thought she could smell the alcohol seeping through the receiver of her phone.

Tala went to the window again and saw Valerie had been jumping up and down on Mark's trampoline as she talked on the phone. She stopped when she saw Tala looking through the window and beckoned her. Tala pulled her window up, the music sounded concert level.

"What are you waiting for?" Valerie screamed and raised a beer. She got off the trampoline when Lance came from behind, grabbed her, and tossed her into the pool, beer and all.

Tala wanted a change, alright. She wanted friends, and here they were.

Beggars can't be choosers.

15

TALA KNOCKED SEVERAL TIMES, but no one answered. The Handler by Muse blasted out of multiple jumbo speakers. Tala felt like the ground was shaking, but of course, it wasn't. Maybe it was her head. Yeah, that was it. She felt a mild headache coming on. She thought about turning back and going home. But that was what the Old Tala would do.

She wanted to make friends. She wanted to be normal. She kept knocking to no avail. She wondered if The Hawks invited her over as some sick joke. Like the whole school was peering through the window blinds laughing at her. She knocked harder and harder. Her knuckles got red, but the sound drowned out like screaming in a soundproof room.

She fished her phone from her back pocket.

She texted Mark:

TALA: *Hey, I'm here.*
     Mark: *The doors unlocked; all you have to do is walk in.* ;)

．　．　．

SHE HADN'T EVEN THOUGHT of checking if the door was locked. These weren't Urbana norms. She walked in and closed the door behind her. She stepped into a tight foyer that led into the living room. There were grizzly bear rugs on the floor, giant Moose heads on the wall, masterfully conserved. The animals looked alive.

She studied the living room, taking it all in. She didn't know why she was so drawn to the dead animals. She hated trophy hunters but seeing the animals up close like this had a macabre sort of beauty. There were buffalo heads, exotic stags with crown antlers that crawled up to the ceiling.

She felt claustrophobic and sullen. She wanted to go outside where the people were. She liked how rustic and old fashioned the decor of the house was. It reminded her of Urbana. An old wooden tree trunk sat at the center of the living room with wooden picture frames of Mark, his father Ben, and another man about twenty years old. They were dressed in green camouflage.

Ben Bradshaw was shorter than Mark, had a beer belly and short salt and pepper hair. He looked military, and he was, Tala inferred from several frames with military honors, including a Purple Heart.

Her eyes came up again and couldn't believe it. It was bad enough to kill these animals, but then it got worse. Tala saw on display a gorgeous lion. It had to be fake. What kind of person kills a lion for sport? What kind of person displays a lion like some trophy? It was enormous. Beautiful and melancholy.

"Are you almost done?"

Tala turned. "Fucckkdddge..." Her hand was on her chest. "I was just looking."

"Scared you?" Mark said. He was holding a Yuengling beer. He took a sip, then pointed at the lion with the can as if referring to nothing of importance.

"Shot that bastard at about 200 yards."

How long was Mark standing behind her?

"Where did you?" but she wanted to say was *why would you.* "Limpopo, South Africa. Small village. We had been in Jeeps' all day. No luck. We were about to head back to the lodge when I looked through the binoculars and saw him pop his head up the sawgrass. He was beautiful. I could have stayed quiet. I debated it. But I told my dad. You know, that's why we were out there. Hunting big game. I told him lion, six o'clock." Mark smirked. Although he seemed sad. "Five seconds is all it took. I heard the gun go off. The beast fell."

"Everyone in the Jeep, you know, the tour guide people and other hunters started celebrating like our team had just won the Super Bowl. But every time I see it, I feel guilty. Sometimes it's better to look the other way."

"You like hunting?" Mark asked.

"I never been," She wanted to yell.

How could you and your sick father do that?

Someone opened the rear doors because the music got really loud again.

Yin popped his head. Looked at Tala.

"Hello Mexico, will you be joining us in our debaucheries?" He flashed a brilliant smile, and his jet-black hair was perfectly spiked.

"I'm here, aren't I?"

"Shall we?" Mark offered his arm formally to escort her. Tala obliged. Mark took her to the back yard where the party was. The yard was big, about the size of Tala's, and had a pool with neon purple lights around its rim. And a trampoline. The landscaping was immaculate. A tall oak tree reminded Tala of Pleasant Valley. The oak split into a massive V- shape, where it held a large tree house in its mouth.

The tree house was wrapped in thick vines like veins that pump blood to keep us moving. To keep us talking. And of course, breathing. There were teens hanging out she had never seen but not too many. Most were faces from school. The same crew from the Hialeah Racetrack, The Hawks, beckoned her from the tree house windows.

Tala looked up at the beautiful tree house, she imagined Mark and his dad must've built it many summers ago when he was a kid. The tree house was made of varnished redwood and pine and had weathered well with the years. The tree appeared godly, a testament of its strength, weathering storm after storm through the turbulent hurricane seasons of South Florida. Lance popped his head out a window. "TALA! Up here!" He waved her up.

"I didn't lose anything up there," she said.

The music was still on, but it had been lowered. Valerie shoved Lance to the side and popped out her head. "Come up, Redhead! We got something to show you!" Tala sized up the tree and couldn't imagine anything that would make her climb it. The Hawks continued hollering.

"You going up?" Mark said.

"I like it down here."

"Suit yourself." Mark went up the makeshift ladder with acrobatic ease. What would they think if she didn't go up? She didn't want them to know she was scared of heights. The makeshift ladder didn't help. It consisted of pieces of wood screwed together unevenly. How could someone who created such a beautiful tree house create such a shitty ladder? The thought almost made her laugh, but instead she smirked, biting her lower lip. She ran her hand through her hair as she began to feel her anxiety rise.

"Looks dangerous," she said.

"It's a tree house, not a watch tower. We're not at war or anything. Get up here," Lance said. Tala saw smoke coming out of the treehouse windows. Lance held a beer over the railing with a goofy smile. "One step at a time," he said. "You can do it!"

She imagined stepping on one of the last steps, slipping and falling to sudden death. As preposterous as the thought was, there it was, lingering in the back of her mind. Lingering like the ravens in Pleasant Valley.

"What are you waiting for?" Lance said, his cheeks as red as a lobster's. "Get your ass up here! We have to initiate you!"

Tala looked up at the treehouse. Her hands had begun to sweat. "I'm coming."

The closer she got to the tree, the higher the treehouse seemed. High like a skyscraper. Her ears got hot. And that damn headache came in and out like an ocean tide. *Just breathe. In and out.* She wanted change, *damnit,* and change was here.

This stupid tree wasn't going to stop her from making friends, from starting over. She put her foot on the first step and grabbed the next rung with her hand. She hauled herself up slowly taking both feet off the ground now. She made sure her foot had proper grip on her soles, then pushed upward. She took step after step. She controlled her breathing. She thought about nothing except for the next rung. Going up wasn't hard. She had ran track, after all.

When she put her foot on the twelfth step. She looked down. She didn't want to look down; that wasn't part of the plan, but she couldn't help it. Instantly, she felt different.

Outside of herself. Her heart pounded faster and faster. She thought of an engine overheating and giving out, and the blood overflowed to her hands, and she felt lethargic.

She held on. She closed her eyes. She wasn't climbing a shitty ladder anymore. She was running through the woods somewhere. Running from the wolves. There were so many of them. Biting. Tearing something to pieces. A wail. A horrible wail. She opened her eyes and—

"Come on, you're almost here," Valerie egged her on, reaching down for her hand. Tala couldn't move; the blood flowed through her veins, and she imagined her veins stuck and clogged, and her brain lacked oxygen. She took another step up, and the air became thinner.

The whole world's oxygen seemed to be gone, sucked away by a giant vacuum. She thought of a woman falling from a hotel in a polka dotted dress. After the woman hit the ground, she walked up to her as people ran for cover. She saw Yona's face. She was only a child.

Tala let go.

When she opened her eyes, she saw Yin standing over her. Mark, Valerie, Lance shouldered in closer to look.

"Holy shit balls, I thought you were dead," Lance said.

"What happened?" Tala said.

"Are you okay?" Mark said. "Can you move?"

Tala sat up despite her back hurting.

"You're such a buzzkill," Valerie said.

"How many fingers do I have up?" Lance said. Pointing his middle finger at her.

Tala said, "You're an asshole." They all laughed. The fear she had really hurt herself went away.

After a few seconds, Tala said, "You have a really nice lawn." She extended her arms and legs out wide as if to make a snow angel.

"She's alive!" Yin said.

"Are you okay?" Mark said, kneeling next to her. His voice overpowering their laughter.

"I'm not much of a climber," Tala replied.

She saw kindness in Mark's light brown eyes. His look made her feel vulnerable, like he knew her secrets. Mark offered his hand. She took it and he pulled her up. She felt the power of his pull and felt for the first time in her life like she was with a man, not an insecure boy from Urbana.

"We usually perform our ritual in the tree house." Lance sarcastically cleared his throat. "But since we have a ladder-challenged friend here tonight, and Mark's dad is out cutting trees, it only makes sense we initiate her right here. *Oh no, this can't be good. What if I say no?* She didn't know if the new Tala would be open to an initiation, whatever the hell that meant.

"I'm not smoking pot," Tala said. Cigarettes were the furthest she'd go.

"Who said anything about smoking?" Lance said with a mischievous smile.

Jaen said, "Tala's face tells me she ain't up for it," she said. "Although it's the only way to join The Hawks."

They had all succumbed to the ritual. Tala thought Mark was cute ever since he showed up at her front door, but for some reason tonight the word wasn't cute anymore. The word was sexy. She didn't want to appear child-like. Or be a buzzkill, in Valerie's words. The fluorescent lights reflected off his glasses. He was damn sexy. Yin pulled something out of his pocket.

"Well, Tala, since you like books. Tonight, you get to choose. Do you want to go to Wonderland or to Oz?"

"What are you jabbering about?" Makayla said. Yin

held something in his hand. Makayla took a closer look and started laughing. "It's perfect. The illusion of choice."

Makayla said, "Wait, not so fast. We have to vote, remember?"

"That's right," Valerie said. "It has to be unanimous. This is the first step."

Tala couldn't see what Yin was holding. Did she want to try it? She didn't know. All she knew was that the Old Tala didn't want to.

16

MARK, Jaen, Lance, Valerie huddled underneath the tree house, giving Tala speculative glances. They called Yin over. "Put that down, man. Come here."

Yin put his beer down and obliged.

Tala sat by the pool. She wondered what they were whispering about together. She felt like an outsider. They were all smiling mischievously. Whatever it was, it wasn't good.

Yin came back.

"Well, good news, sort of. They wanna know if you'll join The Hawks."

"Which part of my soul do I have to sell?"

"All of it. Just kidding. But there is a cost."

"What kind of cost?"

"You won't know the cost until you decide to pay it."

"What are you talking about, Yin? What's the mystery?"

"Say the word. And you're in."

Tala looked past Yin and saw The Hawks waving while smiling mischievously. This couldn't be good.

"In or out?"

Tala didn't like surprises, but she relented.

"I'm in."

"Awesome."

"She's in, guys!" Yin yelled. The Hawks came over.

Yin took a joint off the top of his ear.

"I'm not smoking," Tala said.

"Who said anything about smoking?" Valerie said.

She pulled something from her back pocket. "This is for you."

Val revealed small pieces of blotting paper cut intricately in squares with different cartoons and designs. She ripped two stamps apart.

One was a yellow brick road. The other, the Cheshire Cat from *Alice in Wonderland*.

"Pick your poison."

"Is that LSD?" Tala looked frightened.

"Lucy is safe. Very fun. Oh, come on—we've all done it once, some of us." She elbowed Lance. "A little more."

Yin smiled. "You don't have to do it."

Makayla said, "If I did it, she has to."

Tala didn't like the idea of feeling outside of her body. She had enough of that without the aid of drugs or alcohol, but this, this was unheard of. "Doesn't this crap make you crazy?"

"This is a small amount. It'll alter your perception for a couple hours. We'll be here with you—to make sure nothing happens to you."

Alter your perception...

To make sure nothing happens to you...

Mark said, "Listen, you don't have to do it. I'm still going to be your friend."

"She has to." Makayla took the stamps from Valerie. "We've all done it."

She offered Tala both stamps. "Come on, Redhead, live a little."

Tala felt the pressure building. She could say no.

Don't people respect you when you say no?

She nodded, "I'll do it. Just tell me what to expect."

"Don't expect anything. You'll be fine," Yin said.

"What's it gonna be, Redhead?" Makayla stepped closer. "Will you follow the yellow brick road to Oz or follow the white rabbit into Wonderland?"

"What's the difference?" Tala asked. Her palms were sweaty. She hoped something would egress her from this awful situation.

"It's an illusion of choice. They both take you to the same place." Makayla laughed.

"I'll take the yellow brick road. That cat scares the shit out of me."

Tala took a deep breath, took the stamp, and put it on her tongue.

"A fine choice," Makayla said. She raised her hands victoriously. "Say hi to the wicked witch for me."

Tala felt pretty much the same. Nothing happened, at least not right then, but then the yellow brick road disintegrated into her tongue. The chemicals ebbed into her bloodstream like an injection. She was in a storm, in a field somewhere, maybe it was Oz—but there was nowhere to go and no red slippers to bring her home.

She took a selfie photo of herself and saw her pupils dilated, her mind afar.

"Well, she'll be gone a while." Yin pulled the joint from his ear. "Any takers?"

"I'll take a hit," Valerie said. Putting her flask into her purse.

"I'm good with beer. I have a feeling I'll be on babysitting duty tonight." Mark said.

Tala's mind wound back like a mechanical clock, and she started thinking of the day she stood at Urbana airport looking at the 757. She skipped back to the eighth grade, when Nancy Regal had asked her on the basketball courts during Physical Ed what her family had planned for Mother's Day.

"My mother's dead," Tala had told her. The words came out heavy and distant, like if someone else had uttered them. Those words repeated inside her head like a drum.

My mother's dead.

My mother's dead.

My mother's dead.

Tala never forgot the next words Nancy Regal said. "She killed herself, right? Because she couldn't stand you. Stay away from Michael Parga. He's mine."

How could she had been so cold? Michael Parga? I don't even like him. You hurt me like this because of a boy?

Nancy took a final blow.

"Face it, she hated you!"

She hated you.

She hated you.

She hated you.

Tala grabbed Nancy Regal by the hair and rolled on the ground with her, and so her rebellion and downward spiral began. Those hateful words were etched into the cortex of her mind.

She hated you became *she hated me.*

The LSD brought her back to—

When she was eight years old, in Urbana.

She heard the shower come on. She packed her Mickey Mouse backpack, closed the old wooden door, and ran down the street to Pleasant Valley. It's dark and it's snowing. She knelt in front of a peculiar grave.

She rubbed the snow off the tombstone.

What did it say?

GL—

GLEN—

GLENN URT—

GLENN CURTISS

She read it.

She couldn't remember before. Was this really Glenn Curtiss's grave she'd been to as a child? Eight-year-old Tala cried because her mom was dead and she knew she'd never see her again, but why?

The ravens squawked and took flight, leaving an echo behind, a harrowing sound.

David was next to her now. "I'm sorry, baby. I don't know why."

Tala sensed something different; the wolves were near. They ran toward David, attacked him, knocked him over on the snow. They sunk their horrid fangs into his skin, ripped his flesh to pieces, left behind a sprawled snow angel of blood.

Tala couldn't scream.

She came back to the present.

"You okay?" Mark said. He seemed taller than usual.

"Yeah." Tala managed. "I'm feeling weird. Thinking."

"I'm here with you. Don't worry about anything. They're just thoughts, okay?" His voice sounded amplified.

Tala looked terrified. She had broken into a cold sweat.

"How's the wicked witch treating yah? Babe?" Valerie said, laughing.

Jaen chuckled like a hyena. The laugh evil and haunting.

Tala felt scared now. She'd always refused drugs, but she decided she was different now, and that the girl she'd been was long gone and far away in Urbana. Lance took a puff of a joint and offered her a hit. "This can mellow you out. It helps sometimes."

Tala looked at Mark as if saying, is this true? *Will this help these horrid thoughts leave me?* "You're going to be in Wonderland regardless. It's up to you. Sometimes it helps."

She put the joint to her mouth, took a dainty puff, but nothing happened, not what her friends expected anyway.

"Inhale. You're not Clinton, for Christ's sake," Valerie told her. "You're not doing it right."

She wanted to say I can smoke. *I've smoked squares before*, but she said nothing.

"Yeah, take it deeper!" Lance said, laughing. "Take it real deep."

"Ignore him," Mark said at the obvious perverted remark.

Tala tried again to no avail.

Valerie took the joint away.

"Like this." She took a long drag. The end turned a dark orange red. She held the smoke, then exhaled it. Reminding Tala of the cold night when she read the names on the plaques at Pleasant Valley.

Valerie gave Tala back the joint now that she had demonstrated proper form. This time Tala took a long, deep puff. She had inhaled deeply, bringing the smoke to her chest, and that was made apparent when she started coughing hard. She put her hand to her neck and coughed violently like she was choking.

Lance, Valerie, and Makayla laughed hysterically.

Yin knelt beside her pool chair and asked if she was okay, but Tala kept coughing. They all took turns puffing, and Tala got the hang of it the next time it came around. She wouldn't cough as much. They laid on the grass. Mark turned off all the lights in the house.

They smoked, looking at the stars. Tala went in and out of Oz. Up down the yellow brick road. She spilled some beer on her jeans, and didn't care. She felt different. Her heart raced and she could feel her pulse in her ears. This sensation would often make her panic—leading to full blown panic attacks—but her mind was too dissociated to be afraid.

She saw Mark's grin sharp like a knife, with a hint of malice. Makayla and Valerie's voices seemed far away, like they were in a tunnel somewhere. Tala felt like the laughs turned on her, following her down a dark corridor, cornering her in a room with no windows. In that room, Tala saw a woman sitting at the end.

She walked toward the woman, who sobbed and shivered. Tala reached out to touch her, and when the woman turned, she saw her mother, Yona. With gentle blue eyes. Tala realized her mother was just another stranger whom she knew nothing about. Tala went to caress her longing face, but then it transformed, turning evil. Her eyes changed to a sick, jaundice yellow, jerking, her mouth salivated with blood, then she transformed into a wolf.

Tala sat up gasping for air. She was back at Mark's house.

She was lost in thought and had forgotten to breathe.

"Whoa! Relax. Don't freak. I'm here. It should wear off soon," Yin said, stepping and twisting on the last of the joint.

Her friends laughed at whatever it was that teenagers laughed about when they were drinking and getting high. She felt serene again. Happy not to be alone.

The evil images were gone, and Mark's grin was his

again. She felt excited. The feeling of euphoria grew strong, and she wanted to laugh at everything now. She did, even though she couldn't remember at what exactly. No one paid attention to the stupid grin on her face. Her friends were all trapped in their own worlds. Tala fixed her gaze on the North Star. She whispered, "Miss you Mom."

"Did you say something?" Mark asked.

He lay next to her. He walked his fingers on the grass bed as if they had legs and crept up to her hand, then went to her belly. Slowly he went up her stomach. He picked his fingers up and pretended they had legs, jumping over the mountain hills of her breasts landing underneath her neck, then up to her lips.

Tala was happy he didn't touch her breasts. It was chivalrous. Although under the circumstances, she wouldn't have really minded.

"What are you doing?" she said, giggling.

He turned her hand over and held it. It felt good. Tala felt secure. Held. Strong. He didn't answer her question. He didn't have to. Mark's eyes seemed to wander. She wasn't sure where he was, but she hoped he was here. On this grass bed, with her. Forever.

"I'm doing what I want to do," Mark said.

There was a distant rumble of thunder. The night got cooler. The mood changed. Everything was still slow, but more nostalgic. As if everyone was lost in deep thought, contemplating the meaning of life. Jaen came back from the bathroom holding a Yuengling with a grave look.

"I just saw on TV." She waited for everyone to look at her and, when they did, she blurted, "Another active shooting, man."

"Where?" Yin asked.

"Some town up north. Bath, New York."

Lance checked his phone. "The Counterfeit News Network is reporting it. Somehow these fuckers have news people there already."

"Counterfeit News Network?" Tala said. She was confused.

"Ignore him. He only gets a hard on for FOX news. He's talking about CNN," Jaen said. "They're already calling it a *Blood Bath*, Jesus. How fucking original. Three dead so far. You know how that goes. The count will go up."

"You sure it's an active shooter?" Valerie said.

"That's what they're saying."

"It's probably some small dick loser. Why can't they just smoke weed and mellow the fuck out?" Lance said.

Yin looked concerned.

The mood had shifted.

Mark got up, went to the 4k TV mounted on the wall of the backyard terrace. He turned on the TV and put on CNN.

Sure enough, Anderson Cooper was reporting on the incident. The marquee title at the bottom of the Breaking News Alert read: Bloodbath in Bath, New York, four reported dead. Active Shooter fled in a dark SUV.

"I thought you said it was three," he said.

Jaen said, "Like I said, the count always goes up."

"Damn, we just had one of these few weeks ago," Mark said.

"At least it's not here," Makayla said. "Where the hell is Bath, New York anyway?"

Tala looked dumbfounded.

"I know exactly where it is," Tala said, breaking her silence.

They all waited.

"Where?" Makayla inquired. Tala didn't want to say it.

She didn't want them to know for some reason. Like it would somehow reveal something about her. It felt personal. It just came out.

"It's the town next to where I grew up. I used to ride my bike there all the time."

"Wow, what a fucking coincidence," Yin said.

Fucking happenstance.

Tala felt exposed. Like if someone wanted to send her a message somehow, some higher force. When had such a small town like Bath made the national news? Never, probably, and here it was, on the screen thanks to some deranged gunman.

CNN played a cell phone clip of a woman running, multiple shots heard in the background but no visual of the shooter.

"I used to walk there with my dad. He'd take me to Pleasant Valley."

Her friends looked like they had no clue what Pleasant Valley was.

Tala said, "It's this big cemetery filled with ancient tombstones, mausoleums, angel statues, some from the Civil War, some older. They're fascinating."

"Your dad took you to a cemetery when you were little?" Jaen said, as if that was the strangest thing she had ever heard.

"Well, there's not much to do in Urbana. It's kind of a tourism thing." Jaen's expression of disapproval didn't change. Tala said, "It's actually beautiful."

"That's pretty wicked," Lance said. "Your mom was cool with that?"

"My mom's dead."

There was a long moment of silence.

Anderson Cooper got an "update" from his earpiece. He

said, "This just in. Our CNN sources on the ground say, eleven people are confirmed dead."

The count goes up.

"How did she die?"

"She died in a car accident."

"I'm sorry," Mark said. Everyone was quiet. Tala felt a heavy silence envelope her.

She felt a cool stream of water escape from her eyes. It dripped down the hill of her nose, on to her bottom lip, then fell onto her lap. She knew she was crying but decided to go on. It had been so long since she cried. She thought she had forgotten how.

A cold gust of wind came and went.

Jaen parted Tala's hair out of her face. "Jesus, I'm sorry, Tala." She embraced her, but she couldn't stop the tears. She had forgotten what it felt like to hug someone.

Tala wiped some grass from her jeans and stood up. "I think I'll go home now."

Before anyone could muster words, she had walked into the shadows, leaving only the sound from the back gate.

MARK REACHED into his pocket for his cell phone, and made a call, "Hello?" a voice said into his receiver, "Dad, I think it's working." he said, and hung up.

17

TALA DIDN'T GO HOME. It wasn't her home. Just a toy house she and her father had moved into trying to erase the past. Besides, she knew her father would be at work soaring the skies somewhere by now, and she would be home alone again. She was used to it. She was in and out of Wonderland. Or was it Oz?

Up and down the yellow brick road.

Maybe down a rabbit hole?

She was thinking of her mom. Why did she kill herself? Why would she do that? What demons was she fighting?

Up and down the yellow brick road...

Her mind went back to the shooting. The gunshots.

They called it a Blood Bath in Bath. Out of all places in the world, right next door to Urbana? It felt as if God was giving her a sign.

Why was there so much violence in the world?

Up and down the yellow brick road

Her mom died in a *car accident.*

She hated lying, but she had no choice. Miami Springs

was a new start. How would The Hawks see her if they knew?

She wanted change, and now she was acting like someone she didn't even know. She had drunk alcohol, smoked weed, and Lucy. How's that for change? Tala wondered what she would do in Urbana if she were there now?

Eleven innocent people shot dead. Sheriffs from Urbana, Bath, and even Hammondsport, swarming around trying to control an uncontrollable situation. Like stopping the rain but the rain had come to small towns in America. She debated going to the toy house and opening a novel. That's what the Old Tala would do, so she kept walking past the toy house, wrestling with her thoughts.

Up and down the yellow brick road.

She went up the sidewalk with no destination in mind, occasionally hearing dogs bark as if they were using amplified microphones. When she turned the corner of Fairway, two pit bulls barked and salivated ferociously while trying to bite through their fence. This commenced a cacophony of dogs barking like they wanted to tell her something. Tala knew that a young girl walking down dark streets wasn't the smartest thing, but she didn't care. As much as the dogs frightened her, their barking made her feel like she wasn't alone.

Driverless cars drove by, slowing down. Would some maniac jump out and stuff her into the trunk as she yelled and pleaded for her life? No. That only happened in the movies. Or to other people. This was a good neighborhood.

Still she wondered.

The cars kept going. Going nowhere. Possibly going where she was going all the same. She didn't know her destination until she saw *it*. The Curtiss Mansion stood in the distance like a black elephant. She went up Deer Run, walking alongside the black iron gate that divided the dead from the living.

She wanted to stand at the front gate, where she and her dad had parked and shared a cigarette. Now she was back, in the dark, its black iron gate sentinel. She ran her fingers along the bars and felt an electricity flow through her body. It was static of some kind, but it could have been her drugged mind playing tricks on her.

It was colder. A gust of wind sent chills up her neck. She was suddenly afraid. She kept trudging forward. When she made it to the front gate, she examined the giant padlock and wondered.

Are they trying to keep us out? Or keeping something in?

She felt fear. Could someone be inside? That was a ridiculous notion why even—

"It'll drive you crazy if you let it," a man said from behind her.

Before she turned, cold hands wrapped around her neck like a snake preparing to eat its prey.

She knew she was in trouble. She couldn't yell either; her voice had forgotten how to make sound.

"I used to come out here and stare at the mansion a long time ago." The man's voice was deep like a bass chord. His grip tightened more. She choked back a scream. "Steady now," he said. "Steady." She felt sharp fingernails pressed into the sides of her neck. He shoved her against the front gate, her face between the iron fence as if she were imprisoned. His grip tightened.

"Don't scream. I won't hurt you, girl."

"Let me gooo," Tala pleaded. She was crying too. As if he had squeezed the tears out of her.

"Let go, please. I won't—"

The man leaned down. He whispered into her ear, "Quiet down. I know yur scared."

She felt his hot breath. He smelled like rotten garbage. This was a man from the streets, a homeless man. She knew the smell. She'd done volunteer hours in New York, two summers ago, in a homeless shelter and could not forget the smell.

Tala saw from her peripheral that he was a black man with white facial hair.

She squeezed the iron gate harder, bracing herself. Sure he would rape, maybe kill her.

This is a good neighborhood, her father had said.

If I could only break free, I could run. He won't catch me. I could run—

"You can't, Tala," the man said, as if reading her mind. "You can't run from them." His voice cracked like he was fighting back tears. "You just can't. The house has eyes. There are eyes everywhere."

How does he know my name?

There was a moment of silence where she could feel his breathing on her neck. He was whimpering. She wanted to calm him, say something to make him let go, but she feared saying the wrong thing. The wrong thing could set him off—

"Stay away from here. This is a bad place. The house has eyes."

"I'll leave. Please let me go," she managed.

Tala wanted to break free and get away. She wanted to fight back, but instead she did nothing. Her fear and his strength overpowered her.

He bent down, whispered, "I saw the wolves too. A long time ago."

He let go of her neck. She gasped for air. He then grabbed her by the shoulders, put his chin over her left shoulder. She didn't dare look at him. She kept her gaze forward as did he. She kept her eyes on the mansion, trembling. She felt a warm sensation falling between her legs. The man took a step back. He must have noticed she wet herself.

"They say when you stare into the mansion, the mansion stares back into you." He pulled back and let go of her shoulders. Tala turned. She saw the tallest man she'd ever seen walk away into the shadows. Tala ran home as fast as she could. No dogs barked.

18

DURING LUNCH THE NEXT DAY, Tala bought a slice of greasy pepperoni pizza even though she wasn't hungry. She replayed the night's events, questioning the whole thing. She had made it home, locked her doors, and fancied calling the police. Maybe she would have, had she not been drinking and visiting Oz.

How could she tell her dad what happened at the mansion when she wasn't supposed to be there to begin with? She had laid on her bed crying and shaking until she fell asleep.

"Earth to Redhead," a girl said with a snarky attitude. Tala realized she was holding up the line. She got her pizza and water bottle and found an empty bench in the court-yard. She couldn't stop thinking about the party, the music, falling from the tree house, Mark running his fingers up her lips, the yellow brick road, the shooting in Bath, New York, thirteen dead, and that deep insidious voice.

It'll drive you crazy if you let it.

She'd been assaulted. Why?

The assailant made no sexual advances. He didn't steal

anything from her, not that she had anything to steal, besides maybe her phone.

When you stare into the mansion, the mansion stares into you, he had said in that horrible deep voice. He had warned her.

She put her pizza on the table and pulled out her phone. Her CNN notifications showed the headline: BLOOD BATH IN BATH, NY. She figured they couldn't come up with a better clickbait title. The shooting in Bath was the flavor of the moment. It was all over the web, trending on Twitter, Facebook, and YouTube. Cell phone videos were being released. The hideous shots echoing as people yelled frantically for their lives. A volley between Anderson Cooper and Don Lemon with 'the latest' breaking news. A sight too often in America. This time it felt so close.

"Looks delicious."

Tala looked up but couldn't make out his face; he was standing in the sun.

He sat down and peeled an orange with a pocketknife. His face came into focus. She had never seen him before. He had a fair face, with unkempt blond hair, intelligent hazel eyes, light scruffy beard. He had a colorful sleeve tattoo of the three wise monkeys.

"That can't be good for you," he said, looking at her pizza.

"Do I know you?"

"We're in American Government together. I'm Jax."

"How come I've never seen you?"

"I don't go to class much."

"I'm Tala." She looked down. "This pizza looks delicious. I'm just not hungry."

She quipped, "Are you on a diet?"

He smiled, leaned back, extended his arms, showing his

body. "Oh yeah, I'm trying to lose weight." He was thin, toned, muscular. He looked like a sophomore in college.

"My uncle has a farm in Homestead. I grew up on them." He referred to the orange. "Old habits die hard, huh?"

Tala looked around to see if anyone was looking. "Are you allowed to have that knife?"

"It's just a pocketknife."

"That doesn't look like just a pocketknife."

"Well, if it was a gun, I'd see your concern. With the shooting last night? What's your name again?"

"Tala Stone."

"Why are you so on edge, Tala Stone?"

"What's your name again?" she asked.

"Jax Riggins."

"I'm not on edge, Jax Riggins."

She could tell him several reasons why she was on edge.

"If we have American Government, I should have seen you at least once by now," Tala said.

"Well, maybe because my goal in life is to be here the absolute least amount of time possible. I hate this fucking town. Everyone is so fake, entitled, and rich."

Jax said, "What's your dad do? Stocks? Doctor?"

"I'm not rich," she said. "My dad's a pilot. He just got like a settlement."

"A pilot? Right. You're not rich. Keep telling yourself that, doll."

"I'm not a doll. You're being a jerk, and someone is going to see you with that." She gestured at his knife. "You should put it away."

"I think I will. When I want to." Her eyes came off the blade and back to his face. He made her feel like the girl from Urbana. Like he knew she was an outsider too.

"You're pretty cute. I like your freckles." He said.

Tala looked away to hide the redness in her face. She turned back. "Anyways."

"Beautiful. Actually," he corrected.

The freckles on her face looked like they were sitting on a beach of red sand.

She got up and tossed her pizza into a nearby bin. Anxious to get up, change the conversation. She came back and realized Jax hadn't taken his eyes off her.

Jax cut the orange and gave her half.

"These are juicy," he said.

When she took the orange, she thought of the Hialeah Racetrack. *Citrus Mental Hospital.*

"You know, a few nights ago someone dropped a bunch of these into my friend's Jeep."

"At the racetrack?" he said with a mischievous smile.

"Yes," Tala managed.

"I don't know anything about that," he said. With his hands up like he was surrendering.

"You were there?"

Jax laughed.

"Yeah, me and some friends went to the track to dump some of the rotten oranges we couldn't sell. I saw Lance's Jeep with the top down. It was fate."

"How do you know Lance?"

"He's one of the few Hawks I'll hang with. I haven't confessed my crime yet, waiting for the right moment to break the news." He was laughing.

Tala looked past Jax. "Speak of the devil's twin."

Lance spied them and joined their table. "You know this guy?" He pointed at Jax, patted him on the back.

"Just met him," Tala said.

"Sorry to hear it," Lance said, then gave Jax a bro-hug.

Lance flipped his Miami Dolphins cap backwards.

"Mr. Jax Riggins. What's up, man?" Lance said.

"He dumped the rotten oranges into your Jeep," Tala said.

Jax's jaw dropped. His face revealed he didn't expect her to blurt that out.

"Aren't you the bus driver?" Jax countered.

Lance punched him in the arm. "You Sonofabitch. I had a feeling it was you. Asshole! My car smells like oranges mixed with fertilizer shit."

"Cry me a bridge and jump in the river," he quipped.

"You're lucky you're bigger than me." Lance punched him in the arm again. Jax laughed and rubbed his arm.

"I'll get you back. By the way, Red, this is the only Prairie boy I trust." Lance seemed pensive for a moment. "Where did you get all those oranges?"

"My uncle, remember? I was making deliveries for him. I went to the track to dump the rotten ones, saw your Jeep, and thought, there could be no better place!"

"Asshoooole!" Lance said.

"You scared Mark pretty good." Tala bit the orange. A fresh citrus flavor exploded on her tongue.

"Mark Bradshaw?" Jax said.

When Lance concurred, Jax shook his head slightly and said, "That guy is garbage."

"C'mon, man, he's alright," Lance said.

"I don't like him. Rubs me the wrong way."

"You take things too personally," Lance said.

Tala was surprised to hear someone didn't like Mark. Mark had been nothing but kind to her since she got here, and he had shared his friends with her. Made her a Hawk. To hear someone talk about him like that made her wonder how much she knew him at all. Was there another side to

Mark? Of course there was. Everyone had other sides, even her.

"What happened with him?" Tala asked.

"He's a little too cocky for my taste. That's all I'm saying." Jax looked away. It was obvious he didn't want to talk about it.

Tala nudged, "Care to elaborate?"

Jax glanced at his watch. "I got to go. Take my number."

Tala punched his number into her phone.

He stood, shook Lance's hand, then leaned down to Tala's face. She pulled back a little, confused. She looked into his hazel eyes and swore she saw herself. He smiled and quickly kissed her on the cheek. She felt the stubs from his five o'clock shadow.

"Not sure where you're from," he said. "Down here, we kiss the girl goodbye." He walked across the courtyard and got into an older model white Ford pickup. He drove off like the road and everything on it belonged to him.

"He's not going back to class?" Tala said.

"He's a senior. He's got work-study."

"If he's a senior. Why are we in American Government together?"

"He's probably making up credits he needs. He trans-ferred late last year. I think he got expelled from Hialeah High for fighting."

"Where does he work?"

"Why so interested?" Lance teased.

"Just curious."

"Mechanic shop in Hialeah. He also delivers produce for his uncle. You guys would probably get along. He delivers farm shit."

"I'm not from a farm." She rolled her eyes.

"He works two jobs?"

"Yeah, I guess he's a jack of all trades. He installed my train horn. He's not a bad dude, takes care of his niece. I think she's autistic."

"I like him," Lance said. "But Riggins can be trouble. Doesn't like to follow rules."

"Who does?" She had broken more than one since she got here.

She wanted to say, aren't rules supposed to be broken? But that was too cliché. Her phone chimed. Tala glanced at the CNN app. The count up to 16. They were releasing the names and photos of the victims. A collage of faces, she turned pale.

"You alright?" Lance said.

"No. No, I'm not."

19

DAVID UNFASTENED his tie and opened the front door. He glanced at Tala, who was sitting on the couch watching CNN. He went to the kitchen, poured himself some water. "Gosh, it's hot." He tried to talk about the weather as if people in a nearby town back home hadn't been slaughtered.

His face was flushed.

Tala barely acknowledged his presence as the victims' names from the BLOODBATH massacre scrolled on the TV.

VICTIM, 12

Victim, 45

Victim, 32

Victim, 41

Victim, 18

Victim, 38

Frances E. Gumm, 47

Victim, 29
Victim, 13
Victim, 58
Victim, 44
Victim, 22
Victim, 71
Dexter Reeves, 18 Shooter (Suicide)

FRANCES GUMM WAS Dr. Moss's secretary since he took Tala there as a kid. Ms. Gumm was one of the closest people Tala knew back home; he couldn't believe she was dead. She was a kind woman.

Dexter Reeves murdered his victims with a custom-built AR-15 assault rifle with an extended 100 round capacity magazine. He wasn't even old enough to buy a pack of beer, but he could purchase a military style weapon designed to kill without drawing a second glance.

David felt his phone vibrate; he fished it from his pocket as he poured himself another glass of water.

He answered.

"Hello? Yeah, Ben—You're breaking up. Yeah, I hear you now. I'm holding up. Tala's fine. She gave me the news yesterday. Can't believe it either. I'll be heading there tomorrow. We knew Frances, one of the victims. No, it's alright."

Tala seemed consumed by the television, so he went upstairs to finish chatting on the phone with Mr. Bradshaw.

———

TALA'S MIND played back the gory details of the massacre

back home repeatedly. Why did Dexter Reeves kill those people? Anderson Cooper said the shooter's neighbors thought he was a swell kid. They showed clips of several neighbors stating so. George Rivers said, "He was a good kid, always waved hello and said goodbye. I don't know how this could have happened."

Arthur Bosch said, "I've known Nancy and Tom for years, Dexter's parents. Kid wouldn't hurt a fly. We had 'em over for dinner all the time. He was fine boy. Lots of friends; girlfriends too. I don't get it. Something must have happened."

He was a fine boy. Lots of friends, girlfriends too.

Something must have happened.

They were talking about the killer like he was the victim. *He was a fine boy.*

What kind of *fine* boy goes out and buys a rifle to hunt human beings? He killed a twelve-year-old, for Christ's sake. He killed fifteen other people! People with mothers and fathers, broken families forever.

He wouldn't hurt a fly.

Well, he killed Mrs. Gumm just the same, the kindest woman she knew. Her friend.

What about the victims?

Anderson Cooper reported Reeves was on the Honor Roll at Elkton Hills High School. They had tidbits of his classmates talking to reporters with positive comments about him, save for some eerie observations. "I guess he seemed withdrawn lately," or "He was staying to himself. He had run away for a few weeks. No one knew where he went." Nothing concrete. Nothing firm. The shooter was smart, handsome, had friends, and girls liked him! How do you go from that to an AR-15 extended magazine 100 rounds, locked and loaded?

It was a blood bath in Bath, alright. No, it didn't make any sense. These active shootings never did.

The statements whirled inside Tala's head, giving her a headache.

Something must have happened.
He was a fine boy.
Had friends, girlfriends too.
Wouldn't hurt a fly.
Always said hello and goodbye!
Something must have happened.
Yes, but what? What happened to him?
What *changed?*

They were showing Dexter's high school photo now, a young man, eighteen years old. He had brown hair, gentle brown eyes, spotted acne, he was thin, and yes Tala agreed; He was handsome. He smiled in every photo. A real smile. Tala knew a thing or two of fake smiles. She knew Dexter Reeves's smiles were genuine laced with joy.

Something must have happened.

What happened to you, Dexter? She thought about Ms. Gumm bringing her chocolate chip cookies. *Just breathe.* She felt the onset of an anxiety attack.

Just breathe.
In and out.

Think about the white sand beach with lions. Her happy place. She muted CNN and closed her eyes, but the sand wasn't white. It was black like ash, and the lions were there too—but they couldn't move. They were dead. Stuffed like Mark's dad's Africa trophy lion hanging on his wall. The lions were hunted and long ago slain, preserved with the secrets of Dexter Reeves. She wondered; how well do you really know your neighbors? How well do you really know anyone?

He wouldn't hurt a fly.

David came downstairs.

"I'm going to Urbana."

Tala turned around. "When?"

"Tomorrow. I'm gonna pay my respects to Frances. I know you don't like flying but I promise it will be safe. If you want to go see Richard. He called me. He asked about you. He wants you to call him."

"I'm not ready, Dad. Don't make me go."

David seemed pensive. "It's so strange," he said. "I had a stop there a few weeks ago. I landed in Elmira Corning, it's a small airport about 25 miles from Bath."

David seemed like he was debating something inside his mind. Weighing the pros and cons.

"Remember when we moved here? The first night. I told you there was something I wanted to tell you?"

"Yeah, I remember."

David said, "This isn't the best time, but I figure there is no best time. We're here one minute and gone the next."

Tala seemed concerned. A thousand bad thoughts flooded her mind. He was sick. My God, something was horribly wrong with—

"I want you to meet Olivia."

Her.

"Oh." Tala felt immense relief. "Your girlfriend?"

"Yeah, Red, my girlfriend. We've been talking for," He trailed off. "Years, actually, friends first."

"I see," Tala said. Grateful he didn't have some malignant cancer.

"She's flying with me to Urbana. I just want you to know that. No more secrets, remember? We should be talking to each other. I love you. She's not your mom and she'll never replace her. But I'm alone Red. I've been alone and—"

"You don't have to explain. I get it."

Tala didn't say anything else.

"Her name's Olivia Pace, and she's wanted to meet you for a long time."

"I guess I have no choice." She turned around to watch the TV.

He came around the kitchen counter and sat on the couch next to her. "Red," he said. "I know Frances meant a lot to you. If you want to talk about it. If you want to talk about Olivia or anything, you know I'm here, right?"

She nodded. "Yeah. I just want to watch this for a bit."

David looked at the TV. There was cell phone footage of people running, several shots being heard in the background that sounded like rapid fire.

"It's the same thing over and over, negativity on repeat. Maybe you should get some fresh air. The news makes money on people's misery."

"I know. I'm okay." She forced a smile, like she had for many years.

He held her knee. His phone rang.

"Excuse me." He stood, took the call.

The big house started to make sense. The thought of Olivia or any woman in the house made her cringe. She knew she was being selfish but couldn't help it. She barely spent time with him as it is. How could she compete with Olivia Pace?

She felt a migraine coming on.

DAVID SPOKE with Olivia on the phone. His mind went to when he had met her at the Hotel Statler, the same hotel where Yona had committed suicide. David found solace in getting drunk and walking the hotel corridors. He paced the halls and often went out to the pool deck looking up to see where Yona had shot herself and fell from. He looked thin, pale, and broken. He reclined on the pool chairs outside on the deck, drunk and angry; he got thrown out by security many times.

They knew him as the man whose wife offed herself. Even though he wasn't a hotel guest, they let him be. The guards felt pity for him. He told everyone about his loss. About Yona shooting herself, then falling from the top floor, imploding as she hit the deck. About how Tala had witnessed it. Tears in his eyes, alcohol protruded from his pores.

The Hotel Statler brought him rage and sometimes a serene peace. He felt close to Yona there. He just wanted to see her one last time, talk with her one last time, Ask her... WHY! Why, Babe? Why?

On one of those nights, while in a drunken stupor, one of the security guards gave him the look, which said, *My friend. It's time for you to go.* David walked out of the hotel toward the beach, with a bottle of cheap whiskey in his hand. He ended up on the wooden boardwalk that connected the hotels.

He listened to the crash of the waves. His vision blurry, all he saw was the dim orange glow from the boardwalk lights, the flash of white like teeth from the crashing waves. He felt drunk, sure. He wondered if he should swim out until his muscles fatigued and he was sure he wouldn't make it back to shore. Maybe the pain would be gone then. Maybe he wouldn't hurt anymore. Tala would be better off.

Olivia, one of the new concierges, went out there on a cigarette break. She asked if he was okay. He didn't know why she started a conversation with a drunk man. Most were jerks trying to get laid. Plenty of drunks polluted Miami Beach, but he was grateful she did.

She locked eyes with him.

David imagined she must've seen pain and chaos in his eyes. A ship with its captain sleeping, heading toward the rocks.

She told him she too knew pain.

David never told Tala where they met. He feared it would be too weird, too hard to explain, and too difficult for a little girl to understand. It was too soon, he fretted. And then the years passed. And he always felt like it was too soon.

When David first tried to tell Tala about Olivia, he tried to show her a picture on his cellphone, but Tala darted out of the house.

She muted the TV.

"Dad, I want to meet her."

David looked startled.

"Are you sure?"

"Yes," she said. "You seem to like her."

"Well, I do," he said. "I do like her."

He took his glasses off and wiped them with his fiber cloth.

"How about dinner? You know, when we're back from Urbana. I'll make something."

David knew it was time. You were here one minute and gone the next. Tala was changing. He deserved to be happy.

So did she. Tala thought about something Dr. Moss had once told her. Life was about transformation. *It's not how you're born that matters, it's what you become.*

Tala smiled. "If you want her to stick around, maybe I should cook."

20

Tala stayed busy doing homework and settling into Miami Springs as her dad went back home to Urbana with *her*. When he got back, he asked Tala if they were still on for dinner. She nodded.

David and Tala were in the kitchen when the doorbell rang. He started to wash his hands, but Tala put down the tejolote she was using to mash the guacamole.

"No, finish what you're doing," she said, went to the door, and opened it. It was finally happening.

Olivia Pace stood in the doorway. She had sharp cheekbones, dark brown eyes, her hair in a ponytail. She wore a black V-neck shirt with faded jeans. She couldn't look more casual.

"Hello, Tala." She smiled. She looked half her father's age.

Tala offered to shake her hand, although her palms were moist, and she had butterflies in her stomach.

Olivia ignored her hand and wrapped her arms around her body like she was a small child. The woman squeezed. Tala felt surprised and overwhelmed. When was the last time she had been hugged? Olivia loosened her embrace, pulled back to see her face, and looked directly into her blue eyes. "David was right. You have his freckles," Olivia said.

"You're more beautiful in person," Olivia added.

Tala felt odd, unsure of what to say. This strange woman hadn't let her go.

There was a moment of heavy awkwardness when Tala didn't reply. David said nothing either, Tala imagined it was because he had visualized this exchange so many times that now it seemed lost on him that it had become reality.

He finished drying his hands and leaned against the kitchen counter, crossing his arms, his face revealing a small smirk, like a flash of happiness.

"You gonna let her in?"

Tala stepped aside. "Sorry. Yeah, come in."

Olivia came into the toy house.

David kissed Olivia on the cheek, which made Tala smile. The hesitation of the kiss, Tala noticed, suggested they had been kissing on the lips for a long time now. David's last second turn of the head caught Olivia off guard.

Tala finished setting the table. David brought trays and bowls with homemade salsa, lean beef, homemade corn tortillas, mozzarella cheese, refried beans, sour cream, and Tala's guacamole in its molcajete bowl. She joined Olivia and David at the dinner table.

They made small talk, and Tala saw in Olivia what every man saw. What David must have seen. Beauty. Not just the pretty face and nice body, but something inside, soft and natural. She was fun and easy going. The food was delicious, and meeting Olivia wasn't nearly as bad as Tala had thought. The only hiccup was her age. She looked so young.

My God, how old is she?

Tala didn't want to dampen the mood by asking because she was afraid of the answer. Olivia asked the appropriate and expected questions. How was your day? How do you like Miami? Do you miss Urbana? Yadda yadda. Tala knew her dad was happy. He couldn't take the stupid smirk off his face. Olivia's demeanor changed to grave.

"I'm sorry about your friend, Ms. Gumm," she said. "Your dad said you really liked her. This must be hard for you."

David gave Olivia a look that said *I told you not to talk about that.*

Tala noticed, but Olivia didn't seem like she did what other people wanted her to do.

Tala had almost convinced herself Ms. Gumm wasn't dead. She would see her again sometime and they'd have chocolate chip cookies together. Ms. Gumm would sneak her candy and cookies behind Dr. Moss's back. When Dr. Moss would catch her, he'd say, "Frances! You're going to give this girl diabetes!" And Frances would holler back, "What's life without a little sugar?"

"I'm okay. It hasn't really sunk in," Tala said.

"It will. When it does. David and I are here for you. Right, Dave?"

David nodded.

She was so damn direct it made Tala want to squirm out of her chair.

"Thanks. How was everything, you know back home?"

"Sad. It's a broken town. I'm kind of glad you didn't come. When your dad said you weren't going, it surprised me. I thought you'd like to go back, but I'm glad you didn't.

It wasn't a pretty sight. There were a lot of vigils, lots of tears, balloons, and stuffed teddy bears." Olivia cleared her throat. "There was a short service for Ms. Gumm. People from Urbana and Bath and the whole county came to see her and the other victims. The community brought candy and chocolate chip cookies."

What's life without a little sugar?

"That animal ruined so many lives," David said. "For nothing. Damn guns in this country. Somethings gotta give."

The mood had turned heavy.

"You're here one minute, gone the next," Tala said.

They continued eating. "The food is delicious. That's some mean guac," Olivia said, changing the conversation. "I love the bowl." She referred to Tala's molcajete bowl, made of volcanic rock.

"Thanks. The bowl was my moms," Tala said, and Olivia's smile became a straight line.

"She got it in Mexico, where I was born. Right, Dad?"

"Yes, that's right. A little town off the beach called Zihuantanejo. She fell in love with it. Said it had character."

"It's lovely," Olivia said.

When dinner was over and she said goodbye to Olivia, she knew something had changed. David had laughed in ways she had never seen. If she had seen him, she'd long forgotten. There was no use in being bitter. That was the Old Tala. The new Tala wanted happiness for everyone. Especially her father, who really deserved it.

Tala walked over to the kitchen window and saw Olivia and her dad standing just outside the porch on the rock cemented walkway and watched them hug with their eyes in a magnetic tug of war. How they looked like high school-ers, she thought. Teenagers with the world ahead of them. They glowed out there in the moonlight. Tala bit her lip and felt sad. She wanted someone to hold on too. She wondered what Mark was doing. Wishing he would hold her like that.

She didn't know why life had turned out the way it did. From Urbana to Miami Springs. The people back home murdered by a random psychopath with a gun. This new woman in her life. This big house with empty rooms and her new pot-smoking friends. She didn't know why anything happened anymore. Happy for her father she was. But for the life of her, she couldn't explain why she was crying.

21

TALA WOKE up and rubbed her eyes.

Darkness.

Why wasn't it morning?

She leaned over the bed and hit her angel nightlight. Hadn't she left it on? The nightlight was an ornament she had brought with her from Urbana. She liked to think it was one of the last things her mother gave her, although she had no recollection of it.

When she looked forward, she saw a shadow—no, it was the halo of a man sitting there. She pushed herself against the bed rest, screaming in a fevered panic.

"Dad! Dad!"

The man didn't move. He was in the shadows. He raised a finger to his lips, "Sssshhhhh..."

She couldn't make it to the door. She had no way of bypassing him.

"He's not here," the man said, his voice so calm it could only be inspired by madness.

"It's just me." He stood, towering over her. His height and deep voice registered as the man who had assaulted her at the Curtiss Mansion, the night she walked the yellow brick road.

She wanted to yell, but her voice seemed useless, like a child learning to speak.

"Them wolves are back, you know. The wolves are always watching because their house has eyes."

Her breathing became faster and irregular. There was a madman in her bedroom.

"Please don't hurt me," she managed. "Please don't. Take whatever you want."

"If I wanted to hurt you, I could have slit your throat as you slept. Do you dig? I'm not psycho. I'm not psycho."

"What do you want?"

"You're in trouble. This place is bad. My name is Rodnam Jackson. In the streets they call me Psycho Jordan because I'm tall and crazy. But I'm not crazy for real. That's what they want you to think. When I saw you looking at the mansion, I saw myself. I told you to run. Someone told me to run too, but I didn't listen. Will you?"

These were the ramblings of a mentally ill man. How could she escape?

Yes, I'll run. I'll run faster than ever. I'll run from here to the end of Earth; just please don't kill me.

"The mansion will break you like a wheel. It's no place for a girl like you. A weak girl. Stay away from Curtiss's house. You dig? NEVER GO BACK!" he yelled.

"Please don't—"

Fragments of moonlight seeped through her window blinds. The house as silent as a tomb.

"You know the story. Glenn Curtiss burned his family. About me, though, I don't remember everything. I mean, it's in the Dead Zone, lost, maybe forever, but I know they want you. There's no place like home, Tala Stone."

The freakishly tall man turned and ducked his head as he walked out of her bedroom. She heard his footsteps descending the stairs. When Tala decided he was gone, she tiptoed downstairs, looking for the intruder in all directions.

She grabbed a weapon from the kitchen, turned on all the lights and sauntered to the front door, afraid to look out the window. Afraid to open the door. She fell to her knees in the foyer, crying and trembling with a butter knife in her hand, questioning her sanity.

22

TALA CALLED DAVID, but it went to voicemail.

"FUCK! Why don't you ever answer?" she yelled into the phone.

She called Mark, but he didn't answer either. She pulled her curtain back, peering to his house. No sign anyone was home. Or awake. Or alive. His house suddenly gave her the chills.

She thought of the dead animals hung on the wall like a murder gallery. What kind of person takes pleasure in killing? A faraway thought came into focus, how well do you really know your neighbors?

She scrolled through her contact list and stopped on "Dr. R. Moss," his name and number still there...

Would he pick up if she called now?

She pressed the phone icon, dialing him.

"Hello?" a man answered on the second ring.

She hung up.

Her phone rang. Only it wasn't Dr. Moss calling; it was Jax.

———————

JAX SAT UP IN BED. "Did you just call me?"

Tala told him she must have misdialed, which was true.

He heard the fear in her voice.

"Everything good?"

"Yeah, of course," she said, she sounded scared. She told him about the man in her bedroom with the insidious voice.

"Tala, it sounds like a bad dream."

"I wasn't dreaming," she said. "I've seen him before."

"Text me your address," he said. "I'm on my way."

———————

JAX CHANGED INTO JEAN SHORTS, a white tank top; he ran water through his hair to try to flatten its unkempt look. He went downstairs and got into his battered Pickup. *Is this girl crazy?* He was about to find out. Her story didn't make sense. He pulled into her driveway. Her house was almost the size of the apartment building where he lived. *Yeah, you're not rich Tala, keep telling yourself that.*

He knocked on the door three times.

She slowly opened it.

"Are you okay?" he said.

She shook her head.

"How did he get in?"

"I don't know," she said. "I'm scared."

"Why don't you put that down?"

She was still holding the butter knife.

"Are you going to call the cops?" Jax wasn't convinced this wasn't a bad dream. It didn't make sense.

"Did he hurt you?" Jax tried to understand. "Did he steal anything?"

"No," she said.

"Well, what did he want?"

"I told you. I don't know, okay?"

"Show me where you saw him."

Tala led him upstairs. She pointed at her dresser chair which faced the bed.

"I'm not crazy. I didn't move it. Why would I sit facing my bed? He was sitting there. Watching me. He said his name was something Jackson. He said they called him Psycho Jordan. He knew my name. He told me to stay away from the mansion. That he was sorry for grabbing me the other night."

"Grabbing you? You've seen him before?"

"The night I did Lucy."

"You mean drugs? With your precious Hawks? Some friends you've got."

"I'm going to ask you again. Don't get mad. Is there any way you dreamt this? Hallucinated it? A bad trip?"

"No! There's no way. Look at the chair. He said to stay away. The house has eyes." She was shaking and, yes, it sounded crazy.

"Okay, sit. Relax. Let me think."

"Why didn't you call 911?"

"They'll think I'm crazy, right?"

Jax was no fan of the police. He wanted to say:

YES! THEY'LL THINK YOU'RE BANANAS AND HOSPITALIZE YOU UNTIL SOME SHRINK SHOVES PILLS DOWN YOUR THROAT FOR THREE DAYS.

Jax wanted to believe her.

He almost asked her again if this was a joke, but her fear made him reconsider.

"Where's your old man?"

"Working, God knows where. I called. He's always fucking gone when I need him."

"Did you tell him about the first time? When this creep assaulted you at the mansion?"

"He wasn't home that night. Besides, I was high. I questioned it myself. He's happy here with his new girlfriend. I don't want to mess everything up again."

Mess everything up again? He wanted to ask but it wasn't the right time. He made a mental note and moved on.

Tears ran down her freckled nose.

"Listen, if you say it happened. I believe you. I'll call the police. I'm just scared of what they might do."

He caressed her arm, sitting next to her. "I'll do whatever you want."

Jax pulled out his phone.

"Forget it." She put her hand over his. "Don't call. They're going to think I'm nuts. My dad's going to freak and put me on meds again."

MEDICATION.

"You saw a shrink?" Jax said. The situation took form in his mind.

Tala nodded. "I'm not crazy."

"I didn't say you were."

Jax tried to understand.

"Maybe I'm just tired."

Tala reasoned, "Maybe it was a nightmare."

"I've had worse," Jax offered.

"You're really shaken up."

He stood, took her hand, helped her up.

"C'mon, let's get some water. It'll calm your nerves."

They went back downstairs. Tala exited the room first. Jax looked at the chair, which faced the bed like it was laughing at him.

Tala got two glasses of water.

While standing in the living room, Jax felt a sudden rush of fear creeping up his spine. He looked around and saw the back-sliding glass door had the blinds open. Nothing but darkness outside. He felt it.

Fear.

Could some psychopath be watching them right now? Peeping through the window? He did his best to look unphased. He wanted to convey strength.

"I'm glad you called me." Jax walked to the kitchen and saw a drawer pulled open with a large kitchen knife on top of the counter. The feeling of eeriness grew stronger. He closed the blinds as if to say, no, as if to yell, *STOP LOOKING AT ME!*

He turned back to Tala, who stood in the living room with her arms crossed.

"Did you pull out this knife?"

"Yeah, I guess. I must've," she said.

More validity. She had drawn a knife. She freaked.

Fear.

There it was, churning inside his stomach, coming up like he would vomit. He went to the back-sliding door. Tala noticed the door was unlocked as Jax slid the glass door open slightly.

"You should really lock these sliders when you're alone."

"That's a good idea. My dad doesn't leave doors unlocked. He's anal, guess he hasn't been the same," she said.

"I can sleep over. Even for a few hours till your dad gets here."

"Sure! When he gets here, we'll hold hands and sing *Hakuna Matata* together." Tala smirked. "I thought *I* was crazy. My dad will ground me for centuries if you're home when he gets here."

Jax smiled. "Only centuries?"

"For a boy to be home alone with me, yeah, centuries." At least she was cracking jokes.

Jax's mind raced. None of it made sense. Did Psycho Jordan follow her home? How did he get inside her house? How did he know her name? How come she didn't tell anyone? Why did she call him?

They sat together for what felt like hours. Jax felt protective of her. He hadn't stopped looking at her lips. He leaned in and kissed her. It came from nowhere and everywhere at once. Tala kissed him back, drawing him close. His intensity grew like embers from a fire. All he could think about was the moisture her lips as she panted for air and their bodies became hot and inseparable.

If someone was lurking outside the house. If some psychopath wanted to harm them—none of that mattered now. He wanted only one thing, *her*.

Jax pushed her onto the couch. He was on top now, taking off his shirt. The heat in their bodies reached a fever pitch. Tala kissed him back like a tug of war. He heard the knob of the front door turn, and when she pulled away, he saw her father standing in the threshold with his keys in hand.

Tala got a long chat about sex that night. At sixteen, David figured she knew a thing or two about it. Even though he tried to convince himself she'd be a virgin forever. This all seemed so soon. Sex was everywhere now. Not like when he was a kid.

It seemed every television show glorified teenage sex and pregnancy. David became appalled watching the Family Channel. What happened to the good old shows? *The Full Houses, Saved by the Bells* and *The Family Matters* of the world? Shows that were fun and clean?

Fun and clean, seemed like a world that had passed on by.

He knew it was only a matter of time before some boy tried something. Geez, the hormones raging through that kid. *Not with his daughter.* To make matters worse, he was a Prairie Boy. Didn't he tell her? Stay away from Hialeah boys! David blamed himself for working odd hours and spending time with Olivia. Christ. He deserved a social life. Didn't he?

He was a single father with a teenage daughter, and he

had no clue what to do. He didn't have a comedian best friend and a Rockstar uncle to chime in and fix the problems. That only happened on good television shows, which had passed on by.

Her cheeks were flushed red with embarrassment and anger when David shunned her to her room. She told him how embarrassing he was as she slammed her bedroom door. David sent Jax packing. TAKE A HIKE, BUDDY! DON'T FORGET YOUR SHIRT!

He didn't remember exactly what he told him, but it was something along the lines of, "Stay away from her and this house. She's better than a prairie punk like you."

Jax apologized and left.

───────

TALA GOT UNDER HER COVERS. When she heard her father's bedroom door close, she called Jax right away, wanting to apologize. He didn't answer. She constantly turned in bed, unable to sleep.

Hours later, she got out of bed, still angry, still full of adrenaline. Her mind replaying the nights events, waking up to the silhouette of a man watching her sleep. Psycho Jordan had been in her room. She was confused of how strange and horrible the night had turned out.

She pulled her curtains back again, spying out her bedroom window. How different would the night have turned if Mark had picked up the phone? She saw Ben's Bumblebee Lawn Inc dump truck parked alongside Mark's house. The truck had a cartoon yellow and black bumblebee on the hood.

Tala thought it odd how Ben was never home. He could have been a pilot. David had said they had gone to the same schools but never really spent much time together.

That faraway thought, the neighbors of that shooter in Bath, they had said, "He wouldn't hurt a fly." Another added, "Great kid. Something must have happened."

Jesus, how well do you really know your neighbors? How well do you really know anyone?

Her phone vibrated on her night table. She had silenced it, fearing Jax would call and David would take it away.

"Jax . . ." she whispered into the phone.

"No. It's MMMark. You okay? I got up to use the bathroom and saw your calls . . . ."

"I'm fine. Sorry, thought it was someone else."

"Look out your window," he said. "I want to see you."

"What—"

"Look out your window," Mark said.

"We're kind of far away," she said.

"I have binoculars. Open your blinds."

She wanted to tell Mark what happened. Tell him about Psycho Jordan, his warning, and what happened with Jax and her dad, but she knew he wasn't fond of Jax. He probably wouldn't believe the story of the man with the raspy voice.

"Why'd you call so late?"

"I was up bored. I wanted to see what you were doing. Yeah, that's why I called." Her voice trailed off.

"So you're a nighthawk."

"I guess so," she said.

Tala decided not to share the night's events with him. Suddenly, her curiosity took charge, she wanted to stay on the phone.

"How come your dad's never home? Reminds me of my dad," she said.

He replied, "Same reason yours is never home. Work. Someone's got to bring home the bacon, like the ole man says. He's in Orlando."

Yeah, I know what you mean, my dad's never home either until you start making out with a Prairie Boy on the couch.

"He went to Disney World without you?"

"There's conferences for landscapers, if you could believe it."

She said, "Interesting." But she wasn't interested. She just didn't want to hang up the phone. Anxious she hadn't heard from Jax. What was he doing? Jax would never talk to her again after the fiasco with her dad.

Tala saw the driver's door of the Bumblebee truck wide open.

"Is your dad home?" she said with a sense of urgency.

"No, I told you. He's in Orlando. What's with you?"

"The door is open."

"What door?"

"The truck in your yard. The one with the Bee. The driver's door is wide open."

"You sure?"

Tala saw movement inside the truck.

"Someone's inside," she said.

The phone went dead.

"Mark, hello?"

The porch light came on, and Mark walked out of his front door with no shirt and boxers on, aiming a Remington 798 at the driver side door of the truck.

Tala ran into her dad's room and shook him like an earthquake.

"Dad, get up! Get up!"

"I'm awake! What is it? What's the matter, Red?"

She told him what was happening. David registered:

Next door.

Breaking in.

GUN.

David told her to call 911 and ran downstairs. Tala dialed and told the operator what was happening.

"He has a gun. My neighbor—Mark is being robbed—4560 Fairway. Hurry!"

In a span of minutes that felt like hours she heard the wail of sirens. Red and blue lights bounced off the walls in a hypnotic trance. David and Mark were talking in the front yard. The burglar had fled. The deputies had secured Mark's rifle.

Tala went outside. There was a young deputy looking so green his uniform probably still had the price tag. He had a crew cut and was writing down notes anxiously in his whippet pad. He was next to a veteran officer, who was a burly African behemoth of a man. His uni looked about three sizes too small. The rookie officer looked nervous, not inspiring much confidence.

"Who saw the guy?" the senior officer said.

"Come on, boot, you should know this already."

"Sorry, Sir."

"Apologize one more time and you'll be walking to the station."

The rookie deputy said, "Who saw him?"

"I did," Tala said. "Sort of."

The rookie officer had his jaw clenched. He was stressed. His training officer had embarrassed him.

"Come on, boot," the training officer said.

"What'd ya see?"

"I was talking to Jax, I mean, Mark on the phone ...."

"Mark is your neighbor? Right?" the rookie deputy said.

Tala was about to answer. The veteran officer interrupted, "You already know that. C'mon, boot, turn the page."

The rookie officer took a deep breath, closed his eyes, exhaled, reopened them. He looked like a firecracker about to go off.

He pushed on. "You're on the phone with Mark, then what'd ya see?"

"The bee truck door was open. It was closed when we started talking, then it was wide open. I'm not sure, but I think I saw someone rummaging inside. I knew his dad was out of town. So I told Mark."

The rookie deputy turned to Mark and said, "I don't wanna add insult to injury, I know you have the right to protect your property and you came out with a rifle. You didn't do anything wrong. But sometimes it's not worth it. The guy may have stolen some tools, at most. It's replaceable. Your life ain't."

The rookie officer stood a little straighter when he said this. His field training officer, who was a few feet away texting and spitting tobacco onto the sidewalk, seemed to be listening.

"Don't worry," Mark said. "I know how to handle a gun." He looked to Tala, then back to the new officer. As if he was reaffirming his masculinity.

"He could have been armed. It could have been more than one."

"Well, I almost got the guy, didn't I?" Mark said, Tala thought he felt challenged. "I wasn't afraid." He said.

The young deputy gave Mark a stern look. Like saying, I have the badge. I'm not afraid either, punk. I'm just not an idiot. At least, that's what Tala surmised.

David agreed with the deputy.

"He's right, Mark. You could have been hurt. I admire your bravery, son, but over what? A radio or some tools? Nothing inside that truck is worth your life."

Mark surrendered. "Yeah, I guess you guys are right."

"I already spoke to Benny. He said he was on the way back. He knows you're okay. But when the deputies are done, lock up the truck and give him a call.

Mark nodded again. "I will."

The young deputy gave him a case number.

Mark said, "Any chance Miami Springs' finest will catch this guy?"

"No one could I.D. him for now. CSI is dusting for prints. If he's in the system, it'll be like hitting fish in a barrel. Otherwise, there's not much to go on." The young deputy said.

A female crime scene tech who had pasty white skin came up to the senior deputy, removing her latex gloves. He waved her off, pointing at the rookie. "Talk to him. He's in charge now. This is his scene. I can't hold his hand forever."

The crime scene tech read the deputy's name plate. "Deputy Hunter, I got a couple partials. They might just be the owner's, though."

"Thank ya," Deputy Hunter said and smiled for the first time. The natural color in his face started to return.

"I reckon we'll canvass the area and keep an eye out for anything suspicious."

David shook his hand. "We appreciate it, Officer."

Deputy Hunter shook everyone's hand.

"So I guess that's it, huh? Mark said. "Back to the doughnut shop?"

Deputy Hunter sized him. "Nice boxers, but it's getting chilly might wanna put pants on."

"Well, there's hope for you yet, boot," the senior deputy

said. "That's not all, folks. Thanks to our good mayor, there's surveillance throughout the city. There's always an eye in the sky."

"Okay, Hunter. Let's start the report," said the senior deputy. Taking another wad of tobacco into his mouth. The young deputy went back into the police cruiser.

"I'm sorry if I sounded like a jerk to the kid," he said to David. I realize it's not very professional. But he's training, and I'm trying to get under his skin. It's part of the job. I have to stress him. There's not much crime in this town."

David said, "It looks like it's working."

"Didn't catch your name," David said to him. David made no attempt to shake his hand since it had been dipped in the tobacco can. The veteran deputy didn't offer it. He pulled back his jacket, revealing his name tag. "I'm James Hogg, but around here they call me the sheriff."

24

DAVID TOLD Mark to stay with them until his dad got home. He didn't want another boy in the house, but all things considered, he had no other choice. He left them in the kitchen and went into his room knowing what he had walked into early in the night wouldn't repeat itself, and he made damn sure of it by giving Tala a death stare before he went upstairs.

The adrenaline had not subsided. They chitchatted. Mark told her of the family business. Bumble Bee handled commercial landmarks like the City of Hialeah, Opa-Locka Airport, and The Springs Country Estates, basically a huge golf course adjacent to the Curtiss Mansion. Because that's where the money was.

"Someone should do the mansion. That place is going to shit," she said.

"My dad has that contract too."

"Really? How come it looks like crap?"

"He hasn't had it long. Dad said he gave the town a pretty high bid. He didn't really want it. It's a massive project, takes a lot of resources. Now he's stuck with it."

He seemed pensive. "Listen, I'm sorry. I don't want to lie to you. The truth is, we lucked out with the Curtiss Mansion and we're lucky to have gotten it. My dad gave a low-ball offer. We lost most of our contracts. The Curtiss Mansion is keeping us afloat. A few years back, my dad started betting the ponies at some Indian casino off Chrome Avenue. He lost it all. My mom included."

"I appreciate you telling me. I guess there is some good with that place then. Your friends were saying how dangerous it is."

"There's nothing dangerous about it. Just urban legends."

"Truth is, some things have happened, but nothing that couldn't have happened anywhere else, you know? It's all folklore. Stories spiral here as tradition. Makes the boringness of this town seem more tolerable."

There was silence.

"Isn't life funny. I asked you to go to the window so I could see you with my binoculars, and now it's God-knows-what-time and here we are face to face."

"What kind of creep has binoculars?" Tala said.

He smiled. "Remember, I grew up with a family of hunters. It's nice of your dad to have me over," he added.

"Didn't think he'd be home tonight. Must have been with Olivia."

"Who's Olivia?"

"His new girlfriend."

"Right on. Daddy getting his freak on."

Tala looked bewildered. "Please never say that again. Like ever."

"Sorry." He rubbed his eyes. "Don't know why I said that. I think I'm tired."

Tala laid out his sheets on the couch with pillows,

although there were spare bedrooms, they lacked beds, not that dad would approve of having them on the same floor.

"You never told me . . . ."

"What?"

"Do your binoculars still work?"

"Yeah."

"How did I look?"

"Not as beautiful as you do now."

Tala rolled her eyes. "So smooth."

"Shall I sneak up so we can cuddle?"

"Sure, if you wanna cuddle in a body bag."

"Are you going to tell your dad about us?"

"What is there to say?"

"I like you," Mark said.

"Let's keep that to ourselves. My fathers had a rough day."

25

LIGHT SEEPED through Tala's window blinds, forming a triangle over her left eye. She woke up without much effort, went absentmindedly into her closet for her sneakers. She had woken up with the muse before, and that inspired her to run. Some people painted, wrote, sung, but Tala ran.

It had been months since she put on her running shoes. She felt somewhat strange and elated, like seeing an old friend. Running had always helped her cope with stress and anxiety. She felt a hub of boundless energy inside that needed to be released. Tala tiptoed past her dad's room and heard him snoring. The sound so loud and obnoxious it made her smile.

She looked downstairs and saw Mark was gone. Ben must have picked him up while she was sleeping. She was hungry but decided the road came first. The hub of energy inside her needed to be addressed. She could eat later. She went outside to a blue morning sky. The clouds had taken refuge somewhere far away. A cool wind rustled her hair. She popped in her earbuds, started her Runners playlist, and found inspiration in the orchestral opening of *Masquerade Ball* by Axel Rudi Pell.

Tala's best moments came from running track. She had won medals. Respect. What she couldn't win was people forgetting she was the girl whose mother had committed suicide. Not all the medals in the world could make people forget a thing like that.

The medals never made her happy. What made her happy was the trance running brought. The exertion of energy, the sweat, the moment. The trance helped her clear her head, and she felt in desperate need of that now. Jax and Mark were on her mind, in a strange tug-of-war. So she jogged around the block and became bored of the same houses, the same cars, the same driveways.

She veered north and saw *it* in the distance.

STAY AWAY! THE HOUSE HAS EYES!

The Curtiss Mansion was old, bruised, but beautiful in a majestic sort of way. The broken structure made Tala think of the history contained inside its walls.

"He burned them alive," Lance had said. "The horses too."

She began to tire but challenged herself to make it to the front gate, then back for brunch without resting. As she got closer, the rock 'n roll stopped. Her phone shut off. She pulled out her earbuds as she made it to the front gate.

She tried restarting her phone, but it wouldn't turn on. She could have sworn she had a full battery. She used her sleeve to wipe sweat off her forehead. The black lion statues on the wrought iron gate looked like guard dogs for the devil that had lived inside. Or *lives*.

Tala took deep breaths, trying to lower her heart rate. She put her phone inside her pocket. She stared at the mansion like she did that night. Had someone really grabbed her? That deep hateful voice. Was it real? Of course it was real, she had wet herself.

When you stare into the mansion, the mansion stares into you.

Maybe she was dreaming.

The house has eyes.

The weather couldn't be better. The dopamine made her feel blithe. On a weekday, the roads would be congested with traffic, horns blaring. Ruckus. The calm and quiet this Saturday morning was something to marvel at. She came out of her daze when she heard a metallic slam! The beep . . . beep . . . beep . . . of a truck reversing beside the mansion.

It was a Bumblebee truck.

There were men with olive skin in blue matching overalls cutting grass and trimming branches around the mansion. She remembered Mark's dad owned the contract. Tala saw several men, maybe six or seven of them with straw hats to block the sun, hauling black trash bags into the garbage port of the dump truck.

Someone tapped her shoulder.

He was back.

"Howdy!" the man said.

She almost fell out of her shoes.

"Whoa! Nelly!" Ben Bradshaw said. "Didn't mean to scare you."

Ben wore blue jeans and a uniform shirt which read Bumble Bee Lawn Inc in red cursive letters.

"I'm Benny. Mark's dad. You're Tala, right?"

"Yes."

"I seen you a couple of times over there. Been meaning to say hello. Mark told me you were pretty." He took the toothpick out of his mouth. "But you're prettier than I thought. That kid usually has horrible taste. Gets it from his mother."

He chuckled. He had a goofy affable way about him. "I see you're exercising. That's good, most kids your age are sleeping their lives away."

"Yeah, I felt like jogging," Tala said.

"That's good. I love exercising. Run in my sleep all the time." Ben guffawed.

He used both hands to hold his protruding belly. "Can't lose this figure."

Tala laughed.

Ben looked over her shoulder. "What you want with her?" he said, referring to the mansion.

"Looks like you're staring," he said, his face stern. "She don't like it when you stare."

"What makes you think it's a she?"

"The most evil things are female. Believe me, I know. Been married twice." He smiled. "Had a Yorkie Princess made it a point to pass water next to my bed every morning. She missed the wee-wee pad by about eight feet. If I didn't know any better I'd say she was in cahoots with the ex-wife."

"It's nice meeting you." He cracked a smile. "Gots to get back to it. Be careful with this place now. Legend says there're monsters inside." He winked. Tala liked him. Although he seemed nothing like what she had imagined. When she came to Mark's house for the party, she remembered seeing him in the pictures, except then he was holding a rifle in most of the photos, and his hair was dark brown.

How could someone as nice as him do something like that?

"Why do you like killing animals?" she blurted out.

"I beg your pardon?"

"I saw the animals you shot."

"I reckon you've been over the house then."

Tala nodded. She brought her hand up to her brow to block the sun.

"I don't like killing animals. I like hunting. It's the hunt that life's about—the process—not the end result. If you're not hunting something, something's hunting you."

"What about the lion?"

"Actually, my son shot that lion. It's a beauty. If you ever want to go huntin' let me know, you'll see. That's what life's all about."

My son shot that lion?

Why had Mark lied.

"Think I'll pass."

"Well," Ben said. "Lots of work to do. Bear with me. We'll put lipstick on this pig in no time."

Tala kept her gaze on the mansion.

"Make sure you stay off this property here. Locals bug out about it. You have a good jog now, yah hear? He smiled and turned around. But his voice had been sterner. Tala saw him reach for a huge key ring on his belt. He unlocked the wrought iron gate and let himself in. Nothing scary about a gate. Or an abandoned house in the daytime, she thought. Just silly stories.

"What's in the black bags?" Tala said.

His eyes narrowed.

"Dead bodies," he said solemnly. He smiled a few seconds later. "Didn't your mommy ever tell you that curiosity killed the cat?"

"No," she said. "My mom's dead."

She felt that if her dad and he were friends he should have known that.

"Really sorry to hear it. Car crash, right?" he said, the sternness in his voice returned.

Tala didn't answer, she looked deep into his eyes.

Does he know?

"I see," he said. "Well, we're taking out the trash is all. Branches, twigs, debris, foliage. Junk, really. It accumulates with time. You be good now yah, hear?"

Ben looked at her one last time and waved. Tala waved back but found her eyes on the mansion.

"You mind if I go inside and look around?"

Ben was locking the gate from the inside.

"No can do. Like I said, locals bug out about this place. They see someone in here but Bumble bee they're gonna come calling."

She felt compelled to walk inside. To stroll the halls where the gruesome murder occurred. She didn't know why. She wanted to see it up close. To touch its walls. It looked huge even from where she stood. So many acres away and she envisioned that she would seem insignificant next to it. Who would care if a little redhead like her walked its halls?

"Tell Dave I'll see him soon."

She didn't say anything else. She watched him take a few steps toward the Curtiss Mansion. He looked back. He waved. She waved. Her phone powered on. She started the music and jogged back home for breakfast.

26

WHEN TALA OPENED THE DOOR, she smelled fried green onion, peppers, and veggies. David was scrambling eggs, making Tala's favorite: a western omelet, French toast with a side of strawberries, and freshly squeezed O.J. He was a poor cook, but who could screw up breakfast?

"Glad to see you're back at it," he said. "You're as red as a lobster."

"It's hot!" she said. "Need some water." She was breathing hard. She poured herself a cup from a glass pitcher on the counter.

"How was your run?"

"Not bad. Takes a bit to get into the rhythm, then it's muscle memory."

"Speaking of memory," he pushed the omelet into a plate, started scrambling another batch for himself.

"I spoke to Benny," he said.

"He called me. He said he saw you by the mansion."

"When? He called you now?"

"Yep. Just got off the phone with him."

"Yeah, did you know his company does the lawn there?"

"No. I didn't. But I don't see why it matters. However, what matters is that I specifically told you not to go by there, and that's the first thing you do." His voice had changed. She could sense undertones of anger.

"Relax, Dad. I didn't go inside. I just ran by it. It's kind of hard to miss." She walked back to the living room. Wanting to get some space from him. Now she raised her voice. "I can run by it, can't I? It's just a house. I don't see what the big deal is anyway."

David put the fork down and slightly tossed the plate onto the counter. Enough to make an impact. "I don't appreciate your attitude." He pointed at her with a wooden spoon. "And the big deal is this I told you no." He lowered his arm to his side, picked up the eggs again, and continued to scramble. His forearms were tense.

"You asked him if you could go inside? Why would you want to go in there? I told you what happened there."

"I was just runni—" She cut herself off, grabbed her plate, and stormed upstairs, giving David a nasty look on the way up.

"You're welcome," David said.

Tala didn't see the big deal. Yes, maybe she was intrigued by the mansion. Maybe she wanted to go inside, but it didn't mean she would. The more people told her to stay away from the mansion, the more she would want to go. She was just built that way.

As she laid on her bed, exhaustion took over. She wondered what the Curtiss Mansion's rooms looked like, the ceilings, the windows. Had furniture survived the fires? Were there ghosts like so many people around this town seemed to believe? The notion was ridiculous but fun to think about. Her imagination had always been her greatest foe.

"Do you believe in ghosts?" Tala asked the reflection in her bedroom mirror.

"Are you talking to me?" her reflection in the mirror replied. Surprised someone had noticed her.

"Yes, I'm talking to you. Do you believe in ghosts?" she said back to her reflection.

"Sometimes I do," the reflection replied.

The girl in the mirror ran her fingers through her own hair and asked very calmly, "You don't believe the mansion is haunted, do you?"

"No. But I had a weird dream. It felt real. Some man grabbed me. Then snuck into my bedroom watching me sleep. He told me to leave the mansion alone. He said the house has eyes—"

"Sure you were dreaming?" the Tala in the mirror asked, smiled wickedly.

The Tala in the mirror pulled a knife from the drawer and said, "You were awake." She sliced her neck open. Blood oozed out, dark red, like bittersweet wine. Tala tried to yell, but there was no sound. She tried to run, but she couldn't move.

She was frozen.

Everything around her was frozen—save for the blood spurting from her neck like a shattered water main.

The phone rang.

Tala woke up startled with a hand on her thumping heart. She saw the framed checkered butterfly on her nightstand, took in the rest of her surroundings, and realized she had dozed off after her jog.

27

SHERIFF HOGG GOT into his patrol car and called his boss.

"Emma, we got a problem."

"What now?" Mayor Sosa was exiting a town council meeting.

"David's girl. The redhead. She's been running around the mansion, asking questions," Hogg said.

"What kind of questions?"

"She asked Benny to go inside."

Sosa walked into her office, smiled at her secretary, a young college girl she'd been bedding and closed the door.

"Ben wouldn't let her go inside, now would he?"

"Of course not. But he said she had a stupid look on her face. Like what happened to Charlie. Kids love telling scary stories about the place."

"Well, James, make sure she finds something else to do."

"I know," Sheriff Hogg said. "Remember, I'm your partner. I'm just keeping you informed."

"I know, Jim, I'm sorry. I'm just trying to manage this town, campaign, and do our work. Our important *work*."

She said, "We can't have Tala or any other brat poking their noses."

"We're on the same page."

"Keep an eye on her."

"Will do."

"Thanks, Jim. Meet me at the lab later tonight," the mayor said.

"For what?"

"To discuss our investment strategy."

"What's there to discuss?" Hogg said. "Every time we strike, our bank accounts go up."

"Excellent, then let's make sure everything continues according to plan."

28

Tala received her online order of *The Aviation Handbook* and read the forward which said Glenn Curtiss died in 1930 in Buffalo, New York due to complications of an appendectomy. His wife, Lena Pearl Neff had outlived him.

Tala read this several times. It didn't make sense at all. It was obviously a mistake. The information online contradicted it. Glenn had locked his family in his mansion and burned them alive. The horses too.

When David peeked into her room and said he'd be flying to Hocus, Texas, Tala thought of hocus pocus. It fit. He could have been a magician, always disappearing. She put the book down and decided to invite The Hawks over the house. When she asked her dad how things were going with Olivia. He gave her the thumbs up. He didn't talk about his personal or intimate affairs.

She didn't want to stay home alone again.

What if *he* returned?

The man in her imagination.

YOU WERE . . . AWAKE . . . .

The book kept her mind occupied, and before long she was fast asleep, running in fields of rye.

———

She bumped into Mark after shop class. He gestured at an object Tala held sheepishly.

"What the hell is that?"

"It's my bird cage."

Mark took it. He laughed. "Think you mean birdhouse, and you forgot the door. How does the bird get out?"

"What's life without its challenges?" she said.

She analyzed her creation. "Definitely needs a door," she added.

"Ya think?" He laughed and inspected all its angles.

"What are you doing later?" she said, wanting to change the subject.

"Nothing planned," he said.

It took great courage for her to say this. The fear of rejection loomed over the tide. She nearly stopped. "I was thinking of inviting some people over tonight. To my house."

They walked down Ref Hall, short for Refugee because it was full of ESOL classes for non-English speaking students, recent arrivals from wealthy families in Latin American countries.

"Am I one of those people?" he asked.

She nodded, giving him the cutest look she could muster.

"Time?" he said.

The fear of rejection washed away like footprints in the sand. "Whenever," she said. "You're next door."

"Right, who else is coming?"

Tala made a group text and added The Hawks, and Jax

too. She hadn't talked to Jax since her dad walked in on them on the couch. Lance, Yin, Valerie, Jaen and Makayla all said yes. Jax didn't reply.

Whose number is 786-834 . . . Valerie asked in the group chat.

She ignored Valerie's inquiry.

A troublemaker, Tala thought. She pushed away the thought of Jax on top of her, kissing on the couch.

She wasn't Jax's type. He probably dated seniors or college girls. Instagram models with perfect bodies and a million followers. She wondered if he had thought of her, of that night. Tala could see he started texting, then deleted it. She thought of calling him but that seemed pushy.

No, dad wouldn't approve.

She thought of how her dad had said Jax was a good for nothing Prairie Boy. A bad influence. She was already making poor choices. What happened with Jax wasn't a poor choice. It felt right. It felt real.

The text bubbles of blue and green danced on her phone in an upward procession.

> *Lance:* PARTY AT TALAS!
> *Valerie:* REDHEAD WANTS TO SEE
> THE WICKED WITCH
> AGAIN LOL!
> *Makayla:* WHO'S BRINGING BEER!!
> *Jaen: YELLOW BRICK ROAD TIME . . .*
> *Lance:* PARRRTTTTYYYYYYYYY
> *Valerie:* WE GONNA PARTY TALA
> OR WAT!
> *Tala:* K
> *Valerie:* DON'T K ME!
> *Yin:* I'M SO THERE!

It went on and on.

The messages made her happy. The one about the wicked witch made her squirm. She wouldn't walk the yellow brick road again. She wouldn't.

> *Yin:* WHAT TIME??
> *Yin:* WHEN SHOLD WE BE THERE?
> *Yin:* SHOULD*

She didn't want to write *whenever* because it felt lame when she said it to Mark.

"Be at my house at seven," she said. "We can tell ghost stories."

The bell went off and the birds started exiting their cages.

TALA FELT APPREHENSIVE, like she was acting in a role where she hadn't memorized the lines. She had never 'hosted' friends. By seven, she had made her favorite Guac in her mom's molcajete bowl. No one was there by then, which brought deep feelings of anxiety, she tried to convince herself people were fashionably late, and no one arrived on time.

To her relief, half an hour later, Yin knocked on the door. Jaen arrived next. By eight, The Hawks had all trickled in. Except for Jax. He wasn't a Hawk, and he never replied to her text. She saw Mark looking at her from across the room. He was talking with Yin. Mark wore a camo hunting shirt with khaki cargo shorts. Tala tried not to think about his claustrophobic living room congested with deer, moose heads, and other exotic game.

My son shot that lion.

Why had Mark lied?

She wondered if he saw her like another trophy. Valerie rummaged through her Blu-rays, separating possible choices of movies to watch.

Lance eliminated most of her movies as "Never heard of this crap before," and "I wouldn't watch this if you guaranteed me a date with Jessica Alba." Tala stood in her hallway for a moment, analyzing her friends.

She was grateful, despite the disappointment of Jax not coming. A year ago, there was only Frances Gumm and Dr. Moss. Dr. Moss was paid therapy. Now Dr. Moss was replaced with a bunch of teenage misfits. She heard The Hawks laughing at something Valerie pronounced wrong. How they wailed.

"It's DONKEY!" Jaen laughed hysterically. "Not Dunkey!"

Jaen held her crotch. "I'm going to pee myself!" Valerie, as clever as a dog whistle, always had problems with the pronunciation of basic words.

"That's what I said." She couldn't help laughing either. She really believed she was right. "I said Dunkey." It had to be a disorder of some kind.

"Pleaseeee stop!" Jaen wailed. She ran to the bathroom, her abs sore from laughing.

When some of that laughter subsided. Tala went over to Mark.

"You looking for game?"

He looked down at his shirt and gave a faint smile.

"Put on the first thing I saw."

She wanted to bring up what Benny had said.

My son shot that lion.

Tala didn't want to sour the mood. Another time, perhaps.

"So what's with the outfit?"

"My brother always wore camo. He died when I was ten."

"Wow," she said. "I'm so sorry. I know how hard it is to lose someone. He was the man in the hunting pictures at your house?"

Mark nodded.

"Me and you have been through some real pain." He pointed to the other side of the wall where their friends were hanging out laughing. "They're unable to comprehend the pain."

"How did he go?"

"Down the rabbit hole." Mark shook his head. "Sorry, my dad says that all the time. Don't know why, just does. It's a habit now, I guess."

She examined the imperfections on his face under the fluorescent light of the hall, but there weren't many. He took a deep breath.

"My bro was in a fight with his girlfriend. They split. My dad convinced himself it was an accident. He was cleaning his gun. I think he shot himself. It was ruled an accident, though, thank God. For my father's sake. But I always wondered...."

Mark said, "We'd go hunting in October. Haven't been back since."

Something clicked inside Tala's mind. *My son shot that lion.* Maybe it was his *other* son. Maybe she had Mark all wrong.

"We got some things in common, I guess," he said. Tala hadn't said anything but was leaning in listening intently.

"Wish I could read your mind," he said.

Mark picked a strand of red hair out of her freckled face.

The doorbell rang.

"Pizza's here!" Valerie said. She put the movie case down and ran to the door.

"Damn, fat ass!" Jaen teased.

Valerie looked out the peephole. She saw no one. She cracked the door slightly, revealing a girl of about eight or nine years with dirty blonde hair holding a small axe. Her face powder white, blood smeared on her chin like she had just chewed a beating heart. Valerie screamed. She ran behind Yin.

"What the hell—" Yin said.

The little girl used the axe to push open the door. Her eye sockets were black, her pupils looked sowed on, she had torn clothes, blood dripped from her mouth.

All the girls screamed in unison.

The little girl said nothing.

Tala wondered if this too were a hallucination. Was she back on the yellow brick road? Had they spiked her drink so she would visit the wicked witch?

The girl's eyes revealed nothing. They were as dead as the game on Mark's wall.

Jax revealed himself from behind the door, laughing.

"She's my niece," he said, smiling. "Good job, Casey." He gave her a high five. He was concealing something behind his back.

Casey smiled. Appearing human for the first time. But she looked off to the corner of the room, making poor eye contact.

"Jesus, fuckin-mother-of-Christ!" Valerie said.

Tala knelt. "Who might you be?"

"Casey." She pointed to her face. "I'm a zombie."

"Wow! I see that!" Tala looked up at Jax and shook her head. "Come on in."

When Casey crossed the threshold, Tala whispered to Jax, "Isn't it a little early for Halloween?"

"She wanted to dress up. I can't say no to her."

Tala rolled her eyes.

"Howdy, Hawks," Jax said to Tala's friends.

When Jax was out of earshot, Makayla told Tala, "You're aware Jax and Mark are archenemies, right?"

"Look at what the cat dragged in," Mark said. He sat at the couch with his legs spread-eagle, sipping a Yuengling.

"Look at what the dog threw up," Jax responded without hesitation.

"Ouch," Yin said. "You've been served." The Hawks chuckled uneasily at the comeback. Tala could almost taste the hostility in the room.

He looked at Tala. "Hope it's okay I brought my niece. I'm babysitting tonight. I wanted to see you." He stared down Mark. As if saying *and what.*

Tala blushed. Her skin as hot as a curling iron.

"I'm glad you came," she said, composing herself. She liked the hostility in the room between the two guys. Her being in the middle of two hot guys excited her. She brought her attention back to the zombie.

She knelt down to Casey's eye level. "You're not going to kill or eat any of us, are you?"

"Not if you do what you're told." Casey panned the room, examining the new faces.

"She's adorable," Makayla said facetiously.

Lance added under his breath, "Yeah, in a demonic sort of way..."

Tala opened her eyes at him. As if saying, shut up, she's little.

"What was that? Care to speak up?" Jax asked Lance.

"Disregard." Lance said.

Jax gave him a suspicious look.

"Anyway, she gave me the sad face when I told her I was leaving. She wanted to try on her costume. I can't say no to her. I hope it's alright I brought her."

"Are you kidding me? Of course it's okay," Tala said.

He looked at Mark and waited for the uniform response from the girls.

All the girls said, "Awwwww."

He glared at Mark victoriously.

"How sweeeeeeet. . . ." Mark put his legs on the coffee table. "I feel like puking."

"Be nice." Jaen poked him on the ribs.

Jax gave him a stark look.

"She's adorable," Jaen said.

Casey gave Yin a high-five. There was something different about her, she clenched her fists and bit her hand excitedly while making poor eye contact. Tala suspected she could be mildly autistic.

Casey sat on the rug in front of the couch with the case of Blu-rays on her lap. She flipped through the plastic sleeves reading bootlegged movie titles.

"I wish I had a cool name like Casey," Valerie said, sitting next to her. "Casey, Casey, Casey," she whispered.

Casey laughed, rummaged through Tala's collection of movies. Her books and movies were two things she never threw away. Tala believed they said a lot about a person.

"What's with the box?" Valerie said, looking at Jax, who was carrying a dark wooden box with a golden handle. Valerie had confided to Tala that Jax reminded her of a rugged version of Zack Morris from an old TV show her mom used to watch. Mark was cute too, but they had grown up together, it wasn't the same.

"Full moon's out," Jax said. "I heard Tala likes a good ghost story. If the movie sucks we could always summon the dead."

"What are you blabbering about?" Mark said.

Jax gave him the look. *Don't piss me off.* He put the wooden box on the coffee table. The box had a gold handle with matching hinges, which suggested it opened and expanded. He looked at Mark. "Move your feet."

Mark showed him his teeth. "Make me."

"Does anyone have a ruler? So these guys can measure their peckers? I don't see the point. We all know I have the biggest," Lance said. He put his arm around Jaen. "I'm black from the waist down."

"You have a tiny penis. I've seen pictures," Jaen said.

"Those were photoshopped!" he countered. "It was a botch job."

The Hawks laughed. Even Jax chuckled. "Guys." He gestured at his niece, who was rummaging through the Blu-rays.

"Right, Sorry," Lance said.

"C'mon, move your feet, Mark," Yin said heartily. He seemed to be trying to ease the tension. "Let's see what's in the box."

Mark reluctantly moved his feet off the coffee table, piercing Jax with his eyes. Jax discarded his look as trite. He reached into his collar and pulled out a gold key that he was wearing around his neck. He unclipped the key, which looked massive in his hand. So large, it looked unproportionable for the lock, but somehow, it fit.

He turned it and they heard a click. Time seemed to slow down. Jax looked at every one of them, dragging out the moment. The silence was heavy and the room, suddenly seemed darker, sinister and macabre.

Casey gave her attention to the Blu-rays. Flipping repeatedly through the movies. Not affected by the apparent severity of the situation. As Jax unfolded the box, no one knew exactly what it was. They all saw a large red hardcover book. Old, burnt, ancient looking. There were no letters on the cover, and the weight of the book apparent, rough textured, with blotches of ink, or blood.

There was something malevolent about the way the red candles were positioned inside the box. They looked like eyes staring back at you, reaching into your soul to charge you the fare to the River Styx.

"It was my grandfather's," he said, breaking the silence. "It's a spirit game. *El Juego Del Libro Rojo*, The Red Book Game."

"Put it away," Jaen said.

"Wicked," Lance said. "How do you play?"

The mood changed; Tala felt like she had been wrapped in a blanket of despair.

Jaen crossed her arms.

Casey said, "You ask the book questions and it tells you its secrets."

Mark said, "Tell me you don't expect us to play with this lame book?"

"It's okay, you don't have to be afraid," Casey's voice was high and haunting, like a forbidden lullaby.

Tala sensed fear in Mark.

"Listen, I'm not down with the Ouija Board or any spirit game. So I'll just watch from over here, thank you very much," Valerie said.

Tala couldn't shake the feeling of despair. "Why did you bring that God-forsaken book here?"

"I thought you guys liked ghost stories," Jax said. Matter of factly.

"Aren't you going to frighten your niece?" Makayla walked closer to the door, a cue she wanted out.

"Why would I be afraid? I'm the one who talks to them," said the little girl dressed as a zombie.

"To who?" Tala said.

She bore an obvious look on her countenance. "To the dead."

No one knew how to respond to that.

Jax looked around. "What are you guys so worried about? You don't believe in ghosts, do you?"

Tala thought about the man who grabbed her. The man who watched her sleep. The man who told her to stay away from the Curtiss Mansion. Was he real? Was he a hallucination? The man in her imagination? No, he was real.

"It's time to stop the wolves," Casey said.

"How could you know—"

Jax interjected, "She's a special girl. If you're up for it. She'll show you."

29

THE HAWKS LOOKED at each other, confused.

"What is she talking about, Tala?" Yin asked.

"I don't know," she lied. "I'm sure it's part of the game." She tried to divert attention from the wolves.

"Let's play," she said.

How could she know?

They gathered around the book. The power went off, and they were suddenly standing in pure darkness.

The girls gave a high-pitched wail.

The lights came back on. They hadn't seen Yin creep off to the corner of the living room and hit the light switch. He was laughing like a madman.

"This is too easy," he said.

"Jesus fuckin-mother-of-Christ, really? Asshole!" Valerie punched him on the shoulder.

"That's not funny," Jaen said. Although she was laughing.

The guys thought it was hilarious except for Jax. Who maintained an air of seriousness.

"You're trying to give us a heart attack!" Makayla joined in. Giving Yin a death stare.

Tala just shook her head. Not really surprised.

"He wants to talk," Casey said. Her voice a whisper.

The laughter faded. Everyone looked at Casey, who was now standing at the edge of the coffee table looking down at *El Libro Rojo*. No one had seen her stand up. She startled everyone. Even Jax seemed taken aback.

Tala's palms were sweating like they had when she boarded the plane from Urbana. *Just breathe.* Her friend's nervous laughter echoed in the room. Thunder struck.

"Rain's coming," Mark said.

"Of course it is," Casey said with that same high haunting voice. "It always rains on nights like this."

The power went out again, and they were all in darkness. The girls wailed again.

"Yin, stop it! Turn them on."

"I'm right next to you. Have been. That really wasn't me."

"Transformer blew," Lance reasoned.

"The transformer is fine," Casey said.

The girls yelled again.

"Your niece is freaking me out, Jax," Valerie said.

"HEY! Calm down," Jax said.

"This is important." Casey's voice sounded like someone else. Someone older. Someone wiser.

"Ooh, scary," Mark mocked and made a scary noise. "This is stupid. She's just teasing. The girl's six and knows how to have more fun than you guys."

"I'm nine."

Lance used his phone and went around the room, helping Tala light the red candles she had taken out of Jax's wooden box. Lance turned them on and made mocking gestures as if ghosts were in the room. When the room was lit by nothing but candlelight, they all gathered around the coffee table and sat Indian style to play the game.

Everyone looked at each other.

Fear.

"Why are we doing this again?" Makayla said.

"Casey insisted we bring the book. My grandfather used to play when he felt like there was something he wanted to know. Casey hasn't insisted this much before. I've tried to forget it. But she says we must play. She's special."

"You got that right," Mark interjected sarcastically.

Jax's fists landed on the table.

"Don't be an ass. I'll—"

"Guys, knock it off. We're here to have fun. You don't have to play if you don't want to, Mark," Tala said.

Everyone looked at Casey, who sat front and center as she picked up the Red Book, which looked massive in her tiny hands.

The tome was heavy, dark red. It smelled like sulfur. Or maybe the passage of time. The more Tala analyzed it, the more she realized it wasn't a book at all; it was a hideous thing that seemed to grow as if it were feeding off their fear.

"Where did you say you got this book?" Tala said.

"My grandma bought it in Mexico," Jax said. His eyes were glued to the book. Casey hadn't blinked and looked like she had fallen into a trance with no hope of returning.

"I was born there," Tala said.

"Zihuatanejo," Casey whispered.

"How could she—" Tala said.

"Ready?" Casey spoke in her normal nine-year-old-girl voice.

She put her hand on the book and said, "Tala, it seems

you have the most questions, so ask. But first, you must enter the game."

"How do you do that?"

"You ask."

"Ask who?" Tala tried to sound confident, like this was nothing but a silly game, but she didn't feel silly. She felt fear. Of course, she didn't believe in any of this. How could she?

Jax explained how the game was played.

"Ask *El Libro Rojo*," Casey said. There was no sound. No laughing. No mocking. A conversation between dead bodies at a mortuary. Rain began pattering the windows. A veil of doom fell over them.

"Storm's coming," Makayla said. "Maybe staying home wasn't such a bad idea tonight."

"Staying home is always a bad idea," Jaen said.

Tala steadied her hand on *El Libro Rojo* as much as possible and asked, "Red Book, may I enter your game?" Her voice cracked, trailing off at the end. She hoped no one noticed. She had her eyes closed. She opened to a random page and pointed. As Casey had instructed her.

Casey leaned in and read the sentence her finger indicated out loud:

> My hour is almost come,
> When I to sulphurous and tormenting
>   flames
> Must render up myself.

THE WORDS BROUGHT a chill to her spine.

"You're in," Casey said.

"No way," Valerie said. "How the hell is that a positive statement?"

"Okay, no offense to the little zombie. But this is stupid," Mark mocked. Lance joined in. A nervous laughter trickled around the room and died off. Casey's eyes rolled back, white as freshly picked eggs, something sinister was at work.

"I think I'm with Makay on this one," Lance said.

"Shut up and let it be. This is for Tala," Jax said.

The photos on the walls fell simultaneously against the floor, shattering to thousands of microscopic pieces. Everyone instantly stood. Panicked. Only Jax and Casey kept their composure, as if they were expecting it to happen.

They had been down this rabbit hole before.

"Sit. The game has begun," Jax said. "Do it now!" They all complied fearfully.

"I want to stop!" Valerie cried. "I want to stop!" Her hands trembling.

"You don't have to play," Casey told her in her nine-year-old voice. Her eyes still hideously white.

Casey unrolled her eyes, craned her head, and looked at Tala, who sat to her left.

"We can stop if you want, Tala. It's up to you. You're the one with the bad dreams."

"Who told you that?" Tala asked, glaring at Jax.

"*They* told me." Casey said.

"Stop. Please. I'm scared," Jaen pleaded. "Can we stop this? Me and Makay don't want to play."

"Tala decides," Casey said.

"We play," Tala said. She was tired of the bad dreams, tired of running from the wolves. If this had something to do with it, she wanted to know why.

The boys had their eyes wide. Yin looked petrified. His hands were the steadiest.

Valerie concurred in tears.

Lance, who had been mocking since he showed up, hadn't said a word.

Mark seemed unconvinced. How could this be true? It's a game, right?

Tala closed her eyes, raised her voice. "Who's here?" Her hands on the Red Book. She opened to a random page and pointed.

> Never to speak of this that you have seen,
> Swear by my sword.

THE ROOM now lit only by red candle light, made the mood eerie. The lines in the hideous Red Book seemed almost conversational like she was talking to something or someone.

"I swear I won't," Tala said, then looked at Yin, who stood next to her.

"I swear," he said. He looked at the rest of The Hawks.

"I swear," they said in unison.

"Mark?"

"This is stupid."

"Just say it, for me."

"I swear," he said reluctantly.

Jaen put her hand on the book and tried to enter the game.

The response:

God be wi' you; fare you well.

IF THE ANSWER didn't make sense, or was interpreted negatively, the player couldn't play until it changed.

YIN TRIED. Failed:

Nay, but hear you, goodman delver,

LANCE TRIED. Failed:

I know you are not ignorant.

Which got some questionable laughs.

AFTER FORCING HER, Jaen tried despite her fear. Failed:

Give you good night.

ONLY TALA WAS in the game. As Casey had said, this was for Tala.

Her turn again.

"*El Libro Rojo*, answer my question. Who is here?" She

opened her eyes, turned to a random page, and pointed. Casey leaned in again and read the line aloud. It was only one word, "Uncle."

Tala closed the book and tried again.

The Hawks inquired, "You have any uncles?"

"No, I don't think so."

"*El Libro Rojo*, who is here? Uncle who?"

She opened again to a random page, and again only one word was under her finger. Casey read it aloud, "Strings."

UNCLE STRINGS.

"WE ALL HAVE AN UNCLE STRINGS, don't we?" Mark said jovially. Still spreading doubt. Maybe convincing himself this was inconceivable.

"UNCLE STRINGS. If you're here, if you're *really* here—prove it," Mark said.

Casey's voice darkened, reprimanding him. "You are not in the game!"

Tala looked at her friends, and the darkness of the room whose only friend was the red candlelight. Tala decided to ask questions. For some reason, something was happening. She felt it since she got here. She was suddenly thrown into this new world, this new town—active shooter near her hometown. The man grabbed her at the Curtiss Mansion, then watched her sleep. Threatened her to stay away. He warned her. Why? Was she dreaming?

YOU WERE AWAKE!

"Uncle Strings. Tell me what you want from me." A cold wind surged through the room, and the doors upstairs opened and closed, slamming hard. The wind put the red candlelight out, and they were in the belly of the whale. The only light was that of the full moon outside, which crawled in through the half open window blinds. Valerie and Jaen yelled and ran for the front door, but it wouldn't unlock. They were trapped inside the house.

"Come back to the book!" Jax yelled.

"I can't," Jaen cried.

"Follow my voice," Jax said. "Here." He extended his arm and guided them back to the sinister book.

"Get it together. You're going to make it worse," Jax said. *Fear. Fear. Fear.*

Yin tried again. *"El Libro Rojo,* may I enter your game?"

Jax read the line his finger landed on:

It is offended.

"No ONE ELSE BUT TALA. He wants to speak to her only," Casey said gravely.

Tala closed her eyes and went through the mantra again. She opened the book, pointed, and read the sentence herself:

> Before my God, I might not this believe
> Without the sensible and true avouch
> Of mine own eyes.

Tala felt panic. Why did the answers make sense? What were the odds?

"Who is it?" Valerie asked.

"I don't know," Tala said.

"You don't have an Uncle Strings?" Jaen noted.

"No, I don't."

Tala didn't know what else to say. She sensed the fear in all of them. In some more than others.

"There's something he wants to tell you," Casey said.

Tala nodded. "What do you want?"

Once again, she pointed to a random page, random line:

> So you shall;
> And where the offence is let the great axe
>   fall.
> I pray you, go with me.

She didn't understand. But the accuracy of the answers were bewitching. She could have been talking to someone from another time.

She tried again:

> The soldiers' music and the rites of war
> Speak loudly for him

Jaen, who had been sitting quietly by the coffee table, flinched and knocked over a red candle. The book's pages caught fire, and Mark quickly took off his shirt and plowed it down. Although *El Libro Rojo* had burned, no damage could be seen on it when the fire was finally out. The whole thing felt like a sick joke to Tala. Another prank by Jax?

How? She couldn't say if it was a trick or not. She had finally connected with something that lurked deep here. Something that had been bothering her since she arrived. And now, she believed it existed.

It was real.

30

TALA SAW her father pull up in the white Porsche as she got dressed for school. When she was done changing, she met him in the living room.

"How was work?" she asked him.

"I wasn't working. I stayed at Olivia's. They changed my schedule again."

"You spent the night?"

"Yes, is that okay?"

She felt a pang of jealousy.

"You're a big boy," she said. "Getting serious, huh?"

"Little bit. I'm not exactly a spring chicken anymore. Trying to figure it all out again."

You're old. She's young. What's there to figure out?

Tala was going to say something but trailed off.

"You sure everything's okay?" he asked.

"Yeah, everything's great." She didn't want to share her concerns and worry him. She knew he'd been through hell and back, with losing his job and the lawsuit. Maybe Olivia wasn't after him for his money. She seemed well off too.

David looked at his watch. "I can still make breakfast."

"David, you've burned eggs," she said. It was one of her real smiles.

Tala saw him in the window as she left for school. He waved and smiled. As much as he got on her nerves, those moments made her appreciate him. Even though he was always working and never there. He was there. He never abandoned her. He stuck it through. That was what family did.

She forgot to mention the 'Get together' but David always said she suffered from selective memory, so she knew he'd understand. She kept the *El Libro Rojo* ordeal to herself. Besides, he would chop it up as nonsense. But was it? Was it a prank by Jax? Another trick up his sleeve? Was his niece complicit? She could have been.

Tala didn't know who Uncle Strings was, but something about her compulsive nature told her she'd find out. It was only a matter of time. She just needed to know where to look. Uncle Strings could be anyone. She didn't pay attention in class, thinking of the possibilities: long lost uncle who left her a fortune? Unlikely but would be nice.

She almost broke Google, punching in "Uncle Strings" over and over but found nothing. She looked up from her phone when a paper plane hit her face. She sat up in her chair, saw Mr. Wilson, an obvious conservative, was still rambling on and on about how we should fight for our second amendment rights in spite of the string of active shootings around the country, including Bath.

Tala scanned the classroom for possible suspects and saw Yin, whose face had turned as red as a fire hydrant. He was biting his finger, laughing. Despite being hit on the face, the sight of him, so enthusiastic and happy made Tala happy.

"Mr. Vo," Mr. Wilson said. "Would you like to share a joke with the class?"

Mr. Wilson looked about ready to make another phone call. His tripping in class stunt earned him a month of detention.

Yin cleared his throat. "Sorry, sir." He said, composing himself. Tala doubted he could afford another phone call to his parents.

Mr. Wilson narrowed his beady eyes and looked at all his students like miscreants.

"This is why they're taking our rights away. Everything's a damn joke to your generation. We're more interested in keeping up with the Kardashians than we are with knowing our own history."

When Mr. Wilson turned around, Tala flipped Yin the bird.

Tala wanted to find out what happened at her house and what Jax and Casey knew about it. They left abruptly and wouldn't elaborate. Jax told her they would talk later. She was hoping to hear from him first, but he hadn't called. She gave in and sent him a text after American Government.

> *Tala*: Meet me by the Golden Hawk 4
>   lunch.
> *Jax*: I can't. Listen, don't take this the wrong
>   way, but I think we should stop talking.
> *Tala*: WHATS UR PROBLEM?
> *Jax*: Just leave it alone.
> *Tala*: LEAVE WHAT ALONE?
> *Jax*: Me. Just leave me alone. Bye
> *Tala*: R U KIDDING?

TALA WENT to the Golden Hawk hoping Jax would show. The Golden Hawk happened to be their school mascot. The statue was made of bronze and stood arrogantly as a display of wealth and superiority. What the hell was Jax's problem? The sun felt like a torch on her face.

Beads of sweat ran down her forehead. Just as she made it to some shade underneath some palms, she saw Jax walking toward her in a white tank top with jeans. He had a black shirt over his shoulder. He walked with his head high and his chest out. Boys back home didn't walk like that. If they did, she never noticed.

He stood closer than she felt comfortable with. She took an involuntary step back. He stepped closer. She looked up at him with one hand over her eyes. She saw through the sun's rays that he hadn't shaved. It added that ruggedness to him that she liked.

"I thought you wanted me to leave you alone," she said.

"Well," he said. "I shouldn't have taken the book to your house. That was a bad idea." He paused for a minute. Took her hand and walked her to a palm tree providing more shade. "The thing is." He searched for words. "Casey insisted. She wanted to see you."

"How did you and zombie girl do it? You got us good."

"We didn't do anything. It was real, Tala."

"No." She gathered her thoughts. "You owe me an explanation. You just left. Who the hell is Uncle Strings?"

"I don't know."

He leaned on the palm tree and took a deep breath with his eyes on the Bronze Hawk. "Casey sees things. My mother was the same. She had the gift."

Tala looked perplexed. "What do you mean, gift?"

"She sees things no one does. Sometimes she predicts the weather. She talks to spirits. Ghosts. Whatever you want to call them. She's done it all her life. My mother did it too. Casey insisted I bring my grandfather's book. She thinks you're in *danger*."

Tala looked unconvinced.

"This is serious, Tala," he said.

"She thinks there's something wrong with the town and you're connected to it. I know it sounds crazy."

"Where's your mom now?"

"Gone. Last I heard she was committed somewhere in Ocala." Tala didn't want to say anything about the credibility of a 'committed person.' She didn't know how Jax would take that, and her own mother's suicide was a non-discussion topic, so she left it alone.

"Why me, Jax? She doesn't even know me. Did you ever think of that?"

Jax looked away.

"How would Casey know who I am? I just met her the other night. Why would she think I'm in danger?"

"She said a girl's in trouble. She has red hair and runs from wolves . . . You're saying that's not you?"

"No. It's not me. I haven't dreamt of wolves." She spoke louder, a good affirmation of her annoyance. She wanted to say maybe once she did dream of wolves but not anymore. At least not lately. That was the Old Tala.

"Is this another practical joke, Jax? Are you going to pull a rabbit out of your ass?"

Jax just shook his head.

"Jesus, were you not there?" he said. *"El Libro Rojo*. The frames falling. The fire."

"You saw that too?"

"Of course. We all did."

"Who is Uncle Strings?" she said.

"That I don't know. It may have to do with your mother."

Tala felt something rise inside. She pushed him with everything she had.

"You're one sick fuck. Don't you ever talk about my mom."

"I knew you'd be mad," he shouted as Tala walked away. The sun cowered behind the clouds, shielding the sun.

"I know what happened to your mother," he said. "I know she didn't die in a car accident."

Tala stopped and turned around, and she knew he knew before he said it.

"I know she killed herself." He said.

31

EVERYONE LOOKED up from their quiz as the door slammed behind Yin, who walked into Tala's Spanish class with his signature smile and waved a yellow pass at the teacher.

"Bring it here." The teacher looked it over briefly.

"Tala. Looks like you're going to your *casa*."

To my casa?

Home?

Something was wrong. She Christmas treed the remaining multiple-choice questions, gathered her things, and tried to contain the slow and steady rise of panic in her chest. She grabbed the pass from the desk and followed Yin into the hall.

"Is my father okay?" she asked desperately.

Yin shrugged. "I don't know guess he's fine. I just got you out of that bat cave. You welcome." Yin's part-time work-study consisted of working the principal's office as an aide, which had its perks.

"How did you get that pass? Will we get in trouble?" she said.

"Relax," he said with a sly smile. "I own this school." He winked at her.

His face changed expression; it bore deep concern.

"There's something I wanted to talk to you about. I had a breakthrough, I think. I need your opinion."

They were now standing in a deserted hallway from an annex building being constructed for the following year.

"After *El Libro*-whatever-the-hell, I couldn't get Uncle Strings out of my head. I was seriously freaked out. I slept with the light on. Anyway. When I was home, I couldn't stop thinking about it. I started researching UNCLE STRINGS. I googled it a thousand times, but nothing came up. No person. No place. Nothing."

"I did the same thing," Tala admitted.

"I have this thing with my brain. Where I remember a lot of useless information, and I remembered an article I read about how Edgar Allen Poe used to write short stories in the Baltimore paper. He used to include cryptograms and offer people money if they could solve them."

"Like a riddle?" Tala said.

"Sort of, yeah. So I started messing with the letters, and I came up with some possible names. None sounded real good, but names nonetheless. So after breaking my head for like an hour on my notebook. I went back to Google and found an anagram solver. I inputted UNCLE STRINGS and it gave me hundreds of results." Tala had no idea where this was going.

"Guess what name popped up?"

"What name?" she said.

"GLENN CURTISS," he said.

Fear.

32

TALA PROCESSED what she just heard.

Uncle Strings is Glenn Curtiss?

Jax had told her at the Golden Hawk:

Uncle Strings is connected to your mother.

No. No. This was madness. How could anyone know a thing like that, even if Casey is special?

Tala hadn't said anything.

He clarified, "Glenn Curtiss from the Curtiss Mansion, the guy who burned his family alive a hundred years ago," he said. "I freaked the fucking fuck fuck out. You know. What are the chances?"

"Yin," she finally said. "What the hell is going on?"

"There's more, Mexico. Lance told me about when you guys went to the racetrack. He said he told you the story of Charlie Owens. He said, last he heard, Charlie's at Citrus permanently committed. There's a chance he might be allowed to see visitors. But there's also a chance he's brain dead."

"He's brain dead?"

"I don't know. I guess. He never talked to anyone about

what happened on the night he disappeared. Or about his whereabouts for months. The police tried everything. Psychologists. Medication. Psychiatrists. Hypnosis. You name it. His friends say he was a happy guy."

Something happened.

Something bad.

"Everyone knows Charlie's story. He went to tag up the mansion. Then boom. He's gone for months. Out of thin air. When he comes back. He's like in a trance. Some think aliens took him and revamped his brain. Messed with the wires in there."

"Please don't tell me you believe that," Tala said.

"Aliens? No. No chance."

Tala thought this over.

"We have to talk to Charlie," she said

"I thought you might say that. If he can see visitors, it's probably just family," Yin said.

"They'll let us in. Use your charm," she said. "Flash that smile."

A teacher walked in their direction reading the newspaper. Tala and Yin started walking in the other direction.

"We can try but I wouldn't get my hopes up," he went on.

"It's a lead. Something's going on. Come on. What we saw. That wasn't normal. And all these clues. All these signs."

Yin agreed with her.

"So we just show up there," he said. "Let's say for some miraculous reason they actually let us talk to this mental patient, whom we don't even know. Then what? Hey. Mr. Owens. You don't know us, but remember the time you disappeared from the Curtiss Mansion? We know you haven't talked to anybody about it. Not even the cops. But you mind telling us what happened that night? And this is supposing that he can even talk back."

He was right, it was a stretch.

The walk took them out to the courtyard. Where she had stood with Jax a day before. She went over to the Golden Hawk, which seemed unphased by time and had a stoic beauty. Tala touched the beak.

"We ask him about the mansion and about, I don't know; *El Libro Rojo*, objects falling off walls. You know, stuff like that," Tala said.

"What if he's crazy?" Yin said.

"What if we're all crazy? I'd hate to burst your bubble, but most people won't believe our story either. You have a better idea?" she added.

"No."

"Then it's settled. We'll say we're his cousins. It's the only way we may have a shot at talking him. Maybe we should ask The Hawks to tag along," she said.

"No. Me and you and no one else."

"Why?"

"That's the way it has to be," he said.

"Why?"

"Just trust me on this, Mexico. I have my reasons." That look of deep concern returned.

"Talk to me. Why just us?"

Yin looked deep into her blue eyes.

"I had a bad dream."

He looked away.

Tala turned his face by the chin.

"It's okay. Tell me."

"Guess I was thinking about him. In my dream, we went to see Charlie Owens. It was dark out, for some reason. We walk into Citrus. Then the rest of The Hawks show up. I guess we were meeting them there. We came in separate cars, I remember. Point is, when we walk in, the receptionist, or nurse, or whoever she is; some fat nasty looking woman, smiled and let us through. But it wasn't a regular smile. There was malice to it. You know what I mean?"

Tala nodded. "Go on."

"We walked down the corridor where people yelled frantically and banged on the doors in these heinous screams like caged animals being beaten. The walk down the corridor seemed eternal. The sounds and scratching coming from behind the doors seemed inhumane. The fat nurse walked ahead of us, showing us to his room. In the dream, I remember looking up because I heard static. I saw sparks of electricity coming from the fluorescent lights. When we got to Charlie's room, the fat nurse used an electric keycard to open the door. She let us in. Charlie stood there dressed in a white hospital gown, staring outside a window at a concrete wall."

"And?" Tala said eagerly.

Yin took a deep breath.

"When he turned around, Charlie wasn't human at all. His face was long and his jaw wide. His eyes were black holes with worms, and when I turned for the door, it was locked. We were trapped inside. Just us. Me and you. Mark, Val, Makayla, Lance and Jax had locked us in. They were outside laughing hysterically at us. It's hard to explain but it was like it was all a big sick joke. We had been fooled, you know?

"Then Charlie grabbed you, and I woke up sweating in bed. I nearly pissed myself, Tala. I don't remember the last time I had a nightmare. I don't know what it means, and sometimes when you've had a nightmare, you wake up and forget it, but not this one. I could close my eyes now and see the thick black worms jutting out of his eye sockets."

"It's just a dream."

"Dreams have meanings."

"What's it mean, then?" she said.

The bell rang, and students were heading out for lunch hour.

"It means, no word to anyone. You and I go alone. Deal?"

"How many times have you had this dream?"

"Enough times to know we go alone."

Tala thought it over. "You have a knife?"

"Of course I have a knife. I'm a ninja, remember?"

"Bring the knife. You got a deal."

DAVID HATED FLYING CARGO PLANES. But when Dotted Blue called him with the job offer, he accepted the interview, hoping to fly again. The perks of flying the big commercial airliners was gone. No eye candy flight attendants. No air of respect from travelers. He was smalltime. Flying cargo was a step back. In and out of Opa-Locka airport for half the pay.

He wished he could get his life back. He often thought about his happiest moments: When he, Yona and Tala were all together. Those moments felt so foreign and far away that the thought of being unable to experience them again made him want to break down and cry. But mainly, it made him want to drink. He tried to think about it less. But at times, the mind had a mind of its own.

There was Olivia. He knew he was a handsome man for his age, but she was much younger. Did people gossip when they walked by? Thanks to his settlement he now fit the stereotype of the old rich man with the young gold-digging girlfriend.

There was Miami. The hope for a change of pace, warm

weather, and moving his life forward. No more whiskey. No more driving to Angels of Mercy to cry at Yona's grave, the grave of a woman who gave him a child while being a stranger all along. It wasn't his fault, damnit. How could he have known? She seemed happy. Most of the time.

There was now. Tala with friends. She seemed happy, but was she? He was obviously no expert on the subject. Her happiness made his new and unfulfilling job more bearable. Less money. Less perks, but he hoped his reputation of being a drunk would stay at bay in Urbana. He knew things like that haunt a man.

David contemplated going back, not for the money, no. Just for his reputation. Just to feel whole again. So he could soar the skies again on the Boeings he was destined to fly. The old idiom that you never know what you have until it's gone felt so true that he had to say it aloud to himself several times in a therapeutic way to hold back from yelling.

Tala seemed happy, he reminded himself, and thank God they had moved before the horrific shooting in Bath. Miami had changed considerably from when he lived here as a boy. He had told Tala on the plane she could expect the sun every day, but that wasn't true.

Yona always said Tala got her selective memory from him. How could he have forgotten the days of massive rain, flooding, and the power of hurricanes? Miami's tropical climate had always been a seesaw of unpredictability.

After only months in the Sunshine State, the dark and stormy clouds of Urbana had tracked him down and brought the cold for company. This brought him unease. Some things have a way of following you.

David was in his office now. He looked out his window and saw a grayish sky. Drops of rain pattered his window like darts. Was it five o'clock already? His door was ajar, and he heard Tala open the fridge.

He raised his voice. "I thought we might go for a drive today, but the damn weather." He was finishing a job application for American Airlines.

She popped her head into his office. "Were you going to tell me about it?" She narrowed her eyes.

"I'm telling you. I woke up this morning and felt like taking a drive."

He felt guilty for not spending more time with her.

"Now you like driving," Tala said.

"I don't, but I feel like I haven't seen you since we've been here. And I'm off today. But I can't seem to stop working."

He almost told her he was thinking of applying to a new airline but didn't.

"Looks like we both have homework." She expected him to smile, but he didn't. He seemed bothered.

"How's Olivia?"

The question surprised him. It made him feel like it was okay to talk about Olivia.

"We had a little disagreement," he said.

"Anything I can do?" Tala said.

"No Red, it's nothing serious." Tala read his face. David, much like her, was terrible at hiding his emotions.

"Why do I feel like you did something wrong?"

"I didn't do anything wrong," he said defensively.

But he had. He had asked Olivia to 'hold back' where they met. Olivia didn't like to lie. "Holding back" to Olivia meant lying. Plain and simple. David argued the contrary.

"Take her out, get her flowers, apologize. You're probably wrong."

"I know I'm wrong," he said, smiling meekly.

"If I take her out, what will you do?"

"Me and Yin are going to the library," she said. "That's okay right?"

"That's fine. Is the Hialeah kid going?"

"No."

"You know, Tala. You can talk to me. I don't want you to —" He almost said *lie* but instead said, "hold back."

"I'm not holding back. It's just me and Yin."

"What are you guys doing at the library?"

"We're hosting a book burning bonfire. I have homework, David."

"Must you inject sarcasm into everything?"

Tala shrugged.

David took her at her word about Jax. He understood she was sixteen, blossoming, beautiful, and that kids were going to do *those things*. He was young once too, for God's sake, but not yet. Unsure of what to do after a father's worst experience with a teenage daughter ever, he asked Olivia for her two cents.

"She's smart—you just gotta trust her. Don't snoop. Don't lock her up. If you do, she'll never tell you anything."

He remembered things he did in high school with girls and thought it ironic that now his daughter seemed to be the prize.

David apologized to Olivia and asked her out on a "date." The word never spoken before. Olivia burst into a laugh attack.

"So is that what we're doing now. We're dating?" she quipped.

It terrified him to be "dating" when the woman he loved, left them forever. He couldn't lose someone he loved again.

Spending time with Olivia made him think less of the

past and helped with the pain. Olivia could be something special to him and Tala. A new chapter in their lives.

OLIVIA ARRIVED BEFORE YIN. She came into the house looking more dressed than Tala expected. Her hair was blow dried straight; she wore pastel makeup with silver earrings. She wore a black dress with red stiletto heels. Stunning was an understatement. David kissed her on the lips. David and Olivia made some small talk, said goodbye, and left.

Tala called Yin, who was supposed to be there twenty minutes ago.

He picked up.

"Hello, Mexico. I was about to call you. My car is dead."

"What?"

"Battery is shot. Maybe I left the lights on. We're going to have to reschedule."

"Let's call one of the girls and have them take us," Tala insisted.

"No. No one else. Remember our deal?" he said.

Tala peered at the wooden key holder in her kitchen and saw the Porsche keys. David never left his keys behind.

"You have my knife?" she asked.

"Do you like chrome?"

"I love chrome."

"Text me your address," she said. "I'll be there soon."

34

TALA TOOK the keys and sat on David's La-Z Boy, twirling them in her hand. Should she go? How mad would he be? She told herself, *you only live once*. Before she really decided, she was inside the white Porsche with the key in the ignition, butterflies in her stomach. She turned the key. The engine roared. She made a mental note of how everything looked before she adjusted the seat so she could reach the pedals.

I'll just put everything back the same way.

He'll never know.

Tala punched in Yin's address into Google Maps, learning that he lives ten minutes away on Hammond Avenue. She drove onto Deer Run, The Curtiss Mansion looming in the distance. She felt hypnotized by it as dark thunderclouds congregated above it like a wicked crown.

She had to make it back home before David's date ended. As she passed The Curtiss Mansion, she saw a flash of orange in her peripheral, like a blur. She slammed on the breaks, jerked forward. Her tires screeched and left the appropriate marks on the road.

What was that?

Had she seen a ghost? She checked her rearview and reversed slowly back to the entrance. What she had seen was still there. No. It wasn't a ghost—it was worse. Fear ran up from her stomach to her throat. She almost vomited.

She heard a loud honk.

In her rearview, a car sped around her. She pulled off the road, parked at the front gate where she had shared a cig with her dad. She got off the car and walked toward them. There they were in all their contrast. A kaleidoscope of monarch butterflies took refuge on the mansion's gate. Their orange wings made her think, *proceed with caution*. Made her remember mom, who wore a monarch domino mask on the day she . . . .

Mom.

The police report and photos from the masquerade party showed Yona wearing an orange and black butterfly domino mask. Her autopsy revealed Lexapro, Zoloft, Ketamine. Two antidepressants and "Special K," a hallucinogenic. David's sworn statement said he had no knowledge of Yona taking prescription drugs. As their investigation went on, it was later determined Yona may have been mentally ill and self-medicating.

SHE HATED YOU!
SHE HATED YOU!

Why did Psycho Jordan warn her to stay away? There were hundreds of monarchs climbing on top of each other, moving like the spiral of a hypnotic trance. One of them landed on her hand. She inspected it. Did it remind her of mom? She didn't know anymore. She cupped the butterfly and took it with her.

She followed the GPS to Yin's house. The butterfly refused to fly away. When the GPS narrated her arrival, Yin was waiting outside and started toward her once he saw the Porsche. She cupped her hands and handed him the butterfly once he sat in the car.

"You shouldn't have. Wait, what is—"

Yin took the butterfly in his hands, analyzing it.

"You catching butterflies now?" Yin said.

"No, I'm just trying to set them free."

Tala debated explaining what it meant. It could be nothing. Her brain was connecting things that had no business being connected. She was becoming paranoid.

"Nice ride." He pulled a chrome Balisong knife with a white bone handle out of his pocket.

He swung it open. "How about this butterfly?"

"A deal is a deal," he added.

"I have a bad feeling about this. About everything," she said.

"I know what you mean."

"What's up with this little fellow?" The monarch was standing on his index finger and refused to fly away. He jerked his finger up and down and it wouldn't budge.

"It's poisoned," she said.

He handed her the knife. "So is this one. Let's go," Yin said.

Tala rolled down her window, took the monarch butterfly from Yin, and set it free.

She searched for Citrus Mental Hospital on the GPS and followed the pink line on the screen without saying a word.

35

Citrus Mental Hospital sat beside the Palmetto Expressway in Hialeah. The building was old and painted a forgotten orange color. Tala parked in the section labeled VISITORS ONLY. She had her windows down. Yin and Tala listened to the swoosh from the cars as they zoomed by on the highway.

Yes, she parked in the lot labeled *Visitors*, but she didn't feel like a visitor; she felt like an *Intruder*.

She put the windows up to drown out the sound of the cars.

"What's the plan?" she asked.

"We go in, ask to see to Charlie. We say we're his cousins. Who's going to know?"

She didn't want to lie but it was their only shot. They walked into the small facility and made their way to the front desk.

Yin said, "Hi. I'm Chesnut and this is Elizabeth. We're here to see cousin Charlie."

"Charlie?" the nurse said with an inquisitive look.

"Charlie Owens."

"Oh, that Charlie," the nurse said. The nurse wasn't the woman from Yin's nightmare. She was younger and thinner. Her hair was pulled back into a ponytail, and she had black framed spectacles. Cute even.

"Charlie's been my patient for the last six years." She looked at her clipboard. "Can't say I've seen anyone come in here but his mom and the Sheriff."

"Which sheriff?"

"Sheriff Hogg. Who else? He's the one who found him," the nurse said.

"Sheriff Hogg visits him?" Yin said.

"Yeah, here and there. It's been a while. I guess he feels sorry for him."

Yin spoke in his most non-confrontational voice and flashed his smile like a weapon.

Yin read her name tag. "Marjorie, we just want to talk to Charlie for a few minutes. We just found out we're family."

Marjorie looked down at her clipboard again.

"There's no Chesnut or Elizabeth in the visitors log. I'm afraid I'll have to get approval from his mother."

Defeat came across Tala's face.

"He's not your cousin, is he?" Marjorie said.

Tala shook her head.

"I know Ms. Owens very well. She's been through a lot. She's here almost every day and has made it crystal clear that Charlie has no one else but her. And no one has ever come to see him since I've been here. So how about you tell me what you really want before I make this an issue?" Her voice had become stern.

"Journalist? School reporters?" she went on. "Completely off limits. His mother has made it clear. I'm sorry, but you need to leave. He's *sick*."

"We're not reporters. We just need to talk to him," Tala said.

The nurse lowered her voice and leaned in. "No. I could get in *trouble*." She took a deep breath. Her eyes went to the corner of the ceiling. "So come with his mother or don't come back at all."

Tala followed her eyes, looking at the corner of the ceiling. There was a bubble surveillance camera just like the one at The Circle.

As they turned to walk out, a frail, thin woman walked in wearing all black, like she was visiting a funeral. Marjorie asked Tala and Yin to wait. The frail woman stopped and appeared to analyze the teenagers as faces she had never seen here before. She continued to the front desk to speak to Marjorie. The nurse eyed them and told this woman that these two wished to see her son. That they claimed to be his cousins.

"Is that right?" Ms. Owens said. Turning around to face them.

Ms. Owens called Tala and Yin over to the counter.

Tala looked into Ms. Owens' dull grey eyes. She asked Tala and Yin why they wanted to see Charlie.

"Do you work for a paper?" she said politely.

"No, ma'am. I wanted to ask him some questions about the mansion. That's all."

"That wretched place. I see." She put the crevice of her palm to her neck.

"The mansion upsets my son. He has his moments of lucidness, but he still rambles about things and people who don't exist. I'm afraid my son is very sick. He's improved in the last couple of months. I don't want to see him regress."

Tala and Yin looked at each other.

The woman spoke solemnly, "I take it you won't be back."

Tala and Yin nodded. "We're sorry to bother, ma'am," Yin said.

"What was your name again?" she said, extending her arm to him. Yin took her frail hand, shaking it. "My real name is Yin Vo." No point in lying anymore.

Marjorie gave him a scrutinizing look. "So, it's not Chestnut then," she said sarcastically.

"No, ma'am."

Ms. Owens then offered her hand to Tala. "And you, dear?"

Tala shook her hand, feeling the frailty of fingers that had been cried into for many years.

"Tala."

The woman continued shaking her hand and didn't let go. The woman seemed to be looking through her as opposed to at her.

"Pardon me?" Ms. Owens said.

"My name is Tala. Tala Stone."

The woman still hadn't let go of her hand. She smiled but it appeared to be out of discomfort, not happiness. "Oh dear," she said.

The woman let go of her grip. The crevice of her palm went back to her neck.

"Ms. Stone. It seems my son has been asking for you."

Yin, Tala and Ms. Owens followed Nurse Marjorie up an elevator to the second floor. They went through a long corridor of the psychiatric ward. Yin smelled a strong stench of cleaning chemicals. The halls were darker than the main entrance of the hospital, and the farther down the hall they went, the dimmer the lighting became.

They tried to keep up with the nurse, who was very much ahead, leading them to Charlie Owens; however, they found themselves eyeing into the rooms that faced each other like hotel rooms with one small plexiglass window.

Yin was shocked at how similar the place was to his nightmare. That kept him on edge. Tala glanced inside several rooms, as did Yin, as they walked by, and saw men and women wearing white robes in padded rooms. People living here made him feel stupid that he could ever consider himself lonely.

They were caged like animals, but Yin imagined their minds were far away in some happy place—he hoped—maybe in places where there were children laughing on Ferris wheels, maybe in places with talking cats and wicked witches. Anywhere but here. The thought of these patients cognizant of the padded walls made him want to weep. No one deserved this.

Nurse Marjorie slowed her harried pace. She stopped at the last door of the corridor and took a scrutinizing look inside before swiping her security card. A green light came on at the top of door, and she pushed it open. Colder air seeped through the crack.

She stepped back, giving Ms. Owens a nod. Ms. Owens came into the room first and saw her son standing against a window, whose only view was a concrete wall. He hadn't moved an inch since the door opened behind him. Yin thought about his dream and looked at Tala. They read each other's minds.

"Charles, it's Mom. Some people are here to see you today," she said.

Could he even hear them? He didn't turn around. He stared at the concrete wall and began to run his fingers up the back of his neck and over his bald head with such pressure his fingertips turned white. He appeared to be wearing something on his face.

They could see a black strap holding it up. Could it be a muzzle? Surely not. They could see his wide shoulders and muscular frame underneath his white hospital gown. He kept his back to them. The room was also padded but it had various artwork on the walls, some in paint, some sketches in pencil, and some blank canvases yet to be touched.

When Yin turned to the corner of the room, his heart stopped. He saw a canvas with Tala's name in black and red letters. *Tala Stone.*

"The hell," Yin pointed at the painting.
How could he—

The canvas mocked them like everything else had mocked them since she arrived in this God-forsaken place.

Ms. Owens lifted her eyebrows, as if her son had never heard such words.

Nora Owens asked, "How does my boy know you?"

"I was hoping he could tell me that," Tala said.

"Did you not come here looking for him? How do you know him?" Her voice had become hoarse.

"I don't know him."

Ms. Owens's voice became strangled, as if holding back a scream. "Liar," she said, pointing at the corner of the room. "Are you not Tala Stone?"

"Everyone hold the phone," Yin said defensively. "How about he turns around and tells us."

"He can't talk," Nora snapped. "He's not well. Don't you know where you are? This is a *hospital*."

Charlie turned around slowly and deliberately.

He wore a white venetian bauta mask. He was skin bald, and Yin saw his emerald green eyes, and rampant tattoos that ran up his neck, arms, legs. Most of his ink were words like a newspaper. He had an involuntary neck twitch. It was minor, but Yin was seeing Charlie Owens through some type of filter, every feature stood out on him. He read the words, "RUNNNNNNNNNNN." By his aorta. It didn't seem like a bad idea but he stood his ground.

Charlie stared at them with contempt. His square jaw clenched. His eyes narrowed. He sat down and picked up a pen which made Yin and Tala take a step back. His forearms were huge, his veins vascular like snakes.

Who knew what he could do with that pen? He ignored everyone in the room.

"Ask him," Yin prodded Tala.

"How do you know my name?" she said.

"He can't talk." Ms. Owens stood farther than the guests.

"Why did you let them in?" Charlie said. His voice was deep and monotone.

"So he does talk," Yin said.

"You're a good artist," Tala said.

Yin looked at the paintings and sketches hung on the walls. Wheels. Old fashioned barrel wheels. Ferris wheels. Covered in black and red graffiti.

Yin thought it strange that this mentally unstable patient would be allowed art supplies. All these items seemed like a hazard to someone who had an unstable mind. Maybe he wasn't as unstable as he had imagined.

"He's not dangerous," Ms. Owens said, more to herself than anyone else.

He looked at his mom. "We're all dangerous, Mother."

Tala and Yin looked at each other uneasily.

His mysterious intelligent eyes went to Tala. "You've just killed me Tala. You're the most dangerous one of all. Don't you remember?"

Tala seemed confused.

When Tala walked in the room her attention had been on Charlie. She had seen the paintings that hung above the window and at the corner of the room. Her eyes peeked every now and then back to the painting with her name on it. There was a painting with a woman flying with angelic white wings.

Tala said. "Who's the girl flying?"

Charlie chuckled. "She's not flying. She's falling."

"I call it Wings Break," he said.

Tala seemed lost in thought like she was remembering something awful. The electricity in Charlie's eyes seemed to fade now, almost to gentle understanding.

Owens leaned back in his chair. Then he said something that brought her to tears, "Did you ever wish your mother had wings?"

Tala stepped toward him, her legs moved like they had been tied down to cinder blocks.

"What do you know about it?" she said.

Owens said nothing else.

Yin said, "What's he talking about, Mex?"

Tala yelled, "I said. What do you know about it? What the hell happened to you at the mansion?"

In almost a whisper he said, "Don't you remember?"

"I-I just want to know—" Tala said.

"Leave!" He slammed his hand down onto the table. He looked into her eyes like he could snap her neck like a pencil.

"Enough," Ms. Owens said. "It's time you go." She opened the door. "You've upset him! Off we go."

"What happened at the Curtiss Mansion, Charlie?" Yin said.

Charlie stood and cleared everything off the table with one powerful sweeping motion.

Yin grabbed Tala's hand. "Time to go."

As they turned to leave, Charlie said, "Something to remember me by." He walked over and took off the Bauta mask and handed it to her. She saw his face for the first time. He looked like a man who had been beaten. His green eyes were full of sorrow, longing, sadness. "Try to remember."

Owens started laughing like an evil maniac.

"You've killed me!" he yelled.

Tala was breathing hard.

Yin pulled her arm. "Time to go, Mexico."

Charlie laughed louder and harder. The vein on his

forehead bulged like a snake. His laugh so wicked and loud the patients in the east wing started to pound on their doors. The screams brought nurses and security guards running down the hall. The guards and nurses tried to calm the patients around his room. Tala dropped the mask. The strength in her hands must've given out, paralyzed with fear.

Yin picked up the mask.

"Come back here with that," Mrs. Owens yelled.

An alarm went off, a long wailing siren like a fire alarm. Security guards raced up the hall.

Yin and Tala ran down the stairs.

"Let's go. Let's go!" Yin said.

"You get back here!" Ms. Owens' voice echoed in the stairwell.

Tala and Yin hurried into the Porsche and sped off.

TALA CHECKED HER PHONE: two missed calls. One from Jax. One from Mark. The phone rang again. Mark.

She picked up. "Hey."

"Hey, I called you earlier," he said.

"If I didn't pick up it probably meant I was busy," she snapped, sounding winded.

"Okay. Are you exercising? You're breathing hard."

Tala almost hit the horn when the car in front of her turned without signaling as if the driver were manning a yacht.

"It's not a good time."

"Where are you? I thought maybe we could hang out tonight."

"Can't," she said. "Homework."

"Where are you?"

"Library," she lied.

"I'm at the library," Mark said.

"Which one are you at?" she said.

"The one in school. Where else?" he said.

"I'm at the other one. I'll call you back." She hung up.

"Dad?" Yin asked.

"No. Mark."

"Remember our deal. Tell no one," he said. "You can slow down. No one's following us." She had been driving like she was in a high-speed chase.

"I'm sorry. I don't see why we can't tell them. They're *your* friends."

"Just don't," he said. "For now, anyway."

"Okay." she said.

"That was weird," Yin said. "Owens is definitely a psychopath."

"But at least we got a souvenir." Yin held up the mask. "This thing is creepy."

They stopped at a red light on Hialeah Drive. He turned the mask around and found some writing. "Look at this. He inscribed it."

Yin read her the message:

To: Tala Stone

$2 + 2 = 5$

"Two plus two equals five," Tala said. Her eyes on the road.

She looked over at the first red light and read the message herself.

"What the hell is going on?" Yin said.

"What does this mean?"

"I don't understand," she said. Tala cut through traffic by taking backroads.

"How does he know you?"

Tala shrugged.

"Two plus two equals five?" Yin asked. "I'm not a math whiz, but I'm almost positive that's wrong."

Tala became lost in thought as she drove. Her body was driving on autopilot because her mind was elsewhere.

She said suddenly, "Have you ever read Orwell?"

"No, but I've read Dr. Seuss."

"It has to be Orwell," she reassured herself.

"Do you wanna share?"

Tala pulled up to Yin's house. An Asian man and woman unloaded groceries from a blue Dodge Caravan.

"Mom and dad?" she asked.

"What gave it away, the eyes?" he jested.

"No," she said. "The smile."

"So are you going to tell me or keep me in suspense?"

Tala waved at his parents and they waved back. Yin's mom gave her one of the warmest smiles she'd ever seen.

"They seem happy. Like really nice people."

"They're a little old school, but I love them. I'm really lucky."

Tala debated with him on who should keep the mask. Yin didn't want it. She didn't want it. She feared her father would ask where she got it, having her name on it didn't help. How could she tell him it came from a mental patient at Citrus whom she met today for the first time in her life?

How did he know my name? Could two plus two equals five really be from Orwell's 1984? If so, what does it mean?

She couldn't tell her dad about Citrus or borrowing his car. He wouldn't understand. How could he understand when she didn't understand? In Urbana, she was plagued by nightmares. In Springs, she didn't know when she was dreaming. How could they be dreams when she felt so awake?

Her visit to Charlie at a mental hospital was evidence enough that she had been awake all along. A painting with her name on it. A mask inscribed to her with a false mathematical formula. Another clue to decipher. Was Uncle Strings Glenn Curtiss? Could it really be the murderer? Calling her? The monarch butterflies on the mansion's gate like her mother's mask before she—

"I can't take it home," she told Yin, shoving the mask toward him. She couldn't sleep with that thing in her house.

"What if it's cursed or something?" He said.

Tala gave him the death stare.

"Fine," he reluctantly agreed.

"I'll put it in Yin's Box of Fun."

"What's that?"

"Just a place where I keep stuff I don't want anyone to see. I have some pipes, weed, old porn mags."

"You're gross."

"Oh please, they're classics." He laughed.

"You better tell me what the two plus two thing is about. The Orwell thing. Because this is getting weird."

It's been weird.

When Yin got out of the car, he popped his head back in the window. "Tala, do you know what's going on?"

"Not yet."

He put the mask on before going into his house.

"Do I look like a serial killer?"

"A little bit." Tala looked at the time. "Crap. I gotta go."

She held up the knife.

"Thanks for the weapon."

"That's not a weapon. That's a knife. You're the weapon. That's just an extension of you."

Tala seemed surprised.

"Say it," he said.

"Say what?"

"Say you're the weapon."

"Why?" she said. Giving a half smile.

"Because then you'll believe it. Remember Tala, attack the things you fear the most."

"What? You look crazy. Take that thing off. I gotta go."

She backed out and drove home with her mind racing a million thoughts a second. Hoping David wasn't home looking for his car. And yes, she may have whispered it once.

I am the weapon.

37

Sheriff Hogg met Mayor Sosa at the Happenstance Bookstore. He got a black coffee and bought a paperback copy of *A Clockwork Orange.* He told the clerk he always wanted to read the book and how much he loved the movie.

Mayor Sosa took a couple of photos with the employees, which would soon be posted on social media, great PR in a re-election year. The mayor sat down with James, who was off duty. He wore a bright white polo and khaki pants. He looked like a bodybuilder wearing a shirt from the kids' department.

"Gosh, it's hot," Hogg said.

Sosa ignored the weather formality.

"How do you drink that without sugar? That coffees' as black as you," she said.

James ignored the sugar question.

"What's this about?" Sosa said.

Sosa took a sip of her coffee and burned her tongue.

"Fuck!" She lowered her voice, glanced around thankful no one heard her.

"We got a problem."

"What is it now? I'm trying to run a campaign."

"I got a call from Marjorie."

Hogg gulped down his hot coffee like it was lemonade. The temperature didn't seem to affect him. Most things didn't affect him. Sometimes Sosa wondered if he was human.

"Who the hell is Marjorie?"

"Marjorie. From the Cuckoos' Nest."

"Citrus?" Sosa asked.

"Yes, turns out the pilot's daughter and her fish-head friend paid Charlie a visit."

"Our Charlie? Charlie Owens?"

Hogg nodded and put his coffee down.

"Why would they do that?"

"I'm telling you, Emma, these fuck heads are up to something, and they're putting their nose in the shit."

"What are the facts?" Sosa referred to her college years and applied the scientific method to everything, which annoyed Hogg.

Hogg chuckled. "My god you really are a politician now. You're being sloppy, Em. This isn't a witch hunt. No one should be visiting our subjects. Especially Charlie."

"Is that what we call them now?" Sosa asked. "Subjects?"

"Do you have a better word?"

"Yes. They're soldiers."

Hogg finished his coffee. "Fine, soldiers."

Sosa waved at an elderly couple who came into the bookstore. She took another sip of her coffee. It tasted bitter.

"Did Marjorie say anything else?"

"They wanted to talk to him. They said they were Charlie's cousins. Which tells me the kids *really* wanted to talk to him."

"Reporters have tried talking to Charlie for years. Kids from school—"

"That was years ago. Owens isn't news anymore; hasn't been—"

"What are you worried about anyway?" Sosa said with sudden finality. "He can't talk. His mind is shot."

"Is it really?"

"Oh, Jesus, you think he's faking? It's been four years since he said anything to anyone, including his mom. Believe me, we would know."

Hogg sat back in his chair, took a deep breath, his massive chest expanded like an air mattress.

"So you want me to leave it alone?"

"Only family can see Owens, and I don't think Marjorie is stupid enough—" Sosa reasoned.

"Mom walked in as the redhead and fish-head were leaving. She let them through. They saw Charlie."

Sosa took another sip of her coffee and gazed out the window at The Circle. A young couple were sitting on a bench talking, kissing. She thought about how she never let anyone love her. How she pushed everyone away. She thought about the country. What was at stake.

"I'll ask you again, Em. You want me to leave it alone?"

"No," she said. "Review the tapes. I want to know everything."

38

MARJORIE VARGAS SNAPPED out of her daydream when Sheriff Hogg entered Citrus Hospital. He went to the front desk like an eclipse blocking the sun's rays from the glass doors. He told Marjorie he needed to review the surveillance video due to a nearby crime, but Marjorie knew he was lying. Marjorie had been under his *control* for some time.

She called him "Papa Bear" when no one was in earshot. He had trained her since she was fifteen years old. She had been one of his first soldiers, and now he trusted her more than the others.

She had been highly susceptible, suffering multiple traumas as a child. Sosa made her the nursing administrator at Citrus ten years ago, right around the same time Charlie got admitted. Mayors can do stuff like that, especially when people owed them favors.

She escorted Papa Bear to the security room and asked Jamal, the security supervisor to step out so the sheriff could review the tapes.

Jamal did as he was told. He even suggested grabbing them a coffee on the way out.

"That would be great, Jamal. Thanks," Hogg said.

He sat down and got to work but he noticed the way Jamal looked at Marjorie before he left and didn't like it. He was more interested in Marjorie than in the surveillance video. He had already seen it. He had his ways.

Hogg had an eye for detail.

That's exactly what he'd been focused on, details.

While he reviewed the surveillance footage of Charlie's room, he noticed a couple things.

First, Tala's keen interest in The Curtiss Mansion. Just as he had suspected. She wanted to know things that could expose them.

Second, Charlie-boy was yapping away. Although his prognosis said he would never speak again.

Third, Charlie handed them a mask. How long had he been talking? Jimmy felt a dark anger manifest in his stomach. His ears were hot. But he took a deep breath because he understood the mind and its many doors. Finding Charlie was happenstance. It took two years before they took Marjorie. He and Emma had experimented with Charlie, but they were still raw. Still learning. Charlie wasn't as susceptible as Marjorie. Who gave up her control almost willingly and took on split personalities, thanks to a decrepit father who loved her like no one else could.

The doors were there. All Sosa and Hogg had to do was push them open. Charlie escaped somehow. When Hogg found him at the Hialeah Racetrack there were too many people around. Charlie became a local media sensation. But there was something wrong with him. He wouldn't talk or respond. Hogg and Sosa believed he could be bluffing.

But with years of silence, an uphill political career, and clandestine experiments resolved to move *The Checkered Butterfly* forward. Their great mission had to go on. When they admitted Charlie into Citrus, Marjorie Vargas became the Citrus watchdog. The Harvard Duo had peace of mind. Charlie's condition didn't improve. It was possible starvation, isolation, LSD cocktails, and electroshock therapy, even for a short time had somehow short-circuited his brain.

Fucked with the wires in there, as Hogg liked to say.

Now, in the Citrus security office, he wondered, had his awareness shifted? Had he focused on the *others* too much? Of course, he had. The Checkered Butterfly had to go on. It was God's work. Hogg couldn't remember the last time he gave Charlie Owens much thought. Not until the pilot's daughter came to see him and Marjorie called. *How was he talking? Why now?* But the most important question of all. What did Charlie Owens, *remember?*

The wheels inside James Hogg's mind turned and turned like a mechanical contraption. He sat there in reverie, thinking.

"Is everything okay?" Marjorie asked.

"Are you my doll?" Hogg said.

Marjorie's eyes narrowed slightly. Her gaze was far, staring into the nothingness. She looked like a spirit took hold of her body.

"Yes," she said, her voice metallic, almost robotic.

Sheriff Hogg deleted the CCTV video and stood, facing her.

"Doll, do you like Jamal, the security guard?"

"No," she said. In that same flat metallic voice.

"Does Marjorie like him?"

"Yes. They're engaged."

"Engaged?" Hogg said. How long had it been since he

checked on her and Charlie?

"Why did you not tell me, Doll?"

"I didn't think it mattered, Papa."

"EVERYTHING MATTERS!" He grunted, holding back a yell. He questioned how much of Marjorie took hold of his doll. The doll he and Sosa created, programmed to tell him *everything*, but she hadn't. Someone had to pay.

"When Jamal gets back. You're going to tell him he's a worthless *nigg*— You're going to tell him he was hired to be politically correct but that he's useless, and you never want to see him again. Your engagement is officially over."

Her eyes didn't flicker. Marjorie hadn't blinked.

As if summoned, Jamal came back in with Dunkin coffee and doughnuts. Jamal bought extra for the sheriff. He had turned in his application to the Miami Springs Police Department last Friday.

"Aww, thanks, son. You didn't have to," Hogg said. "Got everything I need now." He gestured at the coffee. He patted Jamal on the back and bit a jelly doughnut.

"This is delicious."

"Glad you like it, Sir."

"It's Jamal, right? Call me James."

Jamal smiled.

"Sheriff—I mean, James, did you find what you were looking for?" Jamal said.

"Found everything I need." He winked and shook Jamal's hand. "You ever thought of being a deputy?"

Jamal said, "I just applied to Springs P.D."

"Wow," Sheriff Hogg said. "I'll be sure to keep my eye out for your application!"

"Thank you, sir."

"You're Darnell's boy, right?"

Jamal nodded. "Yes, sir."

Hogg looked at his watch. "Oh gosh, I gotta go. Time flies." He walked out. "Nice meeting you, Jamal. Bye, Doll."

Jamal said, "Babe, did you hear that? That's great, right? He's going to look for my application."

Marjorie didn't respond.

Marjorie was no longer there.

"Babe, you okay? That's great news, right?" Jamal said, somewhat confused on why she hadn't responded with enthusiasm. They had talked about him joining the force.

Doll turned to him.

She said it to him. She said it in the same metallic life-less voice. Hogg made his way back to his patrol vehicle. He leaned against his patrol vehicle—like all cops do, and took the cellphone from his front pocket. He made the call.

As the phone rang, he saw Jamal exit the hospital through the front glass doors, bawling in tears of rage. Tears of outright anger. Resentment.

The phone rang three times.

"Go," Sosa said, sparing the introductions.

"I don't know what the redhead knows. But she's asking questions that don't favor us."

"Listen, Jim, I'm juggling eight things at once. Call me back when you have something solid. When it warrants action—if it warrants action." Her voice was slightly conde-scending, and Hogg had lately begun to feel tired of that voice. That superiority.

"Stocks are down. We need another one. Let's be politi-cally correct," Sosa said.

"This isn't about the money, is it, Em?"

"God damn it," Sosa said with anger. "Don't ask me that. Don't you ever ask me that."

"I'm sorry," Hogg said. Regretting the question.

There was silence.

"James, make it big. Use two if you want to. Use Jordan. It's time he pays his debt to me. Make it loud. Coordinated attack. Multiple states. Let's bring this country together."

"Fine. It's time to paint the world black," Hogg said.

39

JAMAL STEPHENS DRIED his eyes before he went home. He wiped his eyes because he didn't want to cry, not because he expected anyone to notice. His parents would be off to some gala or political fundraiser for the mayor. They were never home. His sister Makayla would be out with The Hawks.

If she was home, which was rare, she would be glued to her smartphone or shooting makeup tutorial videos for her YouTube Channel. So when he came in and found her in the living room, he was glad he had wiped his tears.

"Hey, what's up?" Makayla said.

"Nothing much."

"You off early today?"

"Yeah, actually. I quit."

"You quit? What? Why? Did you tell, Dad?"

"No, I don't have to run everything by him, Kay. I'm a big boy."

He seemed distraught. He took his tie off.

Makayla stood. "Jamal, tell me what happened. You look like shit."

"Jesus, nothing happened. I'm just tired of it. I'm taking

a break. I've got some money saved. I'm thinking of going somewhere new. Starting over."

"What are you talking about? Dad's getting you into Springs P.D. That's what you've always wanted."

"Well, maybe I don't want it. Maybe I don't want Dad doing everything for me. Maybe I want to disappear."

"What about Marjorie?" Makayla said.

"We broke up too. Everything's off."

"What? I thought she was the one. Just last week you guys were—"

Makyala's phone chimed. She turned to get it and hesitated.

"You might want to check that. It could be a new follower."

"Why do you have to be such a dick? We're talking, aren't we?"

"I'm done talking." He plodded past her.

———

MAKAYLA WANTED TO GRAB HIM, shake him, tell him she loved him. That she was his sister and she was always going to be there for him. No matter what. But Makayla didn't grow up that way. No one told her those things. Speaking such words would sound foreign, and she didn't feel she could do it. So Jamal went to his room and slammed the door. Makayla checked her phone. Yes, he was right. Her Instagram feed showed she had a new follower.

He told his parents he needed time away. That the relationship with Marjorie had ended. She dumped him and he couldn't work at Citrus anymore.

His father, Darnell Stephens III, told him in front of Makayla, that Stephens men didn't get dumped. Marjorie wasn't good enough for him to begin with. What Jamal needed was a good strong black woman to build a home with. There was nothing wrong with having fun with white women, but when it came to getting serious. He had to think about his image.

The Stephens were the wealthiest family in Springs and the prospects would line up from Swan Avenue to Hialeah for a chance to date him. Makayla knew it was true. He had never had a hard time meeting girls. Her brother was handsome and rich.

She thought Marjorie and Jamal had something special. He had told Makayla that Marjorie saw him, the real him. Race and money had nothing to do with it. He was in love. They were in love. Or so it seemed. Jamal Stephens made good on his word. He packed his essentials and disappeared. He didn't tell anyone where he was going. His mother tried to stop him but Darnell told her to let him go. He was a man now.

He had to find his way.

40

TALA READ a text from Valerie asking to meet at The Cozy Corner. When Tala walked into the diner, she felt time traveled into the past. It wasn't just the old school booths or retro decor. The place felt different.

There were black and white photographs on the walls showcasing historical Hialeah and Miami Springs developments dating back from the 1920's. Everything looked so different back then.

She smelled coffee and ham frying. She also saw the clicks high school movies were known for, jocks, cheerleaders, nerds, misfits, losers, you name it. They were segregated in their own tables having burgers and milkshakes.

Tala wondered which group people put her in. The Downright Weird seemed just fine, as she had told Mark on the first day of school. That seemed ages ago. She saw Valerie sitting alone at a corner table. Tala expected to see Makayla with her. Valerie was never alone.

As soon as Tala sat down, Valerie blurted, "I'm worried."

"Why?"

"I've tried reaching Yin, but he isn't answering anyone's calls."

"Maybe he's busy," Tala reasoned.

"It's been days, Tala. That's not like him."

"Have you talked to him lately?" Valerie asked.

"No," Tala lied. "Haven't seen him."

"That's weird," Valerie said.

"Maybe his parents grounded him again." Tala suggested.

"Maybe. They're always up his ass about something."

Valerie's phoned chimed. She fished it from her purse.

"Oh shit," she said

"What?"

"Yin's block is roped off with crime scene tape, and there are cops everywhere."

Tala felt a slight rise in adrenaline. She became mindful of it. She slowed her breathing. "I'm sure he's fine."

One of the teachers hurried in wearing his grey suit and red tie looking down at his phone. He went over to a group of students and whispered something to them. One of the students covered her mouth in utter shock.

Chatter crossed the diner like a wave of energy. People reached into their pockets for their phones. The talking escalated, and a girl in the far corner started to cry uncontrollably and fell to the ground. Her friends tried to pick her up. But she was in a panic.

"Jesus, what's going on?" Tala said.

"I don't know," Valerie said. "Let's go look."

Tala grabbed her arm. "Don't be nosy. Give her space."

Jax ran into the diner with Lance, both breathing hard. Tala saw Lance looked worried.

"YIN'S GONE!" he said.

Tala felt her throat lock. It was one of those moments

that nothing made sense, but everything came into perspective. She asked who, what, when, why, where, how. She got nothing in return. The news spread like wildfire.

Yin's high school picture circulated every news outlet.

Who, what, when, why, and how?

Jax tried to explain, but the words didn't make sense. She felt her body go numb. She thought of her mother buried under dirt and mud. Her body decayed, rotting away. She got a flashback of her funeral at Angels of Mercy. Yona falling from a hotel. Yin was next. She held on to the table's edge to stabilize herself and her breaths were shallow.

SHE HATED YOU.
SHE HATED YOU.
SHE HATED YOU.

She rubbed the bone handle of the knife in her jeans. The next thing she remembered, she was looking up at her friends from the floor. She was sweating but cold.

"Tala, snap out of it!" Jax shook her gently. Lance came from behind and helped sit her up.

WHEN A TEACHER CALLED DAVID, he weaved in and out of traffic lanes, trying to get to The Cozy Corner as soon as possible.

Why did I bring her here?
Why did I bring her here?

David hugged Tala and took her home. He stood in his living room looking out the window, wondering how he had failed her. He just wanted her to be happy. He wanted her to be *fixed*. Tala came downstairs and turned on the TV. The crime was all over the news now, and the honorable

Mayor Sosa, city Council members, Sheriff Hogg and other high-ranking officers held a press conference, announcing an investigation was underway. They would provide more info as it became available. There was a crime scene on Hammond Avenue, and the whereabouts of seventeen-year-old Yin Vo were unknown.

The local media speculated the teenage boy from Filipino-Vietnamese origin had been killed in a burglary gone awry. Headlines read: *Springs Burglary Gone Awry.* They used that very word: *Awry*. There were no signs of forced entry, only an apparent struggle. The living room looked like a masterpiece of red with swaps, sprays and blotches of blood.

There was even blood on the ceilings, the news reported. Nothing taken. The police speculated someone may have followed the Vo family from one of their nail salons and for some unfathomable reason were calling it a possible hate crime. Other theories were lowlife Dogtown crackheads broke in looking for their next fix and found Yin instead.

They panicked and a fight ensued.

When Tala asked her dad what Dog Town was?

He had said, "It's a really bad part of Hialeah."

THE REPORTERS SAID preliminary information suggested Yin was severely hurt. The police found no shell casings. Yin's body was missing. The blood trail ran from the kitchen through the living room and out over the threshold of the front door.

The suspects dragged him out like they were taking out the trash. Yin's mother told police Yin would have fought back. That worried her. She knew her son. Taking him seemed impromptu, unplanned and messy.

Hammond Avenue was roped off with yellow crime scene tape and was swarming with detectives and local news reporters looking for a sound bite.

THE NEXT EVENING, The Hawks came back to talk to his parents, to offer support. When they arrived, they were taken aback by the amount of people. There was no parking, not even on the street, and the house was full of people crying.

David pulled up with Tala. He couldn't find anywhere to park. Tala saw so many people she recognized from school.

Teachers, students, faculty.

"I still can't believe it," she said. "You don't think he's dead, do you?"

"I don't know, but it looks bad," David said.

"Why don't you get off, and I'll try to park around the corner."

She took a deep breath. Taking in the whole moment.

She undid her seatbelt and exited the Porsche.

She closed the door and looked up as if to ask God why this was happening. An ink blue sky with no stars whispered she wouldn't understand. A meditative silence lingered, even with so many people around. The small chatter sounded like the rustling of leaves. Finding words in times like these were hard, and she didn't want to say the wrong ones.

Tala walked closer to Yin's house and had begun to cry.

She used her sleeves to wipe her face. Her feet felt heavy and uncoordinated. The Hawks were talking to Mr. and Mrs. Vo. They were dressed in black as if this were a funeral, but the Vos wore white. The Vos stood on their porch, greeting people who came to pay their respects and offer support.

Tala almost didn't recognize Casey without her zombie costume. She was handing out colored lanterns from a white box. Tala looked for Jax in the crowd. Many people were crammed together. She could almost see the weight on Yin's parents. They seemed older and fragile. How brave they were.

"Tala!" Mark called from the porch.

Tala had never met Yin's parents and had only seen them a few days ago when she dropped him off after Citrus. They had waved hello. She had waved back. They were strangers. And now, their son was gone.

Mrs. Vo made eye contact with her through the crowd and beckoned her with a nod. She whispered something to Mark, and he came down the porch steps, cutting through meeting Tala on the sidewalk.

"She wants to talk to you."

"Why?"

"She just said she saw you with him."

Tala didn't say anything.

"I thought you hadn't seen him."

"I must have forgot."

Mark rubbed his fingers through his hair. "Well, she wants to ask you something."

"Mark." Tala grabbed his arm as he turned to walk back up the steps. "Don't make me go over there. I don't know what to say."

"Is everything okay?" David put his keys into his pocket. As he walked up behind them.

Tala turned. "Everything's fine."

"Hey, Mr. Stone," Mark said.

"Call me Dave. Is your pops coming?"

"He's on his way. He can't believe it."

Tala remembered the night of the burglary. Mark came out with a rifle in his boxers. She wondered if Yin would still be here if he had a gun. Tala didn't like guns because of *what happened* to Yona. But sometimes she wondered.

"I'm sure no one can," David said. "Any word on the investigation?"

"Just the same stuff plastered on the news," Mark said. "Detectives already started talking to people. But as far as they're concerned, Yin's dead."

"How are they so sure?" David asked.

"Too much blood loss, I guess."

"How do they know it's his?"

Mark shrugged. "Beats me."

Tala said, "Maybe they know something we don't."

Tala made eye contact with Yin's mom again. She held her gaze and nodded slightly. As if saying, *may we talk?*

"Dad, Yin's mom wants me to go over there, but I don't know what to say."

"Say how you feel."

"Dad, I have no words."

"Then tell her that," he said.

41

TALA WALKED up the driveway through a crowd of people. She felt the weight of their eyes on her. Mark grabbed her hand, leading her through the crowd. Shoulder to shoulder cutting through. A line of people had formed from the sidewalk to the steps of the house, townies waiting to offer their condolences to the Vos.

People said the same thing over and over. Something along the lines of, "I'm so sorry this happened." People offered hope. Fewer said, "He'll come home," Scared to offer optimism, which may make the inevitable truth harder to bear.

The news spread through a whirlwind of social media posts, teachers, students, neighbors, alumni, friends, family and the whole town of Miami Springs perched on Hammond Avenue in support of Yin and his family.

Jaen and Valerie propped up a blow-up picture of The Hawks hanging at Mark's house, smiling, young, alive, and happy. Tala was in the photo too but didn't remember taking it. It was the night she walked the yellow brick road. There was an old couple ahead of her talking to the Vos.

The way cleared, she stepped forward, making it to the top step. She felt the gentlest hand caress her chin and raise her head.

She gazed into Mrs. Vos small sad eyes. It was her turn to speak. No words came. Instead, the welled up tears ballooned and popped. Mrs. Vo hugged her. Tala felt like a little girl who had been in trouble for something. Tala felt this woman's heartbeat as well as her own and wondered how two broken hearts could beat.

"You knew my son."

"Yes." Tala tasted the salt from her tears.

"What did he tell you last?"

"I told him you guys looked like good people," she cried. "He said he was blessed. He had some great parents. He was really lucky."

"Where's my son, Tala? Where is he? Do you think he's dead like the police?"

"I don't know."

"Of course you know."

Mrs. Vo placed her hand over Tala's heart.

"Tell me from here."

Tala closed her eyes. She saw Yin's smile, heard his laugh, saw him trip in class. The whole class laughing and cheering after he got up and bowed.

Yin's father cleared his throat like he was fighting off a cold. He sat on a wooden rocking chair. He appeared lost in thought. He was hand drawing a flyer with his son's picture. Reward $50,000. The Hawks were speechless. Together, Tala imagined, in the same horrible dream.

Mrs. Vo escorted Tala inside the house. Mourners lay on the couch. Asians in white clothing. Tala had a flash of her mother's funeral and pushed the thought away. This was about Yin. Mrs. Vo led her into Yin's bedroom.

She knew it was his room because of the Japanese swords, knives, balisongs, Swiss Army blades, and ninja stars. The walls had posters of Bruce Lee and Conor McGregor. Mrs. Vo opened a wall-mounted knife display cabinet. There was a knife missing. It was in the section of his Balisongs.

"My son must have liked you."

"Why?"

"I came here when he took knife out of frame. My father gave it to him. The last gift to his grandchild. The detectives ask me about it," Mrs. Vo said. "When I came into his room to bring laundry. My son told me he wanted to gift the knife to friend. He has many knives." She put her hand on her heart.

"He got knife when eight years old in Philippines. We were sitting by campfire, and my father told him the story of the Balisong."

Tala felt guilty.

"I have it. I can give it back."

"No," Ms. Vo snapped. "No, no, no." She shook her head. Tala was confused.

"His grandfather told him gift the knife to someone special. Because knife is special. So *you* are special." She smiled. Tala thought maybe the stress was getting to Mrs. Vo and maybe she was on the verge of a mental breakdown.

Mrs. Vo paused as if she had an abrupt thought. "Where is the knife?" she asked.

"Home. I can bring it back," she offered.

She looked sadly into her eyes. "Home not good."

"I can go home and—"

"Tala, the knife is yours. He gave you knife like he knew something would happen to him. Like my father did to him before he died. Legend says every Batangueno from Tagalong province in the Philippines carries one. If you are gifted with Balisong, you must carry it everywhere you go. Otherwise, it certain the knife will not be with you when you most need it. And that if you carry knife everywhere you go and knife taken from you. It will come back."

Mrs. Vo, who had a solemn face, gave a faint smile and wiped a tear from her eye.

"Silly stories," she said.

Mrs. Vo walked over to his desk and grabbed a frame with his family in the Philippines during a vacation a couple of years past. Yin was photobombing his parents with his arms extended, the epitome of happiness. His infectious smile radiated cheer. So alive. So happy. So in the present. He looked much younger.

"Will you honor him?" Her eyes never left the frame.

"Yes."

"Does anyone know you have it?"

"No," Tala whispered.

She put the frame down. "Tell no one."

42

TALA ASKED her for the restroom even though she had no intention of using it. Mrs. Vo pointed at the end of the hall then went outside again. Tala imagined, she needed to be by her husband. Tala could see hundreds of people gathered outside from Yin's bedroom window, including local news outlets interviewing people.

They were lighting the colored sky lanterns and wrote messages on them for Yin. Some messages of love, some of faith, some of hope. The lanterns were slowly being lit, and Tala could see them coming to life one by one with their orange glow. It was beautiful.

A thought struck Tala like lightning. Clean Yin's Box of Fun; she didn't want his parents to find it. Tala feared the detectives who had searched his room had already found it. When Tala heard Mrs. Vo go back outside, she quickly shut the bedroom door and peeked under his bed. Nothing but a set of Archie comics. She checked all his drawers, careful to put everything back in its exact place. She didn't find any contraband.

With the help of a chair, she rummaged his closet,

moved his shoes around. Checked his shirt pockets, for some reason. Nothing. His room was spartan. She went to the living room looked out the back window and that's when she saw it.

Yin's Box of Fun was spray-painted on an old shed in his back yard. Yin must've played there as a kid. It was dark out, and she knew she had to get to the back yard to get rid of the dope. She didn't see the mask Charlie Owens gave her either, so it should be in the shed as well. She wanted to see it again. Maybe there was a clue she missed. She hadn't stopped thinking about it. Even now. Even after all this.

Tala needed a diversion. She went back outside and saw more town folk gathered to greet the Vos. David was chatting with Benny, which made her think, *good, more time.* She employed The Hawks to help her discard Yin's contraband. Mark said he hadn't thought about the shed in years. He knew where it was because they had played there as kids.

"There's an alley out back," he said. "I'll sneak in the yard by hopping the back fence. I'll get the dope and any other incriminating stuff," he said.

He just needed someone inside the house to keep cover. Make sure no one went outside. Make sure no one looked out the back windows. Tala insisted she'd go stand guard, but Mark waved her off. He pointed at Valerie. "You do it," he said.

Valerie nodded. "Say no more."

Tala accompanied her. They ushered themselves into the house and poured themselves pop while keeping an eye out in the kitchen, making small talk. Tala saw Mark jump the back gate, and creep into the shed. Mr. Vo came into the house and started pacing like a zombie.

His eyes small and distant. Somewhere else altogether.

He poured himself green tea and spilled some on the counter. He forgot to clean the mess and stopped in front of Tala and Valerie. Acknowledging them, as if this was the first time he had seen them tonight.

He said hello with a curt nod. He went back to his thoughts.

Tala used her peripheral vision to make sure Mark hadn't come out of the shed yet. Mr. Vo went to the back window, sipping his tea. Valerie started talking to him and turned him, so he wouldn't look outside.

"I'm so sorry," Valerie said, and even though she wanted to distract him, Tala was sure she meant it with all her heart.

"Will you help me draw signs? For Yin?" he said. "My wife helping."

"We'll find justice for Yin." He nodded, looking at Tala.

"If anyone knows *something*, he must tell sheriff." No words came to Valerie. No words came to Tala. Mr. Vo said thank you and went back outside. Tala imagined he needed to be with his wife. Tala and Valerie saw Mark going over the fence again, holding something. Once he cleared it. They went back outside to meet up. They cut through the crowd when someone tapped Tala on the shoulder. She turned around and saw Jax holding Casey's hand.

"Hello, Jax," Tala said.

"We have to talk," he said. "It can't wait."

Casey held out a white candle. "Want one?" The flame turning her little face orange.

"Sure." Tala took it from her small hands, but she didn't really want one. Candles reminded her of *El Libro Rojo*.

She saw Mark eyeing her.

"Give me a second." She walked a few steps to the side to talk to Mark.

"Did you get it?" she asked.

"Yeah. I got it. Don't worry. He didn't have much."

"Was there anything else?" Tala said.

"What do you mean?"

"I don't know. Anything," she said.

"Just his pipe." Mark and Jax made eye contact and nodded in dry salute. "What's he doing here? I'll be back. I'm gonna leave this in my car. It reeks."

Mark walked off.

"I can't stomach him," Jax said. "Where's Lance?"

"He's around."

"You won't find what you're looking for, Tala. They took it," Casey said.

"How—How could you?"

"They took the mask," Casey said. The orange glow hadn't left her face.

Tala raised her voice. "*Who* took it?"

"Lower your voice. What's the matter with you?" Jax said. "You trying to make a scene?" People were looking her way.

"I'm just tired of all this. I don't know what's going on."

Casey saw people turn to watch. Her cheeks flushed.

She took off running up the street.

"Wait. Oh shit, I'm sorry," Tala said, and was about to start off after her.

"Damnit," Jax said. "Tala, we have to talk! There's more. It's serious," he said. "I'll call you. Pick up."

Then he was off behind his niece.

"I'm sorry," Tala said, but there was no one close enough to hear it.

43

THE DRIVE back home reminded Tala of the drive when her mother died. Her dad hadn't said much. She knew why. What do you say when your wife climbs thirty-three flights of stairs, gains access to the roof top of a hotel and shoots herself point blank in the head, falling over like a rag doll to meet the rising ground? *What do you say?*

How could she do that?

Why would she?

How could I have missed the signs?

The random strikes of lightning and rumbling thunder aided Tala's insomnia. When Tala's phone rang at 1:00 A.M, she was nowhere near sleepy.

"Hello?" she said.

"Come downstairs. I'm outside."

Tala pushed David's door open and saw him sleeping with Olivia.

She called Jax back. "I can hop into your truck, but I can't be long."

"This won't be long."

She checked her hair in the bathroom on the way downstairs.

She ran to his truck in the rain and saw Casey, asleep in the cab.

"She wanted to apologize," Jax said. "But she fell asleep."

"She's just a little girl. I'm the one who's sorry for yelling."

"Can you turn off your AC? I'm freezing."

"Yeah, of course. We need to talk," Jax said. "This is serious."

"You keep saying that."

"I wanted to ask you something. But before I do, I want you to know you can walk away."

"What are you talking about, Jax?"

"You can either know or not know. If you chose not to know, I'll never bother you again. But Casey insisted I tell you."

"What are you rambling about, Jax? Just tell me."

"Are you sure?" Jax said.

"Tell me."

"I think you're right about the mansion. There's something wrong. What happened to Yin. It's not random. He knew something was wrong. The suicides at the mansion. Charlie. Your mother. You're right about it all. You're connected. I think we all are."

"Connected how?"

"The mask is gone, Tala. Someone took it. Someone wanted to read what it said."

"What do you know about it?"

"Yin told me."

Tala shook her head. "No. Yin didn't want anyone to know."

Jax looked at Casey, who was fast asleep, holding her

teddy. "Yin told me. Remember, I'm not a Hawk. He was suspicious one of The Hawks knew more than they were letting on. The Hawks have strong ties to the town."

"Why would someone hurt Yin? Everyone loves him."

Jax said, "Yin told me you two went to see Charlie Owens. I think you're digging up graves someone wants buried."

"Casey is special, right? Why doesn't she know what happened to Yin?"

"It doesn't work that way," Jax said.

"Why not? She has visions, right? She has her little red book." Tala demanded.

"Stop it, you're going to wake her."

"She sees pieces, not the puzzle."

"Okay, who sees the puzzle then?"

"You do," Casey said without hesitation. "Don't you see that? That's why you're here. This town's upside-down."

"It's okay Casey. Sleep time. We're about heading home."

"This is crazy. I don't see a puzzle. I don't see anything. All I see—all I think about—is my mom," Tala cried. "A mom I barely remember. What do you want me to do? Just tell me."

"Yin trusted me," Jax said. "I want to help, but you gotta let me in."

"How do I do that, Jax?"

"What was in the mask?" Jax said.

"You already know."

"Walk me through everything. What is two plus two equals five?"

Tala told him about the first night she came to Miami Springs. When Psycho Jordan whispered into her ear. She told him how Charlie Owens' name came about and how Yin had come to her. Because of his dream. "He had this gothic mask on. Sad intelligent eyes. Charlie Owens seemed like he wanted to yell. Like something inside of him wanted to get out. His green eyes went to the corner of the room often. There was a camera there. He gave me the mask before we left. I told Yin to keep it. Charlie asked me if I remembered? I don't know what he's talking about. It creeped me out. The mask . . .my mom wore a mask the night she died. We were at a masquerade ball in Miami Beach. Some event. It's weird, like it's connected."

"It had my name, *To Tala*: $2 + 2 = 5$"

"Anything else? Any detail?" Jax asked.

"Oh, yeah, Charlie's mom said he'd been asking for me. It makes no sense. How could he know me?"

"Anything else?"

"Wait." She closed her eyes to think. She was forgetting something.

Tala's mind went to *El Libro Rojo*. The Red Book Game.

"The game said Uncle Strings needed my help. Yin used an anagram solver to rearrange the letters and found a name." She paused.

"What name?" Jax said.

"Glenn Curtiss," Tala said.

"Shit, Glenn Curtiss needs your help?" Jax reasoned.

"It seems so."

"That's odd, because he's been dead a hundred years."

"Tell me about it."

Tala thought it over. No ideas came. No reasoning.

Casey opened her eyes. She sat up, sleep-eyed, and yawned. "Can we go home?"

"Sorry, Casey, we're leaving."

Tala said, "I better go too before my dad and his girl-friend wake up."

"Yeah," Jax said. "The rain's going to pick up."

Casey said, "Tala, things are gonna get worse."

Tala didn't know what to make of that. When Jax drove Casey home, he passed by The Curtiss Mansion and had an epiphany. They would all have to work together. He tucked himself into bed knowing he and the people of Springs would have a hard time sleeping. He knew the Vos' may never sleep again.

WHEN TALA SNUCK BACK in the house, she almost yelled when she saw a silhouette on the couch.

"You okay?" Olivia said. "I got up to use the bathroom and saw you weren't in bed. I've been debating whether or not to tell your dad."

"Please don't," she said.

"You've been a busy little bee, Tala." She said. "But remember, bees can be stung too."

44

THE NEXT DAY, Jax picked up Tala with Casey in the back seat. On the radio, CNN's Don Lemon commented on the recent surge of active shootings across the country and how, despite that, the President vowed to protect the second amendment even with gun control legislation at the apex of congressional discussions.

"Fucking shootings never stop," he said.

Jax changed the station and turned onto Deer Run.

They could see the face of the Curtiss Mansion built of adobe rock standing sentinel through years of hurricanes and abandonment. Jax decided to scope out the mansion before planning the break-in. It was time to face Glenn Curtiss. As they approached, they saw a deputy parked near the front gate. So Jax put his windows up and drove by knowing his dark tints would conceal them, as if they had a reason to hide besides the obvious, that trespassing on the property was a big no-no. Highly enforced.

The deputy appeared to be reading a paperback.

"He's reading," Tala said. "I don't get it. Why is he parked there?"

"Something's up. There's never a cop there," Jax said.

"We could wait. But something tells me he isn't going anywhere," she said.

Casey popped her head between the seats. "We could ask him."

"Ask him what?" Jax said.

"What he's doing there. And when he's leaving." That made *sense*.

"She's right," Tala said.

"That's beyond suspicious," Jax added.

"It's suspicious if *we* ask. Not if she does."

"I can do it," Casey said, biting her hand.

Jax was making his way around the mansion on Curtiss Parkway when he hung a right on Deer Run again and said, "Here goes nothing."

"Or everything," Tala whispered.

The deputy hadn't moved and didn't seem to be going anywhere. Jax wondered if the deputy noticed them circle the block. Jax could see him eyeing them from his rearview. He imagined the gun out of his holster, rested on his lap.

Jax's F-150 pickup pulled up alongside him, and Tala put her window down.

"Excuse me, officer," she said. "Someone wanted to say hi."

Tala saw it was Deputy Hunter, the young officer who responded to Mark's vehicle burglary.

Casey leaned over enthusiastically from the rear passenger side. She smiled. Jax put her back window down.

"Didn't think anyone was back there. Howdy," Deputy Hunter said, with a jolly voice.

"What are you doing here?" Casey used the cutest voice she could muster.

Deputy Hunter held up his book, laughed and said, "Can't you see? I'm working, sweetheart."

"Are you protecting us from the ghosts?" Casey said.

Deputy Hunter started coughing; he was a bit under the weather. He looked quickly at the mansion and back at Casey.

"Nonsense. There are no ghosts." He paused, and his voice became grave. "Only monsters." He laughed and winked at Jax and Tala. "Don't yah be scarin' this little girl with them stories now. Yuh hear? There are no ghosts and *no* monsters," he clarified.

"Truth is," he added. "There's been complaints of kids jumping the fence. Town's afraid someone's going to hurt themselves, you know, everything's liability. Sheriff Hogg and the mayor are being extra cautious with what happened to Yin and all."

Tala said, "Anything new with the case?"

Deputy Hunter said, "No, nothing yet."

Jax said, "Anyone making trouble here?"

"I haven't seen a soul, and I've been working the post for about a week now. We're rotating it day and night. Easiest money I ever made. Biggest crime here is when I cash the check. No worries, it's all good here. Anyway. Yah be good now. And get that gurl some ice cream."

Deputy Hunter radiated good Southern cheer. He could have been anyone's brother. It was too bad they had to get past him. They parted ways, saying goodbye, and Tala gave him the traditional, "Thank you for your service," with a salute.

Jax drove back and parked around the corner of Tala's house.

"All of a sudden there's a cop at the mansion," Jax said.

"Someone doesn't want us there. There are too many coincidences for this to be a coincidence," he said.

"You're right. This doesn't make any sense," Tala agreed. "He said people are complaining of kids jumping the fence? I don't buy it," Tala said.

Jax reasoned, "He can't be there every night."

Tala got off the car. "We'll figure something out."

She said bye, started walking away, then came back.

"Thanks."

"For what?"

"For believing me. You too, Casey. You betta get that gurl some ice cream," she jested, mocking the deputy's Southern accent. She waited at the window of his truck, looking at him. Jax thought of when they kissed on her couch, him on top. He felt his body temperature rise. She looked deep into his eyes like she knew all his secrets.

"I'll be sure to do that," he said, glancing back at Casey through the rearview. Casey gave him a high five. "Sundae with sprinkles."

Jax said, "Come around."

Tala went around the truck to the driver's window.

Jax caressed her face, pulled her in. He felt the soft moisture of her lips.

"Be safe," he said.

"You too."

He saw her walk to her red door. As he drove away, from the corner of his eye, he could have sworn he saw the blinds at Mark's house move just an inch.

45

Jamal's head was throbbing.

He felt like he'd been hit across the head with a shovel. How did he get here? Didn't even know where *here* was. Was this a hospital? His vision began to stabilize. He was in a padded room. It looked like Citrus, but the lighting was all wrong. It was too bright. Had he suffered a breakdown? A deep feeling of dread ebbed inside of him. He felt worse than when Marjorie called him a ....

He tried to move his arms and legs, but they were strapped to a torture device. He was like a fly caught in a spider's web. The Catherine wheel was spoked, made of oak and could have been from the eighteen century. Some called it the breaking wheel. Jamal's wheel still had blood stains on it.

How did he get here?

He heard a mechanical noise and a projector screen lowered before him. It was a projector screen that at one time could have been found in any classroom in America. The bright lighting went off. Jamal was in total darkness. He wanted to yell but his vocal cords felt swollen, strained and exhausted. He felt hoarse, like he had been yelling for hours. He mumbled gibberish. He didn't have the energy. How long had he been here?

The projector screen turned on and illuminated the backdrop, as white as eggshells. The number 100 came on the screen. The countdown began. The numbers descended, ninety-nine, ninety-eight, ninety-seven, down to one then zero. The wheel began to spin slowly.

The programming began, a cocktail of hypnotic suggestion commenced, and he saw a string of various unrelated images on the projector, such as footage of the *The Wizard of Oz*, bombings of Hiroshima and Nagasaki, incinerated children, thousands of dead bodies, *Alice in Wonderland*, child abuse, rape and military training videos.

The metamorphosis of cocoons to butterflies of different shapes and colors. The programming continued. More unrelated images. The music of the Rolling Stones' Paint it Black thundered and was deafening, and in intervals, the voice reminded him. Of who he was. Who he now was. Thanatos. Say it, the voice suggested. Say it aloud. I am Thanatos. Say it. I am the reaper. The God of Death. He must paint the world black.

Next to him, in an adjoining padded room, was a man whose mind split long ago. He was tied to a Catherine wheel of his own. Psycho Jordan was strapped in leather belts, his mind more open to suggestion, more open to control, and how could it not be?

He was broken.

They broke him years ago.

The voice reminded him. Of who he was. Who he now was. Hypnos. Say it, the voice suggested. Say it aloud. I am Hypnos. Say it. The God of Sleep. He must paint the world black. He and his brother Thanatos must bring human souls to Hades in the underworld. Their programming commanded them on their mission to paint the world black.

It wasn't easy. It took time. It took starvation. LSD injections. Electroshock. The hypnotic voice explained how Hypnos and Thanatos must carry out their mission. They were subject to the same programming. The same isolation, the same starvation and pain. They almost died before it begun. The wheel would spin them faster. They vomited several times.

The electrical pads connected to their temples and the dog collars on their necks electroshocked them with excruciating pain. So much so they smelled their burnt flesh like rubber. They were both screaming in soundproof rooms. They looked like actors in a silent film. The pain and projector images never stopped. Jamal Stephens and Psycho Jordan bore trauma no human beings should've ever felt.

They were isolated for months and observed through two-way mirrors by their handlers. They begged for food but were starved. Given only enough nutrients to keep them alive. Barely. They had to identify themselves to eat.

I am Thanatos.

I am Hypnos.

Say it again.

I am Thanatos.

I am Hypnos.

Their pictures on the screen.

Again.

I am Thanatos.

I am Hypnos.

Paint the world black.

The more you say a thing, the more you believe it. Their handlers came and went, never at the same time, and never revealed themselves. They were masked and came into their

padded rooms to inject them with hallucinogens and disso-
ciatives like ketamine and China White.

Like the butterfly, Thanatos and Hypnos slept in a
hammock-like cocoon bed so they too would transform.
Voices whispered their new identity.

Thanatos.

Hypnos.

When the order came, they would paint the world
black. Of course, they would never remember any of this.
Not the Catherine wheel, isolation, starvation, electroshock
therapy, hallucinogenic drugs, nor the checkered floors. All
of that would be filed away in the deepest recesses of their
minds.

A nightmare.

Nothing more.

46

TALA SAW out her window rain and dark clouds congre-
gating in the sky. She went downstairs and saw a stranger
she sometimes referred to as Dad. He was on his lazy blue
chair watching the news, not really watching, but it was on.
He was working a word puzzle.

"What you watchin'?" she said.

"Gun control stuff. It's all over the news."

"Dinner's in the micro."

Tala opened the microwave. "David, this is a hot
pocket."

"You're welcome," he said heartily.

"Back to your old ways, I see. How was work?"

"Nothing like flying cargo across the states," he said.

"You ever miss your old job?"

"All the time."

"You ever think of going back?"

"I have. Olivia thinks I should. I think I'm ready. But the
black mark on my resume doesn't help."

"You weren't guilty," she said.

"I know," he said. "But I was guilty."

Tala poured herself fresh orange juice. She joined him on the couch, crossed her legs Indian-style, and raised the volume on the local news. The weather woman spoke in Spanish and had an hourglass figure. She wore a dress that looked molded to her body. She pointed to a cluster of green, orange, and yellow hues that represented heavy rainfall and the brewing of a storm. Tala realized the news station was in Spanish.

"It's in Spanish," she said.

"I'm learning. Besides, the weather girls are easy on the eyes."

"That's so grosssss." She made a barfing expression.

David chuckled.

"Weather's horrid lately. It's only going to get worse. I'm just trying to stay informed."

"What happened to summer every day?" Tala countered.

"Listen." David fixed himself in his chair. He turned to her. "I know Yin was your friend. But things like that happen everywhere." David stopped talking, it looked like he was looking for the right words. "What I'm saying, Red, is things will get better."

Tala thought about what Casey had told her.

No.

No, they're not.

Things are gonna get worse.

47

TALA TOLD Jax if they wanted to find out what happened to Yin, they would need help. The Hawks wanted in. He would have to play nice with Mark. Jax reluctantly agreed. This was for Yin, after all.

Tala told The Hawks about her visit to Charlie Owens, the eerie two plus two equals five inscribed on the mask he gave her, the Uncle Strings cracked code by Yin. She even told them how Psycho Jordan grabbed her by the neck at the Curtiss Mansion and how he snuck into her house to *warn* her.

The house has eyes.

When you stare into the mansion. The mansion stares into you.

She even told them the truth about her mother. Yona Stone hadn't died in a car accident. She had killed herself at a masquerade party. She had fallen from a building. She had worn a mask. Tala saw it.

The Hawks were speechless.

She told them she believed Casey was special, she had a

clairvoyant gift. Tala talked and talked and Mark, Valerie, Jaen, Makayla, and Lance listened. Leaning on every word. But she never told them about the knife with the bone handle.

That was her little secret.

48

Tala delegated research to Val, Makayla, and Jaen. The girls knew a thing or two about the net, with a combined social media following of 3.4 million followers. With their social media savviness and experience stalking ex-boyfriends, they were the perfect trio for the job. They huddled at the Cozy Corner with their laptops.

Jaen Googled CHARLIE OWENS, hoping to find more information on his case, on his doctors, his disease, anything that could help. After clicking *next* several times through thousands of search results. Some related to Charlie, some not. She stumbled onto an old article from the *Miami-Herald*:

LOST BOY FOUND DISORIENTED AT HIALEAH RACETRACK
June 2, 1999
Melanie Marie

A Hialeah High School teen reported missing for two months was found by an off-duty Miami Springs Deputy in Hialeah, FL on Wednesday night. Charlie Owens, 17, was found inside the Hialeah Racetrack dehydrated and disoriented. Miami Springs Police Sergeant Hogg, who found him, said he pulled into the racetrack one night when his shift was over because he had a 'gut' feeling to take a stroll around. The abandoned racetrack is frequented by underage drinkers. "Most of the kids are locals from the rivaling high schools." Sergeant Hogg said. Sergeant Hogg saw someone with a white t-shirt pacing through the pines.

"It looked like a ghost just floating around," the sergeant said. He put on his spotlight thinking the person would take off, but instead the person kept walking and ignored him.

Sergeant Hogg, a nine-year veteran, said, "He looked like a zombie. I told him over the intercom to stop, but he kept trudging through the woods."

The deputy got off his patrol car and called for backup. He set his emergency lights and followed him through the woods. Sergeant Hogg gave Charlie verbal commands to stop, but he didn't listen.

The deputy finally approached and grabbed his arm. Sergeant Hogg stated, "He had a blank stare in his eyes. I knew it was the missing kid from the BOLO and fliers plastered on every light pole in the city." Sergeant Hogg said the boy appeared disoriented and mentally unwell. He asked the dispatcher for EMS.

It's unknown if Charlie Owens was under the

influence of alcohol or drugs. Sergeant Hogg's report stated he smelled no alcoholic beverage on his person. Several other teenagers were found at the racetrack, they were subsequently questioned and released.

MAKAYLA FOUND another article in the *Miami Herald*.

She said, "Did you guys know Emma Sosa was a psychiatrist?"

"The mayor?" Jaen asked.

Makayla nodded.

Makayla turned her laptop and showed Valerie and Jaen the article:

MISSING TEEN FROM HIALEAH SHOWS MENTAL INSTABILITY

June 6, 1999

Kayleen Cruz

HIALEAH, Florida —Charlie Owens, 17, brought joy to the community when he was found by police Wednesday night. His mother, Nora Owens reported Charlie showed signs of mental instability. A once gregarious teenager and graffiti artist known for his eccentric artistic murals in the Leah Arts District seemed unrecognizable by his mother, his family and friends. He has been admitted into Citrus Mental Hospital for examination.

"I don't know what's wrong with him," Ms. Owens, told the *Herald*. "The doctors don't know. He's just sick now. Something happened to him. Something bad. He's not talking. It's like he forgot how."

Charlie Owens will be under the care of Dr. Emma Sosa, the Chief Psychiatrist at Citrus. The doctor was not available for comment.

VALERIE FOUND the Dotted Blue article cached in Google. The original article had been wiped. She read it and showed it to the girls.

EMMA SOSA PURCHASES DOTTED BLUE FOR 2.1 MILLION
Jan 08, 2002
Christian Castro

HIALEAH, Florida —Emma Sosa, ex-doctor, ex-police officer, new mayor of Miami Springs and weekend investor has partnered up with Painted Lady Corp to purchase Dotted Blue for 2.1 million dollars. Emma Sosa purchased the cargo airline which is responsible for bringing produce and other merchandise from all over the country to Opa-Locka airport for distribution. Emma Sosa was not available for comment.

THE SNIPPET DIDN'T PROVIDE much information save for the fact that Emma Sosa had bankroll and an impressive resume.

She showed Makayla and Jaen and sent the information to The Hawks in a group chat. There were other articles about Charlie's disappearance. Posters, flyers, but the information was redundant.

When Sergeant, now Sheriff, Hogg found him. Charlie went from a normal teenager to a mentally ill patient with no one having the slightest clue of his whereabouts for six months. Was he kidnapped? Did he run away? What made him sick? No answers.

Tala feared her obsession with the mansion would lead her down the same rabbit hole. What was it about the mansion that had drawn him in? Was it the same thing that was drawing her in? Calling her.

No.

Beckoning her.

She knew she had to jump the wrought iron gate. It was the only way to discover what happened to Charlie and Yin. She closed her eyes and visualized herself gripping the lion's head and hurdling herself over the fence, landing on the frigid land.

The land of the dead.

It doesn't matter how many people come with you when you go to a place like that, she thought. You're always alone.

VALERIE FOUND this article and read it to the girls.

NEW SHERIFF IN TOWN: MAYOR EMMA SOSA APPOINTS JAMES HOGG

June 6, 1990
Robert Cruz

MIAMI SPRINGS, Florida —The citizens of Miami Springs have spoken with the highest voter turnout in the town's history. The citizens have elected hometown hero, Emma Sosa, who vowed to bring 'much needed' changes to the town. Sosa, who retired early from her career in law enforcement, vowed to reduce crime and keep trespassers out of Springs. Sosa's resume includes law enforcement, community organizer, Chief Psychiatrist at Citrus Hospital, and now—Mayor. Mayor Sosa held a press conference and announced she had appointed James Hogg as the new Sheriff. Hogg is a burly intelligent man who graduated summa cum laude from Harvard Medical School. The Sheriff said he entered the world of law enforcement to make a difference. Hogg said, "It would be my honor to work alongside the mayor, an old colleague and friend. It would be an honor to serve this town and protect its citizens."

AFTER VALERIE READ all the articles something clicked inside her mind.

"Somethings off about this," she said.

"What do you mean?" Makayla asked.

Makayla and Jaen both stared at her.

"Don't you see? They're not cops. They're doctors."

Tala and The Hawks masterminded a plan. Mark thought it was a bad idea but agreed, nonetheless. The Hawks stuck together, always had. Tala saw the puzzle, Casey had said. As for Casey, she was too young to go, and when Jax mentioned their plan, she showed no interest in going and went back to playing with her fire truck toys.

The twilight sky looked painted on the horizon. Tala and Mark waited impatiently inside of Mark's car scrutinizing every pair of headlights that came up and down the street.

Mark put his hand over Tala's to stop it from shaking.

"Relax," he told her. "Just a house," he went on. "We'll look around and be gone before anyone knows it." Tala stared back into his brown eyes, which seemed darker now that the shadows of the trees were longer. He sensed her unease. "Ghosts aren't real," he said.

Tala looked away. "I read somewhere that ghosts are real. They live inside us."

"This isn't a book, Tala. This is *real* life."

Lance pulled up in his Jeep and rolled down his tinted windows, revealing Jax, Makayla, Valerie, and Jaen, who looked damn near terrified of the plan concocted earlier at The Cozy Corner.

"We have a little problem," Lance said boisterously.

"What's wrong?" Tala said.

"There's Five-O."

Tala looked lost.

Lance almost rolled his eyes.

"There's a law enforcement officer duly sworn to enforce the laws with his badge and gun at the front gate," he said with a funny voice. Trying to lighten the tone.

It didn't work.

"Geez, I forgot about him. Why's he still there?" Tala said.

Mark replied, "I told you guys this is a bad idea. Maybe to keep people out. We better leave it for another night. This is a heat up."

"No way! We're here. We can go in through The Sea of Trees. It's the densest area," Lance added.

"That little forest is creepy. Do you know how many people died there?" Jaen said.

Tala nodded. "We're already here."

"We have to be quick, though," Jax said. "There's lots of trees and tall grass. God knows what's living there. Snakes, Rats. Roaches. Insects."

"Spiders?" Makayla asked.

"Oh yeah," Lance interjected. "Tons of those. You ladies still up for it?"

The Hawketts nodded.

Mark held Tala's gaze. "Let's hope you know what you're doing."

THE THOUGHT of a spider walking up Makayla's legs was enough to send shivers down her spine. She saw Tala in loose fitting Urbana Track Team shorts. Tala would regret not wearing pants soon. She must've prepared for running. But the Curtiss Mansion's tall grass and dense shrubbery would make that impossible. At least, until they cleared The Sea of Trees.

Lance parked on the east side under an underbrush of trees which hid the Jeep well. He took a few steps back onto the street to analyze the camouflage and approved of how dark and damp the lighting was on this side of the acreage.

It was hard to tell the Jeep was there at all. As they discussed at The Cozy Corner, the bad part was they would have to jump and cut through The Sea of Trees. Lance climbed onto the hood of the Jeep and leaped over the gate, almost losing his balance.

"Be careful," Tala said.

"Nice one, jackass," Mark teased.

When Tala saw Lance on the other side, she felt her

pulse begin to rise. Valerie hoped the deputy stayed put. She kept a lookout for headlights on the dark road.

"Okay! Who's next?" Lance said.

The girls seemed nervous, and Tala leaned on the Jeep, taking deep breaths. She looked like she was meditating with her eyes closed.

Jax saw her rubbing her palms.

"You alright?" he said.

"Yeah, I'm good."

"Just breathe," Jax said.

Lance hollered through the fence, "He-llo. Are you guys coming or what?" He stood in a needle of tall grass. "My balls itch."

"Oh, God." Jaen said. "I can't do this. Sorry, Tala."

"Fan-fucking-tastic," Lance said. "Don't mind me. I'm just here by myself."

"We're going," Tala said. "Just give us a sec." She said *us*. She meant *me*. Give *me* a second, Valerie thought.

"Don't worry about me, guys," he ranted on. "I'm just here with the dead people."

After a minute or so.

Lance walked up to the gate and held the iron bars like a prisoner. "This was your idea Tala. You goin' to chicken out? What are you afraid of anyway?"

"Just shut up," Tala yelled. "Shut up! Shut up!" Her palms were cupping her ears.

Makayla yelled at him, "Damnit, Lance!"

Valerie saw headlights coming up the road.

"Duck! Car coming." They all hid behind the Jeep. The car whooshed by.

"We better hurry," Tala said, taking deep breaths.

Valerie smelled mildew and a stench of burnt wood.

Mark had one foot on the truck and one leg on the fence. He said, "Guys. We have three girls who can't get over the fence and one of them is having a panic attack. Maybe we didn't think this through."

Lance agreed. "Well, in that case, it's time we end this dog and pony show 'cause I'm the only asshole over here."

"I concur," Mark said. "You are an asshole."

"Very funny." Lace said.

"When that cop makes his rounds, we're screwed." Valerie said.

TALA THOUGHT of when she was younger in Urbana, when her peers chanted, *Suicide girl! Suicide girl! Suicide girl!*

She forced a white sand beach to materialize on the surface of her mind. She started to breathe normally again. She thought of what Yin had told her.

You are the weapon.

Attack the things you fear the most.

I am the weapon.

She pictured his face, his smile, his spiky black hair with too much gel, how he had tripped in class for her. How he had believed her. How he had gone with her to see Charlie Owens. She wouldn't let him down.

"Let's do it."

"For today," Lance said.

"I'm with ya," Jax said.

"I can't," Jaen replied.

Tala said, "I understand."

She looked at Valerie. "You up for it?"

"I need a little adventure."

"Jaen, you'll be the lookout. Call me if you see anything," Tala said.

Tala saw the relief on Jaen's face. She said, "I love Yin, but I've never climbed a gate. I have no business in there."

"I understand," Tala said.

Mark said, "Listen, Red, you just freaked out. Maybe it's best—" Before he finished talking, Tala stood on the hood of the Jeep, propped her leg on the side, and jumped over the fence, barely touching it in one swift motion. *Just another hurdle.* She landed on her feet and hands and felt like a wolf as the tall grass spawned up through the space between her fingers.

The jolt of energy came not from the years of running track but from anger. Anger for her dead mother. Anger for Yin. Anger for the night terrors. Anger for the unknowns.

MARK AND JAX set their egos aside and helped boost Valerie over the gate. They eased her over as Lance caught her on the other side. Valerie had a sense of deja vu having climbed fences with her brother at the railroad tracks in Hialeah before he became addicted to meth.

He would boost her over the chain link fences armed with spray paint cans to tag up the trains. She remembered writing their names underneath the bridge CHRIS & VAL. When Chris OD'd, she went back to the trains and wrote his name on as many train cars as she could. As if writing his name would somehow help him *live* a little bit longer.

Valerie was only thirteen when he died, and on nights like this, on nights of adventure, like Chris used to say, she thought of him and wiped away the tears as she waded through The Sea of Trees. She was crying, but it's okay to cry now, because no one could see her. She trudged forward toward the mansion with a spray paint can inside her backpack.

———

THE HAWKS TOOK short steps through the Sea of Trees, all lost within their own heads, questioning their motives for being here.

Some thought of Yin. Some of Charlie Owens. Some of their own family. Some of the suicides that happened here. Some of getting caught.

One of Yona.

All of fear.

Tala thought of all the people who went to Yin's house to mourn. How many people would go to hers if she was gone?

Yin wasn't her friend because he wanted something from her. He hadn't asked her for anything. They were friends because they were friends, and she didn't think people that real existed.

Tala cut through shrubs, leading the pack. She climbed over fallen oak trees long ago slain. Branches and soil that witnessed the last moments of many lives. Dark secrets. The suicides. The fires throughout the years. The hopelessness of broken souls. Tragedy is never forgotten; the ashes always remain. Tala smelled rain in the distance. Thunderclouds were beginning to gather in the sky. She trudged through the ashes.

She saw the moon's reflection off the top of the horizon which looked like a cunning smile slicing through the night sky. The closer she got to the mansion, the faster her heart raced.

Just breathe.

In and Out.

I am the weapon.

Tala waved her friends on, feigning her courage, leading the pack. She sprinted to the nearby trees as if someone could see them out here in the dark of night. The gates around the mansion were black metal columns enwrapped with vines and shrubs. Making it almost impossible to be seen from outside.

Lance looked overwhelmed with the mission before him. Valerie's chest heaved in and out as she wore a reverie smile. Mark bore no expression. Tala wasn't used to seeing him like that, so this worried her. Before they took a step farther into the thick of the woods toward the mansion, Tala felt her phone vibrate in her pocket. She saw red and blue lights coming from the front of the mansion's gates. Tala answered the phone.

"Hello?" Tala said.

Call dropped. No reception.

The police car pulled out of the swale area with its emergency lights on but no siren. The deputy drove along Deer Run, did a U-turn, and headed up Curtiss Parkway toward the Jeep.

"Holy shit," Mark said.

Lance said, "We're fucked."

The deputy put his spotlight on the driver's side of the Jeep before approaching cautiously. Jaen was still there, they imagined.

"What the hell? He went right to it," Valerie said. The Hawks huddled together behind a tree.

"Shit," Jax mumbled. "Let's go."

Valerie said, "We're screwed."

Tala started walking back.

"Wait. Maybe she can talk her way out," Makayla said. "You left her the keys, right?" She looked at Lance.

"Yeah. She's got 'em."

"Let's just wait then," Makayla said.

Mark added, "I'm not gonna let her get burned alone."

"Give it a sec," Jax said, annoyed.

They waited in the dark, crouched behind a tree, less than halfway through The Sea of Trees, feeling trapped like rats inside a maze. They waited and waited. They were too far to see exactly what was going on.

"Have a little faith. If they think people snuck in here, we're gonna be surrounded in no time," Jax said.

"He's right," Tala said. "Wait it out. Jaen's smart." The red and blue lights continued to reign in their hypnotic state. Jaen didn't have a license yet; She failed twice. Couldn't do a three-point turn if her life depended on it.

Another cop showed up with his red and blues on.

"We're majorly fucked now," Mark said.

"No lube. Not good," Lance said.

Everyone's faith dissipated.

After what seemed like hours, the police cars turned off their emergency lights and pulled away as the Jeep's headlights came on and drove off. The deputy turned on the spotlight and pointed it inside the mansion's acreage.

"Get down," Mark said. They all crouched down.

"We're too far," Tala said. "He can't see us."

Tala felt her phone vibrate in her pocket. It was Jaen.

She answered, "What happened?"

She couldn't make what Jaen was saying due to the

reception. She took a few steps forward, trying to better the signal, closer to the gate.

"Cop said they got a 911 call in the area."

"Someone must have seen us," Makayla said.

"Hello. Are you there?" Tala said.

"Hello?"

Call dropped.

Staying was too risky. Something was off.

"We're done. Let's go."

When Jaen came around again they had helped each other hop the gate. They waited in the brushwood, until the blacked-out Jeep pulled up. They could see more police cars beginning to circle the mansion. Their spotlights like rays of light, zigzagging inside the mansion, cutting through the darkness. They had to go. And they had to go *now*.

The Hawks got into the Jeep, and Jax rode shotgun. More police cars arrived to meet the deputy at the mansion. Jaen used backstreets to make it to Tala's house.

"What happened?" Tala said impatiently.

"I don't know. I told him I parked here to think for a while. Because I got into a fight with my mom. He counseled me, which was sweet, told him I left my license and everything at home. Made sure to perk up my boobs. Worked like a charm."

"Really?" Tala said. "Was it the sheriff?"

"Eww, no, it was a younger guy. Officer Hunter. Cute guy."

"That dweeb can't even catch a car burglar," Mark said.

"So now what?" Lance said.

"Take me home. Let's debrief," Tala said.

WHEN LANCE PARKED on the pebbled driveway. The Hawks went inside Tala's house with a certain energy in the air. All of them relieved of having made it out of the mansion without being caught.

"I don't know how they saw us, but something tells me the mansion is on serious lockdown. Someone doesn't want us there," Jaen said.

"That's the idea," Tala added.

Tala sat on the couch. Mark and Jax paced around her living room. In no rush to go home. The adrenaline still pumping in their veins from the night's events. It was just one odd occurrence after another. The Hawks found themselves full of questions. After some time, the adrenaline started to subside, but the sense of excitement hung in the air. Tala felt it too, but she was disappointed.

Only *we* could get busted out there this late, Jaen jested.

WE.

Tala had never really been included before.

WE.

Tala was part of The Hawks. She checked her pockets and realized she had dropped her phone.

"Anyone seen my phone?"

Makayla said, "You had it on the way back."

"You sure?"

Makayla nodded.

Her friends stayed talking as she went out to get her phone. She found her iPhone between the seats. It must have fallen when Jaen made a wild turn as if she were a race car driver. When Tala reached down for it, she saw a small blue light shimmering on the floor. Another phone had fallen. She recognized it as Mark's. For some reason, one she couldn't explain—she felt compelled to look through it and she did. There was no passcode. She went through his text messages and his calls and she almost threw up. In his outcalls folder. The call.

911 1:45 A.M. 10 seconds.

50

THE NUMBERS MOCKED HER.

911: 1:45 A.M. 10 Seconds

She double checked the time and date. It couldn't be. The call made just half an hour ago. She felt like the girl from Urbana again. Like the little girl who walked into a cemetery and found nothing but the ravens.

Why would he do this?

What was he to gain?

Out of curiosity. No. Out of utter anger, she stormed back to the house and waved Mark's phone around.

"Did you forget something?"

Her tone got everyone's attention.

Mark looked like there was a spotlight on his face and he was about to start sweating.

"Why did you do it?" she said.

It felt as if no one else was in the room.

"What do you mean?" Mark said, standing.

"Don't play with me, Mark." She held the phone to him. "Nine-one-one. Really?"

He looked stunned. "Wow, so you went through my phone. I'm outta here."

"Sit down!"

"Don't tell me what to do. DON'T—What—What right do you have to look through my phone?" He was yelling now. His face bloodshot.

"WHY DID YOU CALL THE COPS ON US?" Tala said.

The Hawks looked confused. The idea just started to take form.

"You did what?" Valerie said. "You called the cops?"

"What the fuck, man?" Jax added.

"Tell me why you did it," Tala demanded.

Mark didn't sit. "I don't gotta tell you shit. Or anyone else, for that matter." He snatched the phone from her hands and stormed through the door.

Tala followed him out. "Mark, wait! WAIT!"

He kept walking until she grabbed his arm. He turned with contempt in his eyes.

"Tell me why you did it," she pleaded.

"I did it because I wanted to get out of there," he said.

"I thought we agreed to look around. That something weird is happening here," Tala said.

"The only weird thing that's happening here is you. My father could lose his contract, Tala. I know you think you're doing this for Yin, but that damn forsaken place has nothing to do with it. The Curtiss Mansion is my dad's biggest contract. We've lost a lot of money. If I get caught trespassing, the mayor will take it away. So yeah, I did it. I called. I thought if I got a cop to go by before we jumped the gate, we would lose this stupid idea."

"What about Yin?"

"Whatever visions or dreams you're having—I'm sorry to

tell you—have nothing to do with Yin, or with Curtiss, or the mansion. It's all in your head. That place fucks with people's minds. And it's fucking with yours. You've been buying into this shit since you got here. And now you're making everyone else buy into it too. It's BULLSHIT! And I'm done."

By now, Lance, Valerie, Jaen, Jax, and Makayla stood on the porch listening, and Mark saw them as a halo behind Tala.

"It's all BULLSHIT," he repeated. "Don't you see? Yin's gone. No one knows where he is. He may never come back. And the mansion has nothing to do with it. You do see that, don't you?" he said. "The world doesn't revolve around you. Or around that goddamn house. I loved Yin, Okay? He was like my brother. And I'd do anything to help him. We're chasing ghosts. At my father's expense."

He walked across the pebbled driveway and was home before anyone said anything else.

Tala stood there with her friends behind her thinking about Yin. About her dreams. Casey. She wished this too would be a dream; a long and horrible dream, and that when she woke, Mark would still be her friend. Jax walked up behind her and put his hand on her shoulder.

"Don't worry. I'm with you on this," he said.

Tala didn't turn back. She looked at the dark sky and at the moon that still held its cunning grin.

51

TALA TOSSED and turned in bed thinking of Mark. She called him, but he didn't answer. She opened the chrome balisong as she laid in bed. *What a beautiful knife.* She wondered why she never saw beauty in such things. The cold steel and sharp edge made her feel strong. Safe. The blade made her feel in control. She could thrust it into her body now. She could die if she wanted to, but she would never cower like her mom.

She thought of Yin. He gave her the butterfly knife with a certain graveness that implied she would need it. She opened the knife with a quick fan. The blade shone off the moonlight through her window. She played with the safety latch, then opened and closed the blade with vigilance.

She swung the blade from side to side slowly, then faster and faster. The clicking and clacking, like wings that could take her to places she'd never been before. The sound the blade made as it clicked and clacked as she cut the air sounded like music. A hypnotic rhythm. She felt calm. Meditative. She closed her eyes.

She smelled something burning. She sat up in bed,

alarmed. Smoke seeped from underneath her door. She rushed out and met thicker black smoke. She coughed, covered her mouth, and fought her way through it. Her living room up in flames. She ran to David's room. He was in bed, bleeding from the abdomen.

"Dad, what happened. The house is burning."

David slowly turned over. Ignoring her.

"What are you doing? Dad—" She grabbed his shoulder and turned him.

He spoke as if he had all the time in the world.

"This is your fault, Red. Just leave it alone."

She could smell the fire seeping through the walls. David opened his mouth. A black widow's legs protruded from it and crawled out and down his chest. Tala shrieked, and when she turned around to run, she was in total darkness.

She thought she was dead. Death was like this, a dark place where your mind wandered forever in an endless Ferris wheel of despair. She yelled for help. Crying, begging. Praying to God. To anything. Her voice echoed in a black hole of nothingness.

Lights came on from a racetrack. Stadium lights. She knew these lights. She was at the Urbana Track and Field, and surer than ever she was dead. She had fallen and hit her head. The fire raced up the stairs, had suffocated her, and burned her to ashes like Glenn Curtiss burned his wife, and children.

She had died the same way.

It was poetry.

She took careful, precise steps and felt weightless, as if she were walking on nothing. No floor underneath her. She was floating, she now saw, floating to the light. The light flickered on and off like a hypnotic spiral, and at the center of that spiral was a black chair. The chair from her bedroom, where Psycho Jordan had sat and watched her sleep. She touched her chest to feel her heartbeat. She felt nothing.

She couldn't make out where she was, and she thought she was nowhere. Not heaven. Not hell. Only dead. Only in a place of non-existence. As she approached the chair, she saw someone sitting there. A girl. A small girl with her hands behind her back.

El Libro Rojo was on her lap.

The girl looked up.

It was Casey, with lifeless eyes. She was in her zombie costume. She had no pupils. Only white. The fire must have got her too. Casey brought her small hands forward and opened them, revealing a checkered puzzle piece in one hand and a monarch butterfly in the other.

"Do you see it yet?" Casey asked. "Don't you remember?"

The checkered puzzle piece started to tremble. The puzzle piece turned into a checkered butterfly and flew out of her hand simultaneously with the monarch. The nothingness of the floor opened beneath her and swallowed her into an infinite fall. She cried out. She didn't want to die. She was Alice, falling down a rabbit hole.

Tala woke up sweating and panting.

She gasped for air, holding her chest. Her heart beat rapidly.

She looked around the room.

You were sleeping.

It was morning. She flinched as the wooden bureau started vibrating, as if a monster hid inside its drawers. She came to her senses, *it's just your phone.*

Just breathe.

Jax texted her: CALL ME NOW. SHE'S GONE.

The feeling of falling was still deep in the pit of her stomach. Tala called him back. Voicemail. No answer.

Her phone rang, and she picked it up on its first ring.

"Jax," she said.

She heard a girl crying into the phone.

"Someone took Jax's niece."

"What? Who's this?"

"It's Val! Tala! Did you hear me? Someone took Jax's niece. Casey is gone. Jax is losing it."

"What happened?"

"I don't know."

"Jax won't talk to anyone. Just you."

"Why me?"

"Beats me. He told me to call you. I'll swing by and get you."

"What time is it?" Tala asked.

Valerie said, "Does it matter?"

52

TALA WENT to her window and saw the Porsche parked in the driveway. He was home, which was odd. He was never home. Tala went to his room and saw him sleeping in bed. No smoke, no fire. No spider would crawl out his mouth.

Maybe going out would be a bad thing. Maybe leaving him alone was a mistake. Her dream, a bad omen. She didn't know what to do. But she had to do something. She kissed him on the forehead. Pulled up his sheets to cover him better. A million thoughts ran through her mind.

Casey is missing? What happened to Yin? The Curtiss Mansion? What did her dreams mean?

Tala heard a loud honk. Valerie waited outside in her red Mustang. Tala was leaving when she heard him say, "Hey. Where you off to?" David rubbed his eyes, waking up.

"Out with Val."

"Where to? Gosh, it's early." He stretched and yawned.

"Long night?" Tala asked, wanting to change the subject.

"Where's Olivia?"

"Should be home," he said.

Valerie blasted the horn again.

"Sorry, she's waiting. We'll catch up later." She turned to leave.

"Red," he said. "We used to have fun, right?

He straightened himself against the headboard. "How come we don't talk anymore?"

"There's a lot going on, Dad. You wouldn't understand."

"Make me understand," he said firmly.

"Casey is gone."

"Casey?" he said.

Tala said, "The little girl handing out lanterns at Yin's house. She's Jax's niece."

"The girl with autism."

"Yes, Dad. The girl with autism." Tala hated when he referred to people with status names like that. Yes, she had autism, but that wasn't who she was.

"I didn't mean it like that."

"Wait, is it make-out-with-my-daughter-on-my-couch-Jax? Hialeah-prairie-boy-Jax? That Jax?"

She reluctantly nodded.

"I told you to stop seeing that punk. We talked about this."

"He's not a punk, David." Tala snapped. "You don't even know him. You can't tell me who to be friends with. That's why we don't talk anymore."

"I can and I will. I'm your father. You live under my roof. You'll do as you're told." David got abruptly out of bed.

He pointed at her. "You're not going anywhere. You're grounded."

"For what? Are you even listening to me? Casey is missing. She's special. She knows things. But she's autistic, and she's only nine. He needs my help," she reasoned.

"What can you do about it? Have they called the police? That's what the police are supposed to do. Not you. Let them do their jobs. You think you're going to find her? They have the resources."

"Just like they found Yin?"

Her dad stayed silent.

Another honk came from the Mustang. Valerie held it unnecessarily long.

"Go to your room. I'm serious."

"Am I twelve?"

"I told you. I was emphatically clear. No prairie boys."

"He needs my help."

"I don't care," David yelled. His anger grew. Tala couldn't believe it; he had a soft spot for kids.

His voice was grave. "TALA STONE. Go to your room NOW!"

"I'm sorry, Dad. I love you. But I won't. His name is Jax. And her name is Casey. And they're my friends. My room isn't here. It never was."

Tala ran downstairs, and David heard the front door slam.

GET BACK HERE, he thought. He almost yelled it. But there was no use. She was in the car already. There were burn marks on the road.

53

VALERIE HEADED DOWN FAIRWAY AVENUE, zig-zagging past cars on Circle Drive, racing out of Miami Springs. Tala held on for dear life as she fired rapid shot questions about Casey.

"I don't know what happened. I just found out," Valerie said, with her eyes on the road as she switched in and out of lanes rather unsafely. Tala braced herself and made sure her seatbelt was locked.

She saw dark clouds forming in the east. Nothing but dark clouds and stormy nights since she got here. All the normality she had hoped for seemed non-existent, like she had been transported to an upside-down world of chaos and confusion.

It wasn't summer every day.

Why was this happening? She couldn't fathom why anyone would hurt Yin or take Casey? Did she run away? Things were bad at home? Who knew what the truth was anymore? Tala held on to the recurring thought that someone wanted to keep her away from the mansion. This was no coincidence. All her friends were being targeted.

"Do the Hawks know?" Tala said.

"I sent a group text. Not sure who's read it."

Valerie stopped abruptly at a red light. "Is there something you're not telling me?"

"About?"

"I don't know, anything?"

"You know what I know. Something's going on in this town. We're being targeted," Tala said.

"You and Yin had a secret. You visited Charlie Owens at Citrus. For whatever reason, I don't care. But it was a secret," she said. "Don't you think it's odd that Yin is missing. He could be dead. Now Casey is missing? She's cute, but she gives me the creeps."

"Go," Tala said. The light had turned green.

"At least promise me you'll tell me what Jax tells you."

"I will. Where are we going?"

"Dog Town."

"Isn't that the bad part of Hialeah?"

"It's not bad," Valerie said. "It's the worse."

Valerie drove to Dogtown and parked at the Eastgate Apartments. Tala was thrown aback by the poverty. The chipped paint, cracked walls. The buckets lined throughout the halls to catch the rain leaking from the ceiling. There were beheaded chickens in the corner of the parking lot on a white blanket with black and red beads and coconuts. No doubt some omen of Santeria. A closer look revealed a picture of Casey. The place looked forgotten. There were few cars in the parking lot, but it was mid-day. Tala figured the residents were still at work.

"You sure he lives here?"

Valerie parked, checked her phone.

"Yeah, Eastgate Apartments, #472. It looks a little suspect," she said.

Tala felt unease wash over her. She tried not to show it.

Act normal.

Just breathe.

She pictured herself walking up the uneven stairs of this old building, reaching for door #472, only to be thrown in and captured. Valerie got out of the Mustang.

She poked her head back in. "You coming?"

"Yeah." Tala opened the passenger door and continued to analyze the building. Chipped paint, rotting walls, and only a handful of cars in the parking spaces. Tala walked up the stairs. Even though it was four stories because the elevator was out of order, not that she would've taken it anyway. She followed Valerie up the stairs.

Something felt wrong. Wouldn't there be more cars if Casey were missing? She felt more nervous with every step. She felt a wad of cotton in her throat. She thought of running downstairs until she found out what was really going on. *You're being paranoid.*

Just Breathe.

Valerie knocked on the door.

No one answered.

She banged harder, using the back of her fist.

"No one's here," Tala said.

"He texted me. He told me he was here."

They heard the deadbolt unlock.

Jax opened the door. He wore a white tank top that revealed his muscular frame, tribal tattoos on his shoulder blades that ran down to the three wise monkeys on his forearm. Tala knew he had a sleeve tattoo but had never focused on the details. It was like she was seeing his ink for the first time.

"Hey," he said with a low voice. "Come in."

Tala took a step back and let Valerie walk in first. They

both looked around. Tala saw Jax and Casey in pictures on the coffee table, kitchen counter. Disney World. The zoo. The Sea Aquarium. There were pictures with two people Tala imagined were Casey's parents. The inside of the dwelling was much nicer than the outside.

"Where is everyone?" Valerie said.

"Everyone's at Casey's house. My grandma is over there with the fam. Everyone's losing it."

"Why are you here?"

"I needed to get away. I told everyone I was going to shower and change and head right back. That was hours ago."

Jax tossed an empty pizza box onto the coffee table and sat down with excruciating effort like he had endured a beating. Tala could tell his mind wasn't here but everywhere. He seemed to search his memory. Jax cupped his hands over his face and fought back tears.

"Where the hell is she?"

Tala didn't know. Casey was truly gone. The idea began to sink in like the idea we are as impermanent as footprints on a beach shore. We all wash away with the rising tide. The tide always comes.

She thought maybe it would have been better if she would have opened the door to be kidnapped and killed than to see Jax in this much pain. She felt responsible. She had started a witch-hunt with her theories and obsessions. One bad thing happened after another.

"This is my fault," Tala said. "I'm sorry."

"Don't say that." Valerie put her hand behind her neck and pulled in to hug her as she sat next to her on the sofa.

"It's not your fault. It's mine," Jax said.

"I should have watched her. I should have listened."

"What do you mean?" Valerie said.

"She said it. She said things were gonna get worse. She said bad things were going to happen. I just didn't think they would happen to her."

Jax cupped his hands again. He pressed his face hard until his fingertips turned white. He brought his hands back down to his jeans, rubbed them anxiously. The anger evident in his tense arms. Tala noted tears wouldn't dare run down his face.

"If anyone hurts her, I swear I'll kill them." he said.

Jax's face seemed more focused now, sharp even.

"I have something to show you."

He stood, beckoned her down the tight hallway into a bedroom. He hit the lights. The room looked like a doll house. Displaced from the rest of the apartment, the walls had crisp pink paint, new doors, white shelves. There was a television and a box of toys, mainly battery-operated fire trucks with red and white emergency lights.

Out the bedroom window she could see other apartments and a tennis court with no net flooded with rain. Dark clouds crying as Miami Springs had cried, now it was Hialeah's turn to weep. Murder? Kidnapping? Now Jax, Valerie, Jaen, Lance, and Mark were starting to believe in the girl from Urbana.

"This is her room," Jax said. "When she sleeps over, anyway. I painted it for her because pink and white are her favorite colors."

Tala saw a mask propped against Casey's pillow. It sent a shock through her body so great her legs caved.

She couldn't breathe. She was on the 757 again. Her knees buckled, and she held herself up by leaning against the door to keep her footing. Suddenly, her theories, her ideas once fixated in her mind as an incomprehensible glob came to form.

It was the mask Charlie Owens gave her.

The mask.

How did it get here?

Who put it here?

The connection between Yona, Charlie, Yin, Casey, the mansion, the active shootings around the country, all seemed interwoven like the web of a black widow. Tala had no answers. She hyperventilated. Feeling caught in that tangled web, unable to break free.

"Breathe," Jax said. "Just breathe."

"What is it, Tala?"

"That's it, isn't it?" He said.

Tala pointed at the mask. She couldn't talk. She felt a sharp pain in her sternum like she'd been stabbed and the airflow was uneven like a straw with a hole in it. Her chest heaved up and down. Up and down. Her thoughts raced. The rain outside came down hard, pattering against the windows. Lightning strikes with harsh thunder. A storm brewing. Tala thought about Charlie. Yin. Casey. The reappearing mask. Glenn Curtiss. Her house burning. The mass shootings. Her dad giving her a cigarette. Her mother falling like a ghost. The sound of a gunshot. Her mom had worn a monarch mask the night she died. Two plus two equals five.

How well do you really know your neighbors?

Jax carried her into the living room through the narrow hall. He laid her on the couch. He moved strands of red hair from her face.

"What the hell did you do to her?" Valerie said.

"Nothing. She fainted."

Tala felt outside of her body like she was astral traveling. Unable to control her arms or legs. She hadn't had an attack like this in years, since . . . .

"Tala," he said. "Tala." Moving her shoulders lightly. "You okay? Wake up!"

Her arms and legs felt bound together. She was wrapped in the widow's web.

"Just *breathe*."

She imagined Dr. Moss's office, the drum of the AC Unit on the wall, his soothing voice telling her to picture the white sand beach with lions. "You can be anywhere. Anywhere you want," he had said. "The mind doesn't know the difference between reality and imagination."

"What is it?" Jax shook her. "Snap out of it."

She started to move, but her vocal cords were snapped.

Tala heaved in and out with a dumbfounded look.

Jax and Valerie analyzed her.

"We're in danger, aren't we?" Jax said.

Tala nodded.

"That's the mask Yin had isn't it? The *exact* mask." He said. "The one Charlie gave you?"

Tala nodded again.

Valerie went into Casey's room and came back.

"Who left it there?"

"Whoever took Casey left it there." Jax said. "Whoever took Yin left it there."

After some time, Tala got her bearings, she went into Casey's room again. Jax followed her in.

The mask laid against the pillow.

Tala seemed lost in her thoughts.

Jax and Valerie looked at each other. They were afraid.

"You sure you alright, Tala?" Valerie asked.

Tala picked up the mask.

"Two plus two equals five," she said, reading the inscription.

"What does it mean?" Jax ran his fingers through his hair. "I need to find her," he said.

"I need to find her too. But I need to find the person who hurt Yin. And this mask is the link between both."

She put the mask over her face.

She looked like a horror movie killer. She turned to face them.

"What does the mask mean?" Jax pressed.

"It means, they're watching us. And they've been watching us."

54

THE HIALEAH POLICE found no sign of forced entry at Jax's apartment. Casey lived a block away from Palm Springs Elementary School and would walk home every day after school. Police found her diary inside her book bag on top of her kitchen table where she usually did her homework. The detectives found UNCLE STRINGS and 2 + 2 = 5 written hundreds of times in Casey's handwriting in her diary.

Jax told police he didn't know what it meant. It was probably a homework assignment. Police interrogated Jax like a criminal. It didn't help he had priors for grand theft auto and resisting an officer without violence.

Tala was sure there was a link between Casey's disappearance, Charlie, Yin, and herself, and that link was the mask. Call it intuition. Call it common sense.

JAX STOOD, paced around the kitchen.

"We have to see Charlie," she said.

They waited.

"He gave me the mask. I think he was trying to tell me something. I think he was trying to warn me. He knows more."

Valerie said, "What makes you think he'll help? I thought he didn't make any sense."

"We have no other option."

"Lead the way then, Red," Jax said.

"There's only one problem," Tala said. "He's crazy."

55

SATURDAY MORNING.

The streets were desolate, which made her think of Urbana, that faraway, ordinary place where life was tolerable and simple. The drive back to Citrus Hospital put Yin at the forefront of her mind with a dreamy feeling of Deja vu.

She was going to the same places over and over. Always feeling watched. Yin and Tala had ventured here weeks ago on a gut feeling to talk to Charlie Owens, and days later, Yin had disappeared, his home painted in blood. His block roped off with crime scene tape. Why?

A faded orange building loomed before her. Here she was again.

They pulled into Citrus in a red Mustang. Valerie parked on the swale by the entrance.

Tala said, "This lane is for emergency vehicles."

"This is an emergency and this is a vehicle. See how that works?"

Tala rolled her eyes.

As they got off the car, Tala's stomach rumbled. She

couldn't remember the last time she ate. The automatic sliding glass doors opened, and the three of them walked into Citrus. Tala feared her inquiry might get Jax or Valerie hurt, but she didn't see another way. It was a risk they had all agreed to take. They approached the front desk, waiting for an elderly man with a cane to finish talking to the receptionist.

The woman behind the counter was obese with a look that said she would rather be anywhere but here. Anywhere. Tala wondered if this was the same woman who had haunted Yin's dreams. When the lady finished with the man, she looked at the teenagers like a band of misfits.

"We're here to see Charlie Owens. We know his mom."

The woman's face became grave.

Tala read her name tag: Villalobos

"I'm sorry. I'm afraid he's no longer with us," she said.

"He transferred?" Jax asked.

"No, he's dead," the woman said. Cold as ice. "He overdosed on his medication. I'm afraid he had been storing them. Mr. Owens took a month's worth of meds in a single sitting, dropping his blood pressure to unsafe levels. His body couldn't handle it. When Nurse Marjorie came to check on him this morning, it was too late. His heart had stopped. He'd been dead for hours."

Tala felt so lost. So alone. Jax grabbed her by the shoulder and pulled her into his chest. She found her face buried in his arms, feeling cheated and hurt. Another dead person. Another dead person. No answers. *What's the connection? Am I truly cursed? Do I hurt everyone I touch?*

Tala sprinted down the hall to his room. The fat nurse yelled that she wasn't allowed to go that way. Jax and Valerie followed. The fat nurse ran after them in a half-hearted attempt.

"Call security," she said to a desk clerk.

Tala sprinted up the stairs and found his room. She looked inside the plexiglass window. There was nothing inside. She turned the knob, but the door was locked. She pounded on the door, now screaming hysterically for someone to open the door. Jax stood in front of her to protect her as the fat nurse wobbled up the hall with her face flushed, panting for air.

"This is a restricted area!" she scorned them. "I told you he's gone. I'm sorry."

"Open the door," Tala said.

"He's dead."

"Open the door now!" She banged on the door. Some of the neighboring patients began to yell. The fat nurse obliged. She reluctantly reached into her pocket and swiped the keycard to open the door. Tala jolted in. She smelled chemicals and death.

Jax stood in the room, and Valerie trickled in behind him. They didn't see anything of evidentiary value, it was a padded room.

"What happened to all his stuff? His art?"

"The patients aren't allowed to have art. Dear," she said. "Are you okay?"

Tala looked at Jax and Valerie.

She saw doubt on their faces.

"This is a *hospital*. Not painting with a twist," the nurse went on.

A new security guard who couldn't be more than seventeen walked into the room and looked at Nurse Villalobos for further instruction.

"I need them to leave!"

"Where's his art?" Tala said, more to herself.

"Are you on your meds, honey?" the nurse said.

"I don't take them anymore," she blurted.

"I see." The nurse looked at them with a face that said *Maybe it's time you start again.*

Jax and Valerie didn't know what to say.

Tala felt so confused. Of course she took medication. They were prescribed after Yona—But that was for depression, not hallucinations. Just for the never-ending ebb of sadness.

She asked for Nurse Marjorie, but Villalobos said after Marjorie found Charlie dead, she put in her resignation letter. Tala looked at the corner of the room and saw the bubble surveillance camera.

She yelled at the camera, "You killed him. I know you're watching. I KNOW YOU'RE WATCHING!"

"Tala, Lets go," Jax said.

Tala walked down the hall and back to the counter. She didn't know what to think. As she walked out, she stared at the dome mirror in the corner of the hallway and thought she saw the nurse smile.

56

JAMAL STEPHENS RETURNED HOME.

Makayla was happy he was back, but he seemed different somehow. He was staying in his room for hours and wasn't really talking. Makayla tried to bring up Marjorie, but he said she was dead to him. His father, Darnell barely noticed he was gone. His mother Keisha didn't make inquiries to his whereabouts. She was busy tending to business and keeping up appearances.

Three young men received a letter in the mail with no return address. Jamal was one of them. When Jamal opened the letter, he found a sheet of black construction paper.

No words.

None were needed.

When Jamal went into the bathroom and saw his reflection in the mirror, he saw the God of Death.

"I am Thanatos," he said.

It was time to paint the world black.

He went to The Circle and taped the black construction paper to a Glenn Curtiss mural. Everything was in motion now. Rodnam Jackson eventually saw the mark and met Jamal to purchase two AR 15 assault rifles and ammunition from a local gun shop. Everything needed to be documented. So they picked a place with surveillance video. They practically smiled at the camera and provided proper I.D.

In Hocus, Texas, a young man received the same letter. As did one in Alabama.

It was time to paint the world black.

Jamal and Rodnam bought two rifles with slings, lasers and extended magazines. Enough ammunition to paint a dark masterpiece. They rented a Hertz vehicle and drove up to an amusement park in Orlando. No tickets needed. No one would stop them. Everything happened so fast. Thanatos and Hypnos cut through security like a straight razor.

The rifles came out of their slings. First came the harrowing sound of rapid-fire shots. Parents shielded their kids. Park employees ducked for cover. The disturbing screams. Children fell. It was pandemonium. The sound of two assault rifles firing armor piercing rounds into the atmosphere as hot brass ejected from the heavy nomenclatures of death.

The amusement park turned black.

And red.

There were baby strollers with bullet holes.

Another shooter in Hocus, Texas and his cohort in Frail, Alabama had purchased their own rifles too.

In a span of minutes, there was three coordinated active shootings inside of the United States.

One shooter in Frail, Alabama.

One shooter in Hocus, Texas.

Two shooters in Orlando, Florida.

They painted the world black.

The shooters in Alabama and Texas were programmed to self-destruct.

Before they ate their guns, they killed thirty plus innocent people in their respective states.

Many were killed, but armed security and contracted police officers responded quickly to the amusement park and exchanged gunfire with the gunmen in Orlando. Killing them both. Unfortunately, their weaponry was advanced, and they were mindless drones designed to kill. The twins took fifty-six with them to the River Styx. The social media world went crazy with hashtags about the coordinated attack. The FBI began investigating. There had to be a connection between the shooters. The only problem was all the shooters were dead.

Sosa and Hogg's investment stocks in gun companies skyrocketed over the coming weeks as the politicians in Washington debated gun control legislation. Gun sales went up with the death count, so did their bank accounts.

57

CNN AND FOX NEWS affiliates had boots on the ground within minutes. The rest of the news networks trickled in within the hour. The social media networks went into a frenzy with posts, videos, and tweets from the tragic active shooting in Florida, Texas, and Alabama.

There was shaky cell phone video showing victims running with the sound of gunshots in the background. The story trended number one with hashtags #FloridaStrong, #AlabamaStrong, #TexasStrong and #NeverAgain.

The reporters stated the 'apparent' coordinated attack was unprecedented and investigators were trying to find the link between the shooters. The shooting in Orlando was an anomaly. The first active shooting orchestrated by two African American men. There were conflicting details emerging from friends and relatives of Jamal Stephens who affirmed Jamal and Rodnam Jackson weren't friends nor cohorts. They had never met.

Rodnam Jackson, nicknamed 'Psycho Jordan' because of his height and lanky frame, had his basketball scholarships revoked when he became the target of a sexual abuse allegation involving a juvenile. He was never arrested nor formally charged, but that shadow had followed and haunted him, ultimately ending his career.

People knew Rodnam frequented Hialeah and Springs for years. But Jamal didn't know him.

Makayla spoke to Local 10 and said her brother wouldn't have hurt anyone. Yes, it was true he had a breakup. Yes, it was true he had unexpectedly quit his job. But he couldn't have done this.

Nothing made sense.

They never did when tragedies happened.

There was a whirlwind of questions no one could answer. Rodnam Jackson was a known petty criminal with known mental issues. He was often Baker Acted by law enforcement for forced mental health evaluations.

FOX News and CNN reported he was known to amble between Hialeah and the Springs and was a petty criminal in and out of jail. He had no violent offenses. Jamal Stephens, on the other hand, was a young smart black man from the wealthy Stephens family in Miami Springs.

Jamal was working full-time at Citrus Hospital until he abruptly quit one day. His ex-girlfriend, Marjorie Vargas, said he'd been acting bizarre. She said he had dumped her for no reason. She suspected he was talking to someone else. The news speculated he may have met Rodnam Jackson at Citrus, but that couldn't be confirmed.

Darnell Stephens III and his wife, Keisha Stephens, couldn't believe what FBI agents told them Jamal had done. Why? Keisha had told them. Why? He wanted to be a cop. He was one of the good ones. Since he was a boy, that was all he'd wanted. A badge and a gun. Why?

The FBI said they were trying to put the pieces together. Not everything fit. There was surveillance video of Jamal and Rodnam together at a local gun shop purchasing the assault rifles. The gun owner remembered them. Although one of them was freakishly tall. They seemed normal, the man had said.

He didn't think anything of it. Jamal and Rodnam passed the background check with flying colors.

58

Tala turned the shower handle until the hot water scorched her body. The drum of the water hitting the porcelain created white noise which usually helped her think. But her thoughts were as fogged as the rising steam.

Why had Glenn Curtiss burned his wife and children in that horrible mansion?

She could still feel Psycho Jordan's long fingers and nails pressed into the side of her neck.

Yes, he *had* grabbed her that night. But he didn't hurt her.

He had *warned* her.

Why had Psycho Jordan snuck into her bedroom and watched her sleep?

She remembered some of his crazy ramblings.

The wolves are always watching because their house has eyes.

You can't run from them.

When you stare into the mansion, the mansion stares into you.

She scrubbed soap on her body and analyzed the imperfections on the yellow brick road.

Psycho Jordan's mugshots were on every major news network.

He and Makayla's brother had committed a heinous act.
Why?
No one could ask them.
They were both dead.
Why?
Charlie Owens had said: *Don't you remember?*
Why?
She couldn't ask him.
Charlie Owens was dead.
Why?
The mask.
Two plus two equals five.
Yin's crime scene drenched in blood.
He was gone.
Why?
Casey disappeared.
Why?
And, of course, the greatest question of all.
Why had her mother killed herself?
So many questions.
So many puzzle pieces.

It was hard to say the words even in her mind, but yes, why had her mother *killed herself?* Was she mentally ill? Heavily depressed? Possessed by demons? Did Mom belong in a place like Citrus? Or did she shoot herself and fall from that tall building because of voices inside her head?

Where did she get the gun?
Why would she—
Why why why why why.

No answers came. It seemed life was riddled with whys. She never went to church, but she prayed before bed every night. No. Not reciting Bible verses or hymns, just her words. Just her heart. She had prayed to God because she did believe God existed, that he listened, but Yona's suicide annihilated the notion God was benevolent.

But when she put the covers over her face at night, she still prayed. Grateful for her dad. Grateful for life.

David wasn't perfect but being a dad didn't come with an instruction manual.

The steam blurred the bathroom mirror.

She heard a knock on the door.

"Give me a minute, Dad." She leaned her forehead against the shower wall. Water beads ran off her back. Another knock came with more urgency. She pulled the curtain back through the heavy steam.

She saw the doorknob turn. "Wait! I'm naked."

The door screeched and opened a few inches. A hideous screech, and it wasn't the screech that scared her, it was the silence that followed.

"Dad . . ." she called out. She covered herself with the shower curtain.

A coldness seeped through the open door as steam escaped into the hall.

Fear.

"Dad . . ." She said. "You there?"

No, he wasn't there.

Silence.

He would've said *something* by now.

"You're scaring me . . ."

Silence.

The bathroom steam began to clear.

She turned the water off, reached for a towel. She

wrapped it around her body, looking at the door. The eerie feeling grew and compounded into a shot of adrenaline. Who was there? Her instincts told her to *run* down the stairs, but her iPhone was in the bedroom. The chrome knife Yin gave her was in her room.

Never leave it out of your sight.

If she made a break for it across the hall, she would be cornered upstairs.

Never leave it out of your sight.

Yin's mom had told her. *Never.*

She took a step toward the bathroom door, shivering from the fear.

Silence.

She sprinted to her bedroom, pushed open the door, grabbed the butterfly knife, and turned around, slashing the air. When she saw no one had followed, she ran downstairs on her tiptoes as fast as she could, opened the front door, and ran into the darkness.

He's in the house, she thought. Whoever he is. *He* is in the house. She was on the sidewalk in her towel, soaking wet. She clutched her knife in her hand. Two men approached on the sidewalk. They appeared like shadows, unable to make out their faces. She walked up the sidewalk, in a bath towel, barefoot, with a knife in hand.

"Hey!" a voice said. "Come here."

She was already running, holding on to her towel with one hand and the knife in the other. She ran up Fairway Avenue screaming for help. She glanced back in full sprint and saw two men chasing her. She turned the corner at the stop sign.

"Help!" she wailed.

She glanced back again and saw one man gaining ground on her. Dogs began to bark and run up against their fences. Tala saw lights come on from houses, but no one came outside. She ran as fast as she could, barefoot, in a towel, but then she tripped and fell. The man landed on her. His weight immobilized her. She fell on her side and rolled over. "Help me! Let me go," she yelled. Swinging her arms, punching the man on top of her. "Get off me. Help!" she cried. "Get the hell off me!"

"It's me," the man said. "Hey! Red! It's me!"

Her focus came back. David was leaning over her in a dark sweat suit. He was holding her wrists to stop her punching.

He shook her. "Red, it's me. What happened?"

Benny came into her peripheral. His arms out to his sides, breathing hard. "Is everything okay?" he said. "David. Is she alright?"

She was gasping hard. Her knee ached from the fall. David lifted her, careful to keep her covered.

"Red, you're bleeding," David said. "Did someone hurt you?"

Tala's white bath towel was drenched in crimson blood.

"Dave," Ben said. "I think that's yours." He knelt, "Let me take a look." The bone handled knife was on the grass, painted in red. Which looked more like purple now with the fluorescent streetlamps.

"We better get you to a hospital. It's deep."

Ben removed a red bandana from his back pocket and applied pressure to his wound.

"I stabbed you," Tala cried. "Dad, I'm so sorry."

David didn't feel anything until he lifted his sweatshirt and saw the puncture in his stomach. Dark warm blood oozed from his body. He felt queasy, and Ben kept the pressure on.

"I'm okay," he said. He looked back to Tala. "Are you

okay?" What happened?" He hadn't processed that he was stabbed and bleeding out.

"I don't know," she said.

Ben helped David up. "Let's go, Dave. That doesn't look good."

Tala ran to the house to put on clothes. By the time Ben helped David to his car, she locked her front door. Ben drove them to the Hialeah Hospital E.R., the waiting room was damn near empty. Her mind replayed the bathroom doorknob turning while she showered. *The knob turned. I saw it.* She told herself. *That horrible screech.* Someone turned it and pushed the door open. *What the hell was happening? Was her mind playing tricks? Had the curse of Glenn Curtiss taken hold of her?*

She had almost killed her dad, who went out for a jog. Ben sat next to her for hours reading a *Sports Illustrated* with a busty brunette bikini girl on the cover. He hadn't left her side save for buying a Snickers bar from the vending machine. Ben put a hand on her knee to still her shaking leg. "He's going to be fine," he said. "Two inches to the right and we wudda had a problem. But he'll be fine. He'll just need stitches is all."

"How do you know?"

"Old men know things," he lifted his chin proudly. "Marines know a thing or two about wounds." Some memory seemed to take surface in his mind, he changed the subject.

"I have to ask you, what in the blue hell were you doing half naked with a knife out there?"

"I thought someone was in the house."

"Why?"

She wanted to tell him. I saw the knob *turn*. She decided not to.

"I don't know, just had a bad feeling."

Ben didn't push it.

"You probably spooked yourself. It's a big house for two."

"Yeah, probably," Tala reasoned. She couldn't shake it. She knew what she saw. Someone was there.

"Is Mark home?"

Ben said, "Yeah, he texted me. He just got in."

"I know everyone's on edge about Yin and that little girl. Town's a mess. But they may be out there. I know it's scary." He couldn't seem to find the right words.

"The sun will rise again. Remember that." Ben rubbed the top of her red hair.

Hours later, David came out of the wooden double doors holding his sweatshirt. He had another white T-shirt on. His smile made Tala want to cry. She feared something would go wrong, and she would never see him again. She hugged him now as hard as she could.

David grimaced.

"Easy now, don't break him," Ben said.

"I'm so sorry," she said.

"I'm fine, Red. It was an accident."

"I was just scared."

"I know. I know you were." He looked at Ben. "We'll talk about it when we get home."

Ben gave him a hard slap on the back. "Good as new,

huh?" David's shoulder came forward from the blow. "Ouch."

"Oh, take off the skirt. How ya feeling?"

"I feel fine. Doc says I'll need some rest."

David and Tala locked eyes.

Ben picked up on it.

"I'll give you guys a minute. Be in the car. No rush." Ben exited the emergency room.

David sat at one of the waiting room chairs. Tala saw him try to ignore the homeless man with salt and pepper beard who kept eyeing them with a look of contempt.

"What were you doing outside in a towel?"

"I was taking a shower and heard a noise. Someone opened the bathroom door. I thought you were home, but you weren't. So I got scared. And then I saw—"

David interrupted, "You saw me and Benny and you made a run for it with a knife? Where'd you get that knife?" He looked perplexed.

"Yin gave it to me."

"Why?"

"I asked him for it. Protection."

"Protection? Did he want you to kill your father with it?" David chuckled. "It's a good thing he didn't give you a gun."

Tala didn't laugh but felt relieved. At least he was making jokes.

"You don't need a knife. Newsflash—I'll always protect you. I'm a badass," he lifted his shirt. "I have the scars to prove it."

Tala's smile didn't last long. "You're never home."

"I have to work, Red." What kind of man stays home with no purpose? She knew he was thinking about his father; he had mentioned it many times. The story of the gambler and hustler who never provided for his family.

"You know, the AC could have pushed open the bathroom door, Red, if you didn't shut it right. I've walked by when you're showering, and you don't always close it."

Tala second guessed herself, she knew he read doubt on her face.

"I closed it," she said, standing her ground. "I saw the knob turn. I know what I saw."

"Listen, I'm just glad you're okay. But you've been acting odd since we got down here. I wanted Miami Springs, and by God, I got it. I wanted it to be a good thing for you. For us." The undertone of sadness made her feel horrible.

"It's been hard on you, I'm sorry but life can be a confetti of shit or a rainbow parade. It's up to you. It's what you make it."

"I know, Dad, I'm just scared. Yin and now Casey. I feel like I'm not safe. Like none of us are safe. I've heard the stories of the mansion. People are talking. And on the news, it's a maniac with a gun mowing down people. It was Makayla's brother. It's like everything's connected to this town. Everyone's at war."

"That damn house. Curtiss Mansion stories have spiraled since I was a kid. It's nonsense, Red. You're a smart girl. We have a military vet next door, a hero. Anything you need, Benny's there. When I'm working, I always call him. He knows when you're home alone. He's always watching."

"Dad he's kind of fat," she said.

David said, "Maybe so, but Marines don't fear anything. You've got to be smart. There are bad men everywhere. Women too. All they need is opportunity."

"So much for the good neighborhood," she quipped.

"You have to live your life. You can't live paranoid. You just have to be smart. Don't put yourself in a bad position. That's all I'm saying. What happened to Yin and Casey and this mess with Jamal Stephens. It's terrible—a God damn nightmare—but the sheriff is all over it," he said, trying to make Tala feel better. He didn't know anything about the investigation.

"I love you, Dad."

David leaned in and kissed her on the forehead.

"Love you too, Red."

Tala looked into her father's eyes, "What if the sheriff is a bad guy?"

"Why would you think that?"

Tala looked down at her shoes.

"I don't know. This whole town feels weird. I can't explain it. I think I'm losing my mind sometimes."

"Let's go home," he said.

DAVID'S PHONE CHIMED. He fished it from his pocket, read the local breaking news alert.

His face turned pale.

"Dad, what is it?" Tala asked.

"It's the news," he said. "Jesus, they found human remains."

"Where?"

"At the Hialeah Racetrack."

He thought of Yin or that poor little girl. He knew this wasn't good. He saw a look in Tala's eyes he hadn't seen since she was under heavy medication. Far and distant. All he could think was, he should have never brought her here.

60

ONCE THEY WERE in Benny's truck, David gave him a rundown of his conversation with Tala. "I was just telling her what happened to Yin and Casey are random acts that can happen anywhere. I told her if she sees anything suspicious, call the sheriff."

"Better yet, call me." Ben winked at her. "I'm closer."

Ben came to a red light.

"They found human remains at the Hialeah Racetrack." David said.

"Geez," Ben said. "You don't think it's Yin or that little girl, do ya?"

David said, "The remains were burned beyond recognition. It could be anyone."

"Who else could it be?" Tala said.

Ben took a deep breath and exhaled.

"By god, this *was* a good neighborhood," he said. "Towns up in flames. Me and Mark always got a gun handy. I reckon Yin's been over the house since he was twelve. It's a damn shame. All that Hialeah shit is coming over the canal like a tsunami. And the country, that's another story. Active shooters galore. This thing with the Stephens family's boy and that mental patient. Unbelievable. These pimple faced losers have military grade weapons. They think life's a video game; there's no respect for humanity anymore. No empathy."

"Did you know Jamal?" David asked.

Benny shook his head.

"Small town, I've seen him around. Talked to him a few times, seemed nice enough. His father though, Darnell, that's a real prick. Richest man in Springs, he'll make sure you know it. But his kid, don't see why he would do something like that. Or why he would make friends with that basket case."

David said, "Red, there's nothing wrong with asking for help. If anything happens to you . . . ." David trailed off and looked outside the window at a small Quick Mart like its sign was the most interesting thing he'd ever seen.

When he said that, Tala thought of Charlie Owens. If anything happened to her, would her father be lost like him? Is that what happened to Charlie and Jamal? Did they lose someone they loved? Ben pulled into David's circular driveway, on the pebbled rocks.

Ben put the truck in park and shook David's hand, "Anything you need, bud, I'm right next door," he said. "That goes for you too, Redhead," Ben smiled, revealing his jack-o-lantern teeth.

Tala gave him a half smile. David and Tala walked back to the house in silence. In slow strides. Tala knew David was thinking of Yin. Probably Ben was too. A young Asian boy from the city had disappeared and now his body may have been found confirming her worse fears. A kid from her own school who had befriended her. No, the neighborhood wasn't what it used to be, Tala thought. That could have been anyone.

It could have been her.

DAVID POPPED his head into Tala's room that night. "Can I come in?"

"Well, you're sorta already in."

She was under the covers listening to Axel Rudi Pell on her iPhone. David sat next to her. Tala wasn't sure what he wanted.

"I'm not great with words. I love you so much, Red. And I know we fight, and we disagree. We've been through a lot, and you're going through a tough time now with your friends, everyone is. Whatever happens to you happens to me. I want you to know that I know I haven't been the best father. Even here, I've barely seen you. But if anyone ever tries to hurt you." He paused. He didn't say the words, but his eyes said *I'll kill them.*

Kill?

She had never seen him throw a punch. It wasn't his style. He was smart, clever, nerdy; he'd beat you with his wit. A killer? No, he wasn't capable. But that night, underneath her sheets, in her toy house, as she drifted off to sleep, she asked herself: *How well do you really know your neighbors?*

How well do you really know anyone?

61

THE DAYS at school were a blur. Sitting down in Algebra II, trying to focus on numbers and formulas proved impossible, because all Tala could think about was, the awful things that had happened.

She knew she was the X factor in that unsolvable equation. She sat at the back of the classroom doodling as Ms. Fletcher spoke of theory. Tala sketched the mansion. Large, dark, burned and decayed, with horrible windows that looked like eyes.

The house has eyes.

Tala shaded the black lions on top of the gate. She had sketched a bird's eye view of the haunted land and analyzed the property. The mansion slept at the center. There were deteriorated horse stalls along the back. She wondered how they had survived the fires. Then there was The Sea of Trees, who heard the whispers of desperate souls.

She remembered Ben's lawn company hauling black trash bags onto the Bumblebee truck. Yes, there were acres of land to tend to, but wouldn't they need a bigger crew? Why would deputies be rotating shifts day and night?

Townies believed uttering "Glenn Curtiss" brought bad luck, much like breaking a mirror. Most people in Springs never said his name. As if mentioning it would suddenly make him appear with a tank of gasoline and a match. Parents would often use the legends to instill fear into their children. Even in Hialeah, David Stone fell victim to such threats.

"You better behave, Davie. If not, I'm sending you to the Curtiss Mansion. Glenn Curtiss's ghost still walks the empty corridors," they'd tell him.

The thought gave her the jeebies. Why parents felt the need to traumatize their kids was beyond her.

Tala came back from her daydream when a goth kid with green hair came back from the bathroom and dropped a small folded paper onto her desk. She opened it slowly, keeping her gaze on Ms. Fletcher, who had her back to the class explaining the binomial theorem. The note was written in hard pencil lines.

MARK SAYS MEET HIM AT THE GYM NOW!!

TALA HATED ALGEBRA II, but she couldn't keep ditching class forever. Her grades were awful. She had to find normalcy, as if such a thing existed. After class she headed toward the gym ambivalent about talking to Mark because of their argument.

Tala pushed open the heavy gym doors and saw Mark up on the bleachers. He came down as soon as he saw her, and they met half court on top of a garnet and gold cartoon hawk with a basketball in its mouth. Some students exited the gym lockers, jabbering about Snapchat and Instagram.

"I heard what happened to your dad. Glad he's okay," Mark said.

"Thanks. Is that all?"

"I miss you and The Hawks. It's just this whole thing with Yin. And now Makayla's brother. And, you know . . ." She knew he was embarrassed for calling 911 that night.

"I'm sorry I called. I just wanted to protect my dad. We need the Curtiss Mansion."

Tala said, "Why didn't you tell me the truth?"

"I told you it was keeping us afloat. You didn't care."

She took a strand of hair out of her face. "I didn't think of it that way. I'm sorry too."

"I miss him," Mark shook his head. "Can't believe he's gone. Sheriff said there's no new developments in the case. News said FBI is investigating the shooting in Orlando."

"I know lots is going on, but Yin could still be out there somewhere," Tala suggested. "He's strong."

"Where? Over the rainbow? No. He's dead like Jamal," he said. "For nothing."

"Don't say that!" Tala grabbed his chin.

"Heard about Casey?" Tala asked.

"I saw Val's text, plus it's on the news. This fuckin' town is cursed."

"That little girl's dead."

"Dead?" Tala said. "Who said she's dead?"

"It's just I saw on TV if kids go missing and they're not found within the first couple days, they usually end up dead."

Tala thought that, yes, it's been a few days. But she's a *special* little girl.

"Jax's going through it, I bet. Makayla won't call me back. And I can't blame her. She hasn't been to school," Mark said.

"Jax isn't picking up my calls either," Tala said.

Mark reached for her hand. She felt a nice warmth that made her feel better in the freezing gym. "I miss you," he said. She looked into his longing eyes and at his dimples, and before she knew it, he kissed her.

She pulled back. "Wait."

A security guard poked his head through the gym doors and said, "Clear it out. Time to go home, lovebirds." *Home* is too far, Tala thought. All I have now is a toy house.

"I'm sorry. I just wanted to do that. I'll walk you home if you want. It's not outta my way," Mark said.

"Home is too far. Just take me to my house."

62

ON THE WALK HOME, Tala broke the heavy silence. "What do you think happened that night?"

Mark searched his memory.

"What night?"

"The night we played *El Libro Rojo*," she said.

"The night with Casey," he said. "I don't know."

"Me either, but what do you *think* happened?"

"I try not to think of it. I told myself it didn't happen."

"It did happen. She knows things, that girl. And something tells me that's why she's gone. None of this makes any sense. Who would take her? No signs of forced entry. No fingerprints, nothing to even suggest foul play to police."

"Unless," Mark felt a cold breeze.

He looked up and saw the gloomy rainy sky above. The rain was coming. "Unless she ran away."

"But why, and why now? Don't you find it odd? The timing of everything. Jamal hooks up with Psycho Jordan and shoots innocent people. Casey is missing now. Is everything in this town a big f'ing coincidence?"

"Conspiracy," Mark corrected. "The word I think you're

looking for is conspiracy. That's how everything feels here sometimes."

"It feels like someone is trying to send a message."

"Who?"

"I don't know yet."

Mark said, "When a kid goes missing, it's usually someone who knows her."

Tala stopped walking. Mark turned to face her.

"Are you saying Jax took his own niece?"

"I never said Jax did; I said it's usually someone who knows her. But since you bring him up. How well do you know him? Someone goes missing. The cops look at the husband, the wife, or family. Textbook suspects."

They made it home with a heavy silence. Ben was outside unloading equipment from the back of his Bumblebee truck.

He waved at Tala. "Howdy!"

Mark went to kiss her on the lips, but Tala turned her head. Mark's dimples returned, and he jogged over to help his dad.

"Hang on, you'll hurt your back again."

Ben tapped his chest. "Your old man's healthy as a horse." He winked at Tala and put his hands up in surrender. "You're not armed, are you? Just kiddin', kiddo."

"Mark." Tala waved him over.

"What's up?"

"I need your binoculars."

"For what?"

"I'm going hunting."

63

THE TV WAS ON, but no one was watching it. She wasn't sure if David was home even with his car outside because Olivia sometimes picked him up. He had also taken up jogging again. He hadn't run in years. It's crazy what love made you do.

When she passed the foyer into the kitchen, she saw the rear sliding glass doors open and heard voices laughing outside. She went through the glass door and saw her dad sitting on a pool chair jabbering with Olivia. Olivia wore a white cover-up over her aqua bikini. She saw Tala standing there.

Olivia smiled and waved. "Hey Tala! Come on over."

Her dad turned back.

"Hey, Red! Come here!" He was talking louder than normal, and the daiquiris on the table were the culprits.

Tala felt a nudge of guilt because, besides their dinner, she hadn't tried to talk to her again. She hated playing house with someone who wasn't mom. He'd been sad for years, crying himself to sleep at times. She decided to try. For him.

David sat up in his chair when he saw her approaching. "You're early." A look of surprise crossed his face.

"I got out half an hour ago."

David looked at his watch. "Look at that. Time flies when you're in good company." He smiled at *her*.

"How was school?" David asked, the question that annoyed every student in America.

"Educational." She forced a smile.

"Drinking, are we?" Tala said.

Olivia picked up her strawberry daiquiri and joked she would make her one as soon as she turned twenty-one.

"Unless you want a virgin," Olivia said.

The heat was unbearable.

"Virgin is fine."

"Virgin for a virgin. Words a father always love to hear." David laughed, to Tala's surprise. No question he had some drinks in him. Tala felt rather embarrassed at the comment and disappointed to see her dad drinking. Olivia stood up anxious to serve.

"So, I guess you're drinking again?"

"Today, yes."

"You said you wouldn't drink after—"

"I know what I said, Red."

Olivia had turned on the blender and wasn't in earshot.

"I'm drinking because I'm happy, not because I'm sad. There's a difference. I'm not in a dark place anymore. You have nothing to worry about, and besides, we're celebrating. I survived death." He pointed at his scar.

Despite her reservations about her age, Tala admired Olivia's free spirit. She did some homework and learned she owned an upscale clothing boutique called Ozean, that she started after quitting her job as an accountant. She was a self-made woman.

She walked over to the outside counter next to the stainless-steel barbeque grill and started pouring the drinks. David's cell phone went off.

"Excuse me, ladies, it's work. And I need the restroom." He went inside the house and closed the sliding glass door. Tala hadn't seen him so lax in a long time, first time in the pool.

"Extra virgin coming right up." Olivia said it like a bartender would. Tala took Olivia's seat and looked at the sky, using her hand to shield her eyes from the intense rays. Her mind was distant, in a daydream, the present blotted out by the drum of the blender in the background like white noise.

Olivia came back and gave Tala her drink in a tall slender glass with a sliced strawberry on the lip.

"Wow. Looks amazing," she said. Really impressed with the presentation.

Tala took a sip and grimaced a little. "This has—"

"It tastes better that way. And yeah, you ain't no virgin either. Get the fuck outta my chair."

64

Tala wore a white linen dress, her hair held together in a bun by her knife. She was on a white sand beach. In the distance, the clouds turned dark. Ominous strikes of lightning looked like God was taking photographs of a crime scene.

Maybe Yin's. Perhaps Casey's. No thunder. No sound. Not even the wind. She saw the ocean more still than an ancient painting. The sky turned full dark, no stars, just black. Until she saw the full moon. She looked around.

Where are the wolves?

She knew they would come.

It had been a long time since she'd seen them.

They were near.

She felt them moving through the island trees. Suddenly, they stopped, and this scared her more.

Where are they?

She saw in this darkness. An ocean rose from afar, it rose and rose, the tide grew, the rain came, and she knew that she could go nowhere. She stood in the heavy rain but didn't hear the rain falling; she could only feel it. She felt the rain drench her body like the night at the racetrack.

She stood on the ocean shore in her white dress with her Balisong. She took a step back when she realized the tsunami rising, coming toward her from yonder. She grabbed the Balisong from her bun and her hair came loose, her hair and dress billowed in the wind and she screamed as she held the butterfly knife to the ocean's fierce current. "I'm not afraid." "I am the weapon!" The waves came crashing down. She was drowning.

She woke up sweating. Breathing hard. She puts her hand on her heaving chest. She saw the knife on her computer desk. She focused on it. She calmed her breathing. As she imagined the knife moving. And suddenly, it did.

It moved.

65

HER MIND SHUFFLED thoughts like a deck of cards.

Casey: vanished.

Yin: vanished.

Charlie Owens: Suicide.

Mom: Suicide.

Jamal and Psycho Jordan dead.

Domino mask.

The house has eyes.

Bauta mask.

2 + 2 = 5.

Glenn Curtiss

Monarch butterflies.

What's the connection?

Tala heard David downstairs rummaging through the kitchen. He wouldn't understand. All he would hear is "Jax" and he would shun her for disobeying him with that prairie boy. He could be such a hypocrite sometimes. She wouldn't tell him. He was happy with his toy house and his toy girlfriend. He was okay with his new job and, yes, bad things had happened in Miami Springs, but hadn't he said bad things happen everywhere?

There were active shootings all over the country like clockwork. On every channel there were montages of the victims. The news drank it up like an elixir. Jamal Stephens' high school photo and Rodnam Jackson's mugshot circulated the national news.

There were protests for gun reform around the country. Students marched out of their schools with signs for gun control. More restrictions on gun purchases, background checks, but more citizens demanded a total repeal of the second amendment.

It was time.

⸺

TALA LOOKED out to Fairway Avenue from her window and saw a pack of dogs running up the street. Only they were bigger. Could they be . . .

They were wolves. Between them she saw Casey in her zombie costume. Her skin was pale, her eyes lifeless. Tala heard a window go up fast and, when she turned, Casey stood in front of her, mounted on a wolf with yellow eyes. Tala blinked.

She was gone.

The clock on her computer desk struck thirteen.

El Libro Rojo was on her bed.

David opened her bedroom door. "Everything alright in here?"

Tala was in the middle of the room shaking, nervous, and scared.

"It's that boy, isn't it?" he said evenly. He was cleaning

her knife on a white cloth. Tala saw what might've been blood on the bone handle.

"You can't leave this thing lying around," he said.

"I took care of Jax. I told you he was trouble, Red. That Hialeah scum is coming over the canal like a god-damn tsunami."

Tala kept her eyes on the blade. When she blinked again, he was gone. The air smelled like iron.

Tala went downstairs. Her feet felt like cinder blocks. The TV played Fox News, and Sean Hannity yelled it's time to give up your guns! Tala had no control of her body as if she were a puppet being controlled by strings. The strings took her outside to Casey.

Tala said, "Where have you been? Jax's worried sick. We've all been looking for you."

"I'm where I'm supposed to be. Are you?" Casey said, matter of factly. They were now standing in *The Sea of Trees*.

"The wolves are here. They've been here all along," Casey said.

"What am I supposed to do?"

"Accept who you are."

"And who am I?"

"The one who stops the wolves."

The sequence changed.

They were now standing in front of the Curtiss Mansion gate. Tala observed the frightening detail in the sculpted lions. The gate suddenly opened.

"He's waiting for you," Casey said.

The front doors of the mansion seemed miles ahead. They held hands.

"No vampires. No zombies. Only dead men," Casey said.

"And what do they want from me?" Tala asked. The mammoth mansion that appeared like a hideous shadow of black ink on a white moonlit backdrop.

"He wants what you want," Casey said, her voice as soft as feathers.

Tala looked down at her zombie, lifeless eyes.

Casey's skin changed from rich to pale. Her voice from soft to harsh. Scratchy. "He wants help."

A gust of violent wind came fast and ripped the iron gates off their ancient hinges. Rain came crashing from the heavens. Tala continued her trek again toward the mansion's front door, against the vile wind. When she woke up panting, she remembered what Yin had said. Dreams have meaning. She knew the answer to her questions, the connection—Everything—was at the Curtiss Mansion.

The missing puzzle piece.

66

School had once been bearable, but now she dreaded it more than anything. The days seemed to blur together. Things had changed so much. She barely talked to The Hawks and often questioned her own sanity. Was everything in the world supposed to be devoid of answers?

After Yin, everyone went their own way. Tala thought something like that would bring people together, but it didn't. Yin was the rock that held them together. He didn't care about labels or social classes. He just appreciated the things that made us different. He blew the chalk off the invisible line that divided Hialeah and Miami Springs.

Tala tried to decipher the meaning behind her horrible nightmares. One thought crystalized; she must go to the Curtiss Mansion. Like Charlie, she felt drawn, connected, even obsessed with the house. She feared she was under the same spell that had taken hold of him. Yin said dreams meant something, and she believed that too, now more than ever. The best interpretation of her dreams suggested the mansion was somehow the hub of Yin's and Casey's disappearance.

Tala couldn't go alone. Makayla and Mark wouldn't return her calls. Jax was impossible to get a hold of. She really hadn't seen Lance. She took an Uber to Dog Town. It took a lot to knock on the door. Jax opened halfway. "What do you want, Red?"

"Can I come in?"

He opened the door and threw himself onto the couch. Tala walked herself in and saw the place was a mess. There were newspaper clippings of Casey's disappearance from the *Miami Herald*, *Miami New Times*, and *The Hawks Nest*. There were also clippings of Yin's disappearance and the shooting in Orlando on the kitchen counter and the living room floor.

"How are you?" she said. It wasn't the usual formality. She really wanted to know.

"Can't you see I'm fucking great? What do you want? I'm busy."

"If you're busy, why'd you let me in?"

"Because I'm stuck. I'm out of ideas." Jax surrendered. "I've thought of everything. I've talked to the police. Her friends from school. Their parents. There's no hope. She's gone. This God-forsaken city is hopeless. People are talking, you know. The stupid rumors of the mansion being haunted. And goddamn Glenn Curtiss who killed his wife and fucked us all."

Jax got up and paced around the living room. His hair and clothes a mess. He smelled like he hadn't showered in days.

"People and their legends, their stories; it's all bullshit. The mansion has nothing to do with this," he said. That was the polar opposite of what Tala believed.

Tala could smell alcohol on his breath although it wasn't even noon.

"You've been drinking?"

"Yes, I have. You have a problem with that?" he snapped.

She didn't appreciate his attitude but tried to understand.

"You don't have to be rude. I'm here because I care. I want to help."

"Okay, so help."

"We have to go to the mansion."

"You and this God damn mansion. Did you even listen to what I just said? It's a fucking house that's falling apart. It's folklore. No one lives there, and the people who did died a hundred years ago. Folk stories to scare kids. The other deaths were years ago, and they were mainly idiots who killed themselves." He launched a glass cup across the living room, shattering it to pieces.

Tala winced. "People who kill themselves are not idiots. They were suffering and needed help."

Jax remembered her mom.

"Fuck, I'm sorry. I didn't mean it like that."

It took all her will not to walk out.

"I was supposed to keep her safe. I fucked that up too! Now she's gone. She could be—"

"She's not—" Tala interjected.

"All these sick bastards on the street. Maybe it's too late. Maybe she—"

"She's not—"

He reached for a beer that sat on the floor and took a swig. He grimaced, suggesting it was hot and tasted like shit. Jax didn't like drinking. He just wanted the pain to go away. It had worked for his father before he went out for a pack of cigarettes and never came back.

He looked tired and broken. Tala knew all about feeling broken. She put a hand on his knee.

"I've seen cops," he started saying, then stopped. He composed himself. "I've seen cops all over this damn city patrolling, but Casey is still missing. Yin is still gone. And the news just plays crazy fucks with guns trying to mow down the most people possible, like trying to break a fucking Guinness world record."

He paused. "How is Makayla doing?"

"She's not answering my calls." Tala said.

"Her brother and that psycho killed 56 people. Including kids. Yin and Casey are old news already. People forget and move on to the next shiny object. It almost feels intentional. You ever feel like we're being controlled?"

"All the time."

"I hate this. I hate this place. They could drop a bomb here for all I care. I don't know why you came here. Springs and Hialeah are the same. On your side of the bridge, people fake it better. You shouldn't have come here." He slurred his words.

"I know how to find Casey," Tala said.

Jax expanded his arms with a cynical smile and a helpless expression. "How?"

"Get sober. Then we go to the mansion. Meet me at my house at dawn."

"Why so early?"

"Just do it."

"Tala, is there something you want to share with me?" His voice sounded concerned and suddenly crisp.

"There's a white heat of burning desire inside me that says the Curtiss Mansion is behind all of this. And I'm going to prove it."

67

TALA PEERED at the Curtiss Mansion through Mark's binoculars. She was in Jax's pickup and could barely make out the features of his face, because it was still dark. Good thing, the binoculars had night vision.

The sun's crown below the horizon, a melancholy silence lingered about the town. Deer Run was vacant until a Bumblebee landscaping truck came up the road, as she expected. She peered through the binoculars and focused the zoom, but she couldn't make out the driver nor passenger; they were still too far.

Eventually Ben came into focus behind the wheel with Sheriff Hogg riding shotgun. They were as thick as thieves, it seemed.

"It's Mark's dad and the sheriff," she said.

Black smoke came up from behind the Bumblebee truck, polluting the air. As the truck passed them, they ducked down as a precaution, although they were too far to be noticed.

"So Mark's dad landscapes the place. Right?" Jax asked.

"Right," Tala said.

"So, what's he doing with a cop? Strange."

Tala hoped Jax would find it an odd pair. He did.

"This place doesn't even look landscaped much, but I guess it's a lot of land to cover."

The sun began waking from its slumber. The darkness faded to gray like invisible ink.

Jax took the binoculars from Tala and saw Sheriff Hogg hop down the steps of the truck to open the wrought iron gate. He unlocked the bulldozer of a lock that clung to the gate like it imprisoned a monster. But there was nothing scary about the mansion when the sun was rising.

Jax turned on the radio and lowered the volume. The DJ on the radio was jabbering about the upcoming weekend and how we should all party hard because a storm was heading our way with a vengeance. Tala liked the word.

Vengeance.

Tala said it aloud, and Jax looked at her like she'd been possessed.

"You're bleeding," Jax said.

She put her hand to her face and saw the blood on her hands. The blood trickled down from her nose to her mouth, and she tasted iron. She looked in the mirror and saw one streak of dark red like wine.

Jax reached across her lap to open the glove compartment, brushing against her legs. He used a fast food napkin to wipe the blood from her lips. He stared into her blue eyes, transfixed. They had the windows rolled down, but it was still warm. Now, a sort of magnetism brewed. It was hot. Tala nearly broke into a sweat. Jax leaned over and kissed her.

She pulled away. "Look."

The Bumblebee truck went up the makeshift road that led to the mouth of the mansion kicking up dirt and decay.

The road seemed to go on forever, and the truck turned into the size of a marble. It drove past the mansion, off to the side, heading around to the back by the horse stables that hadn't heard a horse cry in a hundred years. Jax grabbed the binoculars again. "Let me see."

The two men came into view.

"Doesn't look like the sheriff is going to be trimming any trees." He made an observation of his clothing. Sheriff Hogg wore designer sunglasses with a white polo t-shirt and khaki pants.

Looking at the Curtiss Mansion, Tala wondered how much rage it took Glenn Curtiss to burn his family and horses. She imagined the genius aviator locking the mansion's doors and stables while drenching them with gasoline before striking a match. How much rage? The combination of hot flame, rising fire, and screams made her feel sick to her stomach.

"Tala?" Jax said. "Hey, you okay? Snap out of it!"

"Im fine." She wiped her sweaty hands against her jeans.

Few cars passed on Deer Run. She wondered if people avoided the road, since legend said it brought bad luck. She wasn't superstitious, but in small towns people don't like to take a chance on things like that. Tala and Jax took turns with the binoculars, but Ben and Hogg were out of view. A while later, Jax tapped Tala, who was leaning back in her chair.

"There," he said. Passing her the binoculars.

Tala saw Ben and Hogg hauling a black trash bag onto the back of the truck. Whose trash? It looked like they were carrying a body. Debris from the trees? Maybe but unlikely. She couldn't fathom why Ben and Hogg would be here. It just didn't make sense. Maybe Ben and Hogg were friends and Ben called him for help. But it didn't feel right. The day that Ben's truck got burglarized, Sheriff Hogg didn't even mention him. Now they were buddies? No, it didn't make sense.

They dragged another bag using what appeared to be significant lower body strength. The rain from the night before had dampened the soil, making the task harder.

"What are they doing?" Tala asked.

He took the binoculars from her.

"Taking out the garbage."

"What garbage?"

"I don't know. Maybe they're working," Jax said.

"What now?" he asked.

"We wait."

He put the binoculars down.

"We come back at night to find out what's in the bags. This time we don't retreat."

They stayed in the white Ford truck for about an hour, the sun started its climb. The humidity unbearable. Beads of sweat ran down Tala's back. When the Bumblebee truck pulled out, they both got down to hide and left a few minutes later, when people started waking up for work.

68

MOST PEOPLE DON'T FIND happiness a second time. David wore a stupid smile that could only mean love. When Tala got closer, she smelled whiskey on his breath.

This worried her.

Yona's suicide put him through hell. He felt helpless for years, refusing to forgive himself for not seeing her pain. For not being able to save her from her demons. Olivia had re-affirmed it wasn't his fault, and that he was a good man. As if reading her mind, David said, "I'm happy, Red." He felt guilt when the words left his mouth.

"You know I love—" he couldn't say it, but he didn't have too; Tala knew.

"I want to spend more time, I miss you, Red—with Olivia—I've been busy. I'm trying to figure it all out again. I've been lonely. I want you to know that I should—"

His words were like potholes. This was him *trying*. David never shared his feelings. He wasn't a bad drunk. He never hit her nor went into rages. He just ignored her when he drank. That hurt more. David took off his tie and stood in the kitchen, searching for words.

"I'm sorry about Yin and Casey. I know they're your friends. It's been a hell of a year. A hell of a ride. Things have been so crazy."

He gestured to his surroundings. "This is all for you. You know that, right? But it's all backfired."

His eyes were sad.

"You can't shield me from the world, Dad. You were right. Bad things happen everywhere. And I want you to be happy. I think that even Mom would want that."

"You still dream of wolves?"

"Sometimes."

"I want the wolves to go away. I want you to dream of only beautiful things."

A little thought of the white sand beach flicked in her mind's eye.

"Me too."

"I should have been there for your mother. I should have known she was sad. Should have known she was sick. But I just didn't see it. I thought she was happy. I thought I knew her. I thought we were all happy. There were things about her I never knew."

He turned his face as a slow current of tears escaped his eyes. He looked defeated.

Tala embraced him.

"It's not your fault, dad. She left us both."

69

AT NIGHT the Curtiss Mansion was a different beast. It held the secrets of that wicked fire, those brutal murders. It held the secrets of the suicides and disappearances that paved the road to folklore and legends.

Tala heard Yin's mom's frail voice, "Silly stories."

She tried to fathom how someone like Glenn Curtiss could snap and murder those he loved. Not having answers drove her mad. Her mind came to the present. They had said Dexter Reeves was a brilliant gifted young man. How could he start shooting people like target practice? Madness. Something happened. Something was wrong. Something was very wrong.

Miami Springs was under the national microscope. Jamal Stephens, a handsome, rich, smart black man, had coordinated an active shooting with a known petty criminal with mental illness. Makayla's brother. Yes, something was very wrong.

She'd had a slight fascination with the macabre since she was a little girl. She went through a phase of voraciously reading bios of monsters like Ted Bundy, Charles Manson,

Albert Fish, Jeffrey Dahmer, and now Glenn Curtiss and his wicked mansion was at the forefront of her mind.

She wished she could pick their brains. Find out what fucked them up so bad. When she was done, bring back the electric chair, strap them in, and pull the lever.

No, she would never kill an animal. These monsters were less than human.

Tala skipped American Government again. She'd been cutting class since Yin's disappearance. Trying to avoid his empty seat and her hollowed heart. Mr. Wilson was giving his students a break, all things considered. The truth was he liked Yin a lot and the murmurings of his guilt for calling his parents after he tripped in class, made it back to Tala. He was doing his job, wasn't he? He had asked.

Tala peeked inside his class, and it was near empty. She went to the courtyard instead and spied Makayla at a blue bench tossing pieces of bread to a flock of pigeons.

The weather took a turn for the worse. There was something brewing alright, Tala thought.

She joined her.

"Hey, you alright?" Tala said.

Makayla looked away and cupped her hands over her sunglasses.

Tala took off her shades, revealing a bruise to her eye. She put the sunglasses on again and looked around to see if anyone else had seen the secret she held.

"Who did this to you?"

"My brother's not a killer. I don't care what anyone says."

"Tell me what happened."

"No one's going to talk trash about my brother."

Tala's phoned vibrated. She checked the local news

alert. Her mind far and distant. Her brain began to weave a spiral of interconnecting dots.

"What's wrong?"

Tala grabbed Makayla's arm and pulled her toward Jax's truck that pulled up.

"Let's go. They identified the human remains in Hialeah."

70

TALA EXPECTED Yin or Casey to be identified but they weren't. They were either dead or still out there, some-where, because the dental records identified Marjorie Vargas, the ex-fiancé of Orlando shooter Jamal Stephens. She was the ex-nursing administrator at Citrus Hospital who told Tala and Yin, she could get in *trouble* when they pressed on to meet Charlie.

It wasn't clear if she quit her job before or after the shooting. The news reporters said Hialeah Police was inves-tigating her death as an apparent suicide. They didn't release the method to the media.

Jax drove by Yin's house at Tala's insistence. She'd been passing by his house more often on mornings on the way to school. It was like passing by his house helped her remem-ber. Helped the pieces of the puzzle take form. This new piece of information was an anomaly. She wasn't sure how it fit.

Another piece that didn't fit was Ben and Sheriff Hogg together at the mansion? Occam's Razor suggested the simplest solution was usually right. They were pieces. Involved *somehow*.

When David came into her bedroom unexpectedly, she flinched. She was on her iPad researching the Glenn Curtiss murders.

"Didn't mean to scare you," he said.

"Didn't hear you come in."

He looked at her screen. "Reading about our local hero, I see."

"I think you mean local villain."

"Why are you reading that?" He swiveled her chair around with a curious look.

"School," she lied.

"Project?"

"Yes," she lied again.

"Can't you pick something else?" he said.

"That's what Mr. Wilson gave me." She lied once more, but this time it sounded natural. The lie ran off her lips with an effortless flow.

"Well, in that case, you should write about the *good* things he did, which were many. He was a genius. A true pioneer."

"Why do people only care about the bad things he did?"

"All people care about, Red, is when someone fucks up."

His language caught her off guard. He only cursed when he was angry. There was whiskey on his breath again. She didn't dare mention it. She didn't want to argue.

"Remember," he said. "No one is all bad."

With that said, David went back to his study, and Tala went back to Wikipedia. She scrolled down the article and saw a heading for other deaths/suicides. There were photos of the deceased, along with their names. Bodies discovered decades after the Glenn Curtiss murder-suicide. Tala skimmed over their deaths.

Sidney Gottlieb, 14 years old, 1993, barbiturate overdose.

Donald Cameron, 16 years old 1993, self-inflicted gunshot wound.

Norma Mortenson, 21 years old, 2003, and Frank Olson 23 years old, 2003. Both jumped from the Curtiss Mansion's third story balcony to their deaths in an apparent suicide. Toxicology results revealed they had ingested Convallaria Majalis, a highly poisonous woodland flowering plant known as Lily of the Valley.

SUICIDE.
Suicide.
Suicide.
Suicide.

THEY LEFT A NOTE BEHIND:

There's no place like home.
Candy and Ken

They found the note inside Norma's pocket. The investigation was fruitless. No leads. No motivation for the deaths. No reason for them to want to kill themselves. No explanation for using the wrong names. The note had Frank's handwriting. Two drops of each other's blood. What Tala read next brought a cold chill to her body, an electric current up her spine. Everything that had happened since she got here seemed to float in holographic squares before her.

Everything stopped and appeared surreal as she scrolled down and read a snippet from Detective Dorado's police report:

Norma Mortenson and Frank Olson were both found wearing masks. I found no explanation for the masks but it's possible they acquired them for Halloween since the holiday was only two weeks away. Ms. Mortenson and Mr. Olson were engaged and worked in the adult entertainment industry. They both had a troubled childhood and met in the foster care system. They were habitual runaways from Mango Hill in Hialeah with extensive criminal and mental health history.

The familiarity of it made Tala want to scream. Yona shot herself and fell from a building at a masquerade party. There were masks everywhere. It was eerily similar, yet so many years apart. She felt a pang of sharp pain deep inside her stomach.

Everything's a coincidence until it's not.

Three suicides from a fall and a mask in both scenes. Coincidence?

No, I don't think so.

"I know there's something here," she said. "I can feel it."

71

It was amazing how fast the town forgot Yin, Casey and Jamal. In just a few months, the national news zeroed in on yet another active shooting in a small town in California, a bacteria outbreak in Miami Beach, and the heroic tell-all of a transgender sports star.

Despite the conglomeration of news, Tala could never forget her friends. She wouldn't forget Jamal either. She couldn't forget Psycho Jordan even if she wanted too.

Detectives ceased canvassing the neighborhoods, questioning people, and looking for clues. They had exhausted all leads and hoped for a break in the case, but nothing came. Time passed and life went on. The crime in Miami Springs went to the back burner with the incumbent re-election of Mayor Sosa, who vowed to find the people responsible for Yin's disappearance and to conduct an independent investigation into the Jamal Stephens shooting. Mayor Sosa passed gun control legislation in Springs.

They would be an example for the nation. The national news focused on active shootings. There seemed to be one every month. That, and its congruent protest to abolish the second amendment from celebrities and politicians, arguing that the U.K. removed guns and so will America.

TALA HAD A DREAM THAT NIGHT. The moon was a Cheshire smile. The gates of the Curtiss Mansion were open. The unkempt path to the front door was a yellow brick road. Her nose was bleeding, her skin a pale white. Fierce wind billowed her white linen dress, then she glided over the yellow brick road. The doors to the mansion opened.

Finally.

She heard a woman wailing from upstairs.

There was no light switch, so Tala used the moonlight to guide herself up the stairs. The woman continued crying. Tala continued climbing.

Step

by

step

Unsure of where the echoed cries were coming from. Maybe these stairs would lead her to heaven. To see her mom once more. To tell her not to cry. Not to be sad. So she climbed and climbed. The stairway expanded and stretched. She ran up now, looked down over the rail, and saw nothing but darkness. She tired, her breathing accelerated. Her chest heaved. It was the only way to beat the expanding stairs.

"Tala!" a distant voice said.

Finally, she made it up.

"Red! I'm here."

That voice—

She ran down the corridor. Dark shadows shaped like

hands reached up from the floor, ripping her clothes. She pushed and fought through their grasp. She made it to the other end and pushed open a door with checkered tiles. She saw a man standing on the balcony rail. Holding a revolver.

The man sobbed and didn't turn around.

"Dad," she said. "Dad, is that you?"

He turned.

"Nobody's all good. Nobody. Not even me. Not even you. I could have been a better husband."

"DAD!"

He had a bottle of whiskey in his other hand.

"DAD! WHAT ARE YOU DOING? GET DOWN FROM THERE!"

"It should have been me."

"GET DOWN!"

He took a sip. Lifted the revolver to his temple and pulled the trigger. He fell.

Tala screamed until she woke up panting.

Her angel night light was on.

She felt pressure on her neck like someone had been choking her, but her neck was unmarked. She slightly opened her door and listened for her dad. She took a couple steps forward and heard him snoring in his room. After a few hours of tossing in bed, she went back to the dream world but slept with the lights on.

72

TALA WENT to the Cozy Corner because she wanted a milk shake and burger. She needed to eat and think, and sugar always helped. There were missing posters on the diner doors with Yin and Casey's pictures.

She hated thinking about it, but if Yin were alive, he would have reached out by now. We live in such a connected world that nothing else made sense. Their posters were on every light pole in the town. Amber alerts on the radio.

Real.

All real.

The pain was unbearable.

Tala saw Jaen come in.

"Can I join you?" Jaen said.

"Sure."

"What's up?" Tala said.

"Mark. I bumped into Mark. He reeked of booze and was talking nonsense."

"How do you mean?"

"I mean he was out of it, Tala. Like really out. And

acting *weird*. That's not like him. He barely drinks. He said Yin was in a better place and that we all have to die sometime. He told me sometimes, he doesn't feel like himself."

"I think he was in Wonderland."

"Was he alone?"

"Yeah, but it gets worse. He said if he had to choose, he'd pick a gun too. He said death was faster, and there was no pain. I'm worried about him. He's talking bat-shit crazy."

"Where'd you see him?"

"In Hialeah, at the Amelia Earhart Memorial."

"Maybe *you* should talk to him," Jaen urged.

"Have you seen Makayla?" Tala asked. "She had a bruised eye."

"I saw her. She gets those occasionally. Bumps into doors, falls on her face. That's what she says. We know it's her dad. He's unrelenting, and after Jamal losing his mind and shooting those people. I'm sure he's blaming her somehow."

"Unbelievable. We have to do something."

"Everybody knows, it's been going on for years. But you're right. We should do something. You can start by talking to Mark."

"Why me?"

"Well, for one, you guys are neighbors. For two, I know he likes you. But he said you're going to get yourself killed too. He said you can't win." She leaned in and made air quotes. He said, "They control everything."

"Who's they?"

"Exactly. He's talking crazy. I'm worried."

"You should be. Because he's right. They do control everything. And we're gonna stop them."

73

After her burger-sugar rush, Tala made some calls.
The Hawks came to her house like the first night, when
they went to the racetrack. That seemed ages ago. This time
Jax came too.

She felt like she'd always known these people, like she'd
always had these friends, and like they were on an adventure together. Only this time, they weren't telling ghost
stories; they were living them.

Tala spoke to Mark about what he'd told Jaen at the
park. Mark said he didn't remember much that he'd been
drunk. He'd been stressed about Yin and everything that
had happened. He said he'd do anything to help. The
Hawks agreed to go to the Curtiss Mansion one more time.

They dressed in black and rode in Lance's Jeep. When
Makayla reminded them of the stakes and the danger
involved, Lance pulled a Glock 19, .9MM from the center
console.

"It's my brother's," he said. "Just in case."

"The hell you have a gun for?" Valerie said.

"Insurance."

If Tala's theories were true, they were investigating something connected to powerful people.

"You know how to use that thing?" Jax said.

"I've played Call of Duty," he said sarcastically. "How different can it be?" Of course he was joking. He had been to the range before.

There were nervous laughs and awkward silence. The radio was off. Lance drove under the speed limit, waiting for someone to say something. Anything.

Tala took the initiative, "You think we'll need that gun?"

"Probably not. But if we do BANG!" he said with a sly smile. Despite his arrogance, Tala sensed his fear. Everyone did. "But seriously, we don't know what we're up against," Lance said.

He was right. He looked at Tala through his rearview mirror. "Do we?"

"No. We don't."

"Yin and Casey are gone. And if your theory is right, Red, this is all somehow connected to someone using the Curtiss Mansion for *evil*. I'd rather have a gun," he said firmly.

"I don't like this at all. We should just call the sheriff," Jaen said. "Have them handle it."

"How much fluoride is in your water? You listening? The sheriff is compromised. We can't trust em'." Valerie said.

"Speaking of cops, they've been circling the mansion lately like a ceiling fan," Lance said.

Jax stared at Mark. "Let's hope no one calls them this time."

Mark said nothing.

"We're parking blocks away and spreading out. We won't draw as much attention that way, in case an old timer is on the porch or happens to look out his window. A group of us is gonna call attention," Jax said. "That's a phone call to Miami Spring's finest, ain't that right, Mark?"

Mark said, "You made your point."

Makayla said, "When is splitting up *ever* a good idea? You know black people get axed first."

"She's right," Jaen said. "Splitting up is a bad idea."

"This isn't a movie. It's our best shot. What do you think's gonna happen if someone peeks out their window and sees a bunch of teens out past curfew? Any better ideas?" Tala said.

She was right. They had to get into the mansion. If they stayed together as a large group, they were going to be noticed. Someone could ignore a couple of teens walking down the street, but four's a party. The plan was to walk. Not run. Just walk. In pairs. Hide in plain sight. They took the backroads to Deer Run.

Due to the housing bubble, real estate everywhere was being lost to banks, and Miami Springs was no exception. Lance said he knew a string of foreclosed mansions on Hunting Lodge Road. He'd use them to their advantage.

Lance parked in one of their empty driveways. The dim lighting was perfect. After some debate, they decided Tala went north with Jax and Makayla. Jaen, Valerie and Mark went south with Lance.

The girls felt safer with Lance because he had a gun. If he really knew how to use it was another story. When they reached the end of Hunting Lodge, they split and walked naturally, but the closer they got to the Curtiss Mansion, the faster their hearts pounded.

Tala had determination in her stride until she heard the rumble of thunder, then she was afraid of rain, the darkness, the mansion; everything. The night air became cooler, the wind picked up speed. Rain droplets fell from the dark sky like a leaky pen, making them cold. Lance walked slightly ahead leading the pack.

Jax had a flashlight, no weapon. He told Tala a weapon hadn't crossed his mind. He'd been in street fights, his fists had yet to let him down. But when Lance brandished the gun she realized:

This is dangerous.

She walked with him at a brisk pace. She saw only forward. Thought only of vengeance.

Vengeance.

She wanted vengeance more than anything. They split up when they made it to Deer Run. The streetlights in front of the houses across the street were mainly off, some were on providing an ambient orange glow, enough to see, enough darkness to hide.

Jax, Tala, and Makayla circled the mansion on the east side. The gate on that side was high, but they had found a spot that had been caved in with trees and bushes, vines growing from it. Getting over the fence here was easier, but still required a climb. They could use the branches as a makeshift ladder.

They would have to cut through The Sea of Trees again, this time all the way through. The Sea of Trees had acres of foliage, tall redwoods, pines, tall grass, which housed camouflaged snakes, spiders, and God knew what else. A dark and desolate wood, where cell phone reception died. A dead zone where screams wouldn't be heard.

This, of course, was nonsense to Tala, but the posted Suicide Help Signs made her think of mom. Would a simple sign have saved her?

Tala climbed the gate, straddling it with one leg on the

outside and one leg inside the mansion. Feeling between life and death. Between two worlds.

"Here goes nothing," she said, her adrenaline rising, concerned with treading The Sea of Trees, again.

"Put your foot here." Jax held out his hands and interlaced his fingers to boost her over the gate. Tala obliged and felt herself light as a paper plane when she went over.

"Ouch." She held her ankle. "I landed on something."

Jax sprung over the gate like a cat. "You alright?"

"I'm fine," she lied. She twisted her ankle. Possibly sprained it. She wouldn't show any sign of weakness now. She was near the bottom of the iceberg.

Makayla got over with a running start, and now they were in, only yards away from the mouth of the Sea of Trees. Cutting through would swallow them whole. No way around it. Tala analyzed the terrain. Only one way through. Straight.

"Stay close," Jax said.

"I have a baaad feeling. Let's scope it out and get out," Makayla said.

Tala saw trees, high canopy branches, bushes. What lurked in these woods, she didn't know. She took her iPhone from her back pocket and realized she still had cell signal.

She texted Valerie:

> *TALA: 1:45 A.M: WE'RE IN*
> *VAL: 1:46 A.M.: US TOO.*

VALERIE'S BLUE bubbled message came back fast, and Tala

wondered how long they had been inside. Maybe they had been in for a while.

Tala wrote back.

> TALA: 1:46 A.M.: DO U C THE
>   DEPUTY?
> VAL: 1:46 A.M.: NO. HE'S PROBABLY
>   ON DONUT BREAK LOL
> TALA: 1:48 A.M.: LOL OK GOOD MEET
>   IN FRONT OF MANSION.
> VAL: 1:48 A.M.: K
> TALA: 1:48 A.M.: DON'T K ME!
> VAL: 1:49 A.M.: LMAO, WHAT! THIS IS
>   SO SCARY! WERE GOING!

THE CURTISS MANSION was the elephant of the town, on thirty acres of deserted land. It stood how Glenn Curtiss left it after those horrible murders. After that horrible fire. The man-made lake, once home to beautiful pink flamingos and exotic birds Glenn had hand-picked himself, was now home to soot, snakes, spiders, and urban legends. That couple who jumped from the balcony of the mansion to their deaths.

Frank and Norma or was it

Candy and Ken?

God forgive them.

Mayor Sosa had contracted Bumblebee to groom the mansion, but it was a vain attempt at best. Most of it looked ignored among its wealthy residents. But why?

Tala, Jax, and Makayla trudged The Sea of Trees. The

full moon and its disciples provided their only light. They hopped over fallen logs, moving swiftly, remaining as low as possible. The mansion was breathing. It held its breath not to scare them away. No, it didn't want to scare them off.

Come inside.

It said.

Come inside.

74

TALA TRIED to push away the bad thoughts—thoughts of the mansion set afire with children burning. With Glenn's wife burning. *When you step into the mansion. The mansion steps into you.*

She steadied her breathing.

In and out.

In and out.

The air came in uneven gasps like a plane with turbulence.

Not again.

She knelt. Jax put his hand on her back.

"What's wrong?"

"Nothing," she said. Her legs refused to step forward. Her chest heaved in and out. Her hands numb.

He massaged her shoulders. "We're fine. Calm down," he said.

"Red, this is all you. We can leave. There's no one here," Makayla said.

Tala shook her head.

The words sounded foreign leaving her mouth.

"Wrong," she said, "Someone's here. There's someone watching us right now."

She rubbed the knife in her pocket.

"What is it? What's wrong?" Jax said.

Everything was wrong.

"I'm here with you okay. Just breathe." He looked concerned. Makayla was terrified. She looked around, but all she saw was darkness.

Tala hyperventilated. Her chest heaved. The white sand beach turned to black. That man who whispered into her ear was near, here, inside the mansion. Even though he was dead.

Why couldn't she stay away?

Ghosts aren't real.

"Look at me. Red, calm down," Jax said. "You're freakin' out."

He cupped her face with his palms. "Just breathe. You're safe. I'm here."

His voice sounded confident.

Her eyes met his.

"Maybe you were right. What if something bad happens?" She felt wrapped in a cloth of doom.

"I won't let anything happen to you. I promise you, Red."

She didn't believe him.

She wanted to. His eyes poured all his attention into her. It was hard to believe he could ever tell a lie.

Tala wanted to run back the way she came. Out of the Sea of Trees, so he could keep his promise, but she had come this far. She had to go on. For Yin. For Casey. For her mom. For herself.

On we go on the yellow brick road.

Maybe she was crazy. Maybe she was making connections that didn't exist.

Jax helped her up.

The shaking subsided.

"On we go," she said.

"You sure? We can head back."

"No. On we go. The wolves are here."

Tala cut through high grass. Jax followed. The chirping of crickets amplified. Not one to be seen. They too were ghosts, she thought. She heard several loud howls.

Wolves.

"You heard it?" she said. Wondering if she had gone mad.

"No fuckin' way," Jax said. "It sounds like." But he didn't say it.

They kept moving.

Ignoring eerie sounds.

A faded signpost read:

SUICIDE HOTLINE: 1-800-273-8255
THERE IS HOPE. MAKE THE CALL.

THEY MADE it to the mouth of the mansion where they had agreed to meet the rest of The Hawks. The staired porch was wooden and hollow. The double doors were high and made of steel.

They heard some laughing. This brought Makayla relief. The Hawks had made it through and were near.

"That's them!" Makayla said.

They must have caught up. Tala and Jax went toward

the cheerful voices. The mansion's monstrous facade looming behind them. Tala saw an old swing set made of wood. From afar, she saw the seats swinging up and down.

They're in. They made it.

Knowing The Hawks were together again made her feel safe.

As she got closer, she realized the cheerful voices were higher pitched than normal. There were children on the swings. The children stopped, frozen, in mid-swing, defying gravity by some miraculous feat. They panned their heads like a winding clock and stared at the trespassers.

"Why didn't you save us?" they said in unison. Their skin pale, fangs for teeth. "On we go on the yellow brick road."

The children started burning.

Tala yelled and ran back. Jax followed, she looked back to see if they were being followed. She saw no one.

"What is it?" he said. Following her back to the mansion's steps. "What did you see?"

She looked at the Sea of Trees from where she had entered this God-forsaken place and thought about going home. To Urbana.

"We can't leave," she said. More to herself.

Jax grabbed her face. "Tala! What did you see?"

She shook her head.

"What's going on with you? Where are your friends? They sold you out. I knew it. Let's get outta here."

"Go if you want. I'm staying."

"I don't want anything bad to happen to you. There's still time. Let's go," Jax pleaded. Tala felt like she had a bowling ball on her chest.

She checked her phone to see if Valerie, Lance, or Jaen had called or texted. Nothing. The reception was poor. Her phone battery was red, and she had left home with a full charge.

They heard things snapping from inside the Sea of Trees. Jax motioned to her to be quiet with one finger over his lips. Nothing. They knelt to conceal themselves behind the veranda. No sound.

When you're afraid, the mind can play tricks on you. Tricks that may lead to madness. Charlie was proof of that.

Tala stood, re-checked her phone, but it was dead. So was Jax's and Makayla's. The front door and its large windows were covered with vines. Tala eyed the area where the swing set had been, but it was gone. The children were gone too. Tala could still hear remnants of them whispering.

Why didn't you save us?

Lance, Mark, Valerie, and Jaen should have been here by now. Something had to be wrong. Tala's phone powered on again. A text from Val:

3:00 *AM: WHEN U STEP INTO THE MANSION. THE MANSION STEPS INTO U.*

THE TIME WAS WRONG, wasn't it? How long had they been here? Tala showed Jax and Makayla the message. Her phone powered off again. Jax tried his phone. Same thing. On and Off. Makayla's was off too.

"What the hell is going on?" Makayla said. "It's like someone is..."

"Controlling them," Tala finished her sentence.

Tala remembered stories of how reception dropped

inside the mansion. She had no reason to believe these myths until now. How many more were true? What lurked in these woods? What awaited inside the mansion? Vampires? Ghosts? The dark and dead as some had called them? Vengeance, Tala thought. My God,

Vengeance.

75

TALA'S INTUITION told her something was very wrong, but they were too far down the rabbit hole. Jax held her hand, shoulder to shoulder, taking slow precise steps. The moonlight and stars above them watched their every move. The night air became cooler, and Tala smelled rain coming.

Distant strikes of lightning pattered the sky like a silent film. The rain came with vengeance across the vast acreage. The soil dampened, transforming to thick mud. She looked at Jax and Makayla for comfort, but their faces bore none.

The rain brought fierce wind. She couldn't shake the feeling of being watched. Her clothes stuck to her like glue, drenched from the rain. She felt slower, like when she ran track against the wind. Her ankle felt tender and had swelled. Jax kicked and tried to force open the front door, but it was like kicking a concrete wall. When he saw it wouldn't budge, he said, "Let's try the back." The rain hadn't let up.

Tala hopped alongside the mansion with the help of Makayla and Jax, and kept her weight on the good ankle. They went to the horse stalls to use them for shelter.

The mansion was enormous.

"How's it feel?" Jax said.

"Twisted it a bit," she replied, taking her wet hair out of her face. "It's swelling."

Now they were where Ben and Sheriff Hogg had once stood. Where they hauled large trash bags onto the Bumblebee truck. Jax used his flashlight to investigate. The heavy rain pattered the shelter. They went stall to stall and found nothing but dirt and spiders' nests.

Makayla cringed when she saw the tarantulas. They crawled over the stalls. God knows how long they had been here. Jax covered Makayla's mouth when she saw a black rat the size of a mailbox. The hideous creature with red eyes stared her down. Those long yellow teeth could rip her to shreds. Nothing about this rat was normal.

Jax picked up a small rock and threw it to scare it off but missed by inches and the damn thing didn't even move. Was he blind? Jax tried again. He reached down to grab another rock, but the rat took off when it heard a loud metallic slam. They instinctively ducked down. Tala squirmed as a black widow crawled on top of the stall rail only inches from her face.

Don't you move, Jax said with his eyes. Don't you move.

They squatted lower, peered through a hole in the stall, and saw light coming from one of the stalls at the far end. The light was bright and illuminated from the ground up, indicating a possible bunker.

Tala heard some chatter but couldn't make out the words. The bunker door slammed again, and the light was gone.

"Someone's underground," Jax whispered.

Makayla nodded. "No shit, Sherlock."

Tala checked her phone again. It wouldn't turn on. Makayla did the same.

"Mine's dead too. Where are your friends?" Jax asked.

Tala shrugged.

"We don't know what we're up against. Lance had a gun, he's M.I.A. I have a flashlight and a dead phone. Don't you see? We have no offense. No weapon."

Tala mumbled. "I am the weapon."

Jax peered through the hole again, trying to see if anyone came out of the bunker. The voices were gone.

Tala feared leaving and coming back to an empty place like when she looked through the plexiglass window of Charlie's room. He was gone, as if he never even existed. As if he never came to the Curtiss Mansion. She couldn't take that chance. Yin and Casey were counting on her.

"I am the weapon," she said in a voice that sounded distant.

She rubbed the bone-handled knife Yin gave her in her left pocket. The knife was an extension of herself, just as Yin had told her.

I am the weapon.

Tala reached into her pocket with some discomfort as she remained ducked behind the stall. She showed them the knife for the first time. Mrs. Vo had asked her to carry it with her.

Honor my son.

"Where'd you get that?" Jax said.

I have my secrets too. We all do.

The chrome knife glowed a radiant blue like a light saber.

"Holy shit," Jax said.

Tala held it up, examined the blue light. Its magical glow radiated off her face.

"Why is it glowing?" Makayla asked.

"I don't know," she said. "But I like it."

76

EVERYONE KNEW the sound of a racked shotgun.

The men behind them had made no sound. In the darkness, Tala could only see the silhouette of their bodies. One pointed the shotgun at her, the other, looked like a standing grizzly bear holding an axe. By his size, she knew he could only be one man. Sheriff James Hogg.

"No one move," he said calmly, pointing the axe at them.

"What's the toy in your hand, little girl?" he said.

"Nothing," Tala said.

"Give it now."

Jax said nothing. He didn't take his eyes off the barrel.

Makayla raised her hands. "Don't shoot us."

Even in the dark Tala could now see the toothpick in his mouth, and as the gunman took a step forward, the moon's light revealed a hideous scar on his left eye. "Give it now." He took a step closer, aiming at her face. "You all are trespassing."

"Don't shoot. We're lost." Tala made no effort to give him the knife.

He pointed the shotgun at Jax, still talking to Tala.

"Give me what's in your hand before something bad happens."

"Here." Tala tossed him the knife. He caught it with one hand. Gave it an unimportant look, now that the glow was gone, and put it into his back pocket.

"This place is off limits," he said. "Step forward."

They obliged slowly with their hands up. The gunman took a couple steps back, reached to his waist for a radio.

He put it to his mouth. A red light came on by the antenna. "We have more kids down here."

"Send them in," a staticky voice responded.

More kids?

They had them. Lance, Mark, Valerie, Jaen must have been caught.

The gunman, still not much more than a silhouette in the darkness, told them to walk down the horse stalls. He didn't actually say it; he walked behind them and used the barrel hole of the shotgun to push them forward.

"Eyes forward."

They complied. When the moonlight glowed, Tala glanced back and confirmed it was Sheriff Hogg. The gunman was Deputy Hunter. That scar was new. He didn't seem like the rookie deputy who responded to Mark's house on a burglary call. He seemed different, Like someone else —evil.

77

A MIDDLE-AGED MAN bumped his head to a Pink Floyd song about not needing education. He was cruising Fairway Avenue in his white Porsche. David pulled into his driveway and parked, exhausted from his flight to California.

He checked his email on his phone and had no response from his American Airlines job app. He didn't know how much longer he could do this. Something about Dotted Blue felt perversely wrong and unsatisfying. No calls from Olivia either. He was beginning to worry. Was it something he did?

He rolled his suitcase into the house. Went to the kitchen for a beer. A habit acquired since Olivia stopped calling him. You can't always tell the truth, he told himself.

He turned on the shower and peeked into Tala's room as he had every night. He saw her sleeping in bed. Or so he thought. David left the water running and downed his beer. He went downstairs to grab another when someone knocked on the door. He looked at his watch: 2:12 A.M. Odd.

Who would . . . .

He threw a towel over his shoulder and looked out the peephole. No one. He sidestepped and looked out the crease of the window blinds and saw a little girl wearing a dirty baby blue school uniform. She was biting her hand. It was her. Had to be. He had seen her on the news, and her face was on posters throughout the town and social media. Yes, it was the same girl at Yin's house passing out Chinese lanterns. It was Casey, Jax's niece. She was panting and looked terrified. She knocked again.

He opened the door.

"She's in trouble! She's in trouble! She's in trouble!"

"What are you talking about? Calm down." He peered out his front yard looking for an adult. He confirmed this was Casey, the missing girl. The girl from the posters. Jax's niece. Yes, this was her.

"Tala's in trouble," she said.

"Tala's fine. Calm down." David knelt to her. "Tala is upstairs sleeping. Everyone is looking for you. Have you called your parents? Are you okay? Everyone's looking for you. Where were you?"

Casey shook her head no and bit her hand.

"You're Casey. Right?" David said.

She nodded.

"Tala's in trouble," she said it with a frightening certainty. The realization came in a swift panic.

Dad, she knows things. She's special.

He didn't remember running upstairs. He must've. He flipped on the light, pulled the sheets, and saw pillows, sheets, and stuffed bears.

"Damnit," he yelled. He grabbed a bear, looking at it like it would speak and confess to Tala's whereabouts. When it didn't budge, he threw it across the room.

He came back downstairs, confused. Casey stood in the living room.

"Where is she?" he yelled from the stairwell. He had gotten his phone and tried calling her.

"Don't bother. She won't pick up."

"Where is she—"

"At the Curtiss Mansion. I can show you." Casey seemed to look for a word. Going through her mind like a rolodex. "She's in DANGER!" She went on. "DANGER! DANGER! DANGER!"

David stood there in a frenzied panic.

He told Tala he would keep her safe.

"How do you know where she is?"

"DANGER! DANGER! DANGER!" Casey repeated helplessly.

"How do you know?"

"Glenn told me."

"Who's Glenn?"

Casey braced herself. David realized he was shaking her.

"I'm sorry."

"Glenn Curtiss," she said.

Glenn Curtiss? She's mad. She's sick. She's *special*.

He could hear Tala's voice in his mind.

Dad, she knows things. She's special.

David went to the kitchen, grabbed his car keys, and took Casey to his car. "Show me," he said.

He peeled out in the white Porsche, heading toward the Curtiss Mansion with the odometer rising as fast as his blood pressure.

78

Psycho Jordan told her:

The house has eyes.

That couldn't be more true. Mayor Emma Sosa saw The Hawks approaching through the Sea of Trees and by the lake from the hidden surveillance cameras installed throughout the mansion. This gave her the advantage and made a bad situation more manageable.

Having the drop on someone always helped. Everything that moved in this town was under her thumb, especially the Curtiss Mansion. The hub of her nefarious activities.

Lance, Jaen, Valerie and Mark were captured, handcuffed, and brought to the Curtiss Mansion's third floor after they were blindfolded. Hogg and Sosa had been tipped off and were expecting company. Jaen and Valerie cried as they held onto the railing and ascended the stairs. They entered a room through double doors with a painted checkered butterfly.

The third floor was Sosa and Hogg's playground, used for mind control experiments in a clandestine operation dubbed The Checkered Butterfly mind control program.

TALA, Makayla, and Jax had their hands zip tied behind their backs. Sheriff Hogg removed their blindfolds. They saw a black and white checkered floor and walls as white as cocaine. It was a facility with isolation rooms, like Citrus Hospital.

Emma Sosa stood before them wearing a white lab coat, thick framed spectacles, and her iconic crew cut. She looked more intellectual and sophisticated but indifferent to them, like she was about to write them a prescription. Sheriff Hogg walked over to a computer station at the far end of the room and leaned his axe against the wall. He took Tala's knife from his back pocket and put it on the table.

"Tala, I'm sorry for everything you've been through. I tried to give you a chance. I helped your father a long time ago by making Yona's murder look like a suicide," she said. "All these years later, I need a pilot. David owes me his life. His freedom. So here you are," Sosa said.

Tala looked around. "What is this place?"

"Tala. Focus. Did you hear me? David killed your mother," she said.

"No. What are you—" How could she get out of this mess? What was this place?

"No more lies, Tala," Sosa said. "We needed a new pilot to fly assets in and out of different states. David owed us a favor. He killed your mother. All we did was cover it up. Why do you think you're in this town? Why would David come back? Why would he come back to a place that brought him so many bad memories?"

"That's a lie! You're liars!" Tala yelled. "Where are my friends?"

Jax and Makayla were no longer behind her. Where had they gone? Everything seemed so slow.

"We own Dotted Blue, Tala. David works for us. We hired him. Recruited him."

"No. No." Tala shook her head, but she had read the article from the *Miami New Times*.

Sosa came closer. Every footfall echoed like an amplified hypnotic beat. Sosa held her phone up. Showing Tala the same article on how she purchased Dotted Blue. Emma Sosa. New CEO, for 2.1 million.

"After David confessed of shooting your mom, I had to make a choice. I tried to help *you*. I told him about Richard Moss. I hoped Richard, my professor at Harvard, could help you cope with your mother's death. You were just a little girl. How could you live a normal life after what you'd seen? Yona wanted a divorce. David GPS'ed her car. He was stalking her. She was having an affair. He put the pieces together. The puzzle was infidelity."

"These are lies." Tala felt like she had a hole inside her chest. "I read the police reports," she said defensively. "There was nothing about an affair. Nothing like that."

"Oh, Tala. Don't be naive. You're not following. David came to me. We were friends from high school. James, pass me the folder." Hogg obliged. Sosa opened a manila folder and gave it to her. "Read the reporting officer. Detective Emma Sosa #1848, Miami Beach Homicide. I wrote the report. I had to make a choice; arrest David for murder and toss you head-first into foster care or look the other way and give you a somewhat normal life."

Hogg walked behind her, and she felt the zip ties open. She felt a tingling sensation as blood flowed to her fingers. Tala opened the manila folder. She scanned down to the reporting officer.

Detective Emma Sosa #1848. Miami Beach PD. Homicide Unit.

Tala felt her legs give. No. This couldn't be true.

"I'm sorry, but that's the truth," Sosa interjected.

"He loved her," Tala said. Her mind raced.

Sosa and Hogg shook their heads like they felt sorry for her.

"We do terrible things for those we love," Hogg said.

"I know you're doctors. I know you did something to Jamal and Rodnam," she said.

Sosa smiled, looking a bit surprised.

"My my, little red riding hood. Aren't you the little detective? But do you know what he did to me?" she said.

Sosa bit her lip. "You see, it doesn't matter how fast you run. Eventually the wolves catch you."

"How do you know—" she said.

"What did you do to Jamal and Rodnam? Did you brain zap them like you did Charlie? Is that why they shot those people? You killed Charlie didn't you? And Nurse Marjorie?"

Tala wanted to stall. She realized she had no out. She felt lightheaded and uncoordinated.

Deputy Hunter appeared to be in a hypnotic trance. Tala wanted to call out to him, but there was no one there. Not the deputy who had told her to get Casey some ice cream.

"Tala," Sheriff Hogg said. "We turned Rodnam into Psycho Jordan because he was a bad man. The world is trying to control your mind every day. What to buy. What to wear. What to say. What to think. Who to vote for. It's a constant attack. We're using government research. We've all been hurt by guns. All of us. Even you. We're ending it. We're putting the second amendment to bed and stopping gun violence once and for all. We're making America great again."

"You're brainwashing people, aren't you?" she said. "You're ending gun violence by *making* gun violence?"

"David was right. You are smart," Sosa said.

"And Psycho Jordan happened to volunteer for your little experiments?"

"No. He was chosen. It was the least he could do."

"What about Jamal? He was chosen too? Where are my friends? What are you going to do to us?" She asked. Wanting to know the answer. Hoping to stall.

"Whatever has to be done."

"People will know we're missing. A group of teenagers can't just disappear from a small town. People will talk. They'll know something's wrong."

"We'll be sure to let the town know what happened. We'll tell them what to believe and how to feel about it. We'll spin a story. The Hawks left a note. They were leaving home. A mass runaway. People will understand. Kids do stupid stuff all the time. Sometimes they never come back. And if they do, they're not the same." Sheriff Hogg chuckled. "Just ask Charlie."

Tala felt the tentacles of fear crawl up her spine.

She ran back to the butterfly doors that were bolted shut. She didn't have the energy to unlock the doors. Her hands were frail and numb. What had they done to her?

"Help! Let me out of here! HELP!"

"It's no use, Tala," Sosa said. "There's only one way out for you." She stepped aside, pointing to the balcony doors behind her that led to a three-story fall.

Sosa said, "I'm sorry about what David did. I thought I made the right choice. Your friends don't know why they're here. They think they've been stopped for trespassing and they're waiting for us to call their parents. Make it easy. If you jump, we'll let them go. They'll move on. They'll be sad, of course, because of what you did, but they'll move on and have somewhat normal lives. We don't care about them. They're just another brick in the wall."

Tala was crying. Her body shaking.

"Come on, Tala," said Hogg. "You don't want to end up like this." He pointed at Deputy Hunter, who stood sentinel like a mindless zombie.

"No, I don't."

"I'm giving you this courtesy because Yona was a good person. You should be with her."

Something from the 1984 computer surveillance station caught Hunter's attention. He looked at the CCTV video. He opened the balcony door, stepped onto the parapet looking over the rail.

"Doctor. We have a problem," he called out.

"What is it now?" Sosa stepped onto the parapet. She saw a car speeding toward them.

"James! Bring up the cameras!"

Hogg sat at the 1984 surveillance station and started clicking and clacking on a keyboard connected to several monitors in the corner of the room. The 1984 surveillance station was one of their greatest achievements. It allowed audio and video surveillance from every camera in Miami Springs. Hogg used a ball to maneuver the cameras and zoomed in.

"It's...David," he said.

"Good," Sosa said. "He's right on time."

TALA'S HEAD pounded like a sledgehammer. The Hawks had been put into separate isolation rooms. Divide and conquer. The rooms had two-way mirrors.

"What are we going to do about good ole Dave?" said Hogg.

"Leave him out of this. Let us go," Tala said. "He's calling the police."

"We are the police. We're your government. We monitor every camera in this town. Everything in Springs is under our control," Sosa said.

Tala looked around. "What's the point of all this?"

Sosa said, "We have Mount Everest ambitions into the human mind."

Hunter looked at the infrared surveillance video. "He's getting closer."

Hunter's voice sounded unusual, almost mechanical. His southern accent was gone.

Sosa heard him but ignored him.

"Tala, do you believe there are things in life we're better off not knowing? Like what I told you about your daddy killing mom and coming to me for help? Would you have been better off not knowing?"

"That's a lie. My dad would never have done that. He loved her. He cried for her."

"Tears of guilt, maybe. Tears of joy for getting away with murder. For not losing you. For not rotting in prison. Men like David don't make it in prison."

David parked.

"He's on the porch. Trying to look in the windows," Hunter said. "Looks like he's alone."

Sosa ignored him. Hogg walked over to look.

Tala played Sosa's game and ignored the comment about her dad. Maybe they would let him leave.

"Thinking you're someone you're not makes you feel odd and alone. I take it you've experienced the feeling of not belonging. Never having a home. Being teased. The Suicide Girl. It must hurt. *That girl* whose mom off'd herself. It hasn't been easy. Yona didn't hate you. She loved you but David took her away from you."

"He's knocking on the door," Hogg said.

"The doors and windows are bolted shut. He'll never make it inside. Stop worrying."

Sosa took a few steps toward Tala. She stood directly in front of her.

She grinded her teeth. "How did he know you were here?"

"He doesn't know anything."

Sosa chuckled an uneasy laugh.

"I'm not holding him. He's outside. He's free to go."

"He's trying to make a call," Hogg said. He watched him on the night vision surveillance cameras.

"The cell scramblers are up and running," Hunter said.

"De-activate them," Sosa said. "Let him make his call."

Hogg shifted his massive weight from one leg to the other.

"Em, what are you trying to do here?"

"Let's see what he does. Let's see if he calls his little red riding hood."

"That's not a good idea," Hogg said.

She nodded at Deputy Hunter, "Do it."

Hunter deactivated them. Within a minute, Tala's phone was vibrating and ringing on the 1984 table.

Sosa walked over to it. She didn't answer but texted David back:

> I'm sorry I snuck out. I went to a friend's house. I'm fine. Sorry! Don't worry. I'll be home soon. Love you Dad

How could Sosa have known Tala never texted her dad? David despised text messages, and she hadn't texted him she loved him in years.

Sosa and Hogg saw David get into his car and drive around the mansion. They followed him on the surveillance cameras like a hawk in the sky stalking its prey.

"What is good ole Dave up to?" Hogg said.

Tala's phone got a text.

Sosa read it aloud.

"I'm looking for you, Tala. Where are you?"

Tala was scared she might never see him again. She pushed away the seed that Sosa planted in her mind. David didn't kill mom. He also never called her by her name. He was either very mad or sending a subtle message.

He had to know something was wrong.

Hogg told Sosa, "Don't write back. Let him go before this gets worse."

Sosa was a little agitated by their current predicament. This was a problem. An inconvenience. Things had been flowing so smoothly before Tala arrived.

They saw David drive around the mansion, then exit the same way he came.

"He's leaving," Hogg said.

Tala felt her heart sink in relief and fear.

They had no reason to keep her alive.

80

David parked in his driveway, questioning his own sanity. He promised God he'd stop drinking. There had been a missing girl on his doorstep. It was Jax's niece. It was Casey. The girl on the news. She had told him Tala was at the Curtiss Mansion and she was in trouble.

Casey had yelled DANGER! DANGER!

He had driven with her to the Curtiss Mansion. He parked and told her to stay in the car as he walked around looking for some sign Tala might be there. When he came back to the car, she was gone. In that moment he questioned if she was ever there to begin with? He'd been drinking more. Sleeping less.

He wasn't crazy.

Was he?

He looked at his phone in frustration. His mind felt like a vacuum that sucked up all the things he'd never understand. Those doors and windows seemed suspiciously secure for an abandoned house. Circling the mansion gave him an eerie feeling, much like when he was a kid. When he was afraid of the dark. The Curtiss Mansion was still the neighborhood haunted house, but he was an adult now, damnit. He shouldn't be scared.

His phone lit up as he checked his message from Tala.

Love you Dad.

That wasn't something Tala would write. Regardless of how much trouble she'd be in. She knew he *hated* text messages and he'd always told her to call him. I want to hear your voice, he'd say. It felt wrong. Perversely wrong.

He got out of the car, his mind spun like a hurricane. He saw Benny's porch light off. He decided to knock on his door for some unfathomable reason.

Maybe Mark knows something.

Ben had offered help after he dropped him off from the hospital. David brought his hand to his abdomen and felt the soreness and raised skin from the stitches.

He stood on Ben's porch, thinking; embarrassed. What kind of father doesn't know where his daughter is at this hour? Jesus. He was going to ground her for eternity. He looked around. The neighborhood was dark and quiet as a tomb.

He didn't know what else to do. He'd toss and turn all night if he tried to sleep knowing Tala was out. What was the deal with Casey? She surely hadn't come to his house. She'd been missing. He was seeing things. Should he tell someone?

He knocked on Ben's door weakly, like he hadn't committed to wake anyone. Before he knocked again, the front door opened slightly.

"Dave, is that you?"

To David's surprise, Ben was dressed. He had on work jeans, t-shirt, and rainboots. He let the door open all the way and brought his arm from around his back, brandishing a silver revolver.

Ben scratched his beard. "Is she gone too?"

"Yeah." David wrapped his mind around Mark and Tala both being gone. They were probably together. But Yin is gone too, and the conclusion seems to be that no, he's not coming back.

The neighborhood's not as safe as it used to be.

"What are you gonna do with that?" David eyed the gun.

Ben looked at the gun with reverie. "It's quarter past two, someone's knocking on the door. Thought it might be a bad guy," he said. His tone was odd and distant. His words had no real emotion.

"You're not a bad guy, are you, Dave?"

David shook his head. "No. I suppose I'm not."

"Is she like her mother?" Ben asked.

"What?" He was thrown off by the question. His attention, for some reason, was fixated on the revolver.

"Was Tala like her mom?" Ben said.

David nodded and gave a short laugh. "Yeah, tenacious as hell."

Ben looked at the gun in his hand like he wasn't sure how it got there. His mind in a faraway place.

"There's something I have to tell you," he said.

David waited for what seemed like a long time.

"I think you better come inside."

81

Ben invited him in and started the coffee machine. David felt smothered by the slain deer and boar heads on the walls. Sometimes little things reminded you of things you've tried to stow away in the drawers of your mind. Like the bear rugs on the floor made him think of Yona because her maiden name was Highbear.

Yona Highbear Stone.

Ben came back from the kitchen, handed David a mug of coffee and sat. The coffee cup shook in his hand and spilled some onto his pants.

"Remember when we used to go to the mansion as kids? Tell ghost stories. Drink. Just shoot the shit under the stars."

David nodded. "Yeah, I hated that place. Gave me the creeps."

"We were all scared. But that was the spot. Dunno If I told ya this, but I got my first blowjob there." Ben smiled. "I felt like I became a man there. Then time happened. We graduated from Hialeah and I went to the Marines. Haven't felt like a man since."

"What are you talking about, Benny? You're a decorated war vet. You're a hero."

"I ain't no hero! I'm a goddamn fraud. I didn't save anyone. I hid. I hid like a coward and, when they found me, they assumed I had heroically battled off a rebel group in Kuwait. I hid, that's what I did. My commanding officers inferred differently. They figured I had fought off forty rebels and miraculously survived the exchange. They didn't know. And I didn't tell them." He took a long sip of his coffee.

David felt unease wash over him.

"You think Red and Mark are together?"

"I know they are, Dave. Mark's been talking about the mansion more than ever. I've always kept him away. But lately, I can't control him. I'm afraid Tala has gotten under his skin. You're right, she's tenacious like hell."

"Yona always said Tala had the bear inside. It was a Cherokee saying that she's tough and full of heart."

Ben looked at the rugs below them. "Bears can be killed."

David didn't like his tone. "What are you saying, Benny? Where are they?"

"They're at the Curtiss Mansion. Aren't you listening?"

David shook his head.

"I just came from there. The doors and windows are bolted shut."

Ben didn't seem to hear him.

He said, "We dreamed of living here in the Springs, across the canal with the rich folk. I started a business, worked my ass off, networked. I met the right people, business took off. But then the crash came. Economy went to shit, I lost everything. I was weeks from foreclosure. How could that happen? Then the honorable Mayor

Emma Lesbian Sosa and her minions came to the rescue. She passed legislation to restore the Curtiss Mansion. She put a landscaping contract up for bid. I entered the bidding war. It's supposed to be a community center or something, who knows. Maybe a place for the rich wives to gather and gossip about their husbands while doing yoga."

David sat up straight.

"What's your point? You're rambling."

It's true. He was rambling, and he wouldn't stop shifting in his chair. He looked about ready to break into a sweat. He opened a drawer and took out a bottle of Four Roses bourbon. He grabbed David's cup of coffee and poured some in. He then poured in his. This made David nervous.

Ben went on.

"The mayor gave me the contract. She said she wanted to keep the money in house. I figured she wanted a kick-back, it wouldn't have been the first time I paid a politician. But she didn't. Never asked for a dime. I needed the money bad. Emma made it clear that I was to work the land but stay clear of the house. She said to show up a couple times a week. Work slowly. *This is just smoke and mirrors* she said. *Make the town think you're working. That's all you have to do.* I don't know what they're doing there, but I've been around long enough to know you should be fearful when politicians want you to look the other way."

"What? You think it's drugs or something illegal?" David said.

Ben looked on edge. He ran his fingers through his thinning hair.

"Well, they're not making cupcakes. I don't ask questions. All I know is I was told to look the other way, and I've been paid handsomely for it. It kept me in Springs. I did it for Mark. The check's always on time and never bounces."

No, David thought, you did it for yourself.

David sipped his coffee. The bourbon was welcoming.

"So the mayor paid you to look away so she could use the house to sell drugs?" David chuckled and almost burst out laughing. "You're kidding, right?"

"I think it may be worse."

"Listen." David downed the coffee fast. "If Tala is there, I'm going to get her."

"Dave, if our kids are there, they're in danger. And if you went there tonight, believe me. They know you're coming. They have cameras everywhere. The whole town is controlled. Sosa runs everything. When I called you and told you I saw Tala running by the mansion, I did so because I got a call. They're always watching. They told me to keep her away."

"Who called you?"

"Sheriff. His drones are always watching."

"What makes you think they went to the Curtiss Mansion?" David said, he needed answers.

David regarded politicians as white-collar thieves. He understood kickbacks and payoffs but anything else left them exposed. Most wouldn't get their hands dirty like that. It was unnecessary and risky.

"They're at the mansion, Dave. I'm worried. Everything was fine. Mark knew better. But now, now I'm worried."

Ben slowly reached behind his back. For a second, David thought he was reaching for the gun. He pulled out a small piece of folded paper instead. He tossed it across the table to him.

David unfolded the paper.

> Dad, if I'm not back soon, I'm at the Curtiss
> Mansion with Tala. Don't worry. Sorry.

"Where did you find this?"

"On top of his pillow. I crack open his bedroom door every night when I get up. I'm not much of a sleeper. Not since I went into business with the mayor, anyway. Mark's almost grown, but I like to know he's there, you know."

David nodded. He did the same with Tala.

"I've been warned not to let anyone on the property." He looked on the verge of crying.

"What kind of trouble are they in?" David said, getting to his feet.

Ben didn't respond. He was somewhere in a faraway place.

"Hey! I'm talking to you! What kind of trouble?" Ben looked up at David like if it was the first time he'd seen him.

David grabbed Ben by the collar and pulled him up off the chair.

"WHAT KIND OF TROUBLE?"

"The never come home kind. The disappear kind. The Yin kind."

"I needed the money. I was going under," he said defensively.

David was frustrated but needed more info.

"What have you done?" he asked. As if patronizing a child. "What *the hell* have you done?"

"I've looked the other way. This is my punishment. A lot of people have to know." He could have been talking to himself.

"We all just look away. See no evil. Hear no evil. Speak no evil. Right? That's what we all do. We're all guilty."

Ben whimpered like a scared child. He reached into his waistband again, turning to the side so he could take the gun out of his pocket. David felt uncomfortable watching a man crying with a gun in his hand. What the hell had Tala gotten into?

Ben started petting the gun timidly. He smiled. His mind—God knows where.

"You're not going to shoot me, are you?" David said. Half jesting. Half not. He was trying to read him. Reading him now was like cracking a cicada puzzle.

"Don't you want to find Mark? If Mark and Tala are in real trouble. We need to get to them. Can you help me get to them?"

Ben, who had been looking at the gun, finally looked up at him.

"Yeah. I'll help you." He turned the gun over and offered it to David.

"Take this one. I've got another in the truck."

David took a tentative step forward and reached for it, taking the gun. He felt an immense sense of relief when he had control of the weapon.

"Am I going to need this?" David said. Feeling like coming to Miami Springs was the biggest mistake he'd ever made.

Ben ignored his question.

"Get in the truck," he said.

82

EMMA SOSA STARED into the soundproof padded rooms wondering how this could have happened. Everything she'd worked for was in jeopardy because of a group of teenagers. They were sound asleep thanks to a mild tranquilizer, had been for almost two hours.

"The kids should be waking up any minute," Hogg said.

"What did you do to my friends?" Tala demanded.

Hogg walked over and pushed her down onto the chair. "Sit, and behave."

"They're fine. We injected them with a serum to calm them down." Sosa smiled. "Don't worry. They won't remember any of this. Neither will you."

Tala said, "Let them go! This is my fault. My fault alone."

Sosa walked over to the surveillance monitors, grabbed a small remote. When she pressed a button, all the two-way mirrors became translucent, and Tala could see her friends inside different rooms like caged animals. She thought of Charlie Owens in his padded room. Was it so different?

Why is this happening? This is my fault.

She couldn't remember how she got here. She didn't know where they were. Her vision was somewhat blurry. Her mind felt warped, but she felt dirty and exposed, and she didn't know why. Had she been drugged as well? Had they *touched* her?

The feelings she had long ago in Urbana were back and sharper than ever. *Your mother killed herself because of you. You'll always be the suicide girl. You're worthless.* She felt like she was on that 757 Boeing and it was nose diving. *Kill yourself. End it now. Kill yourself. End it now. The wolves are near, Tala. The wolves are here.*

She saw Sosa and Hogg as wolves. The wolves who have been chasing her through a dark wood, the same dark wood as before, and now she was sure the dark wood was the Sea of Trees. It had always been The Sea of Trees; she just didn't know it.

"Tala." Hogg smiled.

His wicked smile made her want to vomit.

What have they done to me? My God. What have they done?

"How are you feeling?" Hogg said.

Sosa was observing her. She held a clipboard. Checking things off a list, Tala imagined. She saw a small bandage on her arm where she suspected a needle with serum had gone through her vein. Much like her friends. Except she wasn't in a padded room like them. Her legs felt like concrete blocks. She couldn't move them. *She couldn't run from wolves. They were faster. They could smell you. They had found her.* She was paralyzed.

She tried to talk, but she drooled instead. She was just talking minutes ago. Now it seemed impossible. Like her jaw and brain were on different wavelengths. Her arms felt like spaghetti.

"Relax, little red riding hood. Or the wolves will come and blow your house down!" Hogg said, cracking that wicked smile. He was wearing a white doctor's overcoat, as was Sosa. The mayor put the clipboard down and shook her head slightly.

"Knock it off," she said. "She's been through enough. The boss isn't going to like it. We need to clean this mess up."

"Are you going to kill me?" Tala managed. It came out like she was talking underwater.

Hogg mumbled under his breath, "Not if you do it yourself."

Tala knew she was drugged. Her vision was blurry. She was in and out of awareness.

But heard him loud and clear.

After some time, Tala managed to say, "I just want to goooo home."

"Ah, there's no place like home, is there? But where is home?" said Sosa. "The house on Fairway? Or the house in Urbana?"

"How do—"

"I know everything Tala."

She looked at Sosa and Hogg in their white coats. Her body felt like jello.

Hogg chimed in, "I'm going to ask you a series of questions now. And you're going to answer with the truth. If you don't. Things will get very bad for you and your friends."

Her lips felt swollen and numb. "What are you going to do to me?"

What have they done to me?

Sosa walked to the wall that divided the rooms with the two-way glass, translucent. Tala saw Valerie, Jaen, Lance, Jax, Makayla and Mark tied up. Deputy Hunter whose scar looked more pronounced stood to the side like a mannequin. An engineered droid. They were calling him by a different name, but Tala couldn't make it out. Everything was distorted.

"Come take a look." Hogg waved her on.

"I can't—"

"No feeling in your legs yet. My apologies. That should wear off soon," Sosa said.

Sosa pointed at the ceiling. Hogg went to the 1984 computer surveillance station. He grabbed a small remote control, pressed a button, and a large HD display came down from the ceiling showing surveillance video from all the rooms. The Curtiss Mansion compound split into various screens.

Tala saw her friends wearing a sort of dog collar on their necks.

"The collar makes them compliant," Hogg said.

"Every time you lie, I press the red button." He showed her the remote.

Jaen was sitting with her legs crossed. Valerie and Lance were both standing, pacing back and forth inside their respective isolation rooms, and Lance was headbutting the glass. There was no sound at all. The rooms were soundproof. Her friends looked like they were underwater, their lips moving but nothing could be heard.

"I'm not going to answer anything until you let them go."

Sosa smiled. That politician's smile. The one that got her elected twice. The one plastered on every billboard in town.

"Here's a reminder of who's in control." She raised the remote slowly to her eye level and pressed the button.

Jaen, Makayla, Lance, Jax, Mark, and Valerie shocked instantly and simultaneously. An unknown amount of electrical current was delivered to their nervous system from their collars. Lance and Valerie who were pacing fell flat to the ground, in what appeared to be agonizing pain. Jaen and Jax did the same, fell on their sides, the grimaces on their faces made it evident they were badly hurt.

Tala hopped over to the screen with her swollen ankle. Most of the feeling had returned in her legs.

"What are you, crazy?"

"You'll do as I say. Or I'll press the button. I'll press the button until one of them dies if I must, but I'll get the truth. Are we clear, little red riding hood?"

"Yes," Tala said.

"Who knows you're here?"

"No one knows."

Sosa pressed another button and the rooms were audible. She heard Valerie and Jaen crying.

This bitch wants me to hear them screaming.

She heard their excruciating high-pitched wails, banging on the glass, begging to be freed.

Lance and Jax were also yelling, "Get us out of here!"

"Let's try again. Who knows you're here Tala?"

"Stop please!"

"Wrong answer!"

Sosa pressed the button again.

Tala heard a wicked zap, like some high-powered electric line had fallen and was writhing on the ground while sparking. She saw her friends fall again and grip their collars; the shocks lasted an insurmountable amount of time.

"STOP IT PLEASE!" Tala yelled. "I'm telling you the truth! STOP!"

"Lower your voice, Tala. You wouldn't want to wake the other side of me." Sosa's eyes were like burning coals, and there was no other place Tala would rather be, than home. In Urbana.

"Good Ole Dave was here looking for you. Someone told him." Hogg said, like he was cross examining her.

"I don't know why he came here. I didn't tell him anything. I swear to God I'm telling the truth!"

"God betrayed me long ago. Swearing on him means nothing. Why are you here? Why have you been hovering around this place?" Sosa said.

"I don't know."

Sosa pressed the button.

She heard the wicked shock from the electrical current flowing through their bodies, bouncing off their bones in a hideous jolt of pain. All Tala could do was watch. Watch as her responses resulted in pain.

"PLEASE STOP!" she yelled. "PLEASE. I'm answering your questions." She cried.

"I need better answers."

"Since I got here. People have been talking about it. How it's haunted. Its history. Glenn Curtiss killing his family."

"What did you find, Tala?"

"I found two of the kids who killed themselves here, jumped off the roof. Like my mother did. I thought it was linked, somehow."

Sosa's cellphone was going off. She took it from her pocket. But kept her eyes on Tala. Hogg was at the 1984 station watching the exchange, looking uncomfortable.

Sosa answered, "Yes, sir, they're all here." She took a deep breath. "Yes of course. We'll keep this contained. You just give the order."

83

THE CAMERAS WOULD SEE them coming and kill the element of surprise. Benny's plan convinced David to hide in the bed of his truck. David did so, clutching the revolver to his chest. He was sure he was headed toward something bad. He'd never seen another man so afraid. What had Benny gotten himself into? Now Tala was in the middle of that web.

He was too.

He felt the imperfections of the road, the truck hopped up and down, and he thought maybe Miami Springs wasn't perfect after all. But now while lying on the truck-bed, clutching a firearm to his chest and feeling the potholes on the road, he felt silly to ever imagine a perfect anything.

The closest thing to perfection he'd ever seen was the day Tala was born. His own creation. He guessed every father felt that way. The truck slowed every time they approached a stop sign. He felt like they might've arrived, which terrified him. The truck jutted forward again, and he felt better, there was more road to travel, more time to think.

After a few more of these stop and go's he realized Benny had parked.

Ben turned off the truck. David felt the driver's door open. They were at the Curtiss Mansion. If Ben was right, there were eyes in the sky. David remembered a fleeting line from a book he read years ago and hadn't thought about since. "The art of all warfare is based on deception." There was no deception. No real advantage. The enemy knew they were here.

Ben pulled out his cell phone, put it on speaker, and leaned against the top covered truck bed. David heard the phone ringing and listened intently.

Hogg answered.

"This is a bad time," a voice said into the phone.

"Where's Mark?" Ben said.

Hogg watched Ben on surveillance video. He stood yards from the front door of the mansion, leaning on his truck. He was alone.

"I'm here for Mark," he said.

"You should know where your boy is, Ben. Have you reported him missing?"

"Don't play stupid, James. I know he's here. I'll be taking him home is all."

David was hiding in the bed of the truck, listening intently to Benny's call.

"I'm sure Mark is fine. He's probably out causing trouble with The Hawks. You know, boys will be boys."

"James. Open the door. C'mon, man."

"Think about what you're doing, Ben. I'm trying to level with you. The boss is on his way. If he sees you here, this is going to get ugly. Turn around and leave. Mark will be fine. Let it be."

"I know he's here, James. Open or I'll call the police, and

no, not your twisted minions. I'll go across the canal if I have to. Hialeah Police will be here with Channel 7 on their tail. I'll bring so much light to this place you'll think it's the county fair."

David leaned himself as close as possible to the side of the truck and continued to listen, clutching the gun to his chest.

"You threatening me, Benny?"

"Mark needs to come home is all. Him and Tala won't be back."

He heard a hoarse voice now, coming from the speaker phone.

"Ben, you stupid man. I wouldn't hurt Mark, you know that. But he was trespassing, and you know how the mayor feels about that."

"I'm here now. I'll take him off your hands is all. I'll make sure him and the redhead never come back."

There were a few seconds of silence. Had he hung up?

"Hello?" Ben said.

David realized Hogg hung up.

Ben said, "Be cool, David. He's coming."

David was sweating profusely.

The sheriff went downstairs to open the door. David started to think, if Hogg opened the door and let Ben in, he'd be stuck out here. He had been here hours before and tried to see if he could get inside, but the doors and windows were bolted. He wouldn't be able to get back in, so the plan was for Ben to unlock the rear of the truck bed so David could get out and they could rush one of them, two against one. It was too bad Hogg was the size of three men.

"Let me out," David said. "Quick! Before he comes."

He couldn't see anything, but Ben had to be standing outside. He just heard him on the phone.

"Ben! Damn it! Let me out, man." He was basically yelling and all he got in return was cold silence. The fear inside began to spread. The wheels inside his mind rotated and began to take him down a dark corridor.

"BENNY! OPEN THE FUCKING TRUCK, MAN!"

This was the last thing he said. The corridor became darker, colder and now he knew. He knew he was betrayed.

"I'm sorry, David. I can't. They have Mark. I lost one son, I can't lose another."

"What about Tala, YOU BASTARD? Let me out!"

"Hey hey now," Hogg said in a mocking tone. He was standing next to the truck with Ben. Piercing his brown eyes with a look of disdain.

"How did you fuck up this big?" said Hogg. "Emma is furious. And the boss is coming. This is a shit show."

"I don't know what got into the kid. He knows better. It's Tala."

Hogg slapped the bed of the truck. "He's in here?"

"Yeah, he's in the truck. I brought him before he did something stupid. Just like I said."

"Good man," Hogg said. He looked relieved.

"How did he know she's here?"

"I don't know. He told me he had a feeling."

"Did you also have a *feeling*?"

"No. Mark left me a note. He said he would be here in case I woke up so I wouldn't worry."

"Well, thanks for calling. They're both safe," Hogg said.

"Let's see how we can fix this. Okay?"

"Don't hurt my son," Ben blurted. Looking straight into Hogg's hateful eyes.

"Jesus, Ben, you're acting like we're not friends. I wouldn't hurt the kid. You just need to understand we do serious work here. We have to protect that work. We don't want to hurt anyone, especially not Mark, especially when his dad is one of our friends." Hogg smiled and patted him on the shoulder. In the dark, his smile looked like a weasel's.

"What are we gonna do about David?" He looked at the tailgate of the truck.

David had gone silent. He felt played. Betrayed. Lied to. Confused. All the feelings he felt when he learned Yona had killed herself. He never knew her. He never knew Ben, either. He never knew anyone. Not even his daughter.

"Did you check him for weapons?"

"Yeah, but there's no reason he'd be armed. He doesn't own a gun. He's scared of his own shadow."

84

Hogg walked to the rear of the truck bed.

"Give me your keys."

Ben tossed them to him.

Hogg unlocked the tailgate, raised the bed cover. David was lying down, curled up like a scared child.

"Get out, David."

David started to slide out, yelling at Ben, "You lying snake."

"Sorry, but Mark's in there," Ben said, looking shameful.

Hogg gave him a disappointed smile. "C'mon, all the way out. Get out of the truck, Dave."

David complied. The gun was on the small of his back, under his shirt.

"I don't know what's going on here," David said. "I just want Tala."

"Tala is fine, Dave, relax. She was just trespassing. No big deal. I'm more interested in why you're hiding in the back of the truck. We were about to call you so you could take her home, but Tala refused to give us your phone number." Hogg took an animated breath like it's been a long night and he wanted to get two dumb teenagers home.

"Emma is inside giving them a lecture on the importance of respecting private property. You guys can get them and go. It's not a big deal. We won't be arresting them for breaking in."

"Why would the mayor be here?" David said.

"Emma saw them hopping over and called me. She was driving home."

David didn't like what he was selling. Ben didn't look convinced either. Hogg had an answer for everything. He put a wad of tobacco into his mouth.

Something was off, alright. Ben wouldn't have made him hide in the truck for nothing. He was terrified coming here.

Hogg looked at David with a strange and concerned face.

"Jesus, David, what's that?" He looked bewildered, pointing at his face. David defensively touched his face.

"What?"

"Jesus, Dave, don't move. I think it's... it looks like—" He stepped closer to him, analyzing his face.

David heard a loud wisp, like a spray. His eyes instinctively shut. He felt intense burning in his eyes, excruciating pain, and immediately felt stupid. He couldn't see, but he heard Hogg chuckle.

"My eyes! It's BURNING!" David fell to his knees.

Hogg said, "Don't exaggerate. It's only five million Scoville units of law enforcement grade pepper spray!"

Hogg's chuckle blossomed into a full throaty laugh. "God, you're something else, Dave. Good ole Dave." David tasted the pepper, his face felt like it was doused in gasoline and someone had lit a match to it.

David was on the ground, rubbing his eyes in agonizing pain, trying to remove the chemical from his eyes.

The more he rubbed, the more it hurt.

"Sonofabitch!" he said. He never felt anything like it.

———

BEN JUST WATCHED, unsure of what to do or say. Hogg put the spray into his pocket and reached behind his back. For a second, Ben feared he was reaching for a gun. Hogg revealed handcuffs instead.

He tossed them to Ben. "Cuff him. Let's go."

Benny cuffed David with little resistance. David was completely disabled. His tears and boogers were intertwined, and all he could do was spit as he knelt on the ground like a sinner at church. Thank God Ben cuffed him to the front. He could still rub his eyes.

David screamed in agony as he writhed on the ground. Hogg hefted him up to his feet.

"Steady now, Dave, you'll be fine." He looked at Ben. "You did good. Let's get him inside before the boss gets here."

———

THE THREE MEN walked into the Curtiss Mansion. Two as prisoners, but only one knew it.

85

LIKE DAVID, Benny had grown up in Hialeah, hearing tales of the notorious Curtiss Mansion and its many ghosts, goblins, and vampires. These stories were favorites on Halloween. Like most kids, Dave and Benny used to sneak onto the property. He had a moment of deja vu. Had this already happened?

Why was he back here?

Ben knew the house was being used for *something bad*. That was the deal. All he had to do was look the other way.

See no evil.

He did his best not to get involved. But it all turned to shit when Tala got here. Ben was more involved than he cared to admit. He was a loose end dangerous people usually cut.

"Just shut up and cash the checks," he had told himself. Money will change most men. Ben was no exception. He enjoyed his fake life in this fake town.

Sosa and Hogg kept him in Springs. Moving back to Hialeah was a sign of failure. How bad had he fucked up by looking the other way? He promised himself, if he got out of this, he'd move. He was leaving Miami Springs for good. He would even go back to the Wynken Blynken and Nod Trailer Park in Hialeah where he came from.

He was following Hogg up the spiraled staircase, walking in front, David cuffed and half-blind. He remembered playing hide and seek here as a kid with other Prairie Boys, most of them dead or in prison. He wasn't positive, but he was pretty sure he was here with David once. Now they were back. Time traveled as their future selves for some ungodly reason.

Up he went, step by step. He passed the second floor and saw the silent flashes of lightning outside. Up he went. The walk was slow. David hung on to the rail and stepped up to an unknown fate. Yona went up stairs too. Before she...

David was still blinded. Eyes tearing.

Up they went.

Ben's mind was racing. Hogg behind him.

I'm a loose end.

You don't have to be a tailor to know loose ends usually get cut.

"All the way to the top," said the man holding the gun. "To the third floor. I'm going to show you your kids. I'm going to show you what we've been doing here."

86

WHEN THEY MADE it to the third floor, David's eyes were still tearing, but he began to see glimpses of light. He thought he saw two large doors spray painted with a checkered butterfly, but he must've been hallucinating. He walked into an area that had been completely renovated and modernized.

The antique architecture of the mansion was no more. Instead, David seemed to have stepped into a modern laboratory. A labyrinth with different rooms with foreign instruments. The walls were perfect white. The floor looked like a masonic lodge with large black and white checkered tiles.

David forced his eyes open through stinging pain and saw Tala, Mayor Sosa, and Sheriff Hogg standing in the middle of the third floor.

TALA ALMOST RAN but felt Hogg's strong hand grab her shoulder.

"Stay here Tala, it'll be fine."

Tala thought of pulling away, but she saw David handcuffed. Ben wasn't.

"Let him go, PLEASE! WHAT DID YOU DO TO HIM?" she pleaded.

"Who's in charge here?" David said. He rubbed his eyes, but he could barely see. The pain came in and out in sharp bursts.

"The boss is in charge," Sosa said. "He's on his way."

"What do you want?" Tala said, looking at Sosa and Hogg.

"We want you to know the truth. David killed your mother."

"I loved her! I didn't kill her."

"You killed her, Dave!" Sosa said. "And I can prove it."

He heard Tala crying. His vision was in and out.

"We forged the flight logs at Opa-Locka for you."

"I didn't kill her! I wasn't even there. Don't believe them!"

"Believe it Tala. We helped him cover it up," Sosa said. "I was a detective for three years when he shot her. I had to make a choice." She looked at Tala. "I decided to give you a chance for a normal life. Your mom was miserable. Yona hated him. She was leaving him! She was tired of him, the typical whore pilot, flying from city to city. Sleeping with flight attendants half his age."

She pointed at David. "SHAME ON YOU! Yona wasn't stupid. She knew."

"I don't believe you," Tala cried. "Dad, that's not true."

David whimpered. "I wasn't the best husband, but I didn't kill her. I loved her."

Sosa said, "Get him out of my sight. He disgusts me."

Hogg shoved David into an unoccupied padded isolation room like the rest of The Hawks. David's voice disappeared behind the soundproof glass.

"He likes them young, doesn't he?" Sosa said. "Believe me Tala, everyone has their breaking point. Women get tired of men coming home with alcohol breath and lipstick on the collar. You may learn that one day."

He wouldn't do that.

He couldn't have killed her.

He couldn't have killed her.

"He shot her and pushed her right off that building. She was leaving him. Good ole Dave wasn't going to let that happen. She was going to take half his pay, half his pension, and she was taking *you*. A Prairie Boy wouldn't let something like that happen. Ain't that right, Dave?"

David banged on the glass, yelling a silent scream. If she could read his lips, she imagined he was saying Sosa was lying.

But was she?

Tala looked deep into Sosa's hateful eyes.

"We do terrible things for those we love," Sosa said.

Ben, who was off to the side like a wallflower, broke his silence. "There's nothing here, Emma. Let the kids go." His voice was shaky. He looked like a man on the verge of a breakdown.

Sosa looked insulted he would even speak.

"Is your name Ben or is your name *Soldier?*"

Ben fixed his posture, standing at attention. His face became blank, emotionless. His eyes dead like those of a voodoo doll. The fear that radiated from his aura was gone. He was someone else.

A mindless drone.

He brought his arm to his head in a formal soldier's salute.

"My name is Soldier, ma'am."

Tala couldn't believe or understand what she was seeing. Ben, who had radiated fear and anxiety, appeared steadfast and calm. Transformed into someone else. Into a moist robot.

"*Soldier*! We need to win the war. Do you agree?" Sosa barked commands like a general.

"Yes, Ma'am." His arm came down from the salute.

"Soldier. Your mission failed. You must redeem yourself," egged on Sosa. Making a spectacle of the whole thing, showing Tala she was more than the mayor, more than a psychiatrist; she was the puppeteer who pulled the strings.

"Go to Mark's isolation room!" Sosa ordered.

Soldier did an about face, turned on his heel, and marched to the isolation room his son was being held in. He turned on his heel to face his son.

"Jesus, Em. You think this is the best way?" said Hogg. This seemed extreme, even for her, and if what he thought was going to happen happened, there was no turning back.

Sosa nodded.

Sosa hit the button on the remote again so the two-way mirror became translucent, and Mark could see his dad standing on the other side of the glass wearing the same shirt he always wore before bed.

"DAD!" Mark ran up to the window and started banging on it! "DAD! Can you hear me?" The sound was audible. Everyone could hear him loud and clear. The fear inside Tala began to expand. Benny didn't seem to be Benny anymore. He was a soldier now, there was someone else inside. Someone else behind the wheel. It was the most eerie thing Tala ever saw.

"What did you do to him?" Tala said.

"I'm controlling him."

"How?"

"The mind controls his body. And I control his mind."

Sosa brought her attention back to Ben.

"Soldier, your mission was to keep all persons off this property. Ben let us down and you must make him pay the price. Soldier! It's up to you to make things right," Sosa barked.

Sosa walked over and handed him a Glock pistol. *Soldier* took the pistol and nodded in understanding.

"Dad, what are you doing? Get me out of here. Dad, can you hear me?" Mark banged on the glass.

"Soldier. Aim!"

Soldier put the gun to the side of his head. To his temple. His eyes were steady. A drop of sweat scurried down the bridge of his nose.

Tala heard a wicked scream. It was Mark. He was screaming, yelling and banging on the glass. Jaen, Valerie and Makayla were crying. Lance looked away. Jax looked confused.

Mark couldn't look away.

Tala could hear their sobs.

"NOOOOOO! DAD! WHAT ARE YOU—"

Someone yelled, "FIRE!" It may have been Sosa, it may have been Hogg! She would never know.

It happened so fast.

Tala wondered afterwards why she hadn't closed her eyes. She saw Benny's head come apart like a pumpkin smashed with an axe. His lifeless body fell with a large thud to the checkered floor. His body gave involuntary spasms before he stopped moving. Blood from his severed head ran for several feet, across several checkered tiles.

"NOOOOOOOOO!" Tala attacked Sosa, clawing at her. Sosa grabbed her hands and threw her to the floor, falling inches from the dead body with half his head blown off. She got some of his blood on her arm.

"I didn't put the gun to his head," said Sosa.

Tala cried, covered in blood. Mark yelled. Valerie yelled. Jaen couldn't stop shaking. It all mixed and sounded like a far-off wail of a siren. But there was no siren, no one was coming.

They were all going to die.

Sosa said, "We've learned mind control is possible through trauma. I believe we may have advanced our counterparts in the U.S. Government. The MK Ultra government mind control program was just the tip of the iceberg. Now we know more. It's important work. We take no pleasure from killing. You understand? These are sacrifices for the greater good. Nothing more."

She had never felt this terror before. The shock before death. Tala cried with her knees to her chest, shaking. How could Ben have just shot himself like that in front of Mark? It didn't compute in her mind. This was a horrible nightmare. She wished the wolves would come so she would know she was dreaming, but no wolves came.

Hogg went over to the 1984 surveillance station and grabbed a USB drive. It could've been any standard USB drive. He held it up and showed Tala. "This is The Checkered Butterfly. This is our work. Our legacy. We've killed people, yes, but it's all for the greater good. The documents on this USB are dangerous. We debated what to do with it. We've thought of providing it to the FBI or the CIA, but I suspect that if we did, we'd be killed. We may suffer one of those accidental falls, or maybe a horrific car crash. Maybe we get depressed and blow our brains out. You see? It happens all the time."

"I just want to go with my dad. Please let us go."

"Your dad? You mean the man who killed your mom?"

She shook her head, crying. "He wouldn't do that. He wouldn't do that!"

"You killed Yin!" she said. "You're murderers."

"I think that's your fault." Sosa looked at her watch and said, "Boss will be here any minute."

"Everyone in this town respected the Curtiss Mansion, Yin never came here. You stirred the beehive. YOU! Bees can be stung too."

"DON'T YOU UNDERSTAND HOW IMPORTANT THIS IS? This is how we change our outdated Constitution. The second amendment is an abomination. It's cost us so much already."

"Are you going to kill us?" Jaen said from behind the glass. She held on to her collar.

Sosa ignored her.

She directed her attention to Tala. "You know the truth about David? How do you feel?"

"I don't believe you," she countered.

"Good. Ignore logic and reason like the rest of society. Think Tala, THINK! Yona wasn't suicidal."

"Ask Dad what he did to Mom. He's here, isn't he?"

"He would never," she reiterated.

"Come then, ask him."

"Does it matter to you if it was true?" Sosa said.

"Of course it matters. She was my mother. And I don't have her anymore." Tala was a cocktail of pain and confusion.

"You've suffered so much. I'm sorry," Sosa said.

Sosa took a deep breath.

"Ask David before the boss gets here. Tell him you know the truth. Go on now. He won't deny it. You'll see we're not the monsters you think we are. The big bad wolf has been with you all along, tucking you into bed."

Tala nodded. "Let me talk to him."

Hogg looked at Sosa disapprovingly.

"Take her." Sosa said.

"Come," Hogg beckoned. "Make it quick."

Tala didn't know what game they were playing. She didn't know the rules. Hogg opened the isolation room with his special remote and Tala walked in. As soon as she crossed the threshold, he shut the door. They were both inside now, father and daughter, isolated in a padded room by themselves.

SOSA AND HOGG went to the 1984 surveillance station to watch the exchange on the monitors.

He leaned on the desk. "What the hell are you doing, Emma? This isn't protocol." Hogg looked at his phone. "The boss is on Okeechobee Road. He won't be long. He won't like this. He won't like any of this."

"It's too late now. We'll clean this mess and spin some story. We always do."

Hogg reluctantly nodded. She could tell he didn't like it.

"Fine, but this is on you."

"Stop worrying." Sosa said, her attention on Tala and David on the surveillance monitors.

"DAD, YOU OKAY?" She was still standing by the door, afraid to approach like a lion's handler. David was sitting with his head between his knees. He had most of his visibility back, but his eyes were bloodshot red. When had they put a dog collar on his neck?

He looked up. "Oh, baby, thank God you're okay." He gave her a broken smile, stood, and she embraced him with such emotion they both cried together.

"Dad what the hell is happening? What is this place?"

"I told you to stay away from this goddamn house. Didn't I? You never listen to me. Oh, Red, you never listen." He was shaking.

"I'm sorry," she said.

"They said you killed Mom. That you shot her, then shoved her off the hotel."

"No, Red, no. That's crazy. I loved her. I wasn't even in Miami. I told you that. You know that."

"How do they know about us?"

"I don't know Red." His words came out weak. He looked away. He was an awful liar.

"Was Sosa the detective in charge of Mom's case?"

David looked away. "Yes, she was. There's a lot I don't remember about that night Red, but I wouldn't have her killed Yona, I loved her more than anything."

Tala pushed away from him; not violently, but she needed space. She wanted to see his eyes, see what they revealed. But he was a jigsaw puzzle and time was running out.

She yelled, "How do they know about the wolves?"

"I knew them a long time ago. You have to believe me. I don't know how they know."

"Why did we come back here?"

David licked his lips.

"I bumped into Benny at LaGuardia, he told me about Springs. I dreamed of living here as a kid. Springs was what we all aspired to."

"So you were all friends?"

"We were Prairie Boys. Then I became a pilot, married your mom, had you. When your mom died, I left this place behind me."

"Mom didn't die. She killed herself. You can't say she died like she got in a car crash. She committed suicide. She shot herself and fell from a building, I saw it. I was there!"

"I won't believe that!" David said. "I'll never believe that! Your mother wouldn't have done a thing like that."

"But she did. I saw it."

Tears were coming down now fast. "Didn't she love us?"

"She was sick. I couldn't see it. But she was. I can't go back."

"Did she have someone else?"

David stopped. He looked up as if trying to summon God to take him from this place. He had never told her. All couples had their secrets.

"No. She didn't. I did."

He had kept this from her. What else had he kept? The doubt took root and spread across her as if it were soil. The doubt that said yes, your dad had *motive* to kill your mom. Did he have opportunity? Was Sosa and Hogg involved like they suggested? Had they helped him cover her mom's murder?

ON THE SURVEILLANCE MONITORS, Hogg saw the boss arriving. His driver parked next to Ben's truck. Olivia Pace exited the driver's seat, opened an umbrella and walked around the car. She opened his door. The boss exited the passenger seat as the rain came down hard and the ground became mud.

"He's here," Hogg said.

Sosa opened the isolation room.

"Tala, come with me," she said.

David held her tight. "Don't take her. PLEASE, EMMA!"

Sosa pulled the remote from her coat pocket.

"Let her go, Dave."

"You don't have to do this," David said. "We can work this out. We don't care about this place. Or what you're doing—"

"You mean what *we're* doing. You're just as much a part of this as me now."

David's muscles contracted, his muscles spasmed. He choked back a scream and fell to the ground, shaking from the electrical shock delivered from his collar.

Tala ran toward him but fell when Sosa grabbed her by the hair and started dragging her out.

"Have her comply Dave or I'll kill her."

"Get up, Red, GO!" David crawled on his knees. "Go with her."

Tala got to her feet.

Sosa looked behind her shoulder. "Is he coming up?"

Hogg said, "He's coming. Get her out now."

In that split second, Tala felt something cold slide onto the small of her back. Something metal.

Tala got to her feet, feeling the weight of the gun in her back. She adjusted her t-shirt to cover it and walked out of the isolation room, leaving David alone once more.

Tala was on the checkered floor again. She looked back and saw David staring at her. He nodded. *Do it, Tala.*

I am the weapon.

Did he deserve to be caged? Had he actually killed her mom? No. Of course not. They were playing with her mind.

Or weren't they?

She heard The Checkered Butterfly doors open behind her, revealing a man she didn't think she'd ever see again.

A ghost.

A stranger.

She was speechless.

Dr. Richard Moss entered the lab in a black raincoat, soaking wet. He looked over at his protégées. He had a polka dotted bowtie and was leaning on a black cane. He looked like he'd aged significantly.

Sosa and Hogg acknowledged him by lowering their heads.

He smiled at Tala. "You haven't called me. I thought we were friends? How many people from Springs are not in their beds? How are we to fix this?" Dr. Moss said, in his same, soft, affable voice, looking at the mayor and sheriff for answers.

"Where's Olivia?" Sosa asked.

"Waiting in the car. This won't be long." He said.

Olivia?

It was that moment Tala questioned everything she ever knew, everything she was ever told, everything she ever believed. What was he doing here?

Who was Dr. Moss?

The boss.

The handler of puppeteers.

Dr. Richard Moss walked over to Ben, who was lying askew with his head torn off from the gunshot to the head. Dr. Moss just shook his head.

"This is a mess." His checkered floor was pooled with blood.

Tala said, "What are you doing here?"

The man she trusted with her deepest feelings ambled over to her with his cane and touched her face with his hand gently.

He looked deep into her blue eyes and said, "The question is, what are *you* doing here?"

He let her face go and took a step back. Pondering.

"Tala, I hope you'll forgive me one day. Yona needed help. She came to me. She felt sad all the time. She suspected David of having an affair. She wanted to feel better. God, she was beautiful. You have her beauty and tenacity. Your mom became severely depressed when her suspicions became fact. I was her shrink. She brought you into my office since you were two years old. I never told you, and I'm sorry."

Tala didn't say anything. She just stood there looking at Dr. Moss with tears in her eyes. The Hawks were contained inside their respective rooms. Sosa, Hogg and Hunter stood behind him like wallflowers. Her focus was on him. The man who taught her about the white sand beach with lions. The man who told her to come to Springs.

"God," he went on. "You were such a happy child. You would chase butterflies all spring. You loved them so much I made a butterfly garden in my yard. You'd run around and snatch them in a makeshift net I made you. You gave me my first butterfly, a checkered white. You were like the daughter I never had. I lost you when Yona died because I'd never see you again. I told Yona we could be a family. But she wouldn't leave David. I loved you so much. Of course, Dave never knew about our affair. He was busy with his own debaucheries, pushing Yona into my arms. She was too afraid to leave. I think she loved me. But love is not enough, it seems. I became bitter and angry. I took my work in mind control and did an unspeakable thing. I started programming her with what I'd learned from the CIA's MK Ultra government mind control program.

Yona became my first subject. I created an alter personality in her called Lola. It took a long time, but what I discovered frightened me. Lola wasn't Yona. Lola was not the woman I fell in love with. You can't force love. So I made Lola disappear. Yona was collateral damage. It was I who instructed her to the highest floor of the Hotel Statler and made her self-destruct. Lola believed she could fly like a butterfly. If she would carry out such a command was beyond my experience at the time. Anger made me do it. After all, I loved you both. Deep inside, I didn't think it would work. But I was wrong."

"You killed her," she said.

"I'm afraid so. I tried to mend the pieces the best I could. When David left with you to Urbana, I had him referred to me so I could watch you grow and steer you in the best direction. I blamed the gun. Not myself. I masterminded The Checkered Butterfly program. I decided to use what I learned from my research in mind control to reform gun control. Once and for all. Everyone here has been hurt by guns. I will ban the second amendment. If that, my work and Yona's death would not be in vain."

"You're crazy." Tala said.

"Maybe but David flies our shooters in and out of Florida. He helps me. I help you. You'd get your fresh start. But my plan backfired. The truth always wants to reveal itself. No matter how hell bent we are on burying it."

Sosa said, "What now, Boss?"

"We have a decision to make."

"Who are you?" Tala inquired, like she didn't know him at all.

"You know who I am. I'm Dr. Richard Moss. Behind me is Dr. Emma Sosa, and Dr. James Hogg from Harvard Medical School. My students. We're the wolves of your dreams. And this rich little town is our pasture. Our citizens, the sheep. Good ole Benjamin Franklin once said *Make yourself sheep and the wolves will eat you*." He smiled. "Well, Tala, the wolves of your nightmares are here and we're ravenously hungry."

Tala reached behind her and pointed the gun at him. She used her other hand to steady the shaking barrel. She tried to sound confidant.

"HOW ABOUT I BLOW YOUR FUCKIN' HOUSE DOWN!"

"Jesus Christ!" Dr. Moss yelled. "How in the blue hell did she get a gun?" he said, craning his head behind. He was leaning on his black cane.

SOSA AND HOGG SEEMED DUMBFOUNDED. Hogg had patted down The Hawks and Tala for weapons, but he realized he hadn't patted David down. He took Ben's word he wasn't armed.

He's scared of his own shadow.

Hogg felt played by a dead man.

Dr. Moss said, "Relax, Tala. Don't do anything stupid.

Don't make a rash decision. You're smarter than that. I just want to talk. There's a way out of this for everyone."

"Now you want to talk," she said.

"Well, you have leverage now. That's how negotiations work. Bring out the boy," Dr. Moss said.

"He's not ready. Sir," Sosa replied.

"Nonsense. Bring him out now. She's not going to shoot anyone," Dr. Moss said, not sounding so sure.

"Bring out Yin."

Yin? Yin is dead?

"I don't think he's ready yet, Sir."

"BRING HIM NOW!" Dr. Moss said, pointing his cane at them.

WHAT KIND of sick mind games was he playing? Hogg told Hunter to fetch him. Hunter ignored Tala who told him to stop. He disappeared into the hall. He returned with Yin who was wearing a hospital gown like Charlie Owens had worn. Yin had two electrical pads stuck to the side of his temples. He wore the same black collar on his neck as her friends.

Yin's expression was lifeless, like when Ben became *Soldier*.

"What did you do to him?" Tala asked, dismayed. Keeping the gun pointed at Dr. Moss.

"He's tough as nails. But we're beginning to disassociate him, isn't that right, *Bruce*?" Dr. Moss said.

Yin saluted. The same military salute Ben gave before he blew his head off. Yin's eyes were dead as dead. Tala didn't know what was worse. Yin being dead or Yin being like this. His smile was gone. What had they done to him? He was emotionless.

"Yin!" Tala called out to him. He didn't even flinch. Like she wasn't in the room. This reminded her of Charlie. These monsters were responsible.

"His name is *Bruce*. Yin died months ago." Dr. Moss smiled. "What did they call it? Oh, yes, A Burglary Gone Awry." His smile was dark, pure evil.

"We're going to make him famous. Isn't that what you kids care about nowadays anyway? He'll be all over the news, Facebook, Instagram, Snapchat. He'll be a star. We have big plans for him isn't that, right, Emma? He'll kill so many people the President will have no choice but to bring back the assault weapons ban for good. That's only the beginning. The outcry in this country will reach a fever pitch. We'll start a goddamn civil war if we must, but there'll never be another school shooting again! We're taking down the second amendment!"

"Give me the gun." Hogg took a step toward her and froze when he heard the gunshot. Tala fired a warning shot into the ceiling. "You reach for the remote and I'll kill him." She pointed the gun at Dr. Moss.

"Think of the white sand beach—"

Tala fired another shot. "Shut up, old man. You killed my mom. You killed so many innocent people! Children! What did you do to Casey?"

"I don't know Casey."

Yin stood lifeless. His eyes were distant, his lips a straight line like an anime character.

What had they done to him? Jesus, what had they done?

"Yin," Tala said, crying.

Yin didn't acknowledge her. There were three people on the checkered floor who wanted to disarm her. David and The Hawks were confined, looking helplessly from the padded soundproof isolation rooms.

Had they messed with the wires inside Yin's head like Charlie? It was too late.

"He responds to Bruce now," Hogg said. "He'll do much better than Rodnam and Jamal."

Tala's hands were shaking terribly. She couldn't still them.

"Bruce, take the gun from her," Dr. Moss said.

Bruce narrowed his eyes at Tala, like he'd never seen her before. He went toward her, and Tala took a few steps back, raising the gun to him.

"Get back," she yelled, back peddling. "Get back or I'll shoot."

"You won't shoot your friend," Dr. Moss said.

Bruce closed the gap. Tala back peddled to the balcony doors. The gun pointed at him. Bruce took the gun from her easily. Tala didn't fight back. She was on the parapet.

Her friend was somewhere inside him.

"You remember when we went into Mr. Wilson's class. How you tripped because I didn't want to go in?" Tala said.

Bruce held the gun to his side.

"Point the gun at her," Dr. Moss called from behind.

Bruce complied. He pointed the gun at her chest. His eyes were pinpointed, distant, narrow.

"Remember when I climbed up the tree, I slipped and fell? You helped me up."

Nothing changed.

"Shoot her!" Dr. Moss ordered. "Then throw her off the balcony! It's time to end this."

Tala held on to the railing, bracing herself. The rain came hard and the wind gusted her shirt.

"Yin. I'm your friend. I'm your friend."

"Bruce! Terminate her!" Dr. Moss yelled.

Bruce took the slack out of the trigger. Tala closed her eyes and her life became a flash, a montage of her mom tucking her in at night. Her dad coming home from work in Urbana in his uniform with the pilot pins on his collar, the run to Pleasant Valley cemetery in the snow with the ravens, the kids teasing her, chanting "The Suicide Girl" Another flash, Charlie Owens giving her the mask at Citrus, Yin tripping in class, the ghost stories at the Hialeah Racetrack, her mother's funeral, the candlelight vigil, the police detectives casing the neighborhoods, everything flashing: The Chinese lanterns, the butterfly mask, Casey with her zombie costume, *El Libro Rojo*, Yin giving her the knife, the yellow brick road, her mom falling from the sky like a ghost.

This is it.

Yin said, "Hello, Mexico."

Tala, who had been ducking her head defensively, waiting for the shot, looked up.

What she saw was glorious. What she saw was Yin smiling. His eyes were human again. Soft, kind.

"Bruce, shoot her!"

Yin turned around.

"Bruce's not here right now, but I'll take a message." He pointed the gun at them. "My name is Yin Vo."

Hogg, Sosa, and Dr. Moss wore countenances of utter anger. Yin grabbed Dr. Moss by the neck and pulled him from Sosa and Hogg, holding him like a hostage with the revolver to his head. Sosa went to reach into her lab coat.

"DON'T EVEN THINK ABOUT IT! I'LL SHOOT HIM DEAD," Yin said. "Put your hands up now! All of you!"

He added, "Hand over the control!"

Dr. Moss said, "Do it." He was sweating profusely. "Don't do anything hasty boy. This is bigger than all of us."

Sosa reluctantly slid the remote. Tala picked it up.

Hogg charged Yin like a football player. There was no warning, no thinking. Just a quick tackle. Yin brought the gun to his chest, protecting it like a football in a fumble. He kicked him and fought. Dr. Moss fell on his side and scrambled on the ground, trying to get away. Hogg knocked the wind out of Yin from the fall. He gasped for air, clutching the gun with all his might.

Hogg stripped the gun from him. It slid on the ground. Tala instinctively grabbed the gun from the floor, beating Sosa to it. She pointed it at her.

"You're not going to shoot anyone. You're just a dumb kid," Sosa said. Dr. Moss didn't look so sure.

Tala pointed the gun at Hogg. "Get off him!"

She took a shot above their heads.

Hogg put his hands up. "Whoa! Easy."

Hogg sauntered to Sosa and Dr. Moss as they huddled together like cowards.

Tala pressed the button on the remote labeled ALL DOORS and the bay doors opened simultaneously.

Valerie, Jaen, Lance came out, still wearing their dog collars. Shaking. Afraid. David came out too. Mark, Jax and Makayla followed them onto the checkered floor. Mark stared at his dead father.

"Oh, my God. YIN!" Valerie said.

They were in disbelief, suspended into a fantasy world where the dead return. Yin, the one they wept for at his house. The one they mourned with a candlelight vigil and Chinese lanterns. Here he was, alive in the flesh.

Dr. Moss said, "I'm sorry about your mom. I loved her."

"I'm sorry about *you*. I loved her too."

"Tala, don't—"

Tala pulled the trigger. Nothing happened. He gasped for air. Dr. Moss cackled.

"You stupid child," He pressed a button on his cane, and the bottom ejected a sharp blade. He charged her. Tala was too far from the 1984 table. It all happened so fast. She looked at the knife on the table.

It moved.

It flung from the table to her as Dr. Moss closed the gap. He swung his cane, but Tala ducked, caught Yin's knife, and uppercutted, stabbing him in the chest. Dr. Moss took a long wheezing gasp, like a concrete pillar had impaled him. He fell to the checkered floor, oozing blood over the white and black tiles.

"Doctor! Doctor!" Sosa and Hogg knelt next to him. Hunter looked shocked, leaned against the wall. He looked like the rookie cop again. Like he didn't know what he was doing here.

"What have you done!" Sosa screamed.

"How many families have you destroyed?" Tala's yelling frightened even her friends. She was someone else. Her face flushed, holding a bone handled knife drenched in blood. She had just stabbed a man. Who was she?

"What have you done?" Hogg cried.

Sosa stood, covered in Dr. Moss's blood. The Harvard Duo cried like he was their father. Their God.

"We do terrible things for those we love." Tala said.

Sheriff Hogg ran to Tala and grabbed her by the neck. He squeezed with all his force, the veins on his biceps bulged. Tala's vision dimmed to black. Hogg was straddling her. Taking the life from her. She heard a yell but it wasn't her and it wasn't Hogg. In the corner of her eye, she saw something swing and hit Hogg on the side of the head. It was a wet hollow cracking sound. Hogg fell next to her. David stood there holding the axe. She knew Hogg was dead.

There were screams.

Tala ambled to the 1984 surveillance station and saw a banner that read: 2 + 2 = 5. The computer station had cameras showing every angle of the Curtiss Mansion, including the Sea of Trees and other parts of the town. She saw a surveillance video of The Circle. Of Charlie's room.

"Jesus Christ."

This was an Orwellian Operation.

They were spying on everyone.

Tala had an epiphany: *When Hogg and Ben were loading the garbage bags onto the Bumblebee truck, they were transporting their assets. The body bags were cocoons for mind-controlled shooters.*

Zombies.

JAEN GRABBED her cell phone and called 911. She asked to be transferred to the Hialeah Police Department. She told them where they were. She told them they were kidnapped. She told them there were dead men. She stayed on the line until she heard the sirens of freedom. Until she saw the distant lights of red and blue enter the wicked mansion.

Until they started banging on the door. The Hawks went out onto the balcony and told the police they were upstairs.

They came up with a tactical SWAT team, shields, long rifles. They entered The Checked Butterfly room.

A room that never existed.

EPILOGUE

HIALEAH, Miami-Dade, Miami Springs Police, along with other local and federal agencies responded to the Curtiss Mansion. The FBI thanked the little fish for their help and sent them on their way. This was something bigger and more sinister than they could ever imagine.

The FBI's Special Agents Paul Betancourt and Kristen Mulder led the investigation into what happened at the Curtiss Mansion. The investigation linked Miami Springs Mayor Emma Sosa, Sheriff James Hogg, deceased and Dr. Richard Moss, deceased to a clandestine operation where they coordinated kidnappings and executed mind control experiments on unwilling citizens.

It appeared they were able to turn ordinary citizens into killing machines. The investigation tied them to Yin Vo, Dexter Reeves, Charlie Owens, Jamal Stevens, Rodnam Jackson, Yona Stone, Norma Mortenson, Frank Olson, Mark Bradshaw, Ben Bradshaw, Roseli Villalobos, Frances Gumm, Betty Paige, Olivia Pace, Marjorie Vargas, John Palmer and God only knew how many victims who succumbed to mass shootings.

The FBI added Olivia Pace to their top ten most wanted list with a reward of $100,000 leading to her arrest. She was a fugitive from justice. The surveillance video showed she had been waiting outside the mansion for Dr. Moss to return. It appeared that when she heard gunshots, she escaped before police arrived. Dr. Moss's rental vehicle was located in the Everglades. No sign of Olivia.

Deputy Hunter was apprehended by local law enforcement. He seemed confused and disoriented. His official statement was that he didn't remember anything. He didn't know how he'd obtained the scar on his face. S.A. Agent Mulder went over Yin's missing person report and after forensic testing determined the crime scene had been staged with pig's blood.

Even though Dr. Moss's operation suggested his motivation was to change gun legislation in the country, his financials showed that he was investing handsomely in several gun company stocks. He had an uncanny ability to predict when citizens would purchase more firearms, which in turn, had made him rich. Several co-conspirators including accountants, investors, and gun company lobbyist were arrested.

The FBI's investigation also determined the "1984" surveillance station had audio/video capabilities and that the citizens of Miami Springs were always being monitored. They located a GPS tracker that had been installed inside of Ben Bradshaw's Bumblebee truck and on David Stone's white Porsche.

S.A. Betancourt's report referred to known MK Ultra methods such as exposure to hallucinogens, psychotherapy, electroshock, isolation and new methods containing a Catherine wheel and visual programming that were discovered and implemented by Dr. Richard Moss and his cohorts, which were highly classified.

The investigation revealed the trio had launched a massive misinformation campaign against Glenn Curtiss which tarnished his reputation. The aim was to keep the town and investors away from the Curtiss Mansion. Thousands of websites were uploaded to the internet with false information about Glenn Curtiss murdering his wife and children.

S.A. Paul Betancourt's report found the trio was successful in dissociating the minds of their subjects and turning them into assets for executing mass shootings across state lines. The operation used Dotted Blue pilots including David Stone to transport shooters from one state to another.

Emma Sosa was charged with a slew of felonies including kidnapping, murder, racketeering, aggravated assault, possession of methamphetamines, torture, false imprisonment, aggravated battery. Emma Sosa gave sworn testimony that David Stone was aware of the operation, but David denied it and there was no evidence to prove otherwise.

Sosa accepted a plea deal that saved her from lethal injection. A federal judge sentenced her to serve 333 life sentences in ADX Florence in Colorado.

WITHIN HER FIRST two months in federal prison, a corrections officer notified Sosa she had a visitor. They took her to a small interview room. One table and two chairs. A two-way mirror on each side of the room. She could tell from the man's baggy eyes, goatee and cheap suit, he was an underpaid cop. He was white with blondish hair. The more she looked into his eyes, the more she realized they were gentle and kind.

"I'm Detective Snuggs. Miami Dade Sex Crimes. Take a seat, Ms. Sosa."

Sosa sat across from him, unsure of what a Miami Dade cop would be doing in Colorado.

He reached into his briefcase and pulled out a file. He fished through it and took out a small stapled packet. He read it over. Buying time, like he was looking for the right words.

"I'm here because something happened to you when you were a little kid. You know what I'm referring to?"

"Yes, Detective," Sosa said. "You can't forget a thing like that. Not even after forty years."

"We got him. Emma, the man who raped you is in custody."

Emma gave a snort-laugh. "You're mistaken. The man who raped me is dead. Rodnam Jackson raped me."

"I'm afraid not, Emma. The man who raped you got arrested three days ago for murder. He killed his wife. We got a positive match from your rape kit in CODIS. He's never getting out, but it's him. It's a one hundred percent match. He used to be the janitor at your elementary school. I'm sorry about what happened. I know you've done some bad things to end up here. But you were just a kid. You're still a victim. Your parents signed a non-prosecution form. I'm aware you provided a sworn statement to the FBI that Rodnam Jackson raped you when you were a kid. I flew here to tell you the truth and to ask you if you'd like to press charges and go forward with the case. There's no statute of limitations, you were under twelve."

Sosa stood. "You're lying! You're trying to brainwash me! You're manipulating me! Rodnam raped me!

RODNAM DID IT! YOU'RE TRYING TO CONTROL MY MIND!"

"You were a child. I'm sorry, Ms. Sosa, it's the truth. Rodnam Jackson wasn't even in Miami Springs. The cops did a shit job and picked the first black kid they saw and pushed it because he wasn't from the area. He gave a false confession. It wasn't him. He was in Springs meeting up with a girl. I know your parents tried to bury this, but eventually, the truth finds a way."

She fell to her knees, crying, bawling.

"Would you like to move forward with this case?"

"No," she said. "I don't deserve justice. Give me the Nolle Pros form."

He did. She signed it.

Detective Snuggs put his paperwork away, stood, and began to walk away with his briefcase.

"Detective," she said.

He turned around.

She was kneeling, with tears running down her face. "I've done so many *bad* things. You think God will forgive me?"

"That's between God and you. But if God didn't forgive sinners, heaven would be empty. Take care, Ms. Sosa."

EMMA SOSA WAS FOUND unresponsive in her cell the following week. The prison released a statement her death was being investigated as an apparent suicide. She hung herself with her bedsheets.

At least, that's what they reported.

What a terrible loss.

It's one of those things that happened when you knew you were never going to get out.

CASEY WAS FOUND by K9 officers in the Sea of Trees during the perimeter search. Unharmed and smiling. Sosa had vehemently denied taking her, and no matter how many forensic interviews she had, Casey smiled and said she was exactly where she was supposed to be, with a friend named Glenn. At her insistence, Jax founded the 'Glenn Curtiss Restoration Initiative'.

The G.C.R.I. was a foundation that secured Miami Springs funds in order to clear Glenn Curtiss's name and restore The Curtiss Mansion. The town named Jax Riggins committee president and the restoration of the mansion was scheduled to begin the following year. The City of Hialeah followed suit. They began working in conjunction with Mr. Riggins and his committee and began a million-dollar restoration project to restore the Hialeah Racetrack.

TALA MENDED her relationship with her dad. Yin, Valerie, Jaen, Mark, Makayla, and Jax had to ironically enough see a court-ordered psychiatrist for months. It took time to begin to understand what they had been through. Mark had the hardest time coping with what he'd seen. He'd witnessed his father shoot himself point black in the head.

This trauma was something that made him darker and numb. Even though he was a senior and had been accepted to the University of Miami he decided college wasn't for him. Instead, he enlisted in the Marines and left for Parris

Island, South Carolina. The Hawks went with him to the airport. He gave them a curt goodbye and never looked back.

AFTER THE HAWKS left the airport, Tala asked Jax to accompany her to Angels of Mercy cemetery. This was where her mother had been buried. She had never been here since the funeral. With some help from the caretaker, she found her mother's tomb.

> R.I.P.
> Yona Highbear Stone
> A loving mother.
> Life's an adventure or its nothing.

SHE TOLD her mother she loved her and that she would see her again someday. Tala took the checkered butterfly frame Dr. Moss had given her out of her backpack. She left it there and started walking away with Jax. She came back, picked it up and slammed it against the tombstone. It shattered. After Tala and Jax walked away, something happened. The butterfly fluttered its wing, stood on a piece of glass, and flew away.

DURING THE SUMMER, Tala and her friends plodded along the Miami Beach boardwalk. Tala stopped in front of the

Hotel Statler. She had to see it one more time. Her friends knew this was where it all began. She looked up at the thirty-third floor where her mother had shot herself and fallen to her death.

She could breathe.

She felt elation. She felt closure. Her and her friends were pretending they were normal teenagers. Just kids having fun on a beautiful summer day.

But they knew the truth. They would never be normal again. The scars were too deep. They probably weren't normal to begin with. Normal is a lie, and to be frank, they didn't care to be that anymore. The truth was so much more invigorating and free, and that's how they felt as they plodded along holding hands, laughing together like friends.

They felt free.

The F.B.I. impounded and classified evidence from The Checkered Butterfly room and redacted the reports. The Hawks signed non-disclosure agreements. The case was highly classified. They spun a story to the media about a corrupt mayor and sheriff, drug trafficking that was linked to some murders, but never released anything about well . . . You know.

Who would believe it anyway?

They never found the USB with the highly classified research and documentation of active shooter experiments. Such a thing wouldn't exist.

Tala might have grabbed that on the way out.

And now, they were on the Miami Beach boardwalk, sitting at an ice cream shop, and Casey was putting sprinkles on her Sundae. Jaen and Makayla recognized some friends and left the table to say hello. Lance, Jax and Yin followed. Tala stayed with Casey at the table and narrowed her eyes at a plastic spoon. She laughed.

"I thought I could move things with my mind."

"You can't move things with your mind." Casey laughed. "You can only move them with your heart." Tala looked down at the spoon again and it began to move. Tala laughed.

"You're bleeding." Casey said.

Tala wiped her nose with a napkin.

Jax sat down with his ice cream. "You okay?"

"Yeah, nosebleed."

She finished her ice cream and told Yin and friends to hang on. She ran to the beach shore. The sand was powder white; the water was blue as it had been in her dreams. There were no lions yet, but that was okay. She had so much more to do before they came. She took a deep breath as the salty air filled her lungs. She took something from her pocket and threw it into the ocean.

Jax came up behind her. "What was that?"

"A seashell."

She kissed him.

She glanced at the blue sky and saw a plane flying like a metal bird through clouds.

"I'm leaving for Urbana tomorrow. It's Ms. Gumm's birthday. I'm going back to Pleasant Valley to leave her flowers."

"I thought you hated flying," Jax said.

"I'm looking forward to it," she said. "Life's an adventure or it's nothing."

ACKNOWLEDGMENTS

To my family for their unwavering support. To my editors, Michael Garret and Robert De La Fé for not giving up on a mess of a manuscript. To my designer, James T. Eagan for making a great cover. To Jennie Lundahl for being right about writing. To my advanced readers, Johana, Kayleen, and Vanessa for their constructive feedback.

And to Bob the Bootlegger, the story wouldn't have been the same without you. Thank you all!

And to you reader,
    For lending me your time
    and
    Imagination.

ABOUT THE AUTHOR

George Ox is an emerging author of fiction. He is a Special Victims Detective and ICAC Task Force member who investigates crimes against children on the internet. He is a member of the Mystery Writers of America and resides in Miami Lakes, FL. This is George's first novel.

 facebook.com/realgeorgeox

 twitter.com/RealGeorgeOx

 instagram.com/realgeorgeox